Praise for Minerva Spencer's Outcasts series:

[DANGEROUS] ***Booklist Top 10 Romance Debuts of 2018***

[BARBAROUS] ***Bookpage 14 Most Anticipated Romances of Fall 2018***

"Minerva Spencer's writing is sophisticated and wickedly witty. Dangerous is a delight from start to finish with swashbuckling action, scorching love scenes, and a coolly arrogant hero to die for. Spencer is my new auto-buy!"

-*NYT Bestselling Author* Elizabeth Hoyt

"[**SCANDALOUS** is] *A standout…Spencer's brilliant and original tale of the high seas bursts with wonderfully real protagonists, plenty of action, and passionate romance."*

★Publishers Weekly *STARRED REVIEW*

"Fans of Amanda Quick's early historicals will find much to savor."

★Booklist *STARRED REVIEW*

"Sexy, witty, and fiercely entertaining."

★Kirkus *STARRED REVIEW*

"A remarkably resourceful heroine who can more than hold her own against any character invented by best-selling Bertrice Small, a suavely sophisticated hero with sex appeal to spare, and a cascade of lushly detailed love scenes give Spencer's dazzling debut its deliciously fun retro flavor."

★Booklist *STARRED REVIEW*

"Readers will love this lusty and unusual marriage of convenience story."

-*NYT Bestselling Author* MADELINE HUNTER

"Smart, witty, graceful, sensual, elegant and gritty all at once. It has all of the meticulous attention to detail I love in Georgette Heyer, BUT WITH SEX!"

***RITA-Award Winning Author* JEFFE KENNEDY**

He cocked his head. "Are you trying to look at my eyes, Signora Stefani?"

Before she could answer he lifted one gloved hand to the delicate frames, removed the spectacles, and carefully folded them, his lashes fanning across his cheeks like icicles on fresh snow as he slipped the glasses into a pocket. And then he looked up.

Portia was too awed to be ashamed of the sound that escaped her; his eyes weren't red, but a translucent violet surrounded by thickets of white lashes that seemed to weigh down heavy lids.

"Glorious," she breathed.

His eyes opened wider, as if she'd said something he hadn't expected. "Signora Stefani?"

"Yes, Mr. Harrington?" Her voice was at least two octaves lower than usual.

"I'm going to kiss you."

"Yes," she said, although he hadn't asked question.

His kid-sheathed hands were cool and smooth on the thin skin of her jaws. He held her face firmly, his eyes heavy and hot as his mouth crushed hers.

The Music of Love

Minerva Spencer

writing as S.M. LAVIOLETTE

CROOKED SIXPENCE BOOKS are published by

CROOKED SIXPENCE PRESS
2 State Road 230
El Prado, NM 87529

Print Edition

First printing January 2020

ISBN: 978-1-951662-01-1

10 9 8 7 6 5 4 3 2 1

Front cover image by Biserka Design
Book design by Biserka Design

Printed in the United States of America.

Chapter One

Bude, Cornwall
1816

PORTIA STEFANI PULLED her gaze from the moonlit countryside beyond the carriage window and stared at the well-worn letter she clutched in her hand. She'd read it so often that she'd memorized it, but she still needed to look at the words.

She'd done the right thing, hadn't she?

Dear Signore Stefani,

The Stark Employment Agency forwarded your letter of interest regarding the teaching position. Naturally your skills and experience are well above what I'd hoped for in a piano teacher. It is my privilege to offer you a one-year term of employment. I require only two hours of instruction per day, six days per week. The remaining time would be your own.

Whitethorn Manor is in a very remote part of Cornwall, so if country living is anathema to you the position would not suit.

The letter's author—Mr. Eustace Harrington—went on to offer a generous salary, suggest a start date and give instructions for reaching the manor. Nowhere in the letter did it say Ivo Stefani's *wife* would be an acceptable substitute if the famous pianist was unavailable, uninterested, or . . . dead.

Portia's hands shook as she refolded the brief missive and

tucked it into her reticule. It was foolish to submit to her nerves, especially after she'd already accepted the private chaise, the nights in posting inns, and the meals Mr. Harrington's money had provided.

She groaned and rested her aching temple against the cool glass, exhausted by the relentless whirl of thoughts. Her head had begun to pound several hours earlier and the pain increased with each mile. Weeks and weeks of living with her deception had taken its toll on both her mind and body. Thank God it would soon be over, no matter what happened.

The argument she'd relied on most heavily—that this deception was her only choice—had lost its conviction the closer she came to Whitethorn Manor. But that didn't make it any less true. Portia had no money, no family—at least none who would acknowledge her—and her few friends were almost as poor as she was. She had nothing but debt since she'd been forced to close the Ivo Stefani Academy for Young Ladies.

She laughed and the bitter puff of air left a fleeting fog on the carriage window. Even now the ridiculous name amused her; Ivo had always possessed such grandiose dreams. It was unfortunate his dreams had rarely put food on their table, even before he abandoned her and their struggling school.

Although the small academy had been his idea and bore his name, her husband had pouted whenever Portia asked for help teaching or tutoring.

"Such work is fine for you, *cara*, but my ear bones," he would shudder dramatically at this point, "they are in danger of breaking and bleeding if exposed to such abuse."

"And how will your ear bones feel when they have no place to sleep?" Portia had asked on more than one occasion.

But Ivo had only laughed at her fears—and then run off with a woman whose very existence meant Portia's ten-year marriage was nothing but a sham. Not that any of that mattered now. Ivo was gone and the humiliating truth with him; it no longer signified what he'd done or with whom he'd done it. What mattered was that Portia needed to survive and the only way she could do so was teaching music.

She could have found work in London, but the prospect of starting all over again in the same city had left her feeling tired and hopeless. If she hadn't been destitute she might have considered the offer to share a house with three friends: Serena Lombard, Honoria Keyes, and Lady Winifred Sedgewick, all teachers from her now defunct school.

Unfortunately, all Portia had to offer anyone was debt, and most of it not even hers. But to the dunning agents who dogged her day and night it hadn't mattered that Ivo had generated the mountain of bills without her knowledge.

No, she'd done far better to accept this well-paid position, even though she'd resorted to despicable—and probably criminal—deceit to get it.

The chaise shuddered to a halt and her thoughts scattered like startled pigeons.

Portia peered out the window and caught her breath. It was not a country *house;* it was a mansion: an imposing Palladian-style structure that loomed over the carriage, its massive portico and immense Venetian windows dominating the moonlit sky.

She had arrived.

THE FOOTMEN HAD just removed their plates when Soames entered the dining room.

"I beg your pardon, sir, it appears the music teacher has arrived."

Stacy Harrington took out his watch. "It's quite late and no doubt he's exhausted after his long journey. I'll wait until morning to speak to him. Show him to his chambers and have Cook send up a tray."

His aged butler did not move.

"Is there something else, Soames?"

"Well . . ."

"Yes, what is it?"

"Well, the thing is, sir, it's *not* Signore Stefani."

Stacy frowned at his usually imperturbable servant. "What is it, Soames?"

"It's *Signora* Stefani," Soames blurted.

"Very well, so he brought his wife with him. I wish he'd let us know, but tonight they can stay in the rooms you have prepared and tomorrow we can move them to a larger apartment."

Soames cleared his throat. "Er, it is *only* Signora Stefani."

His Aunt Frances, who'd been inching closer to the edge of her seat with each new piece of information, could no longer contain herself. "What on earth does he mean, Stacy?" she asked, rattled enough to call him by his childhood pet name in front of a servant.

Stacy didn't mind the slip. In fact, he preferred "Stacy" to "Eustace"—which he'd always thought sounded like an undertaker's name.

He turned from his aunt to his hovering servant. "My aunt wishes to know what on earth you mean, Soames?"

The butler's parchment-like skin flushed. "It appears Signore Stefani is . . . well, he is dead, sir."

His aunt gasped and Stacy sat back in his chair.

"Are you telling me there is a dead body in the carriage, Soames?"

"Oh no, sir, no." Soames stopped and stared a point somewhere beyond Stacy's left shoulder, blinking owlishly. His brow creased and he fingered his long chin. "At least . . ."

"Well?" Stacy prodded when it seemed the ancient man had

calcified.

"I understand she is alone in the carriage, sir. No maid or, er, body." He glanced down at his hand. "She brought this with her and claims she is here for the music position."

Soames held out a folded piece of paper and Stacy took it. His own handwriting stared back at him; it was the letter he'd sent Ivo Stefani offering the famous pianist the position. Stacy put the letter aside.

"Very well, show *Signora* Stefani to her room, have Cook send up a tray, and tell *her* I shall speak to her tomorrow."

"Very good, sir."

His aunt waited until the agitated butler left before speaking.

"Well."

Stacy was amused by how much meaning she put into the single word.

"Well, indeed, Aunt."

"Wouldn't you rather speak to her now? Why wait until morning?"

"She's been in a carriage for almost three days, Aunt Frances. I daresay she is exhausted. Whether I speak to her now or in the morning, she'll still need someplace to spend the night." Besides, the woman had availed herself of a costly journey at his expense; he would question her at his leisure.

"But why has she come, my dear?"

"You heard Soames, Aunt, she's come to teach."

"Was there any mention of this in the correspondence you exchanged?"

"Not a word."

"Can she really expect you to offer her the position after she deceived you?" She stopped, her brow wrinkling. "Unless. . . do you think it possible the hiring agency deceived you?"

"Someone certainly has."

His aunt pursed her lips. "You must send her away."

"I can hardly send her packing in the middle of the night, can I ma'am?"

"I suppose not," she said, grudgingly. "But you must do so first thing tomorrow."

Stacy raised his eyebrows at his aunt's strident tone and she flushed under his silent stare and looked away.

Although his aunt had raised him from infancy, she'd always accepted he was master of both himself and Whitethorn Manor. Stacy couldn't recall the last time she'd told him what he must or mustn't do. She must be far more agitated than she appeared.

He gave her a reassuring smile. "There's nothing to worry about, Aunt Frances. I shall take care of everything in the morning." He took out his watch and glanced at it.

His aunt saw the gesture and stood. "I beg your pardon, my dear, I shall leave you to your port."

Stacy met her at the dining room door and opened it for her. "I'll join you shortly," he promised before shutting the door behind her.

He extinguished all but one candle and poured himself a larger than average glass of port, taking a sip of the tawny liquid before removing his dark spectacles. The bridge of his nose ached from a day of wearing glasses and he absently massaged it while staring at the dining room ceiling, on which sly cherubs lolled and cavorted on clouds, avidly viewing human folly from a safe distance.

He supposed he should have expected something like this. Not that a woman would show up, of course, but that it would be impossible to engage a musician of Stefani's caliber with such ease. When the employment agency wrote to tell him the famous pianist was seeking a teaching position, Stacy had wondered if it might be some sort of mistake.

Apparently it had been.

He couldn't believe the reputable and well-regarded Stark

agency would have lied about Ivo Stefani applying for the position. No, it must have been Mrs. Stefani.

Stacy shook his head. What manner of woman would embark on a long journey under such false pretenses? A bold one? A confident one? A desperate one?

He snorted; certainly a dishonest one.

Stacy could guess *why* she'd deceived him—no doubt she believed he would not engage a woman. He swirled his glass and stared into its warm depths. Would he? His lips twisted at the thought. No, he would not hire a female, although not for the reasons she might suspect.

While men might gawk and stare at him, they tended to overcome their curiosity—eventually. Women, on the other hand . . . Well, let's just say he'd learned the hard way that women were not so forgiving—especially when it came to his eyes.

Stacy could do nothing about their reactions, but he could minimize his exposure to their fear or scorn. Other than his tenants' wives, a few women in the village, and his female servants, he managed to avoid most women. Well, except for the women he visited in Plymouth; those women he generously compensated to ignore his appearance.

It said something about the state of his life that he'd so anticipated the arrival of a music teacher. Perhaps this debacle was a way of telling him his hobby was a foolish waste of time? God knew he had plenty on his plate managing his estates and businesses. But was his life to be devoid of any personal pleasure? He'd already accepted that he could never marry and have a family. Must he also give up playing the piano—one of the few things he loved—just because of his freakish appearance? Was he asking too much to engage a music teacher without fuss and bother? People did it all the time. True, it was usually for their children, but why should that matter?

Stacy put down his glass with more force than necessary, and the crystal clattered on the polished burl wood surface. The more he thought about the woman's deception, the angrier he became. How *dare* this female muck up what was supposed to be a simple business transaction? His aunt had been correct. Stacy should have summoned the woman before him, no matter how exhausted she was, and called her to account for her outrageous deception.

Thinking about his aunt made him realize it had been unkind to send her away when she was only concerned for his welfare—no matter how unnecessary her concern might be. She worried about him as if he were still a little boy rather than a man of five-and-thirty. Frances Tate was his only relative and had been mother and father to him, burying herself in the country and devoting her life to raising him. She'd never been married or even had a beau, as far as Stacy knew. Not for the first time did he feel guilty that she'd built her life around him. Poor Frances, at slightly over six feet tall, she was almost as great a misfit as he was.

Stacy pushed away his glass, picked up his spectacles, and stood. He would make up for his abrupt dismissal by playing for her—that always soothed her.

THE BUTLER'S REACTION to Portia's arrival had been so comical she would have laughed if her future did not hang in the balance. Indeed, if Mr. Harrington's horror was a fraction of his servant's, Portia would have been out in the road with her bags right now—or standing in front of the local magistrate.

Instead, she was in the middle of a luxurious suite comprised of a sitting room, a bedroom, and an enormous dressing room complete with a copper tub. The rooms were airy and spacious and decorated in a soothing combination of icy blue and warm chocolate brown. Portia sank into a wingback chair, took off her sturdy black ankle boots, and stretched her feet on the plush

Aubusson carpet. Her body ached, she was dusty and gritty, and her brain was beyond sluggish. Thank God she didn't have to face her prospective employer in this state.

She'd been both stunned and grateful when Mr. Harrington decided to postpone their encounter until morning. Tonight she'd take advantage of her brief reprieve and forget about whatever the master of the house had planned for her; tonight she'd enjoy the luxurious comfort of these rooms.

Portia had just opened her portmanteau and was searching for her nightgown when a maid entered with a large tray of food. The girl gave her a shy smile before carrying the tray to the sitting room and arranging the dishes on a table. She bobbed a curtsey when she'd finished, her large brown eyes brimming with curiosity.

"Mr. Soames said I should help you unpack or ask if you wished for a bath, ma'am."

Portia had the good grace to blush; dinner in her room and an offer of a hot bath? Mr. Harrington was treating her with kindness and courtesy despite her deception.

There was no point unpacking but Portia couldn't turn down a chance to bathe in the beautiful copper tub.

She smiled at the young woman. "I am Signora Stefani. What is your name?"

"Daisy, ma'am."

"I shan't need any help unpacking, Daisy, but I would love a bath after my meal."

"Very good, ma'am." She dropped another curtsey and left, closing the sitting room door behind her.

The smell of food made her mouth water and Portia hastened to examine what the maid had brought: roasted fowl, whipped parsnips, fresh bread and butter, a carafe of wine, and clotted cream with fresh berries. It was the perfect meal for a weary, hungry traveler and she descended on it like a ravenous beast.

She had just popped the last berry into her mouth when Daisy opened the door.

"Your bath is ready, ma'am."

Portia followed her to the copper tub, which was full of steaming water. Beside it was a marble-topped table with a stack of fluffy towels and several crystal decanters.

"Can I help you with your dress, ma'am?"

"Thank you, Daisy, but I shall manage." She waited until the door closed behind the maid before unbuttoning the row of fasteners that ran down the side of her worn, brown traveling costume.

Portia glanced around the room as she undressed. A lovely Chippendale cabinet stood against one wall, rich brown velvet drapes flanked floor-to-ceiling windows, and a massive four-poster bed dominated the bedchamber.

She absently ran a hand over the blue silk counterpane, which felt like a cloud when she pressed her hand into it. A sharp pang shot through her as she considered her surroundings. The housemaid was sweet, the rooms were lovely, and the simple meal had been delicious—what a pity she would most likely have to leave all this tomorrow.

Portia had never received such grand treatment before, not even when she and Ivo had stayed in some of the finest houses in Europe. Her husband had been hailed as a great artist and had been much feted before the accident which had ended his career. Men had paid generous sums to have Ivo Stefani play for their peers, and women had fawned over his olive-skinned good looks and warm bedroom eyes.

But the wife of the great artist had not received the same treatment. For the most part, Portia had stayed in tiny garrets and endured the grudging, slighting treatment of servants while Ivo had bedded the mistress of the house, spent a fortune on expensive frippery, and gambled away most of the money he'd earned.

Portia realized she was gritting her teeth.

Relax, she told herself. *Relax and enjoy the unexpected splendor, because the local magistrate will probably be waiting for you in the morning.*

She pushed away the thought and added a generous splash of lavender-scented bath oil to the steaming water before lowering her tired body into sheer heaven.

By the time she finished washing her hair, her eyelids were heavy with fatigue and she lay back against the warm copper and closed her eyes.

I will rest my eyes. Just for a minute…

Portia woke with a start to cold bathwater, pruned fingers, and pebbled skin. It was all she could do to pull her stiff, aching body from the tub and dry herself. She barely had enough strength left to drag a comb through her damp hair and don her threadbare nightgown before burrowing into the decadent bed. She closed her eyes and was immediately in the grip of a tedious half-dream that revolved around an unending carriage ride.

She was drifting in a deep, dreamless sleep when something awakened her. She pushed aside a tangled mass of curls and squinted at the candle she'd left burning across the room. The clock on her nightstand showed it was just past two.

Portia groaned and dropped her head onto the pillow. In addition to leaving the candle burning, she'd forgotten to draw the curtains, and moonlight flooded the room. She would need to extinguish the candle and close the drapes if she hoped to get any sleep.

Grumbling, she pushed off the blankets, heaved herself out of bed, and padded across the thick carpet to the window. She was about to pull the drapes shut when she noticed a small stone balcony beyond the rippled glass. The well-oiled window latch turned without a sound and she opened the casement and stepped out into a wonderland.

A cool breeze stirred her nightgown and the moon cast a magical glow, illuminating the countryside for miles around. It was one of those moons that hung so low in the sky you felt you could reach out and touch it. Even more light came from a series of lanterns that ran from the corner of the house half-way down the drive.

Portia wondered who would need such a brilliant display of light in the middle of the night but shrugged the thought away. Who knew what country folk did, and why?

Although the night was chilly, it was too beautiful to resist. Portia leaned against the cold stone and filled her lungs with crisp, non-London air, a temporary queen of her moonlit kingdom.

To the west lay a sliver of ocean; the shimmering waves were visible, but too far away to hear them crashing against the shore. Formal gardens surrounded the house to the west and south and beyond them lay a wood large enough to be called a forest.

Portia closed her eyes and drank in the quiet of the night. What a lovely, lovely place this was. And what a terrible shame this would probably be her only night to enjoy it. Her regret was so bitter it left a bad taste in her mouth; she never should have lied. She should've written to Mr. Harrington using her own name. She could've provided him with proof of her training, which was every bit as impressive as Ivo's, not to mention her experience operating a school—not that a closed school was a ringing endorsement.

She'd done them both a disservice by not giving him the truth and allowing him to make his decision. Now her deception would stand between them, and rightly so.

Portia gnawed at her lower lip until it was raw, furious at her impetuosity. She was almost nine-and-twenty, would she never learn to think before she acted? She must have been mad to think this would work, and even if—

A slight sound intruded on her misery and Portia opened her

eyes. Something white and ghostly flickered in the trees at the edge of the woods. She took a step back and stood in the shroud of the heavy velvet drapes, pulling them closer around her body. A figure emerged from the woods and Portia caught her breath as the white blur solidified: It was not a ghost, but a person on a large white horse.

Horse and rider picked their way past the line of trees before exploding into a gallop and blazing across the rolling parkland like a shooting star, closing the distance between the woods and the house in a matter of moments.

The spectral pair slowed as they approached the drive, the bright lanterns affording Portia a better look. No, most certainly not a ghost, but a very substantial-looking man. He wore no coat or waistcoat, only a white shirt that must have become damp from his exertions and now adhered to his torso like a second skin. He controlled his mount with long, muscular thighs encased in breeches and tucked into dark boots. The moonlight turned both horse and man and an eerie silver white.

Portia inched closer to the balcony as he approached, hoping to catch a glimpse of his face as he passed beneath the lantern that hung nearby. The drapes moved with her and the light from the candle behind her escaped and cast a dim line across the cobble drive that was like an arrow pointing toward her window.

Horse and rider swung around as one toward the balcony.

Portia gasped, stumbled back into the room and slammed the casement shut, fumbling with the lock. She pulled the drapes and collapsed against them, her heart pounding as if she'd been running.

Good Lord! How was that possible?

Chapter Two

IT WAS AFTER eleven o'clock by the time a servant arrived to escort Portia to her interview with the master of the house.

She'd been awake, dressed, and waiting for hours—in spite of the fact she'd not had much sleep. She'd tried, but every time she'd closed her eyes a haunting ivory face had flashed into her mind.

And those eyes . . .

Of course she knew it had been a man on the horse and not a ghost or demon. Even so, sleep had evaded her. She'd stared into the darkness above her bed, where phantom images formed and dissolved endlessly.

She'd tried to count sheep or think of other more pleasant things. Like the friends she'd left behind, the five women and one man who'd once been her employees but were now her family. Now her friends were scattered to the four winds, each forced to scratch out an existence on society's fringes. It was probable—likely, in fact—that Portia might never see some of them again.

So here she was; alone, once more.

The thought left her morose, restless, and full of self-pity, and she tossed and turned until the pink fingers of dawn crept over the horizon. Only then had she fallen into a shallow, fitful sleep.

Splinters of bright sunlight penetrated the gap between the velvet drapes and woke her just before eight o'clock. The face that greeted her in the mirror had blood-shot eyes with bags beneath them. Portia wanted to cry when she saw her reflection, but that would have made her nose red, too.

So she'd dressed herself and combed out the frightful mess that was her hair, pulling it back into a knot that was so tight it actually seemed to diminish the bags beneath her eyes.

And then she'd placed a cool cloth on her forehead and fretted until a knock jarred her from her worries.

It was the butler, Soames.

"Mr. Harrington will see you in the library, ma'am." In contrast to last night, when the old man had appeared almost frantic, this morning his wrinkled face and rheumy blue eyes were the epitome of butleresque impassivity.

They descended a different set of stairs than the one she'd come up the night before. Soames turned right when they reached the bottom and led her down a wide, dimly lit hall before stopping in front of a set of double doors.

He flung open the door on the right and motioned her inside. "The library, ma'am."

Portia peered into the room, the interior of which was hardly visible. The only light came from a single candle on the far side.

"Thank you, Soames." The deep voice came from the same direction as the light. "Please, come in and take a seat, Signora Stefani."

Portia took a hesitant step inside the room and jumped when the door snapped shut behind her.

"I suppose you find it rather dark." A flare of light followed his words and a pale hand lit three more candles. The nimbus of light grew until a skull with two black eye sockets materialized beside it. Portia gasped and the skull shifted into a mask of scorn.

"Please, don't be alarmed. I'm not dangerous and won't harm you."

Her face flamed, both at her foolish reaction and his mocking tone. She could see now that the two black spots were merely dark spectacles and the skull was just a very pale face—the same face she'd seen last night. The moonlight hadn't been playing tricks: Eustace Harrington's hair and skin were as white as freshly fallen snow. Only his frowning lips had any color.

"I have albinism, Signora Stefani. That means I suffer from a lack of pigment. You needn't worry, it's not contagious."

Portia laughed and his expression shifted from scornful to haughty.

"I'm not laughing at you, Mr. Harrington," she hastened to assure him. "I'm laughing because I'm perfectly aware you're not a contagion. I've heard of your condition before." Portia didn't tell him the only other person she'd heard of had been stoned to death by superstitious peasants in a village outside Rome.

"Then I don't have to worry you will faint or scream?" he asked, his tone caustic.

"Not unless you give me good reason to do either, sir."

He ignored her attempt at levity. "Why have you come to Whitethorn Manor?"

Portia took a deep breath and commenced the speech she'd rehearsed all the way from London.

"You wished to engage a music tutor with superior talent—I am such a person. I trained at the Accademia Nazionale di Santa Cecilia, the most respected music school in the world. My father was an instructor there for many years and I was one of his pupils." She paused. When he didn't speak, she continued. "The Accademia doesn't admit women, but I am, nevertheless, a classically trained pianist. I'm not Ivo Stefani, but I'm good. Very good." Portia stopped before her crushing anxiety got the better of her and leaked through her carefully constructed façade.

The white face across from her remained motionless. Had he expected her to apologize? To beg? Something very close to terror spread through her chest, making it difficult to breathe. Perhaps she should—

"When did your husband die?" he asked the question coolly, much as he might ask what time it was or whether she preferred tea to coffee.

Portia swallowed her irritation at his calm, deliberate manner—which made her feel like a recalcitrant schoolgirl standing before a headmistress. She reminded herself that *he* was the injured party in this transaction; she deserved cool treatment, at the very least.

"A little less than a year ago."

"So it was you who responded to my original advertisement and then sent me a letter, signing your husband's name."

Her hot face became even hotter. "Yes."

"If you are so highly qualified, why did you not apply under your own name instead of lying?"

The word *lying* was like a spark on dry tinder.

Portia opened her mouth, but the shrill voice of reason stopped her. *Be humble, Portia! Grovel! Only last night you promised no more impetuous behavior and*—Portia shoved the voice aside. After all—what did she have to lose by speaking her mind? The man was obviously not going to hire her.

"Tell me, Mr. Harrington, would you have engaged a woman tutor?"

He leaned back in his chair, his mouth pulling into a slight smile. "That's hardly the point, is it?"

The man was toying with her and feeding off her humiliation and fear. She shot to her feet and he stood with her.

"Are you leaving, Signora Stefani?"

"Why should I stay? You've made your opinion of female musicians quite clear."

"Oh? I thought we were speaking of your deception rather than your musical abilities."

Portia ground her teeth, furious that he was correct. Again.

He gestured to her chair. "Please, won't you be seated? I've gone to a great deal of effort and expense to bring you here. Won't you extend me the courtesy of a few minutes of your time and perhaps some answers?"

Everything he said was fair—maddeningly so—but for some reason that did nothing to mollify her unreasonable anger.

"And what will you do if I refuse, Mr. Harrington? Summon the local magistrate?'

He sighed. "I *am* the local magistrate, Signora Stefani."

Portia gave a short, mirthless laugh and dropped into her chair. "Ask whatever you like."

He resumed his seat, ignoring both her rude behavior and angry words. "I'm curious why there was no mention of your husband's death in the papers, Signora?"

She'd expected this question much sooner, but that didn't mean she was eager to begin telling even more lies.

"My husband did not die in England." She paused, "Perhaps you heard of his accident?"

"Yes, his arm was badly crushed and he could no longer play. I assumed that was why he responded to my advertisement."

"I'm afraid my husband found teaching an unbearable reminder of everything he'd lost." That much was true. "He needed to get away from the memories of his past and do something meaningful with his life. He decided the best way to do that was to join the army." *Lies, lies, lies.* Luckily her face couldn't get any hotter.

Pale eyebrows shot up above his dark glasses, a reaction that could mean surprise, disbelief, or some other emotion. Portia assumed it was surprise. After all, he hadn't known Ivo. If he had, he'd be doubled over with laughter right now: Ivo Stefani had not entertained an altruistic thought in his entire life.

"Please continue."

"There's not much more to tell. He went to Naples and died shortly afterward in the Battle of Tolentino." Would he dare to ask which side her husband fought with? Or would he assume the worst and dismiss her on the spot for being the widow of a man some in England might consider a traitor?

"Tell me, Signora," he said, resting his elbows on his desk and leaning forward, the action bringing his fascinating face closer to the light. "What did you think would happen when you presented yourself to me under false pretenses?"

She'd asked herself the same thing—but in more brutal words—countless times. Why, then, was she so angry when he asked her a question he had every right to ask?

Because you're ashamed of what you've done and nothing is more agonizing than knowing one is in the wrong.

The annoying little voice was correct, but that didn't mean Portia had to like it. Still, she *could* control her behavior better.

"I'm sorry for my deception and I apologize." She clamped her lips shut. But then her mouth opened and more words tumbled out. "If you tell me what you spent to bring me here, I will gladly repay you." She stunned herself with the foolish words; just where would she get the money?

Pride goeth before destruction, and a haughty spirit before a fall.

Portia ground her teeth at the smug, but apt, observation.

Mr. Harrington's features shifted into an expression of mild distaste. "We could haggle like costermongers over repayment for your journey or you could give me a demonstration of your musical ability." His pale lips twisted into a mocking smile. "I know which I would prefer."

Portia bristled at his sarcasm but hope surged in her breast. Would he consider engaging her? Or was this some petty form of revenge?

She studied his unreadable face. He reminded her of the famous stone she'd seen in the British Museum—the one named after the Egyptian port city of Rosetta. He bore no *physical* resemblance to the black chunk of rock, but he emanated the same inscrutable quality. Was he toying with her? Raising her hopes just so he could—

Portia seized control of her whirling thoughts. The truth was, she didn't care *what* his motivations were. Playing the piano was far better than answering questions for which she had no answers or at least none that were palatable.

She inclined her head with hauteur to match his. "You are entitled to a demonstration of my abilities. What would you like me to play?"

"I will leave that to your discretion. You are, after all, the expert," he added wryly. "Shall I take you to the music room right now or do you need time to prepare?"

Portia heard the challenge beneath his taunting question and smiled; what a pleasure it would be to shove his scornful words down his throat. She stood. "There is no time like the present, Mr. Harrington."

Chapter Three

PORTIA STOLE GLANCES at Eustace Harrington as he led her down the long hall. His aquiline nose, shapely lips, and chiseled jaw were the stuff of classical sculpture and his skin and fashionably cut hair were whiter even than alabaster. Only his glasses disturbed the vision of a male version of Galatea come to life: Eustace Harrington was the most fascinating-looking man she'd ever seen.

He opened the door to a room every bit as dark as the library and turned to her, a Sphinx-like smile curving his lips. "Pardon my rudeness Signora, but I'm going to precede you and light the way." He lit five candles in the candelabrum beside the piano before taking a seat as far from the light as possible, effectively hiding himself from her view.

Portia approached the instrument and stopped abruptly. "My goodness."

"What is it, Signora?"

"You have a Schmidt." She ran her fingers reverently across the glossy case.

"You approve?" His voice held the first hint of warmth she'd heard.

"It's a piano worthy of a concert dais." Even Ivo had never played on finer.

"There is sheet music in the cabinet behind you."

It was Portia's turn to smile mockingly. "That won't be necessary." She seated herself and ran through a few scales to loosen her hands. The instrument was easily the finest she'd ever played. The pianos her father had used to teach his students had been well-made, but most of them had been abused by hundreds of hands and years of constant use. This piano was exquisite, the sound immaculate.

She launched into Bach's Goldberg Variations, beginning with "Variatio 14. a 2 Clav."

The piece was lively—almost giddy—and the multitude of cross-overs was a perfect way to demonstrate her technical ability for the man who sat in judgment of her.

Portia could claim, without exaggeration, that she'd been Ivo's superior when it came to Bach.

"Of course you favor him," Ivo had taunted her in a fit of pique. "He has no passion, only mathematics—perfect for your English soul." He'd often flung the fact she was half-English at her as if that were some sort of flaw.

Portia moved without pause to "Variatio 15. Canone alla Quinta. a 1 Clav.: Andante." It was sheer pain and coiled itself around her and squeezed and squeezed, leaving her battered and bruised by the time she moved to the last selection.

"Variatio 5" was sweetness and light and it washed over her like a healing rain, soothing her with its gentle, caressing tranquility.

When the final notes left her fingers, Portia folded her hands in her lap and looked into the darkness. A long pause followed, which was something Mr. Harrington appeared to excel at.

"Your playing is exquisite." An almost undetectable tremor ran beneath his cool voice and Portia didn't bother to hide her triumphant smile. Good! Bach should never leave a person unmoved.

"It appears your claims were not hyperbole, you are a very good musician."

Portia refused to acknowledge such faint praise; she was beyond good.

"I was going to suggest a trial period to see if we might suit . . ." his words trailed off, as if he'd surprised himself with the offer. He'd certainly surprised Portia—rendered her dumbstruck, in fact. "But since you appear to have taken me in dislike—"

"I would be honored," Portia blurted before he could retract his offer. "And very grateful." She squirmed in the agonizing pause that followed. The distant ticking of a clock was the only sound and Portia was just about to start babbling when his cool, unhurried voice pierced the darkness between them.

"I think a month would be sufficient. At the end of the trial period I will either extend an offer for the full term of employment or I will pay you for the month and arrange for your journey back to London."

Portia's pride rebelled at the not-so-subtle threat behind his words: She'd better perform to his liking if she wanted to stay.

Fortunately, this time she seized control of her pride, wrestled it into submission, and swallowed her irrational temper. "That sounds more than fair, Mr. Harrington." She hesitated, "A month will give me time to see if I like living in such a remote location."

He chuckled at her small show of defiance, the sound warm and inviting and at odds with his chilly manner and remote exterior. "You've never lived in the country before, Signora?"

"I've done little more than drive *through* the countryside."

"Ah. Well, I should hate to keep you here now that you've seen how rural we are. Perhaps you would rather return to London?"

Portia almost laughed; the clever snake had let her tie her own noose and then insert her neck. It was too bad for him she refused to hang herself.

"I've come a long way, Mr. Harrington. It would be foolish not to give the situation a chance." Her stomach churned in the taut silence that followed.

"How shall you structure my lessons, Signora Stefani?"

Dizzying relief washed through her body and Portia scrambled to gather her wits. "I will need to determine your level of skill to answer that question. Is there a time of day you prefer to play?"

"I usually practice a few hours before dinner."

"Let us keep to your schedule. Today you can play whatever you've been working on, which will give me a chance to assess your strengths and weaknesses."

He emerged from the gloom and stopped short of the candelabrum. "I am less prone to eye strain if the light is dim. Will that be an issue?" He used one long, elegant finger to push his black spectacles up the bridge of his equally elegant nose.

Portia wrenched her eyes away from his mesmerizing face and stared at his stylish cravat instead. "As long as you are able to see the notes on the page," she said lightly.

"Then I shall meet you here at four o'clock. That will leave you with two hours to rest before dinner. My aunt and I take our mid-day meals separately but meet for dinner. We dine at eight o'clock, which is rather late for the country. You will, of course, join us."

Portia flushed at the unexpected offer—although it was really more of a command—thrilled she wouldn't be banished to her room for the next month.

"I would be delighted."

"Do you ride, Signora?"

"I'm afraid riding was not part of growing up in Rome. I am fond of walking, however, and the countryside looks lovely."

"We have our share of walking paths," he agreed, "but a gig will allow you to access town more readily. I will instruct Hawkins, my stable master, to show you how to operate the conveyance."

"That is most kind of you."

Harrington inclined his head. "I shall see you at four, Signora."

Portia waited until he'd turned before closing her eyes, weak with relief. She could stay—at least for now—and wouldn't have to beg and scrape her way back to London and live off her friends' charity.

"One more thing Signora."

Portia looked up and saw her new employer was standing in the open doorway.

"Yes, Mr. Harrington?"

"As far as I'm concerned the subject of your deception is closed. I will not bring it up again."

She smiled. "Thank you."

"However, I want you to understand I do not tolerate lying from the people I employ."

His cool rebuke crushed the gratitude Portia had been feeling and her hackles rose. But she triumphed over her nature and caught the angry retort before it left her mouth.

"I understand, Mr. Harrington."

He nodded and the door clicked shut behind him.

Portia stared into the dimness, the exhilaration of only a few moments ago now tainted by anger—and fear. His words echoed in her head and she ruthlessly pushed them to the back of her mind. She'd told him everything he *needed* to know. The truth about her past was none of his concern and made no difference to her teaching. All Mr. Harrington needed to know about her life with Ivo was that he was gone.

STACY SAT DOWN at his desk, extinguished the candles, and removed his glasses, letting his eyes rest in the velvety blackness of the library.

What the bloody hell had he just done? He'd gone in there determined to give her a proper raking and send her packing; instead, he'd been stupefied by her playing and then offered her a damned job.

He was *still* awed by her brief performance—a masterful demonstration of passion and precision he could never aspire to.

Don't forget her person, a sly voice in his head reminded him.

Stacy snorted. As if that were bloody likely.

He'd caught only a glimpse of her last night, but it had been enough to pique his interest. She'd looked wild on the balcony, her eyes huge, her full lips forming a surprised *O* when he'd caught her spying. Untamed spirals of dark hair haloed her pale face, her thin garment rendered all but transparent by the candlelight behind her.

Blood rushed to his groin at the memory of her voluptuous silhouette.

Christ. Stacy shifted in his chair.

Last night's woman had been alluring, but so had this morning's, although for entirely different reasons.

Gone were the wild eyes and in their place was a haughty stare. She'd restrained her magnificent hair so brutally Stacy wondered if he'd only imagined her unruly curls. Her serviceable brown dress was high-necked and long sleeved, but it could not hide the enticing body he'd so briefly seen last night.

Her nose, undoubtedly a gift from some Italian ancestor, was her most prominent feature and ensured she'd never be considered a conventional beauty. That said, her dusky hair, creamy skin, and voluptuous body made for a delicious—and dangerous—combination.

But her attractive person wasn't all that captured his interest.

She'd entered the library prepared for battle, armed only with her pride and talent—but, oh, what formidable weapons those turned out to be!

A fire burned inside her and Stacy had seen the flames—hell, he'd been scorched by them—when she spoke of her ability. She'd faced him with an arrogant confidence that had been damn near erotic, and, as it turned out, not at all unwarranted.

And then he'd become aroused when she'd played.

He should be ashamed by his body's earthy reaction, but he wasn't. A man would have to be dead from the neck down *not* to become hard. She'd swung from tightly laced to tempestuous and flushed—like a woman in the throes of passion—in the blink of an eye. The experience had not only been arousing, it had been soul-shattering: Stacy could practice for a hundred years and never play half as well.

But that didn't mean he couldn't *try.*

There was no doubt in his mind Signora Stefani had much to teach him—but would he be able to learn anything in her distracting presence?

You are not some rutting buck sensing a mate. Surely you can control your urges?

Of course he could control his urges, but control or lack of it was not the bloody question. The question was: Would he be able to concentrate on his music or would he spend his lessons fantasizing about bending her over the piano?

Stacy grimaced. It sounded more than a little pathetic when put so baldly.

But the truth *was* pathetic: He was randy. Terribly randy, in fact. He'd spent most of the last two months in Barnstaple, busy with the refitting of two new ships. As a result, it had been ages since his last visit to the Plymouth establishment where he satisfied such urges.

Ha! Establishment?

Fine. The brothel I frequent. Is that better?

Stacy refused to be ashamed of what he did. Paying a prostitute was a far better practice than getting bastards on one's servants or local maidens, a thing the local squire did with disgusting frequency.

There is always a wife.

He didn't even bother to justify that ridiculous thought.

The truth was that he should've set up a mistress long ago, but the notion left him cold. What a lot of bother not only for him, but also for some poor woman. What must it be like to sit around one's house all day waiting for a man to arrive and mount you?

Thoughts of mounting made his body tighten and he dropped his head against the back of his chair. A month was a bloody long time and he was already lusting after the poor widow, a woman who was only here to earn her bread.

Stacy frowned, sobered by that thought. He'd always been sickened by men who preyed on their tenants, servants, or other dependents. So, all he needed to do for the next thirty days was think of Signora Stefani as just another servant. Just a month, and then he would do what he should have done this morning and send her away. Surely he could suppress his unseemly urges for a month?

"Hell," he muttered, squeezing his temples, it was going to be a long month.

Chapter Four

PORTIA RETURNED TO her room and unpacked her portmanteau before writing a brief letter to Serena Lombard—a woman as dear to her as a sister—who would disseminate the news to the rest of their friends.

"Don't do this," Serena had begged when Portia told her about forging Ivo's signature. "Come live with Freddie, Honoria, and me. You can teach piano from our house. There is plenty of room for you."

But Portia loved her friends and could not be a burden to them. It was doubtful she could earn enough to cover her room and board, not to mention make payments on the horrific mountain of debt Ivo had left her. Only a well-paying position like the one Mr. Harrington offered could cover such financial burdens.

Portia wrote a second letter to her London landlady, a grasping woman who'd agreed, for a fee, to store Portia's few possessions until she decided what to do with them.

Ivo had taken everything of value when he departed and none of the items he'd left behind had any monetary worth, but they were all she had left of her parents.

When she was finished, she felt far too restless to read or nap, even though she'd had very little sleep the night before. She gazed out the window beyond her writing desk. The lesson was hours away and it was sunny and crisp outside, a perfect day to seek out a lesson in gig-handling. She slipped on her cloak and tied the wide brown ribbon of her bonnet beneath her right ear before making her way to the stables.

A stout older man was talking to a boy of nine or ten near the entrance to the stalls. He smiled when he saw her.

"Tha'll be Mrs. Stefani, I wager. Come to learn the gig, have 'ee?"

"I have, if it is no bother. You must be Mr. Hawkins?"

"Aye, I'm Ben Hawkins and this be John, my nephew."

"It's a pleasure to meet you Mr. Hawkins, John." Portia smiled at the boy, who flushed and doffed his cap.

Hawkins turned back to his nephew. "Off 'ee go, now. See to master's bitch and that wee 'un without any shilly-shally."

The boy darted off without a backward glance.

"He's good with the animals," Hawkins said, putting aside the harness he'd been working on. "One of the bitches whelped and there be a runt that can't find the teat."

"Oh, there are puppies?" Portia asked, sounding like an excited child to her own ears.

Hawkins gave her an indulgent smile, his brown eyes creasing. "Aye, go to the last stall but one. I'll ready up the gig while ye go back to see."

Portia followed the simple directions and found John kneeling in the straw beside an exhausted-looking hound.

He smiled up at her. "Tha come to see the pups?"

She crouched beside him. "Only if I won't be in your way, John."

"Would 'ee like to hold one?" He offered her a squirming, almost hairless bundle.

Portia glanced at the mother. "Do you think she'll mind a stranger holding her pup?"

John chortled, as if the idea of a dog minding anything was hilarious. "Wouldn't matter if she did. Master wants 'em handled so they be easy with folk. This be the runt. If she don't feed soon uncle will do for her."

"Do for her?"

"Aye, put her down, like."

Portia held the tiny beast closer as the boy's words sank in. "You mean he will kill her just because she is small?"

The boy looked away, clearly uneasy with her flare of anger. "I mun fetch some milk and bread. Cook warms it special four times a day. Would tha care to help feed her?"

Portia lifted the little creature higher and kissed her wrinkled forehead. "I'd love to."

John left and Portia settled into the deep straw. The smell of horse, fresh bedding, and clean dog filled her nostrils. She was humming an Italian lullaby from her childhood when the little dog opened its eyes. Footsteps sounded outside the stall.

"Come quickly, John, she's just opened her eyes."

When John didn't answer she looked up.

Eustace Harrington filled the doorway. He was dressed for riding in tan buckskins and a black clawhammer coat. His glossy, highly polished boots were almost as reflective as his dark spectacles, which were slightly different from the ones he'd worn earlier. This pair was enclosed with leather along the sides, probably to keep out light. A high-crowned black hat sat at a rakish angle on his short white hair, completing his elegant outfit. He tapped the side of his boot with his crop as he took in the scene.

"I thought you were John," Portia said stupidly, her heart thudding as he came closer.

He gestured to the dog with his whip. "That is the sickly one?"

Portia looked down into the pup's clear blue eyes. "She's not sickly, merely small and different. Will you put her down because of that?" Portia bit her lip. Why, oh, why couldn't she keep her mouth shut?

He tossed his crop onto the straw and lowered to his haunches before extending large, leather-clad hands toward her. She gave him the dog and he held the little animal gently while inspecting its body with deft, sensitive fingers.

"Her eyes appear clear enough and she has a good, solid heartbeat." He looked up from the dog, his own eyes two unreadable black mirrors. "But she is half the weight of the others." He handed the pup back to Portia. "If she survives she will always be small."

"These are foxhounds?" Portia asked, careful to keep the disapproval from her tone. She found such activities barbaric but knew the English gentry adored it.

His slight smile told her she'd been less than effective when it came to concealing her distaste.

"I do not hunt, Signora Stefani." He reached out to smooth the pup's wrinkled forehead and the motion brought his hand to within inches of her body. Portia held her breath; for one mad moment she envisioned leaning into his touch and competing with the dog for his caresses.

Idiot!

She wrenched her eyes away from his finger and looked up to find twin reflections of her flushed face staring back at her. He continued stroking, his face unsmiling.

Behind him, John skidded to a halt in the doorway. "Oh, Mr. Harrington, sir."

Eustace Harrington removed his hand from the dog, picked up his discarded crop, and stood. His sudden absence left Portia feeling light-headed, as if he'd taken all the air with him.

"What have you there, John?"

John held out a brown ceramic bowl, his eyes darting between Portia and his employer. "Milk and bread, sir. For the little 'un."

"Ah, it is feeding time." Mr. Harrington inclined his head. "I will leave you both to it."

Portia inhaled deeply as he left the stall, the spell broken. Good Lord he was attractive; *too* attractive. She'd be wise to limit their contact to his lessons and meals.

Yes, that would *be wise. But when have you ever been wise, Portia?*

STACY HAD PLANNED to pay only a brief visit to the Wilson farm and inspect the roof. But afterward, Mrs. Wilson invited him to share a glass of homemade wine to celebrate the birth of their grandson.

He liked the Wilsons, who were kind, gentle people and seemed to accept him for what he was—an excellent landlord—rather than what he looked like. But today the visit left him restless. He chalked it up to either his unfortunate attraction for his new employee or an unchristian covetousness of the Wilsons' happy home—or both.

Stacy might have far more money than the humble farmer, but he would never have the love of a woman or know the joy of children—he'd learned that painful lesson a decade ago, or at least he thought he had; yet when he'd encountered the intriguing music teacher nestled in the straw he'd been tempted to linger near her. Her snapping brown eyes and the fiercely protective way she'd cradled the small animal to her generous bosom had been more than a little appealing. He'd even experienced a stab of envy for the lucky dog privileged to nestle against her.

Stacy snorted; he'd been reduced to envying runty pups.

On impulse, he turned Geist toward the coast. He'd planned to look in at the wheelwright's today but he was just too damned restless to conduct business. He rarely rode for pleasure during the day, preferring his nighttime jaunts, when he could ride unencumbered by glasses, coats, scarves, and hat. His moonlit rides were his salvation. The only other time he felt so carefree was at the piano. But that had changed in the last year, when an invisible barrier had descended between him and the music. As much as he'd practiced, he hadn't been able to find his way past it.

He'd need to keep reminding himself about that barrier in the days to come—his real reason for hiring the woman. An unsolicited image of the music teacher nestled in the straw invaded his mind.

"Bloody hell," he muttered. He flexed his thighs, urging Geist into a gallop, as if he could outrun the distracting vision in his head.

STACY BARELY HAD time to bathe and change before his lesson. He'd ridden until he and Geist were lathered, hoping he'd thrashed his lustful urges into submission.

Signora Stefani was already in the music room when he arrived. She'd lighted the room using two small branches of candles, one on the writing desk where she sat and one near the piano.

She looked up when he entered. "Welcome, Mr. Harrington. I'm ready to get right to the best part of each lesson—the playing."

"I hope you still believe that after hearing me play, Signora."

She laughed and the sound was low, warm, and inviting. "I'm an optimist by nature. I've put out several pieces for you, but first I'd like to hear what you've been working on."

Stacy located the sheet music he wanted and ran a few scales. He forced himself to pretend there was no one else in the room, especially not an attractive woman who was also a virtuosa on the piano. He took a deep breath and began a piece of music that was already part of him.

For a short time, he forgot himself; he wasn't Eustace Harrington the ghostly, violet-eyed freak, he was only sound and sensation. The music worked its magic, feeding his soul and rejuvenating him. The notes drove away his worries, concerns—and yes—even his loneliness, leading him toward a state of being that was sublime.

But all too soon the piece was over.

He removed his hands from the piano and looked up to find Signora Stefani standing beside it. Her flushed cheeks and sparkling eyes spoke volumes; she knew exactly what playing did to him. It was like sharing an intimate secret with a complete stranger.

Stacy looked away from those knowing eyes, his gaze dropping to her mouth. The generous curve of her full lips made his abdomen clench, as if his body was tensing to protect itself from something. Stacy frowned at the bizarre thought. Protect him from what? What the devil was wrong with him?

"Mr. Harrington?"

He looked up. She'd said something while he'd been staring at her mouth. An unaccustomed heat crept up his neck.

"I beg your pardon, Signora?"

"I asked how long you'd been working on the piece?"

"Perhaps four months."

"I am pleased to find you so advanced. With your skills there will be very little beyond your reach."

If Stacy had possessed a tail it would have been thumping wildly against the piano bench. As it was, her praise was causing unexpected responses from other parts of his body. He closed his eyes, once again grateful he could hide behind his spectacles. Was his pathetically grateful behavior what came of keeping too much to himself? Was he now unable to be in the presence of *any* attractive woman without becoming excited or wanting to bed her?

Truly, he must be one of the most pathetic men in Great

Britain.

"I put several exercises out for you, Mr. Harrington. Would you please begin with the one on top and work your way down?" She'd gone back to her desk and her low, slightly accented voice, floated toward him from the gloom.

Bloody hell. Her face, her body, and now her voice?

Stacy stared at his hands as they rested on the keys, briefly tempted to use them to pummel some sense into his skull.

Instead, he played.

Chapter Five

THE TWO-HOUR LESSON felt more like twenty minutes. While Portia's new pupil did not demonstrate that rare spark of genius, he was an exceptionally talented musician and it would be a pleasure to help him hone his skills.

"Hawkins told me you had your first lesson in gig handling. How was it?"

Portia looked up from the notes she'd been making. He'd come to stand by her desk and loomed large over her, the light from the candles on the desk illuminating his stark features.

"I think I may have frightened your poor stable master." Portia didn't see any reason to mention that she'd also run the small cart into one of his rosebushes. Or that she'd come perilously close to crushing Mr. Hawkins's foot with one of the wheels.

"Hawkins is a man of great patience."

"And fortitude. And bravery."

"I shouldn't worry too much about it, Signora. You are not the first to test his mettle. He put me on my first pony when I was six." He smiled, exposing a charming dimple in his right cheek.

A dimple. Portia wanted to weep. How very, very unfortunate. She wished she could see his eyes; did he wear his wretched spectacles all the time?

He bowed abruptly, the gesture making Portia realize she'd once again been staring, probably gawking with her mouth hanging open. *Blast and damn!*

"I shall see you at dinner, Signora Stefani."

His elegant figure was quickly swallowed by the gloom that held sway beyond the piano. He lived so much of his life in darkness, or near enough. What was that like?

That is none of your business, Portia Stefani.

Portia ignored the hectoring thought. She'd always been insatiably curious about the people around her, even when they weren't gorgeous, mysterious men. Why deny she found him attractive? It wasn't as if she had any plans to act on her attraction. Indeed, she had no plans to act on *any* such attraction to *any* man as long as she lived. If her experience with Ivo had taught her anything, it was that her volatile, sensual nature was not something that decent, God-fearing men appreciated.

She assembled her notes and stacked them neatly on the corner of the desk. Dinner was still two hours away, so she would have ample time to review her wardrobe and decide what to wear. Fine clothing was one of the few things she retained from her marriage. It was too bad she no longer had her mother's jewels to go with her gowns.

Portia pushed away the foolish yearning to look attractive and the unwise reason behind it. The man was her employer, not a prospective lover. A wealthy, handsome man like Eustace Harrington would not be interested in what his music teacher wore—especially an older, homely music teacher. Even in her youth she'd never been more than passably attractive, and now she was close to thirty and well past her bloom: a veritable crone.

And finished with impetuous behavior, especially when it comes to men, the nagging voice reminded her.

Portia sighed. *Yes, yes, and finished with impetuosity when it comes to men.*

This was a very well-paying position and she would do well to remember she was an employee here. The only thing her high spirits had ever done for her when it came to the opposite sex was get her in trouble. Look at what had happened the last time she'd acted on her romantic impulses—she'd ended up married to Ivo. Portia snorted. Now she was impoverished, humiliated, and stranded in a country she considered foreign, even though she was half English.

No, this time she'd listen to her brain instead of her body.

THE GOWN PORTIA wore for her first dinner was seven or eight years old but it was her most flattering. It was a lovely carmine silk with dropped shoulders and the bodice was trimmed only with a wide sash in the same shade. She wore a pair of filigree earrings, one of the few pieces of jewelry Ivo had not taken when he left—only because they'd been in Portia's ears at the time.

Mr. Harrington was in the dining room when she entered and, as usual, Portia had to remind herself not to stare. He was breathtaking in evening clothes, the unrelieved black and white a stark but effective foil for his pale beauty.

He took her hand and bowed over it, his lips curving into a welcoming smile. Portia's breath caught and she hoped he did not bandy *that* dangerous look about too often.

"Good evening Signora Stefani, how elegant you look. You will put our country fashions to shame."

"You do not look like a victim of rural fashions, Mr. Harrington," she said dryly as he pulled out a seat for her.

"We have this ludicrously long table but buck convention and dine only at one end of it, *en famille*, if you will."

"Do you speak French, Mr. Harrington?"

"You've just heard a quarter of my French vocabulary." Portia laughed and he poured her a glass of wine before filling his own and taking his seat. "We English are horrible when it comes to learning foreign languages. I daresay you speak several."

"Naturally I am fluent in Italian and French."

"Naturally."

"I only say *naturally* because my father was born on the border and French was his first language. Even so, my accent was deemed horribly rustic by most Parisians."

The door opened and the tallest woman Portia had ever seen entered. When Mr. Harrington stood to welcome her Portia saw the two were almost the same height.

"I would like to introduce my aunt, Frances Tate. Aunt Frances, this is Signora Stefani."

The towering, whippet-thin woman inclined her smooth, sandy blond chignon. "It is a pleasure to meet you, Signora. My nephew says you are an extraordinarily skilled pianist. I look forward to hearing you play."

Regardless of her pleasant smile, Portia felt the woman was not happy to see her. Perhaps she was not as forgiving of Portia's deception as Mr. Harrington?

"I'm happy to play for you anytime you wish. Do you also play?"

"I took lessons as a young girl, but never achieved more than a mere competence."

Mr. Harrington made a small sound of surprise. "Why Aunt Frances, you never told me you had piano lessons."

"I purposely kept that information from you, Stacy. You would have forced me to play if you'd known." She turned to Portia. "My nephew was an implacable youth, Signora. Once he got an idea in his head he could be quite tenacious and always managed to get his own way."

Stacy? The name suited him better than Eustace, which was too stolid for such an elegant man.

"*Tsk, tsk,* Aunt Frances, you will make Signora Stefani think I am a tyrant."

The older woman's eyes glinted with love and affection. "You are—a benevolent one."

The dinner conversation ranged from politics to local affairs to the arts and her host seemed very well informed in all areas.

"I receive a number of newspapers each week, from both London and the Continent. If you should care to read any of them please feel free to do so. The same goes for anything else in the library."

Mr. Harrington signaled the footman to refill her glass of wine. It was her second; she really must slow down.

"My nephew prides himself on his library. You must explore his impressive catalogue of books." Miss Tate's words were warm, but her blue-gray eyes were shrewdly assessing.

"I should like that very much. I was a member of a circulating library in London and feared I would lack for books while here."

Mr. Harrington waved away the footman's proffered tray of desserts and Portia glanced down at her own selection of sweets and flushed; she'd taken a zabaglione as well as several biscuits. If she ate this well every day she'd be in danger of growing out of her clothing.

She took a taste of the frothy desert and barely resisted moaning. It was as delicious as any she'd had back home. When she looked up from the dish she saw Mr. Harrington watching her, a slight smile on his lips. Portia flushed, as if she'd been caught enjoying something carnal.

"What sort of books do you enjoy, Signora?"

"I enjoy anything from gothic novels to travel books."

He turned to his aunt. "What was the novel you just finished reading, Aunt Frances?"

Portia could see behind his spectacles when he turned: thickets of long white eyelashes fringed his lids.

"Have you read it, Signora?"

She blinked, too busy gawking to have heard his aunt's reply

"Er, I'm afraid I have not yet had the opportunity."

"You mentioned one of her other books earlier, but I can't quite recall—which one was it, Signora?" His smile was mocking; he *knew* she had no idea what he was talking about. And he knew why, too. It was mortifying to know she'd joined the ranks of rude people who goggled at him.

"I think it was *Delphine*," Miss Tate interjected, unknowingly saving Portia.

Mr. Harrington's smile grew, exposing his dangerous dimple. "Ah, yes, that was it. Thank you, Aunt Frances."

Portia looked from his amused face to her food, her skin warm. This would be the very last time she was caught staring at the man.

"Your English is very good, Signora, I hardly detect any accent," Miss Tate said.

"My father was Italian but my mother was English. As I was telling Mr. Harrington, I grew up speaking several languages at home."

"How long have you lived in England?"

"I moved to London seven years ago."

"Do you have family here?"

Portia couldn't help feeling she was being interrogated, no matter how gently. Still, she supposed she owed them her history, as she'd come here under false pretenses and was living under their roof.

"My father taught the Earl of Marldon's five daughters piano and eventually married the earl's second eldest daughter."

Miss Tate's eyebrows arched so high they almost met her carefully coiffured hair. "You are Marldon's granddaughter?"

Portia smiled at the woman's obvious amazement. "Yes, that is correct."

"Have you seen your mother's family since returning to England?" Mr. Harrington asked.

"My mother's family was not pleased with her elopement and ceased all communication. When she died my father sent a message to her family but received no response. After I came to England I learned my grandfather had died and the title passed to a distant cousin. The new earl showed no interest in acknowledging our connection." A taut silence followed her disclosure and she almost felt sorry for her hosts. What response could a person have to such information?

Miss Tate's piercing stare didn't waver. "I believe I knew one of your aunts—Cicely."

It was Portia's turn to stare. "Yes, my mother's oldest sister. How did you meet her?"

"We were at school together but were not well-acquainted."

Mr. Harrington cocked his head. "Why, Aunt, you never told me you went away to school."

"It was a long time ago, Stacy, and I was not there above a year."

"What a coincidence. It's a very small world," Mr. Harrington said.

Small world, indeed; Portia could only hope this was the only connection to her past that would rise to the surface.

AFTER DINNER PORTIA played more Bach at Mr. Harrington's request. Both he and his aunt were very complimentary and it was a joy to play such a glorious instrument. Nights like tonight were as close as she would ever come to performing in public. That realization no longer caused her the heartache it had when she and Ivo were together.

"Why do you torment yourself, *cara*?" he'd ask when he found her practicing, his caramel-colored eyes amused and condescending. "Is not my genius enough for the both of us?"

He'd been considerably less amused about her practicing *after* his accident, which had left his hand usable, but unable to play. Then he'd become vicious, rather than mocking, when he'd caught her at a piano. Portia hadn't minded so much; he'd attacked her because he could no longer make music. As a musician, she could imagine how dreadful that would be.

She went up to her room not long after she finished playing. Her body was tired but her mind was still in a whirl so she took Voltaire's *Zadig* from the small collection of books she'd brought with her. But her eyelids became heavy and she abandoned the book and blew out the candle after a quarter of an hour.

Just like the night before, she slept for a few hours before waking. This time she went directly to the window and drew back the curtains. She didn't have long to wait before he appeared, thundering across his land on his magnificent horse, two ghosts under the moonlight.

She kept hidden, unable to tear her eyes away as man and beast moved as one. As he'd done the previous night, he ended his ride by coming beneath her window. Portia didn't think she'd moved and there was no light from a candle, but just as he rode past her balcony he looked up. She froze. He was not wearing his spectacles and under the combined light of the torch and bright moon she caught a faint glimpse of violet.

Not until he'd gone past did she realize he'd been smiling.

"DID YOU SEE the nosy music teacher tonight, Geist?" The majestic horse's ears twitched at the sound of Stacy's voice. He removed Geist's saddle and began the horse's rubdown. Stacy *tsked.* "You probably think she stays up to watch you?" The stallion pawed the floor with one of his forelegs and Stacy chuckled. "I don't think so, my friend. I think she stays up to stare at *me.*"

It was the same morbid interest women always showed in him. Usually their inquisitive stares did not amuse him and never before had he wanted to satisfy a woman's curiosity by exhibiting his eyes—at least not since his debacle with Penelope. He frowned at the memory of his former fiancée and the night he'd learned just how well a woman could hide her disgust at his person in pursuit of his money.

Geist leaned heavily against Stacy's shoulder as he toweled first one foreleg and then the other. Geist made a low grumbling noise.

Stacy laughed softly. "You like that, do you, you greedy thing?"

After he was done he slipped on Geist's halter and led him down the long corridor. Other white heads poked out as Stacy and Geist passed, one his newest mare, Snezana.

The stallion's body stiffened and he stopped and whickered, stomping one hoof on the plank floor outside her stall. Snezana tossed her head but then retreated into the dark recesses of her stall.

Stacy clucked his tongue and patted Geist's rump. "She's not ready for you yet, my friend." Geist followed him with obvious reluctance, his large dark eyes rolling as they left the silent mare behind.

He led the agitated stallion toward his big corner stall, soothing him as they went. "It's difficult to wait, I know. But she wouldn't take you now. I promise, when the time is right, she will come to you."

Another pair of dark, expressive eyes flashed through his mind's eye as he calmly stroked the big horse's flank.

Stacy wasn't sure whether his soothing words were for the anxious stallion or for himself.

Chapter Six

PORTIA'S FIRST WEEK sped by and she rarely saw either of the other occupants of Whitethorn other than at daily lessons and dinner. In fact, she saw so little of them she sometimes wondered if they avoided her on purpose.

But it was far more likely that they each had busy lives. She'd learned from the maid Daisy, who waited on her most often, that Mr. Harrington was a man of business with interests in other parts of the country, not only Cornwall. And Miss Tate ran her nephew's large manor house and also volunteered at the local vicarage.

The only one who had no life to speak of was Portia.

She didn't even get to peek at Mr. Harrington during his midnight rides as those had ceased with the waning of the moon. It struck her as odd that he'd never mentioned her spying; of course she'd never confessed that she watched him. It was almost as if they shared a secret.

Portia snorted at the foolish thought as she rang for the maid her eighth morning at Whitethorn. She'd woken earlier than usual, determined to try her hand at the gig today. She was enjoying her walks, but she wanted to explore farther afield than she could on foot.

When she reached the breakfast room she found it occupied for the first time in over a week. "Good morning, Miss Tate. Are you always an early riser?"

"It is my favorite time of the day, Signora." The older woman smiled but her pupils were small black dots. She was always friendly and pleasant but never lowered her reserve.

Portia approached the groaning sideboard with eager anticipation; it had been many, many years since she'd eaten so well and she possessed a voracious appetite. She'd long ago ceased fretting about her figure, which seemed to remain unfashionably plump whether she starved herself or ate what she liked.

"What are your plans this morning, Signora?" Miss Tate asked after Portia sat.

"I've decided to take the gig to town." Portia looked from the other woman's plate, which held one half-eaten slice of dry toast, to her own, which was heaped with ham, eggs, pilchards, and a thick slice of buttered bread.

"Do you ride?"

"I'm afraid I never learned." Three pots of jam sat on the table, begging her to sample them. "I've been exploring the area on foot." Miss Tate arched her eyebrows, either at Portia's words or appetite. "But Mr. Harrington kindly offered me the use of his gig." She took a forkful of coddled eggs and immediately wished she'd helped herself to more: they were delicious.

"Are you city born and bred, Signora?"

Portia added a generous dollop of cream to her coffee. "I was born and raised in Rome. After I married, I accompanied my husband on his engagements, which were mostly in large cities."

"It must have been an interesting life."

"It had its moments." Portia took a sip of coffee and sighed with contentment; it was dark, strong, and richly flavored.

"Do you think you can be happy living in the country after such a glamorous life?"

Portia chuckled. "I wouldn't say it was glamorous." She didn't tell the other woman her life had actually been fraught with constant stress and insecurity. Instead, she cut a piece of gammon steak while she considered her answer. "Thus far I like living here quite well," she said, and then popped the ham into her mouth, chewed, swallowed, and took another sip of coffee. "Have you lived here your entire life, Miss Tate?"

"I moved here when my nephew was a baby." She glanced down at her plate, where her hands were busy crumbling the remainder of her toast. When she noticed Portia watching her she wiped her elegant fingers on her napkin and lowered them to her lap.

"Where did you live before you moved here?"

The silence drew out for so long that Portia wondered if Miss Tate had heard her.

"I lived with my sister and her husband just north of Plymouth."

Portia waited for more. When none came, she topped up her coffee and gestured to Miss Tate's almost empty cup.

"No, thank you." Her tall body unfolded gracefully as she stood. "I am due at the vicarage. Mr. Harrington's greenhouses provide fresh flowers for the church."

"That is generous."

"Yes, my nephew is generous in many ways—sometimes to a fault. His propensity to think of others' welfare before his own has sometimes caused him . . . discomfort." She paused, as if to let Portia absorb that piece of information. "I hope you enjoy your morning."

"Thank you, Miss Tate." Portia waited until the door shut before resuming her meal. Well. Frances Tate hadn't exactly issued a warning, but she'd certainly let it be known she was prepared to take up the cudgels on her nephew's behalf if Portia overstepped herself. Miss Tate was likely accustomed to protecting her handsome, wealthy nephew from impoverished, fortune-hunting females. Portia wanted to reassure the woman that Mr. Harrington was in no danger from *her*, but she doubted the reserved older woman would either appreciate or believe reassurance from a person who'd already shown willingness to lie to get what she wanted.

And whose fault is that?

Portia ignored her guilty qualms and finished breakfast without further interruption. After fetching her hat, cloak, and reticule she meandered through the spectacular gardens on her way to the stables.

Mr. Hawkins was out front grooming the white horse she'd seen the prior evening.

"What a beautiful animal."

Hawkins smiled proudly, as if the animal belonged to him. "Aye, miss, 'ee surely is. Ready to try tha hand with the cart again?"

"If you think I should, after my disastrous first attempt."

Hawkins gave a good-natured laugh. "T'were only a few bushes tha flattened. Here, let me fetch John to finish Geist and I'll fetch the gig."

"May I pet him?" Portia asked, itching to stroke the beautiful animal.

"Aye, he'll like that."

Portia met the horse's surprisingly dark eye. Geist gave her a calm look and then nudged her hand with his soft chin as she stroked the velvety soft muzzle.

The stable master soon returned with John and when Portia turned to greet the boy Geist nudged her arm with his nose. Both Hawkins and John laughed.

"Tha can niver quit with this one, ma'am. He's a right greedy one for attention."

"What does his name mean?" The word was familiar but Portia couldn't recall where she'd heard it.

"The master says it be some fern word for 'ghost.'"

Ah, that was it: *Geist* was German for ghost, exactly what

Portia had thought he was—a ghost in the moonlight.

"Take 'im back into his stall, John, not the pasture. The master might want him later."

The boy clucked his tongue and led the huge horse into the stables.

Hawkins turned to her. "I reckon tha should take John along these first few times, ma'am."

"I should hate to deprive you of your helper, Mr. Hawkins."

"'Tis naught. He can visit his ma and sisters while he waits."

"I collect everyone knows everyone else in such a small town?" Portia asked, while Mr. Hawkins hooked a placid mare to the small cart.

"Aye, 'tis true. A body can't take two steps without stumbling over family."

"That must be nice."

The old man grunted, his hands deftly attaching the harnessing while his eyes met hers. "It keeps a man from misbehavin'." Mr. Hawkins's eyes flickered over her shoulder and he paused to tug his forelock. "Good mornin', master."

Portia turned to find Mr. Harrington, dressed to ride in glossy boots, dark leather breeches, and an impeccably cut black coat. Unlike on his nighttime jaunts, he also wore dark spectacles, black leather gloves, and a high-crowned hat. The only color in his ensemble was his bottle green and gold striped waistcoat. He was a vision of masculine beauty.

"Tha be wantin' Geist, sir?"

"It can wait, Hawkins." He turned to Portia. "Are you going to try your hand at the gig, Signora?"

"Just as far as Bude, sir."

He nodded, hesitated, and then said, "Perhaps I shall accompany you. I have business at the inn."

Portia's fertile imagination leapt ahead to sitting beside the gorgeous man on the very small bench. "Er—"

"If that is acceptable to you," he asked, with a slight smile.

"Yes, yes of course it is. Mr. Hawkins was just saying that I should have somebody with me." *Of course he was suggesting a boy, and not a paragon of masculine perfection.*

"I think that is probably wise the first few times."

Hawkins stepped back from Buttercup "She'll be a right hand with the ribbons soon enough, master."

"I'm sure she will, Hawkins." His nostrils flared slightly. "Signora Stefani strikes me as the kind of woman who is good at everything she turns her hand to."

Portia couldn't see his eyes, but she swore she could feel his gaze and her body heated; if looking at him did this to her, what would sitting beside him do?

She was about to find out.

STACY STARED AT the very woman he'd been avoiding for days. *What the devil am I doing?*

Apparently you're avoiding her company, the dry voice in his head answered.

He handed her up onto the narrow bench and once she was settled he swung himself up. She'd squeezed all the way to the metal railing that surrounded the seat, yet still his thigh, side, and buttock pressed against hers. She felt good; too good.

Stacy glanced down to find her staring up at him, her face a fetching shade of pink. "Is this uncomfortable for you, Signora?"

"No, of course not." She whipped around and faced forward. And then she sat there.

Stacy's lips twitched. "You need to give Buttercup some indication you are ready to proceed."

"Oh!" Her small hands tightened on the reins and she made a clucking noise with her tongue. Buttercup's head came up, but she didn't move.

"Perhaps you might give her a bit of slack, Signora."

"Oh," she said again, and then loosened her grip so much the reins slid through her fingers.

Stacy's hand shot out and caught them before they could tangle in the harness.

Buttercup, freed from restraint, ambled forward.

"Oh dear." The woman grimaced, cutting him a quick, mortified look. "I'm sorry." Her face had gone from pink to crimson.

"There is nothing to apologize for, you are just learning. Here, take the ribbons."

She shook her head vigorously. "I'd rather you do it."

He continued to hold them out for her and she finally heaved a sigh and took them, this time holding them loosely.

"Is this all right?" she asked when Buttercup had plodded along for a moment.

"It's perfect."

"I suppose she knows the way and doesn't require much steering."

Stacy decided not to tell her that one *guided,* not steered, a horse. "Buttercup could walk to Bude in her sleep—backward."

Mrs. Stefani laughed, a low, sensual sound he'd heard once or twice before. A sound that he decided he liked hearing far too much.

"Your horse—Geist—is lovely."

He raised his eyebrows. Was she finally going to mention watching him on his rides?

"Thank you," he said.

"You have quite a few horses. Are they for personal use or do you breed them to sell?"

"Most of the breeding I've done in the past was for my tenants."

"Oh?"

"Yes, most farmers don't have a use for stallions as they can be temperamental. I own several studs and allow my tenants to use them at no cost as stud fees can often be too expensive. Over the next few weeks you will see farmers bring their mares."

She glanced at him. "That's very kind of you."

"A happy tenant is a productive one. Besides, by providing good sires I'm doing my part to maintain the quality of livestock in the area."

"So Geist's offspring are numerous?"

"Geist is far too valuable to use for draft animals. He is still young, and this is his first season so he will cover only my own mares. But next year I'll stud him for a fee."

Beside him, she shook her head. "I don't understand—I thought you said your tenants couldn't afford to pay?"

"These would be other breeders from around the country."

"And they would bring a horse all the way *here*?" She sounded more than a little skeptical.

"Oh, indeed. I've already got twenty-five owners on my list, some from as far as Scotland."

"That is astounding! I take it Geist is a racehorse?"

Stacy heard the same disapproval in her voice as when she'd asked him about hunting dogs. "He raced for a short period, but only long enough to establish his qualities. When he was put up for sale, I purchased him."

"You bought him because he won races?"

"In part."

"Then why don't you still race him?"

"While it's true he exhibited impressive speed and endurance on the flat he possesses an impeccable lineage so he is far more valuable as bloodstock than as a racehorse. He's also a good-natured horse and fairly biddable for a stallion, which should make him easier to stud."

The brief look she gave him was heavy with censure. "So he's nothing more than a business to you?"

Rather than finding her annoying, Stacy liked her fire. "May I not enjoy him *and* earn money, Signora?"

"You may do whatever you like. It just seems cold to only care about him because of his bloodline. Not to mention arrogant to believe one should control such bloodlines."

Stacy gestured to the two trees on either side of the drive, just ahead of them. "What do you think of these trees?"

"The trees?"

"Yes, the trees."

She shrugged. "They're trees."

"Look closer."

She leaned forward as they passed. "My goodness, are those large things *buds*?"

"Yes, they are. In less than a month you will be gifted with an amazing sight. This year the circumstances have been propitious and our magnolias will flower."

"I've heard of magnolias. They are supposed to be quite spectacular."

"They are. And there are no others quite like these two. These magnolias were planted during my uncle's lifetime. He was a botanist and acquired some of the first magnolias to arrive in Britain. Over the course of many years he worked with them until he created a pair that would not only survive, but thrive, in our climate."

Her smile was wry. "I see where you are going. But your uncle did this to create a tree that would live here. Geist's offspring would survive no matter what mare he was bred with."

"True. But survival isn't the only point of selective breeding—there is also a desire to maintain certain characteristics, perfect others, and eradicate dangerous flaws."

"I'm afraid you and I will have to agree to disagree on this subject, Mr. Harrington. As a person who has been referred to as a mongrel because of my mixed heritage, I'm biased."

Stacy frowned. "I'm sorry to hear you've had to endure such insulting, foolish words, Signora. Horses and magnolia trees are not people and no sane person would ever advocate selective breeding for human beings."

"The English aristocracy do."

Her tart, spirited answer surprised a laugh out of him. "Touché, Signora, touché."

"Oh look," she said, gesturing with her chin. "We are nearing town."

He realized that was her way of ending their conversation.

"Won't you please bring the gig into the inn so I do not run down the poor ostler?"

Stacy opened his mouth to urge her to try it on her own, but when she turned her magnificent—and imploring—dark eyes on him, he found himself doing her bidding and reaching for the ribbons. He'd spent less than half an hour with her and already he was having difficulty denying her.

Yes, he thought grimly as her soft, warm, fragrant body pressed against him, *this trip into town has been a mistake.* The woman's fiery persona and attractive person were proving to be far too enticing. Being in her presence made him forget she was his employee, and that was something he needed to keep at the forefront of his mind: she was pleasant to him because he was her employer, and that was all.

The truth was that spending time with Mrs. Stefani would only yield one result: infatuation at best, and, at worst, deeper feelings. As he'd learned long ago, either result would likely end in disappointment and pain for him.

Chapter Seven

PORTIA WAITED THREE days after her far-too-stimulating gig ride with Mr. Harrington before accepting his offer to use the library.

She didn't want to encounter him—or rather, she was a bit *too* interested in another *tête-à-tête*—and had the feeling that he'd been avoiding her, as well, since their brief trip into town.

It turned out that his business had kept him late that day so she'd not ridden back to Whitethorn with him, but rather a groom from the inn. She'd been of two minds about that. Part of her yearned to feel his hard body wedged up against hers, wanted to inhale the faint, intoxicating hint of cologne, and was eager to talk to him about a rather scandalous topic like *breeding*, even if it was only horse breeding they were discussing.

But seeing him at lessons and dinner was already tempting enough. She *needed* this position too badly to upset the delicate balance between them, so she'd kept her willful nature in check.

But she was out of books to read and she knew Mr. Harrington rarely left his private chambers before noon so she went directly after breakfast.

She dithered about whether she should just march up to the room and fling the door open even though she knew he wasn't in the room.

He told you to use the library.

That was true, he'd told her that more than once. Portia laid her ear against the thick door; no sound came from within. Not that that meant anything. He was hardly likely to be making a racket in his library.

She knocked before her nerve deserted her.

Nothing.

She waited a bit and then opened the door. The room was pitch-black so she left the door open to cast some light while she made her way to the heavy damask drapes and pulled them aside.

The morning light bathed the room and Portia gasped: the ceiling was at least twenty-five feet high, a coffered masterpiece that glinted with aged gilt which picked up the rays of sunshine and warmed the giant space. Floor-to-ceiling bookshelves covered all but two walls, the south-facing wall of windows and the interior wall opposite it, which boasted one of the largest fireplaces she'd ever seen. A mezzanine around the top third held yet more books. It was magnificent and Portia could understand why Mr. Harrington spent so much time in the room.

It took her a few minutes to understand the library's organization and she'd just located the section she wanted when a voice behind her made her jump.

"Good morning, Signora."

She whirled around and found Eustace Harrington in the doorway she'd left open. He looked as inscrutable as ever and it was anyone's guess what he thought about finding her in his sanctum.

"I thought the library would not be in use at this hour." Her tone was abrupt, as it always was when she felt at a disadvantage. "I will return another time."

He gestured to the books in her hand as he came toward her. "May I?"

She handed him the slim volumes and, as usual, took the opportunity to study him while he studied the books. And—as usual—he looked up and caught her staring. He raised the thinner of the two books.

"Have you read anything else by Paine?"

"Only his famous pamphlet—he has many admirers in my part of the world."

He handed her the two volumes and she clasped the books in both hands.

"Thank you. These will serve to keep me busy for a while. I shall leave you."

He gestured to the left side of the room. "You have no novels and I know from our dinner conversations you enjoy them. They are on this side." He gestured to the area she'd just located, but not yet perused. "Let me find you the ones my aunt recommended last night.

"Well, if it is no bother."

"It is no bother at all, Signora."

Portia looked at the sunlight pouring through the window and bit her lip. "Should I close the drapes?"

"That is not necessary," he said without turning.

The pillars that flanked the fireplace were taller than Portia and topped by marble foxes, on whose heads the mantelpiece balanced. She ran a finger across a fox's snout. "Your house is fascinating. When was it built?"

"It was designed and built by Inigo Jones, who completed it 1647."

"It reminds me of one of Palladio's buildings in Vincenza."

"The Palazzo Chiericati?"

"You know it?"

"I've seen pictures. It is well known for its design, which is based on musical ratios." He was running an elegant finger across the oxblood spines, as if searching for a particular title.

"Has the house been in your family long?"

"It belonged to a great uncle, a bachelor who died before I was born. My aunt brought me to live here after my parents died in a fire. I was with my aunt at the time, or I, too, would have perished in the fire." He delivered the tragic story with a detachment that made her heart clench.

"I'm sorry."

He glanced at her, his expression amused. "It was a long time ago, Signora, and I was not even a year old. I don't recall either of them."

"Even so, it is a very unfortunate story."

He plucked a book from the shelf and transferred it to his left hand, where he had two others.

Portia squirmed in the heavy silence. "This room must be lovely with a fire on a chilly evening." She could not take her eyes from his hands, even though she saw them every day during their lessons. They were broad across the back with long, well-shaped fingers. They looked like the hands of a concert pianist, but Portia knew that was mere romance on her part. Ivo's hands had been rather ugly, stubby with large joints and square palms, and yet they'd produced music that caused grown men to weep.

A vision of Mr. Harrington's beautiful hands brushing across her body the way they were moving over the leather-clad books flitted through her mind and she shivered. Her entire body tingled and became more aware, as if her nerves were too close to the surface of her skin.

Portia. . .

I'm not doing anything, she protested, feeling like a fool for arguing with herself.

Mr. Harrington took another book from the shelf, unaware of the turmoil he was causing with his innocent actions. Not until he had four volumes did he turn to her, his spectacles glinting as he handed her the small stack.

She took the books and glanced down at the spines to hide her burning face.

"Are you enjoying your time here thus far?" His question

forced her to look up. He motioned to one of the chairs that stood in front of the enormous fireplace. "Have a seat. Tell me your impressions of Cornwall. We are a proud people and love to hear how others view our little corner of Britain."

Portia could feel the pulse at the base of her throat pounding. Could he see it? Why did he want to talk to her? Why was she behaving like such a half-wit? She cleared her throat and lowered herself rather inelegantly into the chair he'd indicated.

He sat across from her, his body relaxed and graceful, a politely interested expression on his face. Portia couldn't recall speaking with a person more difficult to read. Or perhaps he wasn't. Maybe he really was as bland and emotionless as he appeared. But no, she could not believe that after hearing his playing.

She realized he was waiting. "I enjoy my rambles here; in London it was not so easy."

"Walking in Rome was easier?" He sounded genuinely interested rather than polite.

"I knew Rome very well and was much more comfortable there than I ever was in London." She didn't tell him how she'd wandered every inch of the ancient city by herself when she was young, something a well-bred English girl would never do. Such behavior was frowned upon in Rome, too, but Portia's father had been too busy working to keep track of his willful adolescent daughter.

"Do you ever think of returning to the Continent now the War is over?"

"My father was an only child and we were never close to any of his relations. There is nothing for me there." There was actually too much there, but she could hardly tell him that.

"Do you have plans to travel to Europe, Mr. Harrington?"

"I am not fond of traveling."

Portia opened her mouth, caught herself, and closed it. But naturally it didn't stay closed. "Because of . . . because of your condition?"

To her surprise, he smiled. "That is part of the reason."

Portia knew her face was the color of the oxblood books she held. "People can be ignorant and cruel."

"That is true, Signora." He was still smiling, but his tone had cooled and Portia felt she'd been put in her place.

She got to her feet, her heart pounding with mortification. "I will keep you no longer, Mr. Harrington.

He didn't argue with her this time. Instead, he preceded her to the door. "Until this afternoon, Signora."

Portia inclined her head. It was a struggle to move at a dignified pace, especially with his gaze on her until she turned the corner.

THE DAY AFTER her visit to the magnificent library Portia met Mr. Harrington's old nurse, Nanny Kemble, for the first time. She'd been out on her usual afternoon ramble and decided to take the path into the woods she'd seen Mr. Harrington emerge from that first night. The trail was narrow but fairly well-travelled, proving that her employer was not the only one who used it. The canopy blocked out a good deal of light and made the air cool and damp.

She'd been just about to turn around when the sound of the surf became louder so she kept going.

On the other side of the small wood was a gently sloping hill that led down to a small cottage that seemed dangerously close to the cliffs.

Nanny Kemble was pottering in her small garden when Portia trespassed on her land. The ancient woman greeted Portia as if they were old friends.

"Why, you must be the piano teacher!"

"Yes, I am Portia Stefani." She was no longer surprised that everyone in the area knew of her after having similar experiences in Bude each time she went.

I'm Nanny Kemble, Master Eustace's nanny. I've been hoping you'd visit."

Portia quickly learned Mr. Harrington—or Stacy, as she called him in the privacy of her mind—had not only given his old nurse the snug cottage, but also supplied her with servants to see to her needs. He wasn't just generous with his money; he also called on the old woman weekly, as did Miss Tate. Nanny had no near neighbors and the only other people she saw on a regular basis were the Fants, the dour husband and wife caretakers who lived on the property.

"Miss Tate engaged them," Nanny said, when Portia commented on how efficient the married couple seemed. "They're from *The North*," she said the two words the same way another person might say *under a rock.* "They certainly don't come from where the rest of *her* people live."

"Frances Tate's people?" Portia asked, somewhat surprised. "I was under the impression there was no other family?"

Nanny blinked. "I'm sorry my dear, did I say she had people?" She shook her head. "Miss Tate and Master Eustace are the only two left. It's such a pity." The old lady's mind drifted frequently and some days were better than others. The woman was close to ninety and had come to Stacy, her final and favorite charge, late in her life.

The next time Portia took her walk through the woods the old lady was waiting for her.

"I had Master Stacy from the day he was born." They were having tea in Nanny's cozy sitting room and the older woman was working on a section of intricate lace, which she could make without watching her hands. She stared at Portia with cloudy blue eyes. "What a tiny angel he was. He never cried or fussed, not at all like his brother."

Portia had been winding the thin thread Nanny used to crochet and looked up. "But I thought Mr. Harrington was an only child?"

The old lady's brow wrinkled and her lips parted.

Just then her housekeeper, Mrs. Fant, entered. "I hope you're not overtiring yourself, Mrs. Kemble?" The Fants were the only people who did not call her Nanny.

"Eh?" Nanny appeared startled by the sudden appearance. Indeed, sometimes Portia thought the Fants listened at the door.

"You did not sleep well last night, did you Mrs. Kemble?" Mrs. Fant asked rather loudly. Portia knew the question was meant more for her benefit, as if to say Portia's visit was tiring the old woman and she should take her leave. She glanced at the small watch pinned to her dress.

"What a lovely watch," Nanny said, just as she'd said the first time they met.

Portia gave the same answer. "Thank you, Nanny, it was my mother's. I'd better go if I am to make it back for Mr. Harrington's lesson." That was a bit of a fib. She had at least an hour, but she did not feel comfortable with Mrs. Fant standing watch.

"Will you come back tomorrow, my dear?" Nanny's face was pinched and hopeful.

"Of course I will."

Mr. Fant was doing something beside the cottage as Portia left. He didn't meet her eyes, but she felt his gaze on her back. It was quite gothic the way the Fants drifted about the property, their eyes always narrowed with suspicion. They really belonged in a big, draughty castle.

Portia was still smiling at the vision of Mrs. Fant as the castle chatelaine when Miss Tate came over the rise on a magnificent white horse—some of Mr. Harrington's bloodstock, she supposed.

"Hello Signora Stefani. You are quite a walker to have come so far."

Portia would have sworn her presence at the old nurse's cottage discomposed the other woman.

"I enjoy Nanny's company."

"Yes, she is a delightful old lady but her mind, unfortunately, is not what it used to be. I believe all her charges run together on some days."

"Yes, she mistook me for an old friend and a deceased sister and told me about Mr. Harrington's siblings."

Miss Tate gave a nervous high-pitched laugh and her mount fidgeted. "Well, she is very well taken care of; my nephew treats her like a queen."

"Yes, he does. That is commendable."

Miss Tate looked pleased by her comment. "I should get along. Selene is quite restless today."

The horse wasn't the only one who was anxious.

Portia smiled. "Selene, goddess of the moon. The name is perfect."

"My nephew has his fanciful side. There is a Hecate and Artemis, as well." She nodded at Portia. "Good day, Signora. I shall see you at dinner." She urged her mount into a canter.

Frances Tate was as good a rider as her nephew and dismounted gracefully when she reached the cottage. Both Fants came to greet her and Portia was just about to turn away when all three looked in her direction. They stood grouped together, unmoving until she gave them a jaunty wave. Miss Tate waved back but the other two stood like statues. Portia shivered, almost afraid to turn her back on them.

She laughed at her fanciful thoughts. Really, she did tend to let her imagination get the better of her sometimes.

PORTIA WAS READING in her room a few evenings later when she heard voices below her balcony. She set aside her book and went to the casement window, which she'd left open. Her employer stood below. He'd changed from his dinner garb into riding clothes and was talking with Hawkins, who turned and walked toward the stables. Mr. Harrington glanced up at her window, as if he knew he'd find her there.

"Ah, Signora Stefani. Did our chatter disturb you?" His lips curved into a knowing smile that reminded her that she was wearing a concealing and remarkably ugly dressing gown.

Portia's face heated. "It's still too light out and I was not sleeping yet." She tugged on her sash—even though it was already tight—and glanced toward the stables, where Hawkins was now talking with another man.

He saw her inquisitive look. "Hawkins and I are preparing to introduce Geist to Snezana, my new mare."

"You are breeding horses tonight?" She stuttered a little over the word breeding.

His enigmatic face shifted into an expression she'd not seen before: mischievous.

"No, Signora, they will be breeding each other."

Portia laughed, grateful to have something to cover her wild blushing. "What does Snezana mean?"

"Snow queen. Since you evinced some interest in horses on that ride into town I thought perhaps you might like to come watch?"

"Watch horses mate?" she blurted. Was he mad?

His lips pulled up higher on the right, the resulting lopsided smile beyond charming. "I understand if you'd rather not." There was a distinct note of challenge in his voice and her body tightened in response. Portia had never been able to resist a challenge, a characteristic which had complicated her life more than once.

"In the stables?" she asked stupidly, as though he might have given the horses a room in the house.

He nodded with slow deliberation. "Yes. In the stables, Signora Stefani, where I keep the horses," he added, straight-faced. He bowed, turned, and strode away before she could say anything else.

Portia retreated into her room before she did something embarrassing, like faint and fall off the balcony. She chewed her lower lip. She should forget everything that just happened and go directly to bed. Yes. Nothing good could come from watching animals breed alongside Mr. Harrington. She gave a breathy laugh at the scandalous offer, her entire body vibrating; there was *no* possibility of sleep now. A hysterical giggle bubbled up and she clamped a hand over her mouth. Was watching animals mate a normal activity in the country? It must be. Surely he would not have invited her if it wasn't? After all, breeding horses was a respectable, lucrative business.

Not that it mattered *what* kind of business it was or how normal viewing such an activity was: wild horses could not keep her away from the stables at this point.

Chapter Eight

PORTIA WAS IN too much of a hurry to bother with stays or stockings so she slipped on the day dress she'd been wearing earlier. She could wear her cloak; nobody would ever guess her shocking state of undress beneath it. Once she was dressed, she scraped back her hair, pulling it into a severe knot to give herself courage.

"Courage!" She snorted at her reflection, disgusted by the sparkle in her eyes. "You are a fool, Portia Stefani."

So I'm a fool. What else is new?

Portia flew down the stairs and down the hall toward the side door before realizing a little decorum would not be amiss. She bit back a laugh. Decorum? While watching horses mate?

When she saw her employer standing outside the stables talking to a stranger she balked; just how many people were going to witness this spectacle?

He turned to her and his pale eyebrows rose above his dark spectacles, as if he was surprised to see her. The man he was talking to glanced at Portia, his weathered face registering no surprise at seeing a female. So, perhaps this wasn't such an uncommon occurrence.

"This is Felix Thompson, Signora. He's come to manage Geist and Snezana."

"A pleasure, ma'am." Felix Thompson tugged his forelock. "I'll get to it, sir." He turned and disappeared into the stables.

Portia looked up at her employer. There was a tantalizing curve to his lips and he held out his arm, just as if he were leading her into dinner.

"Shall we?"

Portia laid her fingers on the sleeve of his coat and he led her past a goodly number of stalls to a small area where several men waited with two horses, one a chestnut and one a magnificent white horse who looked remarkably like Geist, but with more delicate bone structure. The animals had their heads together, as if they were having a private discussion.

Hawkins turned at the sound of their approach and grinned, lifting his hat.

"Why good evenin' ma'am. Beautiful night for it, 'tisn't it?" He was an earthy countryman who clearly saw nothing amiss with Portia's presence.

Hawkins turned to their employer. "Lancelot has calmed her down and she's ready to go, sir. Once he's done I thought I'd take him to where Thompson's man is waitin' with the mare."

Stacy nodded. "Very well, you can bring Geist in whenever you are ready."

Hawkins left two men holding and soothing the beautiful white mare.

"Why does she have a blanket on her back and those hoof coverings?" Portia asked, pleased her voice was steady.

"The blanket is to protect her when Geist covers her and the hoof coverings are to protect both of them. This is the first time for the horses and they will likely be skittish; hooves could do a great deal of damage."

"Who is Lancelot?" Portia asked as they leaned against the wooden railing. When she looked down she realized how close they were, close enough that she caught a faint whiff of his cologne. She inhaled the citrusy, clean scent and stared up at the black disks, as desperate as ever to see his eyes up close.

"Lancelot is a teaser stallion." His dark spectacles lent a menacing look to his face in the dimness of the barn.

"Teaser?"

"A stallion used to test a mare for receptiveness to breed. If the mare requires courtship, the teaser is used only until she proves ready. The breeding stallion is brought in at the last moment to do the actual covering."

By the time he was finished Portia could feel every nerve ending in her body. He, on the other hand, looked as cool as ever.

"That seems rather, er, c-cruel. Um, to Lancelot, that is." Her face was flaming, but she still couldn't keep her mouth shut.

He grinned—actually *grinned* at her. "Never fear. Thompson brought one of his mares with him so Lancelot will have his own job to do."

Thankfully Hawkins led in the magnificent stallion just then and Portia clamped her jaws shut. She would ask no more questions, perhaps for the rest of her life.

Geist reared when he saw Snezana, but the man holding his halter brought him back down, where he immediately began pawing the wooden floor to splinters, his dark eyes riveted on the beautiful mare.

Snezana's tail had been wrapped in a long cloth and one man's job seemed to be holding the end. Both horses were restless, pacing and side-stepping and keeping a total of six handlers busy. Even to an uninitiated person such as herself it was clear to see the mare was receptive when she squatted and backed up as they brought the stud closer.

What happened next was unlike anything she'd ever seen.

Portia had grown up in Rome, a city notorious for stray dogs, so she'd seen plenty of animals mating. But those had been dogs, while these were massive animals and the power expended in the process was impressive. Even with the men restraining him, Geist mounted the mare with alarming vigor. He heaved his enormous body off his forelegs and dropped heavily onto the mare's back. The reason for Snezana's wrapped tail was immediately evident as the man carefully but firmly held it to the side, out of the stallion's way.

The room filled with whinnying and snorting as Geist clamped his powerful jaws on the blanket and began to thrust. Portia found it difficult to breathe evenly and thought she might melt into a puddle on the barn floor as Geist violently thrust into the snow-white mare, the muscles in the stallion's hindquarters bunching and flexing.

Although the excruciatingly embarrassing encounter seemed to last a year, Portia doubted it was more than a minute before Snezana abruptly twisted her body and dislodged the stallion.

Geist shook his head and sent his white mane flying as two men led him to the opposite end of the room, where Hawkins carefully examined him from head to tail.

Meanwhile, Felix Thompson did something with the mare's hindquarters, which Portia—thankfully—couldn't see before turning toward Mr. Harrington.

"That took well, sir. Excellent for his first time."

What about Snezana? Portia wanted to ask, but wisely did not.

"You'll be back tomorrow, Felix?"

"Aye, sir. I'll come earlier. I'm sorry 'bout bein' so late this evenin' but—"

"I think you had good reason to be late. Good night, Felix."

The older man pulled his forelock and left.

Hawkins turned from the mare, which he'd also checked for injuries. "Everyone is as fit as a fiddle. I'll have the lads give them both a good rub and some extra feed."

"Very good, Hawkins."

The older man left and Portia swiftly dropped her eyes and stared at Eustace Harrington's glossy black boots as he turned to her.

"The reason we started so late was because Felix's daughter just delivered her first child—a son. Felix stayed to make sure she and the child were well before coming tonight. Rather appropriate for a man in his business, wouldn't you say?"

Portia could hear the smile in his voice, even without looking at him. Which she seemed incapable of doing.

"Signora Stefani?"

"Yes?" She did not look up.

"Is aught amiss, Signora?"

She swallowed and forced her head up. His face was expressionless but his nostrils were slightly flared, as if he were suppressing something, probably laughter.

"So, what did you think of Geist and Snezana's first attempt?" Yes, he was most certainly suppressing laughter.

"That was—" Portia stopped. Really, what could she say that wouldn't sound idiotic?

A slow, delicious smile spread across his face. "Yes, it *was*."

The smile transfixed her more than if he'd produced a pistol. Portia vaguely heard the distant sound of male voices. The men had taken two lanterns but left one behind. There was just enough light that she could see the fine-grained texture of his skin and the pale glints of his night beard. Why did it surprise her that he had facial hair? He was a man, after all. Very much a man. *Too* much a man.

He cocked his head. "Are you trying to look at my eyes, Signora Stefani?" Before she could answer he lifted one gloved hand to the delicate frames, removed the spectacles, and carefully folded them, his lashes fanning across his cheeks like icicles on fresh snow as he slipped the glasses into a pocket. And then he looked up.

Portia was too awed to be ashamed of the sound that escaped her; his eyes weren't red, but a translucent violet surrounded by thickets of white lashes that seemed to weigh down heavy lids.

"Glorious," she breathed.

His eyes opened wider, as if she'd said something he hadn't expected. "Signora Stefani?"

"Yes, Mr. Harrington?" Her voice was at least two octaves lower than usual.

"I'm going to kiss you."

"Yes," she said, although he hadn't asked question.

His kid-sheathed hands were cool and smooth on the thin skin of her jaws. He held her face firmly, his eyes heavy and hot as his mouth crushed hers.

Portia shuddered at the touch of his lips: he wasn't cold like marble—he was *hot*. So very hot that he felt like fire. She wrapped her arms around his neck and pulled him lower, slanting her mouth to take him deeper. Their tongues met and tangled as they probed and tasted, starved for each other like beggars at a banquet.

The voice of reason, so faint she could barely hear it, counseled her to remove her tongue and body from her employer's person and return to her bedchambers with all haste.

It warned of dreadful consequences.

It chastised and pleaded.

And, finally it threatened.

Ultimately, however, the voice of reason buckled beneath the sheer weight of desire and Portia celebrated her body's victory over her mind by rubbing herself along the long, hard length of the man she'd been unable to stop thinking about for weeks.

His hands slid down her sides until they spanned her waist and a low chuckle vibrated in his chest. "Oh, Signora Stefani—no stays." He plunged into her mouth with renewed vigor, as if to consume her. He tasted of port and smoke and heat and she couldn't take him deeply enough. She stood on tiptoes and twisted her fingers into thick white hair, drawing him closer, wrapping her lips around his tongue and sucking him in a vulgar, suggestive fashion.

He groaned and his hands moved lower, his strong fingers

digging into her ample bottom and yanking her close. He thrust his powerful hips, grinding his long, hard erection against her soft belly.

The sinuous, rhythmic stroking snapped something inside her and the last remnants of reason dissipated like smoke.

A BOLT OF heat shot from his groin as she not only absorbed his thrusts but rubbed herself against him. Stacy spread his hands over her generous buttocks and thrust against her, chafing the sensitive skin of his hard cock against his leather breeches.

Logic, self-control, decency, and hundreds of other, more nuanced parts of his mind burned away piece by piece, leaving only a fierce, fevered hunger to be inside her.

So much for avoiding her. So much for keeping your relationship strictly business.

The chiding voice was barely a whisper and he shoved it into the corner of his mind.

Instead of backing away and behaving, he lifted her, propping her voluptuous bottom on the middle railing of the fence and nudging her legs apart with his knee. She spread her thighs wide and yanked up her skirts with one hand. The eager motion made him throb so hard it hurt. He ripped off his gloves, flung them to the ground, and reached for his placket.

But her hand was there before his and she tore at the buttons, sending at least one of them bouncing into the darkness.

A choked laugh broke from his throat.

Rather than be offended, she gave an odd, breathy laugh. "I'm sorry," she gasped, but did not stop, her small, hot hand pushing into his breeches. His hips jerked almost out of their sockets as her tight fist moved down his shaft.

"Great. Bloody. Hell." Stacy didn't realize he'd cursed aloud

until she gave a low chuckle. And then her deliciously callused thumb swirled over his leaking slit, using the copious moisture to slick his hard length.

She began to work him with firm, confident strokes and all rational thoughts fled. He shoved her thighs wider and ran his hands up smooth, shapely legs unencumbered by stockings, garters, or drawers. He was about to kneel and give thanks—and do something else while he was down there—but she had other plans.

Her strong hand guided his eager member toward her sex, tilting her hips to take him. "Now." It wasn't a request; it was an order.

A savage pulse of desire wracked his body at the single word and he struggled to hold onto a slim thread of control. He would *not* spill inside her after one stroke like an overeager boy; he'd been dreaming about her for weeks.

He reached between her thighs and grazed a finger over the hot, damp curls that hid her pearl. She bucked against him and cried out as he began to circle her stiff little nub.

"*Please,* I want—" Her voice was raw with desire as she pumped his primed cock while rubbing her entrance with the sensitive crown, making it clear what she wanted.

"Slowly," he murmured through gritted teeth, his finger still teasing while she rocked against him, harder and harder, until he breached her. "Slowly."

But she had other plans.

Her legs wrapped around his hips and flexed hard, pulling him deep inside her body in one long slide. They both moaned as she clenched around him, wet and tight. Stacy teetered on the brink of control; his crazed, frantic brain was only lucid enough to hold onto one thought: he would *not* spend until he'd pleasured her—even if it killed him. And he feared it might.

He withdrew slowly, his body trembling with the effort of

controlling his thrusts, and then stroked just as slowly back in. This time he held her still and full, sheathing himself to the hilt and reveling in her tight heat.

She squirmed against him. "Stacy."

He smiled at the sound of his name and the way it sounded like a plea.

He lowered his mouth over her throat and flexed his jaws until his teeth marked and held her, sliding his aching cock out of her body with agonizing slowness. She moaned and he covered her throat with kisses and nips while he worked her with deep, vigorous thrusts. The pleasure was overwhelming and he barreled toward the edge far too quickly so he pulled away and stared down to where they were joined.

Good God it was a beautiful sight.

"Look at us," he said in a voice that sounded as if he'd been gargling glass.

They watched in silence as he penetrated her, his stomach clenching at the sight of his shaft disappearing into her body, until all they could see was the stark combination of white skin and curly black hair.

When he pulled out she made an unspeakably erotic sound deep in her throat, grabbed a handful of his hair, and yanked his head up.

Her eyes bored into his, black with need. "Fuck me, Stacy."

His jaw dropped. Had she really said what he thought she said?

"Now," she growled.

Stacy obeyed without thinking and slammed into her *hard.*

"*Yes.*" The word was a satisfied hiss and her eyelids fluttered closed.

He used her with such unrestrained savagery that some part of him worried he was bruising her. But she met him thrust for violent thrust, her body as hungry as his own. Her climax built quickly and he redoubled his efforts, his hips pounding into her faster, deeper. His vision wavered and he began to come apart inside.

Not yet, not yet, not yet . . .

She made a guttural sound and stiffened for an impossibly long moment before convulsing around him, biting his shoulder hard enough to make him wince, screaming her passion into his coat.

Her shuddering body freed him from his tattered restraint and he thrust home and froze, holding her impaled while he emptied himself deep inside her. Pleasure swamped him, eddying and spiraling from the place where they were joined, rippling out to flood the rest of his body.

But all too soon came a bone-deep lassitude that rendered him almost legless and he staggered, holding her against the railing. The sound of men's voices somewhere in the distance yanked him out of his languor quicker than a bucket of ice-cold water down his back and his eyes flew open. *Good God!* They were in the bloody stables—with people all around them.

She must have come to the same realization because her body stiffened, and it had nothing to do with sexual pleasure. Neither did her next words.

"Oh no." The words were barely a whisper but they chilled him to his core.

Stacy gritted his teeth and pulled out of her before lowering her to the ground. She swayed against him, her forehead on his chest.

"Can you stand?" he asked.

"Yes."

"Did I hurt you?" His throat was so tight it was a chore to force the words out.

"No. No, I'm not hurt."

Stacy turned away as memories of the last few moments flickered through his brain with shocking clarity. He'd treated her like a whore—worse. He couldn't recall ever using a woman so hard. Of course never in all his years had a woman used the word *fuck* in his presence—not that the curse excused his brutality. He swallowed hard, his cock twinging at the memory of her vulgar command.

The next few moments were every bit as excruciating as one would expect after one had intimate relations with a virtual stranger in a horse barn. They busied themselves tucking and straightening. Once he'd reassembled his clothing as best he could, he put on his glasses and turned to her.

She was waiting for him.

"Signora—"

She held up a hand, her eyes no longer hot, but severe. "Please, don't apologize. There were two of us, and I'm no blushing maiden." Yet she blushed all the same. "This was a mistake." Her mouth twisted miserably as her eyes swept the room, landing everywhere except his face. "Just because I'm a woman does not mean I'm not equally responsible." She gave a small, bitter laugh. "You didn't, after all, despoil an innocent virgin." She bit her lower lip and met his eyes. "What I wish to know is whether it will be possible for me to continue working here after . . . this."

Any remaining warmth that had lingered inside him fled at her words. He'd violated a woman in his employ—a person whose very livelihood depended on him—the very thing he'd sworn not to do, and now she feared for her position and future.

"This will change nothing between us, Signora Stefani." He spoke the foolish words with a cool assurance he was far from feeling. How could things *not* change? He'd been inside her, for God's sake, and he bloody well wanted to be there again, right *now*, in fact.

Everything had changed.

Everything.

He realized she was still looking up at him, as if waiting for something more—but what?

Reassure her, you dolt.

"I'm certain we can continue to work with each other, ma'am."

Her eyes were veiled, but she nodded, as if his cold, stilted words were satisfactory.

He held out his arm. "Come, I'll take you back to the house." She laid her fingers lightly on his sleeve but did not say a word.

What had he done?

WHAT HAD SHE done?

Portia ran up the steps after her employer left her in the entry hall. When she reached her room she threw herself onto her bed and took her head in both hands, tugging on it as though she could yank it off and exchange it for another—one that was not so horribly bent on destroying her. She'd all but crawled into the poor man's breeches—after tearing them off his body.

Ivo had been correct; she was no better than a rutting bitch.

Fuck me, Stacy.

Portia groaned at the horrid memory and wished she could hide in a crack in the earth and never come out again. How *could* she? Had she forgotten so quickly how her vulgar language and behavior had horrified and disgusted the last man she'd bedded? Would she never learn?

She'd been a naïve and foolish girl of seventeen the first time she'd used such language with Ivo. It had been her wedding night and Portia had not gone to his bed a virgin. If that hadn't been bad enough, she'd used the words her first lover had taught her; doing and saying things no virtuous Catholic girl should have known. Things Benedict had taught her.

Portia fell in love with Benedict Carruthers, one of her father's students, when she was fifteen. He'd been only three years older than Portia but decades older in sin. The youngest son of an English earl, he'd bedded his first woman at thirteen. Blond, blue eyed, and smooth-cheeked, Benedict had looked like an angel but he'd been the devil himself, especially in bed.

It had been Benedict who'd taught Portia dirty English words and then encouraged her to use them liberally when they made love—a habit that was obviously impossible to break. Benedict had been demanding and wicked, but also generous and kind in his own way.

"Never hide your sensual nature," he'd told her not long before he was killed. "Passion is something to be proud of, even though men try to shame women for taking pleasure from their bodies."

Benedict had been English, but he'd had a temper to match any Italian man. His temper had ultimately been his undoing and he'd died in a knife fight a week before Portia's sixteenth birthday: stabbed through the heart with a stiletto and left to bleed to death in an alley.

Portia had been devastated, convinced she would never love again. But then Ivo—a handsome, gifted genius—came to study under her father several months later. Now that she was older Portia knew what she'd felt for Ivo had been hero worship; his talent had blinded her. And then her father had died of a heart attack and she'd been terrified of what the future held. Ivo had been her salvation. Or so she'd believed.

Their marriage was a disaster from the very first night. He never forgave her for not being a virgin and he deplored her sensual nature.

The most recent example of her deplorable sensual nature echoed in her head: *Fuck me, Stacy.*

Portia groaned, pressing a pillow tightly over her face, as if that could block out the memory of what she'd said and done. The cool, aloof façade she'd cultivated so carefully destroyed in a moment. Well, several glorious moments, actually.

How would she be able to work with him after this?

Chapter Nine

THE DAYS PASSED in an uncomfortable blur.

Portia was stilted and correct around her employer—as if that might somehow make him forget she'd spread her legs and then scratched, bitten, and cursed at him—and it was awkward to communicate even the most innocent information.

Stacy—why not think of him that way after what she'd done—on the other hand, appeared as cool and unruffled as ever. His behavior was so normal she might have thought she'd imagined their tryst if she hadn't woken up so deliciously sore the following morning.

Their first lesson had been the most trying. Portia stared at his face, lips, hands—everything—and hadn't been able to stop remembering that evening. *Look,* he'd said, a fierce expression on his chiseled features while his body thrust deep into hers, over and over.

Portia simply couldn't help herself; whenever she looked at him, she remembered how he'd looked when he'd come undone and filled her with his seed: his pale beauty fierce, cruel, and magnificent.

The only times they saw each were at lessons and dinner. Lessons were all business and dinner was pleasant conversation with his aunt present. When they weren't in lessons she took care to avoid accidental encounters and suspected he did the same.

The nights, however, were far, far different. At night she

welcomed his presence in her head as she lay in her big bed and allowed her imagination to run wild. At night he rode her with the same skill, passion, and confidence he'd shown during their oh-so-brief interlude.

The end of her trial period was only days away and Portia fully expected him to present her with a month's pay and send her packing. It wasn't that he treated her any differently than he had before their tryst, but their interactions were so stilted she couldn't believe he wanted them to continue. Besides, he could easily hire another teacher for the money he was offering. The only reason she was here in the first place was because he thought he was hiring Ivo.

On the thirtieth day he came to her desk after he'd finished playing. She was making notes and recommendations for future work. She replaced the quill in the stand and looked up.

"I am very pleased with my progress and would like you to stay."

Portia's mouth opened, but nothing came out.

"I will understand if you'd rather return to London. I will pay you two months' wages and arrange your transportation." His face was a rigid, emotionless mask—but surely he wouldn't ask her to stay if he didn't *want* her here? Perhaps he even *liked* her a little.

Her heart pounded foolishly hard at the thought and she ruthlessly shoved it aside. This was a second chance he was giving her and she would not make the same mistake again.

Portia ignored the mocking laughter in her head. "I would like to stay, Mr. Harrington," she said, proud there was hardly a quaver in her voice. She opened her mouth, and then closed it.

"Yes?" he prodded.

"I hate to ask, but I'm afraid I left things rather unresolved in London." She grimaced. "I didn't know if I'd be staying in Cornwall or returning." The both knew what she meant.

His expression was thoughtful. "A break would actually suit

me as I have to take trips to Plymouth and Barnstaple. You'll need at least ten days for your journey—or perhaps even two weeks."

"Ten days will be sufficient." It would mean a very short stay in London, but Portia could not justify a longer visit.

"Shall we finish out this week? Will that give you enough time to make travel arrangements?"

"Yes, thank you. Monday would do nicely." Portia was so relieved it was difficult to think straight. She waited until the door closed behind him before dropping her head onto her arms and fighting back her tears of joy.

Thank God. She wouldn't need to leave here. She wouldn't need to leave *him.*

PORTIA COULDN'T PAY for her trip to London without an advance on her wages.

She decided to get the unpleasant task out of the way the following morning after breakfast and went in search of Soames. She found the butler supervising a trio of maids in the dining room.

"Could you tell me if I might speak to Mr. Harrington?"

"He is in the library with his steward." Before she could answer he frowned at the maid who was scrubbing the blackened metal dogs in the fireplace. "No, no, Sally, you will need to use salt on that." He turned back to Portia. "Should I tell him you'd like a word?"

"Don't disturb him. I'll try again later."

"I'll let him know once his steward leaves, ma'am." The stiff butler actually gave her a smile. The Whitethorn servants had unbent toward her when they realized she didn't add much work to their lives and had no plans to steal the silverware.

Portia decided to see Nanny before she departed for London.

The last two times she'd gone to the cottage Mrs. Fant had told her the old lady was not feeling well.

When Portia crested the rise that overlooked the cottage she saw both Fants doing something near the shed on the far side of the cottage. Nanny herself was in the small garden on the other side of the house and Portia headed toward her, feeling as though she were racing against the clock—or at least the Fants—to reach the old lady. Perhaps it was just her over-developed imagination, but she suspected they disapproved of her visits.

Luckily, Nanny saw her before the Fants did. "Signora Stefani." She began to stagger to her feet.

"Please, Nanny – don't get up. How are you feeling today?"

"I'm excessively well, Signora." Nanny's blue eyes twinkled, making her resemble a good fairy from some children's tale. She was so tiny a stiff breeze would carry her away.

"You've recovered from your illness?"

"Illness? What illness? Why, I've never been ill a day in my life! I come from fine country stock, you know."

Just then Mrs. Fant came around the corner of the cottage and Portia was positive she saw dismay, quickly followed by annoyance, on the woman's face.

"Hello, Mrs. Fant." Portia gave the sour-looking servant a pleasant smile.

"I have a visitor, Mrs. Fant. Please see to tea for the Signora and me."

"Are you sure you're feeling up to entertaining, Mrs. Kemble?"

The look Nanny turned on her must have been one she'd developed for recalcitrant charges. "Of course I'm well enough." Her voice was icy with displeasure and the housekeeper was wise enough to scuttle off to make the tea. Nanny shook her head before speaking in a stage whisper, "I cannot abide those people."

"Why don't you dismiss them? Or ask Mr. Harrington to do

so? He dotes on you, Nanny. He wants you to be happy."

Any mention of Stacy always put a large smile on her face.

"He does love me, doesn't he?" She preened for a moment and then her lips trembled. "The poor little mite—sent away so young."

"Sent away? By whom?"

"Why the earl, of course; he couldn't abide him." She looked as though she might cry and Portia couldn't bring herself to pursue the subject, even though she was more curious than she should be. Instead she changed the topic.

"Tell me about your childhood, Nanny. What part of the country did you grow up in?"

"I grew up just outside Thurlstone, but you know that Miss Mary. I've known all you girls since you were born. Our family has worked for Harringtons since The Conqueror, my pa used to say."

Before Portia could respond, Mrs. Fant returned with the tea tray. "I thought you might like this calf's foot jelly Lady Watley left for you, Mrs. Kemble."

Nanny's vague gaze sharpened when it landed on the Yorkshirewoman, who was holding said jelly. She gave a dismissive sniff at either the jar or her servant. "Signora Stefani will pour, Mrs. Fant. You may go." She made a shoeing motion.

Mrs. Fant could hardly argue with such a direct dismissal, but she did give Portia an accusatory look, as though to say it was all her doing.

While Portia let the tea steep she picked up the jar.

"The nerve of that woman bringing me her wretched calf's foot jelly."

She looked up at the venom in the older woman's voice. "Who is Lady Watley?"

Nanny's eyes narrowed, making her resemble a rather evil little fairy. "She's nothing but a harlot."

Portia's eyes widened, but Nanny didn't notice.

"She had a chance to marry the best man in Britain and picked that—that, *oaf,* instead."

Portia didn't have to stretch her imagination too far to guess who Nanny considered the best man in Britain. "Do you mean Mr. Harrington?"

Nanny nodded her head vigorously, her eyes glinting with spite. "Wanted him for his money, she did." Her chin quivered and a single tear rolled down one cheek. "Oh how she hurt him. He isn't one to wear his heart on his sleeve, but I know him like he was my own."

Portia wanted to ask her in the worst of ways what this woman had done, but Nanny blinked and seemed to come to herself. "I don't want that," she said, looking at the jar. "The Fants can have it."

The rest of their conversation revolved around Nanny's garden and there was no more mention of imaginary earls or Lady Watley.

The older lady was so chipper that Portia stayed too long and had to hurry to get back in time for her lesson. She'd just entered the foyer when Soames found her.

"Mr. Harrington will see you now, Signora."

"Thank you, Soames." Portia wished she could go up to her room and tidy her hair but she satisfied herself with a quick glance in a mirror before making her way to the library.

Stacy was leaning over his desk when she entered. "Ah, good afternoon, Signora." He gestured to one of the chairs in front of the desk. "Please, have a seat."

The top of his massive desk was piled high with ledgers and rolls of paper. "I hope I am not interrupting you; I shan't take up very much time."

"It is a welcome interruption, Signora." She heard a slight weariness in his modulated tone.

This man has been inside me. The thought sprang from nowhere and Portia's legs went rubbery at the sudden, graphic image that accompanied it. She gratefully lowered herself into the chair.

"How may I help you, Signora?"

"Would it be possible to have an advance on my wages?" Portia swore he looked relieved, as if he'd thought—or feared—she might say something else. But what?

"Of course. I should have thought of that myself, Signora."

"I do not require all of the money, perhaps the amount for two months?"

"I should be very glad to pay you all of it. I trust you enough to render the services promised."

Portia's face heated at the word 'services' and she knew she must look very much like a brick wearing a day dress.

Fuck me, Stacy.

The words ricocheted around in her head, amplifying the heat that was already spreading through her body.

"Two months will be sufficient, Mr. Harrington." Her voice cracked on his name.

He removed a strongbox from a drawer and counted out a sum she assumed to be two month's pay. He rose and walked around the desk to hand it to her. Portia stood and was immediately aware of how close the action brought her to his body. Close enough to smell him, only faintly, but enough to stoke her yearning for him, which seemed to burn hotter every day.

She took the money from his hand, careful not to touch him, as if that might create a dangerous spark. "Thank you."

He propped his hip against his desk and crossed his arms. "Is there anything I can do to help with your travel plans?" His cool, conversational tone convinced Portia that *his* insides were not tying themselves in knots. He was a man; likely bedding her once had been enough to get her out of his system. If she'd ever *been* in his system to begin with.

"Thank you, but I've already seen to everything."

A heavy, uncomfortable silence hung between them and stretched . . . and stretched.

"Will it be just business in London, or will you have some time for pleasure?"

"I am staying with friends, so it will not all be business."

"I'm pleased to hear it." He hesitated and then said, "I understand you went to visit Nanny this afternoon?"

"Yes, I wanted to see if she felt better before I left."

"Better?"

"She was not well the last two times I stopped by."

His brows drew down. "I wasn't aware of that. I'll have to speak to the Fants."

"I do not believe Nanny cares for the Fants."

He smiled. "Well, they are from Yorkshire and thus geographically suspect. But Miss Tate selected them and I have absolute faith in her judgement." He uncrossed his arms and pushed off the desk, signaling the conversation was over.

"Thank you for the advance on my wages."

"It is my pleasure, Signora Stefani." He took several long strides toward the door and opened it for her. "I shall see you at four."

Portia nodded and left the room without looking back.

STACY WATCHED UNTIL Signora Stefani disappeared down the hallway. She moved with a sensual grace which he knew was more than mere promise. Her hips shifted enticingly beneath her simple cotton gown and he couldn't help wondering if she was wearing stockings or if she routinely went without them.

This is not a subject that will lead you anywhere good.

That is certainly true—but it is *a subject that brings me pleasure.*

Even so, Stacy shut the door on both her and his lascivious thoughts.

But when he resumed his seat he found he was no longer in the mood to contemplate the new parcel of land he'd just acquired, a matter that had interested him greatly before the woman had made it impossible to think. He poured a brandy, took off his glasses, and checked his watch: two hours until his lesson. Lord, he was pathetic to look forward to those two hours the way he did.

He slid his hand behind his neck and brutally massaged the taut cords, his mind sneaking back to that night in the stables. Indeed, his mind rarely went anywhere else of late. He doggedly dragged his attention back to the true purpose of that evening, which had not been to seduce his employee, but to breed his newest mare. That endeavor, at least, had proven successful and Snezana was in foal, which Thompson said was not always the case after a young mare's first cover—

"Good God!" Stacy sat up so fast he knocked his leg against his desk. He yelped and then rubbed his throbbing knee. Could Mrs. Stefani be pregnant? How could he not have thought of that possibility until now? He stared unblinkingly across the dim room, his spinning brain yielding very little of use on the subject. He'd only bedded prostitutes—how pitiful was *that*—and they were taught how to prevent conception. Mrs. Stefani was a widow, but did that necessarily mean she knew how to take precautions? What if she were carrying his child? Would his children be like him?

His aunt had told him long ago that his mother and father had both been fair, but not white like him. Lord. How had he not thought of this until now? He reached for the brandy decanter but stopped; he liked to have his wits about him when he went into a lesson.

He slumped back in his chair; he would have to talk to Signora Stefani. It would be a bloody uncomfortable conversation, but he needed to reassure her that she'd not face such an eventuality alone.

Stacy groaned at even the thought of such an agonizing discussion.

Surely it was early yet? Their talk could wait until she returned. Most likely it would never be an issue. While he knew little about human reproduction, he knew it usually took more than one coupling for horses and other livestock.

Thoughts of coupling inevitably brought her image to mind.

She'd looked delectable today and he cursed himself for not having the forethought to open the drapes on one window so he could've seen her better. He'd not seen her in natural light for days—which he knew was a product of them both avoiding each other.

As gorgeous and sensual as her body had felt, what he thought of most often were her eyes: how could eyes so dark—almost black—burn with such emotion?

Of course, he also thought about her expressive, kissable mouth and how she smiled so easily. Indeed, she seemed to *feel* easily, unhampered by the need to moderate her emotions like the typical staid Englishperson—like him, in other words. Watching the parade of emotions that marched across her face was fascinating. In the course of their brief conversation he'd seen curiosity, embarrassment, desire, anger, happiness, sadness, and a host of other emotions he could not define.

When it came to music her face was even more eloquent. Music turned her into a creature of pure passion: driven, confident, and magnificent. Had that passion threatened her husband? Or had he shared the same temperament? Had her talent been something Ivo Stefani viewed as a challenge or something to unite them?

Stacy had no thoughts of competing with her when it came to music. He played well enough, but she elevated the notes into the realm of the divine. Her mastery of the piano was erotic and the lessons had become a two-hour block of delicious agony. Listening to her play was bloody torture, but it was the high point of his days.

He was becoming stiff just thinking about her.

Stacy scowled at his body's base reaction. He'd become the sort of predator who lusted after his employee—and that is exactly what she was: a dependent.

Not only had he engaged in reprehensible behavior with a subordinate, but it was possible she would suffer greatly from those few moments of careless passion. How would she feel about having a child who looked like him or needing to marry a man who looked like him?

Stacy could not imagine her being happy with either eventuality. A momentary indiscretion with a human novelty was one thing, spending the rest of your life with somebody like him was another matter entirely.

Chapter Ten

PORTIA HAD SEVERAL days in the crowded mail coach to think about what she would tell her friends about Stacy, finally deciding she would tell them nothing. What was there to say? She could hardly disclose what she'd done in the stables, nor did she want to confess she was lusting for her employer day and night. So, yes, nothing was better.

When the hackney dropped her off in front of her friends' townhouse Serena Lombard was waiting for her at the top of the steps.

"How lovely to see you, Portia!" The small Frenchwoman folded her into a very un-English embrace.

"I've missed you terribly," Portia murmured, squeezing her friend hard enough to make her laugh.

Serena kissed both her cheeks before picking up Portia's bag and leading her into the small foyer. "You look wonderful, darling."

"Very droll. I've been cooped up in a coach for days—I look dreadful." She hung up her traveling cloak and stripped off her gloves as Serena led her toward the ground floor sunroom that was just off the back garden.

"Tea will be ready shortly," Serena said, ushering Portia into the room.

"Where are the others?" Portia asked, collapsing into a comfortable old wingback chair.

Serena took the settee across from her and curled her legs beneath her. "You *just* missed Honoria, who left yesterday to go to the Viscount Fowler's country estate, and Freddie received an emergency message from her current young lady—something about a bonnet—but she'll return this evening."

Portia tucked her gloves into her reticule and tossed it onto the side table. "And how is Oliver?"

Serena's eyes sparkled at the mention of her nine-year-old son's name. "He is visiting his grandparents right now." Serena's husband, who died during the War, had been the Duke of Remington's youngest son. "He'll be sorry he missed you. Honey was, too, and said to give you her love."

"I'm sorry to have missed both of them. I wish I could have given more notice of my visit, but I simply didn't have the time."

"Ah yes, your new position." Serena grinned. "You've been suspiciously quiet about that. I warn you; I'm going to winkle every little detail from you."

Which is just what Portia was worried about.

Thankfully the door opened and a maid entered with the tray. "Let me," Portia said before Serena—who made dreadful tea—could offer. "What have you been up to since we last spoke? I wouldn't know—since you never answer my letters."

Serena grimaced. "Ah, yes, my dreadful letter-writing skills. But I *know* Freddie tells you everything you need to know, so I don't want to make you pay for more of the same."

Freddie's weekly letters were the glue that held their small circle together. The others in their group were indifferent correspondents, although none of them was as bad as their friend Miles. Lorelei wrote often, but her letters were brief to the point of being terse. Portia suspected her situation was not precisely happy and that was why she didn't speak of it.

"Besides," Serena said, "My life is so tedious there simply isn't that much to tell."

"But Freddie said you had a commission to design a bier or catafalque, or some such thing."

Serena snorted and waved a dismissive hand. "Ah, that, yes—a marble bier for a mausoleum, an item few people will ever see." She shrugged. "But it will pay enough to put food on the table and keep Oliver in automata."

Portia grinned. "Is he still taking them apart?"

"Yes, but at least now he puts them all back together."

Portia heard the pride in her voice. Oliver was only nine years old but he was a clever little boy who seemed wise beyond his years.

"But what you are talking about is *work,* my friend. What *I* was talking about was love and life." Serena smirked as she took the cup and saucer Portia handed her.

"Why are you looking at me like that?" Portia's tea slopped over the side of the cup and into the saucer. Before the other woman could answer her question she asked, "Has Freddie been keeping you busy?"

Serena chuckled at the clumsy change of subject but did not pursue it. "She has indeed. It has been rather busy for dear Freddie and she has several very wealthy—but not particularly promising—young ladies."

Portia made a moue of distaste. Freddie—an earl's widow—had been the deportment instructor at the academy. Now she used her skills and connections to launch wealthy young women into Society.

"Freddie is good at what she does, but I don't think such work is good for her soul." Serena was no longer smiling.

Portia sipped her tea. "No, she is too sensitive to engage in commerce."

"Not like us," Serena said with a smile.

The door opened and the lady in question entered. The Countess of Sedgwick was tall and slender with the silvery blond beauty of an arctic fox. Her lovely face became even lovelier when she smiled. "Portia, how wonderful to see you. How was your journey? Exhausting?"

"I *was* tired, but a few moments in Serena's company was enough to reinvigorate me."

Serena laughed. "I haven't even begun being invigorating, darling." She cut the countess a sly look. "Tell us about your employer, darling, Freddie says he is very, very interesting."

Portia knew she was blushing but decided she was too tired to care.

"She is just teasing you, Portia," Freddie said. "All I told her was that your Mr. Harrington was reclusive and reserved."

"And wealthy," Serena added around a mouthful of biscuit.

"Yes, he's all three of those things," Portia admitted.

"And?" Serena prodded.

Portia shrugged. "And nothing. He has offered me employment—even after my despicable behavior, so I am . . . contented."

Serena's eyes narrowed and she opened her mouth.

"I just received a letter from Miles," Freddie said, cutting Serena a stern look.

The exuberant Frenchwoman heeded Freddie's hint and they spoke about their absent friends for another quarter of an hour, when a huge yawn seized Portia.

"You poor dear," Freddie said. "What beasts we are to keep you awake after that journey. Let's get you to your room and I'll have some warm milk sent up."

"That sounds divine," Portia said, pushing wearily to her feet.

Serena gave her a speculative look. "Yes, get some sleep. I'm busy tomorrow morning, but I will place myself at your disposal and we can spend the entire afternoon and evening together." Her friend's wicked smile boded ill for Portia's peace of mind.

STACY HAD MIXED emotions as he watched the drab, gray buildings flicker past the window. He was still looking forward to a few days in Portsmouth, but it was for entirely different reasons than a month ago. He would visit a brothel, but this time he wouldn't be engaging in his usual transactions.

The brothel in question belonged to Katherine Charring, the madam who'd been Stacy's first lover and was now his dearest friend. Kitty was his *only* friend—at least the only one who knew him—aside from his aunt, his old nurse, and a few tenants. How pitiful was that? His best friend was also his madam, if no longer his lover.

Stacy frowned at the uncharitable thought; so what if Kitty was a madam? She was a wonderful person and—with the exception of Signora Stefani—a damn sight better company than most "proper" females in his experience.

His lips curved into a smile as he recalled that evening in the stables; well, perhaps the Signora was not *entirely* proper. But she was excellent company and he'd enjoyed their many dinner conversations, as well as the discussions about music they had every day during his lessons. Still, he could hardly call her a friend. He had plenty of acquaintances, business associates, and employees, but friends had been harder to accumulate.

Kitty held a special place in his heart and always would. He'd gone to her a bruised and broken young man after Penelope had broken his heart and she'd helped make him whole.

Although it had been years since they'd had anything but a platonic relationship, Stacy still recalled the day Kitty told him she could no longer be his lover.

"You are too important to me to be a client any longer." She'd been lying naked against him, her redhead's skin almost as pale as his own.

He'd been disappointed by her words although he didn't disagree with them. "Tired of me, are you?" he'd teased.

"Don't be daft. As a matter of fact, I was recently accused of trying to keep you all to myself."

Stacy had laughed. "I somehow doubt your girls are lining up for me."

"Yes, actually, they are," Kitty said with no little asperity. "I wish you'd understand that people stare not only because of your color, but also because you are a very handsome man."

He'd been too contented after their last bout of lovemaking to argue. "You almost make me believe you, my dear. You are an excellent madam, madam."

She'd slapped his leg. "When a woman of my experience tells you anything about matters between the sexes you would be *wise* to listen."

Stacy had wisely kept his laughter to himself and she'd continued.

"I've seen more naked male bodies than I care to recall," she'd confessed with unusual candor. "I've rarely had the pleasure of lying beneath one as perfect as yours. Only one other, if I am to be completely honest." He still recalled the yearning in her voice when she spoke those words. "You are special to me, Stacy, too special to be my customer any longer."

"Then marry me, Kitty." That hadn't been the first time he'd asked her. He had no qualms about marrying a prostitute and he refused to despise the woman he chose to lie with.

"You fool," she'd whispered, rolling him onto his back and lowering her body over his. "One of these days I'll stun you by accepting."

That had been almost eight years ago. Stacy still went to her house in Plymouth but now he went to other women, women who were lovely and gave him pleasure, but he had never become friends with any of the others. After he'd sated his body's needs, he always spent time with Kitty to feed his soul. They argued politics, books, or anything else friends bickered about. They went out to plays and once even took a week-long trip to London together. But still she would not marry him.

"You love me, Stacy, but you are not *in* love with me," she'd said the last time he'd asked her, less than a year ago.

Stacy knew that was true. But was it not possible to have a good life together even without romantic love? He could only suppose she continued to reject his offers of marriage because she still carried a torch for another man. Somebody from the time before Stacy knew her—back when she'd been a governess.

The carriage wheels hit a rut of some sort and jolted him from his musings; he was not far from Kitty's now. He already knew he could not engage one of her girls—no matter how beautiful and willing. The truth was he craved Signora Stefani: her humor, her body, her fire, her mystery—her music. No other woman would do.

For the first time he understood Kitty's preoccupation with the man she'd loved so long ago—the man she could not have but still yearned for. Did his own preoccupation with Signora Stefani mean he was falling in love? Or was what he felt nothing more than lust and passion?

He honestly didn't know which of the two possibilities he wished for.

THE JOURNEY TO Portia's prior residence the next morning roused memories of her life with Ivo—memories she preferred not to remember.

Mrs. Sneed, her landlady, was a needle-thin woman with sharp black eyes and an unusually small mouth. Her expression was perpetually pinched, as if she'd just smelled something rancid. She'd become suspicious and unpleasant toward Portia after Ivo had left, but today she greeted Portia—and her money—with a welcoming smile.

"Going to join your husband in Rome, Seenyora?" Her beady eyes were watchful as Portia loaded a few possessions into the small crate she planned to take back with her.

Portia considered telling her about Ivo and then shrugged the thought away—why bother? "No, I'm teaching in Cornwall, at the address I sent you in my last letter."

"That reminds me. A man came looking for you a few days ago and I gave him the address."

Portia looked up from her packing. "A man? Did he leave a card?"

"No. Said he was passing through and wanted to see you; he said he knew your husband."

It was hard to breathe, like something was squeezing her chest. "Did he give his name?"

"I didn't ask for it, did I?" Mrs. Sneed snapped.

Portia forced herself to remain calm. "Well, could you describe him?"

She gave a careless shrug. "Big, dressed poorly, an accent thicker than treacle."

"What kind of accent?"

Mrs. Sneed's bored expression turned mean. "You don't pay me enough to be your personal secretary."

Portia bit her tongue. The woman was horrid and arguing with her was not worth the effort. She stood and surveyed everything she was selling: a piano, some furniture from the school, and other odds and ends. She'd offered the remainder of the possessions to a man Ivo had borrowed money from and he'd grudgingly agreed to take them in return for part of the debt.

"Men will come by tomorrow morning to take away the rest of the things."

The landlady's sharp eyes narrowed. "Anything still here tomorrow evening will be mine."

Portia strode from the house without another word, glad to be done with the sour, nasty woman.

The rest of the day passed in a whirl of drudgery and she spent most of her time calling on the various people she—or rather Ivo—owed money to. She applied small amounts to most of the debts and made arrangements for quarterly payments for the rest. Even with the wages Stacy was paying it would take years to discharge it all. She pushed that depressing thought aside and told herself to be grateful she had employment.

The rest of her trip went far too quickly. Her second night she ate dinner with Freddie and Serena and stayed up too late talking. The third night she was alone with Serena as Freddie had obligations with one of her clients.

Portia had expected to be prodded and poked for information, but Serena avoided the subject of her employer, almost as if she feared what Portia might tell her.

On her final night in town they ate a late supper at the house. Portia was listening to her friends discuss the play they'd just seen when her mind wandered back to Stacy Harrington. It had been a week since she'd last seen him. Tomorrow she would leave London and begin the long journey home.

Home? When had she begun to think of Whitethorn as home?

Portia frowned; she was lying to herself. It wasn't Whitethorn she was thinking of, it was Stacy. She missed their lessons, their dinner conversations, those brief glimpses of him in the moonlight. She yearned to know more about him—not just about his beautiful body, although that intrigued her more than it should—but to get to know the man who lived behind his mask of reserve.

What was she going to do about him? It was clear he'd put that night in the stables behind him. After all, it had been Portia who'd instigated the heated tryst. That was another thing she could not lie to herself about. She'd wanted him and she still wanted him, and he was far too much of a gentleman to show how shocked and disgusted he'd been by her vulgar words and wanton behavior.

Had her disastrous marriage taught her nothing? When would she realize men did not like to be stalked and brought to earth as though they were wild game? When would she learn they went to whores for what *she* provided and to proper women for a wife?

Her mind burned with shame but her belly burned with something else: she would do the same thing with him again if the opportunity presented itself. More than that, she would undoubtedly do everything in her power to *ensure* such an opportunity arose.

She sighed, exhausted and annoyed by her pointless fretting.

"Why the heavy sigh, Portia my darling? Are you thinking about how much you will miss me and my sage counsel and clever wit?" Serena teased.

Freddie gave a delicate snort but Portia smiled into Serena's affectionate hazel eyes. "I will miss you both, *dearly.*"

Serena lifted her wine glass. "I propose a toast—to old friends, the very best kind."

"To friends old *and* new," Freddie corrected, her serious gaze on Portia. Although the reserved, private woman hadn't pried, Portia knew Freddie was concerned about her new life in Cornwall and where it would all lead.

Portia gave the other woman a reassuring smile. "To friends old and new," she echoed.

After she'd taken a drink Portia left her glass lifted a moment longer, silently toasting somebody who was not at the table, but who was present all the same.

Chapter Eleven

PORTIA KNEW SHE was pregnant two weeks after she returned from London.

She woke up before dawn, retching and sweating with an odd heaviness in her pelvis. After vomiting a third time she crawled back into bed and fell into an uneasy sleep. When she woke again it was after eleven and somebody was knocking on her door.

"Signora? Signora Stefani?" It was Daisy.

"Come in," she called weakly.

The maid poked her face into the dim bedroom. "Are you ill, Signora? When you didn't come down to breakfast Mr. Soames worried you might be having trouble."

Portia almost laughed. She was having trouble, all right.

"I'm feeling a little fatigued so I decided some extra sleep would not be amiss. But I should love some tea and toast if you wouldn't mind, Daisy."

"Oh, I don't mind at all. Mayhap you'd like a nice hot bath, ma'am? I know that always sets me up all right and tight."

"That sounds lovely. Perhaps in an hour?" Portia collapsed back onto the bed once the door shut. What a mess. At the very least she would have liked to keep her situation a secret. Not that being ill necessarily meant pregnancy—except to a suspicious mind. She lay in bed and massaged her sore stomach. What on earth was she going to do?

STACY WAS LEAVING his chambers and saw Soames and Daisy conferring outside Signora Stefani's room. "Is aught amiss, Soames?"

The girl scuttled off and his butler turned to him. "When Signora Stefani did not appear at breakfast I became concerned."

Stacy's heart lurched into a gallop. "Is she ill? Does she need a doctor?"

"She's feeling a bit under the weather and asked for tea and toast, sir. She has not requested a doctor."

Stacy looked into the old man's suddenly not-so-vague eyes and nodded. "Inquire as to whether she would like the doctor when you bring her meal. Please let me know what she decides. I shall be in the library."

"Very good, sir."

Stacy didn't bother lighting any candles when he reached the library. He slumped into his chair and stared into the darkness.

"Hell."

Was she ill or was she pregnant? He knew women sometimes became ill during pregnancy. He could hardly breathe for the thumping in his chest. He was still sitting in the same position a half-hour later when Soames entered. The butler did not look surprised to find his master sitting in the pitch dark.

"Signora Stefani thanks you but declines your offer of a doctor. She is feeling much better." He stood in the doorway, waiting.

"Very good, Soames. That will be all."

Soames closed the door without making a sound.

Stacy tried to get work done, telling himself he was acting foolishly. All the same, his pile of paperwork did not diminish and he found himself in the music room an hour before his lesson. He could think of no other way to calm himself other than to play. He'd been restless ever since his trip to Plymouth. He'd only stayed for three days even though Kitty had wanted him to stay longer. But, for whatever reason, he'd been unable to relax. So he'd come home and worked on the new music he'd picked up in Plymouth, a piece by Beethoven, his Sonata 14. It was haunting, riveting, and almost mad. The third segment, the *presto agitato*, was beyond his skill and likely always would be, but he was determined to master it all the same.

He'd just finished playing the *adagio sostenuto* for the umpteenth time when he felt her presence. He stopped but did not turn around.

"Good afternoon, Mr. Harrington." Her voice was hushed, not at all like her usual lively tone. He felt the heat of her body behind him. "A lovely piece of music."

"I find it captivating."

"You are doing quite well with it."

"Ah, but you have only heard the first part. I'm afraid the last of it is beyond my abilities."

"*Presto agitato.*" He heard the smile in her voice.

"Will you play it for me, Signora Stefani?" His voice was raw and husky, like a man who needed a drink of water. Or something stronger.

She hesitated so long he thought she hadn't heard him. But then she sat down beside him. He began to rise.

"Stay." Her voice was low but firm. She moved closer to him and although he gave her room on the bench their bodies still touched.

Stacy had never heard the piece played by anyone but himself. He knew how it *should* be played and he could hear the music inside his head, but he'd failed to imagine its ferocious beauty.

Her hands commanded, caressed, and ultimately beseeched, all the while demonstrating complete mastery of the instrument before her. The music rampaged through his body like a violent marauder intent on wrecking his peace of mind and stealing his soul.

By the end Stacy was sweating, his heart was pounding, and he felt distinctly light-headed. Whether that was from the force of the music or the pressure of her thigh against his, he could not have said.

She removed her hands from the keys and laid them palm-up in her lap. "I am with child."

Not until she said the actual words did Stacy realize how much he rejoiced at her news—news that would surely be a misfortune for her. He turned to face her.

She was waiting for him and her hands went around his neck even as his slid around her body. He crushed her mouth under his. The kiss was the physical equivalent of the music she'd just played: fierce, unbridled, and mad. He couldn't get deep enough inside her, couldn't get enough of her mouth, her taste, her heat. It felt like years since that glorious night in the stables.

She made a gravelly noise in her throat and her fingers threaded into his hair and tugged painfully as her mouth moved from his lips down his face. She bit him on the chin, hard.

Stacy heard himself utter the words he swore he'd not speak. "I want you. Now."

She groaned into his mouth. "I've thought about this—dreamed about it." She removed his glasses, making the same noise she'd made the last time they'd looked into each other's eyes. It was a noise he'd thought of each and every time he'd had to spill into his fist to be rid of her, even if only for a few hours.

He pulled her to her feet and shoved the bench back with his foot before sweeping the music off the piano. She turned, leaned all the way forward, and gripped the edges of the instrument. When she looked over her shoulder at him, her smile the most wanton he'd ever seen.

Stacy pulled up her skirts. Good Lord! She was wearing stockings and garters and a chemise so brief it barely covered her bottom.

"Mother of God," he muttered. She tried to turn around. "Stay exactly where you are," he ordered, drinking in the sight of her. "I believe you are trying to drive me mad," he accused in a voice he didn't recognize. Her answering laugh was low and wicked.

She was pink, shapely, and perfect, her bottom so like a peach he could barely resist taking a bite.

But that would have to wait. Right now he needed her fast and hard.

"Hold up your skirts."

She grasped the fabric, leaned even lower, and thrust her hips back, offering herself to him.

"Bloody hell," he breathed. He needed at least one taste of her. He dropped to his haunches and ran his tongue along the skin above her plain white stockings. She moaned and her feet spread wider, bringing her sex lower. Stacy ran his tongue up the back of her thigh and over her perfectly formed bottom, stopping when he reached the base of her spine. She shivered as he breathed heavily on the fine down, and then whimpered when he slid a hand between her thighs and parted her damp curls. The pad of his thumb grazed her slick, swollen bud and she jerked against him, muttering something he couldn't hear.

An evil imp prodded him. "What did you say?" he teased, stilling his hand.

"Please. . . *please*," the word came out in a hiss and she pushed against him with needy abandon.

He pushed his thumb inside her and stroked, until he found what he sought.

She bucked and bit out a very filthy word and he chuckled, reaching around her with his other hand, stroking between her swollen lips while he began to work her, pumping harder and deeper as she ground against him.

Stacy had just settled into a pleasurable rhythm when her hips jerked and then froze. She gave another low, animalistic growl and then shouted something in another language; something loud enough to be heard down in the kitchens, or perhaps even the stables.

Her climax drenched his hand and she'd not stopped contracting around his finger when she began to push back against him: She wanted more.

Stacy almost laughed at the feline sound of displeasure she made when his hand left her body. He stood up and tore open his placket. "Hold your skirts higher." He pressed his erection against her bare bottom and groaned with pure joy, lowering his mouth to her neck and kissing, nibbling, and licking.

When she was holding her skirts up to her waist he turned her face until her profile was facing him. He traced her parted lips with the hand that had brought her to climax. She sucked his thumb into her mouth without hesitation, tonguing and stroking him with a suggestiveness that made him ache to be inside her.

"My God," he whispered, and then slid his free hand between her legs and found what he wanted. "Tell me how I should fuck you," he ordered, thumbing her stiff, sensitive bud. "I want to hear you say it."

Her body shuddered at the vulgar word and Stacy guided his shaft between her spread thighs and pushed the slick crown against her tight opening, but not enough to breech her. "Tell me," he said harshly, ceasing his suggestive stroking.

She canted her hips even more and shoved back against him. "Hard, Stacy. Fuck me hard."

Stacy lifted her off the ground with the force of his thrust and she fell forward over the piano, one hand slamming down on the keys and filling the room with a clamor that was no match for the one inside him. He grabbed both her wrists and spread her arms until she held the edges of the instrument.

"Stay put."

And then he grabbed her hips and tilted them, holding her just so before pulling out. She hissed and he knew he'd found the angle that would suit them both to perfection. The next time he entered her he worried he might come out the other side of her body.

"Harder," she murmured.

Stacy used her like an insane man, his body and mind beyond his control. When she climaxed he rode the storm of pleasure right behind her, burying himself to the hilt and filling the part of her that already held his child.

Their child.

It was the most explosive orgasm of his life, an excruciating cataclysm that wracked his body with seemingly endless waves of pleasure before leaving him light-headed and weak.

It was possible he actually fell asleep while still on his feet and seated deep inside her. Her body shifted slightly beneath him and reality intruded; he was crushing her against the unforgiving hardness of the piano. He withdrew reluctantly and then shook out her rumpled, creased skirts before tucking himself into his breeches.

She gave a sigh of pure pleasure, her head resting on her forearms, which were crossed on the piano. "Mmmm. That was . . ."

"Yes, it was," he agreed.

She laughed huskily and pushed herself upright, walking with a stiff-legged gait toward the gold framed mirror. Stacy went to the settee in the darkest corner of the room. He watched her smooth her dress and fuss with her hair, which was wild and would take far more than mere smoothing to return to its tidy chignon.

"Please come here, Signora Stefani."

Her shoulders stiffened at his cool command, but she turned, the light behind her obscuring her face. Not for the first time did he curse the ridiculous darkness he'd imposed on his house: he would have given a great deal to see her expression just then.

As she picked her way toward him Stacy lit two candles beside the settee.

She sat and he turned to face her. "I have an embarrassing confession to make."

She cocked her head, her expression haughty. "Oh?"

"I'm ashamed to admit I do not know your Christian name."

Her look of surprise was priceless and her laughter made him smile. "It is Portia."

"Portia," he repeated. "It is a beautiful name and it suits you." He took her hand. "I know this—" he waved his hand in an encompassing gesture, "is not what you expected when you came here to teach music, but we are beyond that now." He paused and she remained motionless. Stacy did not know whether that was a good or bad sign, but he had to press onward. "We are not well-acquainted but I believe we share at least one passion. Well, two, actually." He grinned and her eyes widened and flickered to his mouth; did he really smile so rarely? He shook the thought away. "There are people who marry after far less acquaintance and I do not think we are as ill-matched as many couples." He paused and she nodded slowly, her expression difficult to read.

"Portia, would you do me the great honor of becoming my wife?" He heard her breath catch in her throat and he plunged on. "I think you are not repelled by me?"

Her lips, full and bruised from their recent lovemaking, curved. "No, Mr. Harrington. Repellant is not a word I would use to describe you. You might be the *least* repellant man I've ever met."

Her disclosure sent blood rushing to his groin. Again.

But then the smile drained from her face. "I didn't tell you I was pregnant to trap a proposal from you."

"Trapped is not the word I would use to describe my feelings on the matter . . . Portia." His words were a dry echo of hers. Her lips parted, as if she might say something, but she remained silent. He continued. "I know we are not well-acquainted, but I believe we would deal well together. I would never expect you to bury yourself in the country merely because I do not prefer to go into society. I would understand if you wanted to travel. I will be generous and you would be an independent woman in many ways."

Her prolonged silence made him uneasy. What was she thinking? Was she frightened? Disgusted? Worried?

"And what will *you* get out of the marriage, Mr. Harrington?"

He blinked. Surely she was not serious? Stacy opened his mouth, but then found he could not speak the truth and expose himself. So instead, he smiled faintly and said, "Perhaps a special rate for piano lessons?"

She shook her head, her expression grave. "No, I'm afraid I've given you lowest possible rate I feel comfortable offering, Mr. Harrington." She laughed at whatever she saw on his face and the sound soothed his tense nerves.

"Call me Stacy." He wanted to bite his tongue at the haughty tone of command.

Her dark, velvety eyes searched his face as if she could see every part of him, parts that weren't visible, parts that might not exist.

"Stacy." She reached up and cupped his jaw and he laid his hand over hers, his heart pounding at her sweetly intimate gesture. "I must tell you something, Stacy."

His heart skipped and stuttered. "Yes?"

"I've been pregnant before but I miscarried within the first three months. It's possible you might marry me for no reason."

Stacy swallowed the inappropriate urge to laugh. He didn't want to laugh because she'd suffered a miscarriage, but because she'd not confessed to something insurmountable—like already having a husband or being a mad, escaped convict.

"A child would be wonderful, Portia, but I believe we might find other reasons to enjoy our marriage." He could only hope his words of assurance would soften his stiff, cool tone. He released her hand and she, lingeringly, he thought, released his face.

"I must also confess the last time I was pregnant I was even more emotional and temperamental than I usually am. Which, as my father would have warned you if he were still alive, can be quite excessive even at the best of times."

"Ah, unreasonable. I see. Well, I shall consider myself forewarned. Was there anything else?" he asked lightly.

She smiled and the expression brightened the room. "I agree with what you've said. We are compatible in several ways and I've enjoyed the time I've spent with you. I know I should want more time to get to know one another—"

"A few more weeks would not cause any scandal when the child is born."

"I said I *should* want more time, but I don't. I would very much like to marry you . . . Stacy."

Her gracious acceptance of his offer left him dazed and pleased. "I will do my very best to make sure you never regret your decision, Portia."

"I will do the same, Stacy."

And just like that, they were engaged to be married.

Chapter Twelve

WHEN PORTIA ENTERED the music room the following day she couldn't help thinking about yesterday's lesson and her face heated.

She'd not seen Stacy since dinner last night, when he'd told his aunt about their engagement. Although Miss Tate had given the proper responses and appeared pleased, Portia was not entirely convinced. In any event, she'd gone to bed not long after playing for them. Even if Miss Tate *wasn't* appalled, the two would need time to talk without her.

This morning she'd been alone at breakfast and hadn't seen either of the Harringtons until now.

When Portia shut the door Stacy turned away from the piano, where he'd been playing some scales. A very wicked smile curved his lips.

"If you give me such looks your playing will never progress," she scolded.

His pale eyebrows rose and he wore the inscrutable expression that made her heart pound. "But perhaps my other skills will benefit, ma'am?"

"I think your other skills need no work."

That made him smile. "I posted your letters today—are you sure you don't wish to put the date back, just in case your friends are able to attend?"

Portia had written separate letters to all six of her friends, telling them her news. She'd extended invitations, but she knew how hard her friends had to work. If she asked them, they would find a way to come, but she did not wish to beggar her friends just so she wouldn't feel lonely.

"I think the date we chose is best," she said.

"Very well. I shall set off two days hence to secure the license. I daresay I'll be back by the end of the week. I shall speak to the vicar tomorrow. I can also talk to my aunt about the wedding breakfast, unless—"

"I would like to discuss that with her, if that is all right with you?"

He gave her one of his rare smiles and she could see he was pleased. "Thank you, Portia, I appreciate your thoughtfulness. I know you will soon be mistress of Whitethorn and—"

"Actually, I'm dreadful when it comes to managing household affairs," she lied. "I would love it if Miss Tate would consider continuing in her current role—if she doesn't mind, of course." That second part was *not* a lie. Portia had no interest in managing a huge house and could see it was important to Miss Tate. The woman would always live with them, so it behooved her to try and get along.

"Thank you," he said simply.

The two-hour lesson—during which only *music* was performed on the piano—passed too quickly. When it was finished, Stacy came to the desk where she was assembling her notes.

"Will you join me in the library for a few moments, ma'am?"

His rather severe expression made her stomach tighten, but she ignored her butterflies. "Of course."

When they entered the library Portia noticed one of the windows was uncovered. It was a window that faced north and was shaded by a large tree. Even so, it was brighter than he usually kept his rooms.

He followed her gaze. "It is my hope to allow a little more

light into the house." The words were simple, but the meaning was clear: he was doing this for her.

Portia took the same chair she'd sat in less than two months ago and Stacy withdrew a beautiful wooden box from his desk and handed it to her.

"How lovely," she said, tracing the fine marquetry with her finger.

He leaned against the front of his desk. "The gift is actually inside the box, Portia."

A little shiver ran down her spine at the sound of her name in his mouth. She bit her lip, afraid of what she would find inside. She had nothing to give to him in return.

"It will not open itself." There was amusement in his quiet voice.

Inside the box was an exquisite pearl choker. The pearls were large and the color of fresh cream. There were earrings and a bracelet to match. Portia had never had anything even a fraction as fine.

"Oh, Mr. Harrington, how beautiful," she breathed, touching one of the pearls, which actually felt warm beneath her finger. She looked up, embarrassed by his generosity. "How can I thank you for such a magnificent gift?"

"You can start by calling me Stacy." He grimaced, "Or Eustace, if you must. As for thanking me?" His pale lips curved. "I'm certain I will think of something."

Portia's face became unbearably hot under his bespectacled stare.

"Will you take off your glasses, Stacy?"

"*Tsk, tsk, tsk.* You know what happens when I do that, Portia."

She laughed. "I promise I shan't launch myself at you like a wanton."

He uncrossed his arms and placed both palms on the edge of

the desk. "Then I hardly see the point."

She rose, took the single step that separated them, and stood on her tiptoes to kiss him softly on the mouth before lowering back to her heels. He stood as still as the statue he so resembled.

"Thank you for the jewels, Stacy, they are lovely."

He reached out and skimmed a finger down her jaw, the feather-light touch sending a pulse of desire directly to her core.

"You are welcome, Portia." To her disappointment, he dropped his hand to his side. "They belonged to my mother. There are several other pieces you are welcome to use. We can go through them at some point but I thought this set would go particularly well with the red gown you've worn on occasion. It would please me if you wore it tonight."

His quiet request took her breath away; there was just something very sensual about a man wanting to see her body wearing certain clothing.

He shifted slightly, as though he needed to put some distance between them, and Portia took a step back, resolving to keep her hands off his body. The next time they made love—or rutted like a pair of wild minks—it would be *he* who initiated it.

"If you change your mind about inviting your friends I shall be happy to send my traveling carriage for any who might need it."

Portia blinked at the offer. "That is *very* generous of you."

"Incidentally, I gave Daisy instructions to wait on you until we can engage a proper maid. She is a pleasant girl and eager to please."

The offer surprised her. "I've always tended to my own needs. Indeed, I should hardly know how to keep a personal servant employed."

His smile was gentle, but firm. "No doubt you will become accustomed to it." He walked toward the door as he spoke and held it open, as though the topic was no longer under discussion.

For the first time Portia realized she was marrying a man who had a mind of his own. He was gentle and soft-spoken, but, she realized now, his servants all obeyed him quickly and without question. She recalled his aunt's words from all those weeks ago: He was a benevolent despot. Portia was fairly certain Miss Tate had spoken in jest, still . . .

Once you are married, he will be your lord and master.

The thought struck her with some force, even though it shouldn't be a new one to her. After all, she'd been married to Ivo for most of her adult life. But she and Ivo had managed their marriage like two squabbling children and there had been no master in their relationship. They'd each constantly struggled to impose their will on the other.

Portia glanced up at Eustace Harrington's handsome, impassive face and a frisson of something—excitement? Fear?—shot through her body as she stared into his dark lenses.

It occurred to her that she actually knew very little about her husband-to-be.

He took her hand, the one not holding the extravagant gift he'd just given her, and lifted it to his lips. "I look forward to seeing you at dinner, my dear." His kiss was hot on the thin skin of her hand. It felt very much like a brand.

WHEN PORTIA SAW the way Daisy dressed her hair that evening—a sleek French twist—she was considerably more sanguine about engaging a maid.

"You've worked a miracle, Daisy."

Daisy laughed. "'Tis easy when a body has hair like you. I've got eight sisters, ma'am, and we all have these same straight as straw mops." She gestured to her own hair, which was braided into two heavy honey-blond ropes.

Portia opened the marquetry box. "Will you help me fasten

the necklace?"

"Oh ma'am, I *never*!" Daisy stared at the glowing pearls with wide eyes.

"Mr. Harrington gave them to me as a wedding gift. Evidently they belonged to his mother." She picked up the heavy strand and draped it around her neck. It did look fine with the low-cut flame silk. While Daisy fastened the necklace Portia screwed on the earrings and clasped the bracelet around her wrist.

"My goodness but you look lovely." Daisy stared open-mouthed at Portia's reflection. So did Portia. She'd never looked better.

On impulse, she said, "I shall be pleased to keep you as my maid, Daisy, if that is what you would like."

"Oh above all things, ma'am. I know Mr. Harrington said it was just temporary-like."

"He has left the choice to me, and I choose you."

"Thank you, ma'am, you won't regret it."

Portia left Daisy humming to herself while she examined Portia's rather pitiful wardrobe.

One of the two footmen, Charles, was waiting at the bottom of the stairs. "Mr. Harrington is in the yellow drawing room, Mrs. Stefani."

"Thank you, Charles."

Stacy was seated at a small writing desk when she entered and he'd just finished sanding something. His lips parted, but it was a moment before he spoke. "You look ravishing, Portia."

Her face heated at his quiet homage. "Thank you." She looked around at a room she'd only seen once before, the day Soames gave her a tour of the house.

"Do you care for something to drink?"

Portia had actually been feeling quite queasy, but it felt uncivil to say no. "Thank you, perhaps a sherry—a very small one." He strode toward a table holding several decanters and Portia couldn't help staring at his muscular legs, encased in black pantaloons that fit him like a second skin. They'd only ever made love clothed and Portia had yet to see most of his body. The memory of the part she *had* seen made her mouth dry. Perhaps it was just as well she'd asked for the sherry.

He turned and caught her staring, as usual.

"Who decorated Whitethorn?" she asked, looking at his hands rather than his face when he handed her the glass.

"I did." The candles behind her glinted off his blue-black lenses, making him appear remote and menacing.

"You have exquisite taste."

"Thank you, but you will be mistress of Whitethorn so you must change anything you like when we are married." His fine nostrils quivered at the word 'married'.

Was he anticipating their wedding night as much as she was? Portia somehow doubted it. Ivo had been convinced she suffered from nymphomania, an accusation he'd flung in her face more than once. Portia had never heard the word before but had been able to guess what it meant. After what had happened in the stables—and again in the music room—she was beginning to suspect Ivo had been correct.

Portia realized he was looking at her, as if waiting for an answer. "I honestly can't think of anything I would change." The house was perfect. He was perfect.

"We've not discussed a wedding trip. Have you anywhere you'd like to go?"

"You wish to go on a trip?"

He looked amused by her surprise. "I have no objection to travel. I merely require certain precautions to make it possible."

Portia decided now was as good a time as ever to discuss those precautions. "What kind of precautions, if I may ask?"

"You must ask me whatever you wish, Portia. You are soon to be my wife, after all."

Portia swallowed at the word 'wife'.

"The precautions are much the same as those I take most days. My skin burns very easily but that does not mean I cannot go outdoors. It just means I must cover as much of my person as possible. My eyes are particularly sensitive and easily damaged. That is why I choose to go out so rarely during the middle of the day. I'm afraid I have rather a fear of losing my sight," he said, sounding as though he were admitting to something embarrassing—like a fear of snails.

"It would be a terrible thing to be deprived of sight." The only thing Portia could think of that would be worse would be losing one's hearing and the beauty of music along with it. "Do your spectacles protect you?"

"I have a pair that are far thicker and enclosed so light does not come in from the sides." He saw Portia's expression and smiled. "I daresay you will hate them, given your curiosity regarding my freakish orbs."

"They are *not* freakish." Portia was surprised by how angry the word made her. "They are quite possibly two of the most beautiful things I've ever seen. Do you never look in the mirror?"

"Rarely." He sounded bored.

"No doubt your condition is a tremendous inconvenience and I'm sure ignorant people—of which there are lamentably a great many—make going out in public uncomfortable. But many people will be looking at you because you are an excessively handsome man. I'm sure my opinion comes as no surprise to you." She flushed as she recalled their most recent lovemaking. How could he not see that she found him desirable?

His lips curved into a slight, tolerant smile. "I thought we might invite the vicar and his wife to dinner when I return."

Portia allowed him to turn from a topic he clearly found distasteful. But privately she vowed to do everything in her power to make him understand just how attractive she found him—both his mind and person—when they were man and wife.

THE DAYS BEFORE the wedding sped past quickly. Portia realized Stacy had been correct when he'd said she would find plenty to keep a maid occupied. Not only was Daisy skilled when it came to hair, but she was also a wizard with a needle.

After Stacy left for Plymouth they spent two afternoons altering one of Portia's dresses into her bridal gown. They giggled like girls and ate too many cakes and biscuits while Daisy embroidered tiny flowers on Portia's simple cream silk gown and transformed it into a stunning wedding dress.

"I wish I'd asked Mr. Harrington's man what color his waistcoat would be," Daisy said as she worked on the hem.

Stacy's valet was a big, barrel-chested man with a severe expression. "I'd be frightened to ask Powell anything," Portia said.

Daisy laughed. "Why he's nothing but a big kitten."

Portia smiled at her blushing young maid; ah, so that's the way it was . . .

The door to her sitting room opened and Frances stood in the doorway. "I've brought you a surprise." She stepped aside to reveal Nanny.

"And what a delightful surprise!" Portia sprang up and hurried toward the two older women while Daisy quickly moved the various garments off the chairs.

"How wonderful of you to visit—both of you."

Nanny smiled at Daisy, her blue eyes clear and sharp today. "It's nice to see you outside of church, Daisy—but you hardly ever visit me."

"I am a working lady, now, Nanny."

Nanny turned to peer up at Frances. "You shouldn't work the poor girl so hard, Miss Tate."

"Oh Nanny, Daisy is teasing you," Frances said, her tone more suited for a small child than a woman of ninety.

Nanny's eyes narrowed and Portia hastily rang for more tea, turning the subject to defuse possible hostilities.

It was the first time Portia had seen Frances with Nanny and she got the distinct impression Nanny did not like the other woman. Portia realized that Nanny, who'd taken to her so quickly, could be a prickly character with other people. Luckily she liked Daisy, whose entire family she seemed to know.

Once the tea tray arrived Portia brought up Nanny's favorite subject—and one dear to her heart as well, she realized—and regaled them with story after story about Stacy. She was in the middle of relating a tale about Stacy and his first pony when she blinked and looked around.

"And where is my favorite today?" Nanny asked.

"He's gone to Plymouth, to procure the wedding license," Portia reminded her.

"Oh, that's right." She shook her head, and then smiled. "He's a caution. He always was. He had you wrapped around his finger quick enough Miss Frances, didn't he?" She shot the other woman a smile that lacked the malice of her earlier looks.

"Yes, he was remarkably adept at getting his way. It's fortunate he wasn't a malicious boy," Frances agreed, her face softening.

"No, he has none of his father in him," Nanny said.

Frances flinched and the two women locked eyes, something unpleasant flowing between them.

"Stacy will back home this evening," Portia said to smooth over whatever was going on. "And we'll both come to visit you tomorrow, Nanny."

Her darling's name was enough to make Nanny stop glaring at Frances and the conversation reverted to the subject of the wedding, the awkward incident forgotten.

ALL THROUGH DINNER that night Portia hoped to hear Stacy's carriage. The meal had been a cozy, feminine affair with only her and Frances and the women retired to the smaller of the sitting rooms and chatted until Portia noticed Frances's head nodding.

Portia was tiptoeing toward the door so as not to wake the older woman when she heard the clatter of wheels on cobblestones.

The sound woke Frances, who blinked owlishly, glanced around until she saw Portia, and said, "I'm pleased that he is home but I really wish he would not travel at night."

"At least it is a full moon," Portia said. "I believe I shall go meet him in the—"

The door flew open and Soames stood in the opening, his eyes wild. "Signora—you must come quickly. It's Mr. Harrington—he's been *shot*!"

Chapter Thirteen

STACY WAS DOZING when Jewell's—his coachman—frantic shout woke him. He'd been enjoying one of those very rare moments in life: a moment of pure contentment.

The Plymouth trip had been a success in all but one area. He'd purchased the common license and then gone to the jeweler he favored. It hadn't taken him long to decide on a large emerald-cut diamond. The stone was exquisite and the setting simple yet elegant. He'd given the man a glove of Portia's that Daisy had filched and then arranged to come by the following morning to collect the ring. On his way out of the shop he'd spied some lovely diamond hair pins and had the man to add a dozen to his order.

He'd then gone to Kitty's and suffered her gloating and preening, as if she, rather than Stacy, was the one who was getting married.

"Was it dreadful when you proposed? Did you stutter like the greenest of boys?" she teased.

"I actually fainted, Kitty. I believe that is the only reason she accepted me, she was too embarrassed to do aught else."

Kitty's shout of joy had almost deafened him when he'd told her Portia was with child.

"Oh Stacy, she sounds like a marvelous woman, perfect for you—fiery and fearless. She won't let you give her that haughty look you specialize in and quiver in her slippers."

Stacy rolled his eyes. "Good God, Kitty, you are an idiot."

His words only made her laugh harder. But she stopped laughing when Stacy invited her to the wedding.

"You're daft—you should be locked in Bedlam. Invite a whore to your wedding?"

Stacy gave her one of the frosty looks she'd just mentioned. "It would please me if you did not refer to yourself with that word, Kitty."

"That look does not work on *me,* your highness. I know what a pussy cat you really are."

"I can see I've been too lenient with you in the past." He gave her the severest of his glares.

But she just shook her head. "I cannot come to your wedding, Stacy. It would not be a good way to start a life of domestic harmony. Have you told her about me—about us?"

"Not yet, but we've hardly had time to talk about much other than wedding arrangements. Besides, there isn't anything to tell other than you are my best friend."

Kitty heaved a sigh. "There is the fact I work in a brothel. There is the fact we were lovers."

Stacy shrugged, refusing to give ground. "We've not been lovers for years."

"Oh, men are so stupid. Trust me, Stacy, she wouldn't welcome my presence at her wedding; she would be insulted. If she is as fierce as you say, you would not survive the wedding night intact. Indeed," she bit her plush lower lip and then said, "you should not visit me again."

They'd argued in earnest after that; through dinner and then through tea, Stacy using every argument he could muster—and no small number of threats—to get Kitty to agree to come.

And all for nothing.

But at least she had relented on ending their friendship.

"I will receive you again—you must know I will, Stacy—but you will jeopardize your marriage if you continue our friendship."

When he'd opened his mouth to argue she'd embraced him fiercely. "My dearest, dearest friend. I am so pleased for you. You deserve nothing but the best and it sounds as if you have found it. I wish you everything that is good and happy."

Stacy pondered her words during the long carriage ride home. Was it an insult to Portia to invite his closest friend? He'd been agonizing over the question for a good two hours when Jewell shouted and a gun discharged, the sounds pulling him rudely from his revelry.

Powell, his valet, was ever at the ready, and handed him a pistol even as the carriage began to slow.

Stacy opened the vent and called out, "What is it?"

"Three men that I can see, sir."

"You're loaded, Baker?" Stacy yelled to the groom seated beside his coachman.

"Aye, sir, so is Freddy," he said, referring to Stacy's footman, who rode on the small perch on the rear of the coach.

Stacy peered out the window but could see little. It was just past dusk and the trees to the west of the road blocked the last rays of daylight. They'd begun their journey early in the day but had stopped to help a wagon that had collided with a gig. There had been two rather nasty injuries and no way to transport the victims other than load them into Stacy's carriage.

As a result of their Good Samaritan actions they'd been hurrying against the darkness.

Stacy chewed the inside of his mouth as he considered the logistics. The lack of light would work in Stacy's favor but not those of his men.

"Can you see well enough to get a good shot off?" Stacy asked his driver.

"Not any worth taking, sir. They're all behind us still."

"Did they hit anything with their shot?"

"No, sir. I believe they were aiming at young Freddy."

Stacy cursed. Freddy was utterly exposed. He took a deep breath. "Listen carefully, here is what we will do."

PORTIA WAS RUNNING before Soames finished speaking and almost trampled the elderly butler. Stacy was between Powell and Jewell, his arms around their shoulders, his booted feet dragging. His face, cravat, shirt, and hair were caked in blood.

She whirled on Soames, who'd shadowed her steps. "Send for a doctor."

"Baker has already gone, ma'am."

"Bring him into the drawing room," she ordered, hurrying alongside the men.

For once Stacy was without his dratted glasses. His eyes were half closed and his lips were curled into a smile.

"Hello, Portia." His voice was slurred and drowsy.

"Where is he hit?" she demanded.

"In the neck and in the leg."

Portia let out a string of the vilest Italian curse words she could think of.

Soames, Powell, and Frances gaped.

Stacy laughed weakly. "Fiery and fierce," he murmured.

"Bring more light," Portia told Soames once they reached the drawing room. She motioned to Powell, "Put him on the settee, Jewell, and then go fetch a basin of hot water. Powell, get me a glass of brandy. Frances, you will help me." She saw Daisy hovering anxiously in the open doorway. "Daisy, find old bedding or something we can use for bandages." Daisy and the men scattered and Frances dropped down beside her, already unbuttoning Stacy's coat and waistcoat.

The men had tied a tourniquet around his leg wound—which was leaking slowly—but the one on his neck only had his bloody cravat pressed against it. Portia removed it and hissed; the bullet had not severed an artery, but the wound was bleeding freely.

Powell came with the brandy.

"Lift his head," she ordered, holding the glass to his lips, which were now as white as the rest of him. "Drink, Stacy, it will help with the pain."

They poured a little down his throat but she was afraid to choke him with more and handed Powell the glass before turning to the other woman. "We've got to stop the bleeding. How are your needle skills, Frances?"

She glanced at the gash, grimaced, and then shook her head. "I am not afraid of blood—but this. . . No, I cannot do it. Are you sure it needs to be done now? Can't we wait for—"

"I will do it."

Frances's jaw wobbled with shock. "Are you sure?"

"I volunteered in soldiers' hospitals in London and I've seen it done many times." Although she'd never done it herself—but why mention that? "It needs to be done quickly."

Frances pressed her lips into a grim line and nodded. "I'll go fetch my embroidery bag."

The next half hour was one of the worst of Portia's life. It took five people to hold Stacy down while she sewed the bleeding wound shut. He was weak from a lack of blood but swore like a sailor. By the time she was finished Stacy was hoarse from yelling but at least the bleeding had stopped.

The injury in his thigh was another matter entirely; the bullet was lodged in the flesh. She had packed the wound with clean cloths before beginning work on his neck, but they were soaked through from all his thrashing, even with the tourniquet.

Portia grimaced and looked up at Frances, whose blue eyes were red from weeping. "How long until the doctor comes?"

"He should be here by now." Soames said. "He only lives on the other side of Bude."

"He must be out on a call. It could be hours." Portia chewed her lip ragged. "It needs to come out. The flesh is becoming more swollen by the minute. It will only get worse."

Frances swallowed audibly and then nodded. "Right, then. I'll clean the wound and make it ready, Portia, you get some of that brandy down his throat." She took the basin of fresh, hot water Soames was holding and began to cleanse the area.

Portia knelt beside the settee and smoothed the damp hair from his forehead. His eyelids flickered. "Stacy, can you take some brandy? We've got to remove the bullet. It will go better for you if you can take some." He opened his mouth and she tipped the glass, dribbling the liquid in slowly, until he'd finished it. "Can you take more?" He nodded and she turned to Powell. "Bring the bottle." While he went to fetch more she looked down at her patient. "How are you?"

"You planned this so I'd take off my spectacles." His voice was a hoarse croak.

Portia laughed, the sound hysterical. "Let that be a lesson to you. Perhaps next time you won't tease me."

Powell handed her another glass just as Soames entered with another basin of steaming water—and the doctor right beside him.

"Thank God!" Portia wiped away the tears that had begun to make their way down her cheeks.

The doctor was a calm, older man who was not about to be flapped by a mere bullet. He commended Portia on her stitchery and substituted a laudanum draught for the brandy. Within half an hour the bullet had been extracted and Stacy was in his bedroom, where the doctor and Powell could go about any business too delicate for females to witness.

Portia realized somebody had ordered tea and took a cup, her hands shaking. Nobody spoke for a very long time. It was Frances who finally broke the silence.

"You are very . . . resourceful, Portia." Her voice held a mixture of reverence, respect, and fear.

"No, merely half Italian." Portia laughed when she saw Frances's confusion. "Stabbings were far too common in Rome. I was nine the first time I helped my father tend a victim. And of course I saw far worse in the hospitals."

The door opened and the doctor entered. "Well, ladies, I hope you don't decide to set up a surgery in my neighborhood or I shall go out of business." He smiled at Portia and Frances, both of whom were liberally smeared with Stacy's blood. "The wounds are fairly shallow and should heal quickly. He appeared much worse because of the blood loss from the neck wound. That was fast thinking on your part ma'am. Powell has a second laudanum draught for our patient if he needs it. Based on what I know of Mr. Harrington and his constitution, he'll be up and about tomorrow. I'll come and see him first thing."

"*Tomorrow*?" Frances repeated. "Surely he should not be up tomorrow?"

"No." The doctor laughed. "But I doubt you'll be able to stop him. It won't hurt him to get dressed and sit up, as long as he doesn't try to resume his normal activities and rip his stitches. Just try to get him to rest, if you can—even if it's just for a few days."

Portia felt a grim, determined smile settle on her face. "Don't worry, Doctor. He'll rest."

PORTIA WOULD REMEMBER that promise often over the next few days.

The doctor had been correct, both when it came to Stacy's injuries and his constitution. When Portia came down to breakfast the following morning Frances had just come from her nephew's room.

"How is he?" Portia asked.

"Eating and complaining in equal amounts."

Portia laughed. "I suppose that is promising."

Frances shook her head, her expression one of frustration and despair. "He said he would stay in bed until Doctor Gates paid a visit."

"I suppose that will have to do. Did he tell you what happened?"

Her expression shifted from frustrated to furious. "No, and when I asked him, both he and his valet could not stop laughing."

"Laughing?"

"Laughing."

What in the world could that be about?

"I spoke to Jewell," Frances said, "but he wasn't talking, either. He said Mr. Harrington should be the one to tell the story."

The legend of what happened had plenty of time to grow before Stacy put everyone out of their misery. He told the story two days later at the dinner party France gave. In addition to the three of them, there were the vicar and his wife—Mr. and Mrs. Lawson—and their son Jeremy, who was a doctor in the neighboring town of Stratton. Jeremy was Stacy's age and Portia had spoken to him several times after church. He was unmarried, attractive, and personable and she felt as if he'd been on the verge of asking her to go walking with him on more than one occasion. She was relieved things had never gone that far or it would have been awkward now. While she liked Jeremy Lawson well enough, he was not Stacy.

Portia wasn't surprised that it was Jeremy—who was friendly, although not friends with Stacy—who demanded to know the truth.

"I say, Harrington," Jeremy asked with a challenging grin, "won't you give over already? We're all dying to know what happened. There is an entire page devoted to the mystery in the book at the Castle." He was referring to the betting book at the inn, which monitored anything interesting in Bude—and plenty that wasn't.

Stacy looked as impeccable as ever. The cravat hid his neck wound and his deliciously snug pantaloons barely showed the surprisingly slim bandage on his leg. He looked at Portia and smiled, clearly enjoying the opportunity to keep them all—her in particular—on tenterhooks.

Portia crossed her arms. "I, for one, refuse to beg."

She was loudly booed by everyone else at the table.

"Very well, very well," she said, heaving an exaggerated sigh. "Will you *please* tell us what happened, Mr. Harrington?"

"Are you sure, Mrs. Stefani?" Portia narrowed her eyes and Stacy laughed and raised one staying hand. "Very well, as you command. You all know it was highwaymen. We had four pistols to their three, and we also had something they never expected." He smirked. "Me."

Portia groaned. "I'm not sure I want to hear this."

"Me either," Frances said.

But Stacy would not be stopped now that he'd started. "Jewell stopped the carriage and gave over his gun, Baker kept the other pistol hidden beneath his coat and so did Freddie. When the robbers demanded we open the carriage Jewell tried to persuade them they'd better not open the door. It was fortunate for us that the sun was almost completely gone.

"Finally, when the three men were threatening to start shooting if they weren't allowed inside, I flung open the door and leapt out of the carriage. I had scruffed up my hair and made it as wild as possible and removed my glasses. The poor men did not have a chance. Our only miscalculation was that their fingers might spasm in fear." He shrugged. "The closest man shot one of his companions by accident and the other two shot me." Stacy took a drink of wine, his black lenses glinting in the candlelight. He didn't notice, until it was too late, that the only one smiling with appreciation was the young doctor.

"Are you *mad*?" Portia demanded when she found her voice.

Stacy raised his eyebrows. "I didn't think so," he said mildly.

"I agree with Portia—you *are* mad."

It was the first time Portia had ever seen Frances angry. Perhaps it was the first time his aunt had ever shown Stacy the emotion either, because his lips parted in surprise as he took in her flushed face and flashing eyes.

"That was beyond foolhardy, Stacy, and we will speak of this later," she promised.

Portia gave the startled man a hard look and nodded. "Yes," she said, nodding with menacing slowness, "we most certainly will."

PORTIA WAS NOT surprised when Stacy insisted the wedding proceed as planned.

"It makes no sense to postpone things. I still have a few more days to recuperate and am more than capable of standing before a tiny group of people and eating breakfast afterward."

He was, in fact, eating breakfast as he delivered his ultimatum. He glanced up from the impressive pile of food on his plate and smiled at Portia. "I thought perhaps you and I might walk over to see Nanny today."

Portia opened her mouth—

"The leg wound is barely even visible and the one on my neck has almost disappeared."

"That is a bald lie."

He cut her a sly smile. "Your needlework is adequate, Portia, but do you think Daisy might add a flourish or two?"

Portia laughed, in spite of herself. "I don't know about Daisy, but Frances is ready to sew you to your bed."

He cut a piece of ham and swabbed it in egg, clearly unbothered by his aunt's persistent anger at his reckless behavior. He paused in the act of levering the food to his mouth. "I would like to visit Nanny. Will you go with me today?"

"Should you walk so far?"

"The good doctor was the one to advise walking."

Portia wasn't sure she believed he'd meant a walk as far as Nanny's cottage.

"I'll take my cane with me. Will you accompany me, Portia?"

He really *was* accustomed to having everything his way. Luckily they would have years together to sort that out.

But for now, she capitulated. "I would like that."

Stacy frowned at her plate of dry toast and turned to the footman. "Are there any strawberries?"

"Cook has the last of them and said she was thinking to make a tart for dinner."

"Ask her if we might have a small portion and some cream?" He turned to Portia once the footman left. "You must eat something."

She grimaced down at her plate; she'd woken up sick again this morning and the food that filled the sideboard held no appeal.

"The last berries are always the best," he added, as if that settled the matter. Portia had visions of him sitting on her and making her eat them, a berry at a time. He saw her speculative look and cocked an eyebrow. "What is it?"

"I believe you always get your way, Mr. Harrington."

He smiled but refused to be drawn. "Shall we leave for our walk after breakfast?"

PORTIA CHANGED INTO her walking dress and half boots before going to meet Stacy in the library. He was waiting for her and took something from a drawer in his desk. She hesitated and bit her lip; he was going to give her something else.

He saw her hesitation and shook his head. "Please tell me you are not one of those tiresome people who do not feel as though they deserve gifts? Come here, *Signora Stefani.*"

"You must stop giving me things, *Mr. Harrington.*"

"Give me your hand," he demanded.

"Don't you know the word 'please'?" He ignored her question and unbuttoned the two tiny buttons that held her glove closed and then pulled it off, finger by finger. He was wearing his walking glasses and she reached up with her free hand to remove them. She stared at his ridiculously long eyelashes, lust pounding through her veins like a torrential river. Something cool slid onto the third finger of her left hand and she looked down. An enormous emerald-cut diamond sparkled up at her.

"Oh Stacy, it is beautiful." She looked up to find his gorgeous eyes on her. "It is also enormous."

"Why thank you." His slight smile was beyond wicked.

Portia flushed, loving his playful flirtation more than the expensive gift. "Please, do stop giving me such lovely things." She gazed down at her hand and tilted it from side to side, the gem catching the light from the window and sparkling. "Not that I have any intention of returning this," she muttered.

Stacy took her chin in strong, warm fingers and forced her to look at him. "I did not get it because I like you, Portia. I bought it hoping it might get me a kiss."

"What an indecent proposal, Mr. Harrington. I'm afraid you'll have to wait a few days for your kiss."

She had the satisfaction of seeing a completely new expression cross his face, one of utter surprise at being denied something he wanted, and then he threw back his head and laughed. She snatched her hand away and plucked her glove off the desk before taking a few steps to a safe distance. When she'd closed the two buttons she looked up to find him watching her with an intensity that made her body tighten. His violet eyes burned and it was all she could do not to fling herself at him. But the next time flinging was done, she resolved that it would be *him* doing it.

"Are you ready, Mr. Harrington?" she asked coolly, cocking one eyebrow at him. He really needed a lesson when it came to expecting her to fawn all over his person. Just because he was all she thought about did not mean she had to give in to her impulses. Denying him might be just as enjoyable.

But somehow she doubted it.

STACY WALKED WITH a cane beside Portia as they entered the section of forest that led to Nanny's bluff-top cottage. His leg *was* stiff and forced him to amble slowly. They walked in companionable silence while he thought about a recent conversation they'd had. Spurred by the realization that he really knew very little about her Stacy had asked her about her friends—the six teachers who used to work at her school.

The tongue of jealousy that had licked at him upon learning that one of them—Miles Ingram—was a handsome young lord had been a surprise, and not a pleasant one. It also made him recall Kitty's warning when he'd invited her to their wedding. Perhaps she'd been correct about Portia not wishing to meet one of his ex-lovers. How could he ask her to accept such a situation when he became jealous just hearing about a mere friend?

Stacy was learning many things about himself, and not all of them pleasant. His possessive feelings toward his bride to be were uncomfortable. He'd never been troubled by such emotions before and his reaction made him realize how bloodless his feelings for Penelope had been.

He watched Portia pick a daisy that was growing in a narrow

strip of sunlight beside the path. She tucked the flower in the velvet band of her bonnet and looked up at him. "There, how is that?"

"Hideous," he lied.

She laughed and resumed walking. "I'm so sorry my friend Annis is not able to come."

"Is she the closest of your friends?"

"No, that would probably be Serena. But Annis is so gentle and sweet I was rather thinking she would enjoy meeting Jeremy Lawson."

"Ah, playing matchmaker?"

"Perhaps a little." She sighed.

Stacy privately thought young Lawson was half in love with Portia. Stacy could not blame him; he was half-way in love with her himself. Maybe a little more than half.

"Lawson is a personable and biddable young man. I am sure he'll find a female eager to manage him when he decides the time is right."

She clucked her tongue at him. "You make it sound so romantic, Mr. Harrington."

Romantic? Stacy supposed he wasn't.

"You know him better than I do, Portia, but I daresay Lawson has more than enough romance in his bosom for two. He needs a wife like his mother—somebody shrewd."

"You think *Mrs. Lawson* is shrewd? She seems so…gentle and vague."

"Do not mistake her lightness of manner for a lack of shrewdness, my dear. Mrs. Lawson manages the vicar with the skill of a military commander. I daresay the vicar needs that," he hastened to add.

Stacy, however, did not. Although Mrs. Lawson was a charming woman she had a distinctly managing gleam in her eyes. He much preferred the look in Portia's eyes: amorous.

"You sound disapproving, *Mr. Harrington.* Do you dislike ambition and intelligence in a female?" There was an edge in her voice that made him smile.

"You willfully misunderstand me, *Signora Stefani.* You know very well I recognize and appreciate both qualities—neither of which are the same as managing. Not that I disapprove of managing qualities, although they are not something I seek in a mate."

"No, I believe you possess that characteristic in abundance."

"I daresay I do; does that worry you?"

She pursed her lips as she considered the question. "I'm afraid my temperament is not always amenable to following orders."

He put his hand on her arm and stopped her, waiting until she met his eyes. "I do not expect to be issuing orders, Portia." Did she think he was some sort of tyrant?

She gave him a rather suspicious look, as if she was only half convinced. "What happens when we disagree on a subject?"

"Then I would try to persuade you."

"And if I remain unpersuaded?"

Stacy paused. What would he do if she did not agree with him? "I suppose it would depend on how strongly I felt on the matter."

She gave a small nod and began walking.

"Portia," he said, waiting until she turned back to him to continue, "We are to be married and I wish to please you in every way. I would never impose my will on you. I would not wish to make you unhappy."

Her shapely mouth curved into a smile. "I know that, Stacy. I suppose I should have warned you how stubborn I can be before you offered for me. My father used to say I could be unmanageable when I got the bit between my teeth."

Stacy could well imagine. She'd shown fire on more than one occasion, the last of which had been the way she'd handled his injuries the night he'd been shot. He'd been groggy, but not too delirious to recall how she'd issued orders to everyone and handled his wounds with impressive efficiency. He'd been very grateful—and always would be—but the steel in her had made him realize she had a will of her own. Stacy knew there had been few instances in his life when anyone had thwarted his will. Both his aunt and Nanny had spoiled him dreadfully as a child, no doubt feeling he deserved indulgence because he lived such a solitary existence. But while he might like his own way, he was no monster.

Was he?

He took a step toward her. "It is true that I am master of Whitethorn, Portia, but you will find that I am gentle with the ribbons." When she flushed and bit her lower lip he knew she was thinking about horses and the first night they made love. Just thinking about that evening made him harden. And the expression in her eyes as she looked up at him only enflamed him more.

But the tenuous voice of reason held him in check: *You've already behaved badly enough. Another few days and you can have her properly. Or improperly—however she wants it.*

Stacy leashed his desire and put his hand on the small of her back, giving her a gentle push before he succumbed to his urges and mounted her against a nearby tree.

They walked in silence, his gaze on her hips, which swayed tantalizingly. He wrenched his eyes from her backside and forced his thoughts in another direction.

"I will teach you to ride," he said, and then realized how autocratic he sounded. Did he always speak with such arrogant certitude? He tried again. "You will be able to explore far more territory than either walking or in a gig."

"I should love to learn to ride. Is it difficult?"

"Not for someone as naturally graceful as you."

"Charmer," she said, but he could hear the pleasure in her voice.

"It will be more pleasant with a good horse and I will enjoy finding you a proper mount." Indeed, Stacy was more than a little excited at the idea of spending time teaching *her* something.

"You mean I can't ride Geist?"

He laughed.

"You are wretched, Mr. Harrington. Perhaps I should have snickered when you first played the piano for me?"

They bickered good naturedly about pianos and horses until they came to the rise that overlooked the cottage.

"It's such a lovely house, Stacy. But wouldn't you rather have Nanny closer? At Whitethorn, maybe?" She took his proffered arm and they walked down the gentle hill.

"My aunt thinks Nanny wants a place of her own."

"I think she wants to be close to you more than anything else."

"Oh?" The warmth in her voice startled him. Was she saying that was what *she* wanted? "We can certainly ask her if she would like to move back to Whitethorn."

Just then Gerald Fant came storming out of the small shed that stood off to the side of the house. He looked furious. His wife stood in the doorway, hands on her hips, and watched him for a long moment before she noticed Stacy and Portia. She raised one hand in a belated greeting and then smoothed her skirt, giving her husband's retreating back a last glance.

What was that about? Stacy mentally shrugged. Probably just a domestic dispute—something he would soon get to experience himself if his wife's confession about her passionate nature was true.

"We've come to see Nanny," Portia called out. "How is she today?"

The older woman gave Portia a stiff, rather sour, smile and curtseyed to Stacy. "She is sitting down to tea. There's a bit of a breeze today so she's in the sun room."

Nanny Kemble was waiting for them at the front door and threw her arms around Stacy as though she'd not seen him in a year. He held her birdlike body in a gentle embrace before releasing her.

"Well, Nanny. I guess you've missed me?"

She squeezed his arm tightly with her slender, claw-like hand. "I thought you'd been killed. Miss Frances would only say you were fine and wouldn't tell me what had happened." Her face wore the bitter look it always did whenever she spoke his aunt's name. Stacy had never understood why she disliked his aunt so much. Especially as Frances had been the one to engage her and did everything in her power to see to her comfort and care.

"I daresay she didn't want to alarm you, Nanny. As you can see, I am fine," he held out his arms and turned around and she laughed.

"I'm so pleased you've come to see me, Master Stacy, even though you should be home resting," she scolded.

"Signora Stefani would agree with you, Nanny."

The old lady gave Portia an affectionate look. "You've a good woman in Signora Stefani."

"I know, Nanny. I'm fortunate." He smiled at Portia and the wicked woman crossed her eyes at him, quickly, so that Nanny never saw. The playful gesture touched him more deeply than he would have expected; how wonderful to have a wife who wasn't only a mate, but also a companion and friend and lover.

He turned to his old nurse, disconcerted by the sudden surge of emotion. "Come, Nanny, I need some sustenance after that grueling walk. I am a wounded man yet Signora Stefani drove me before her most cruelly."

While they sat and enjoyed their tea Stacy told his old nurse a less remarkable version of his shooting. By the time they'd finished the second cup he could see she was tired and had begun to mistake him for some long-past child, murmuring about his sister

Miss Mary and how she ate bonbons until she cast up her accounts in the drawing room.

"She is such a dear lady," Portia said as they began the walk back. "I wish she did not suffer from such confusion."

"So do I, but at least she does not seem much disturbed by it. I believe most of the time she forgets about the brief episodes almost as soon as they happen."

"Did you know the family she was with before you?"

"I only know she was married to Mr. Kemble for barely a year before the poor man died in some tragic accident. She was with child at the time and miscarried from the shock." He shook his head. "It's a shame she never married again. She is the kind of woman who needs children of her own."

"Oh, what kind of woman is that, sir?"

He smiled down at her. "The loving kind."

The look in her dark eyes was unreadable and they walked in silence, each occupied with their own thoughts.

Stacy wondered how she felt about carrying his child, a man she barely knew. He wondered if she'd yet realized their baby might very well be born with his condition. He would need to broach the topic eventually.

"Is your leg paining you?" she asked, interrupting his thoughts.

"Not a bit," he lied. "I believe you must have magic hands, Signora." He held one of those magic hands in his as they came to a part of the trail wide enough to walk side-by-side.

"No, that would be Doctor Gates who has magic hands. If you will recall, all I did to *that* particular wound was clean it and cause you to scream."

"I *do* recall that, actually."

She shivered.

"Are you cold?"

"No, just remembering what you looked like when they

brought you into the house that night." She stopped abruptly and looked up at him, taking his hand, her eyes wide. "It was terrifying, Stacy. There was so much blood you looked as though you'd been mauled by a beast."

Stacy ran a finger down the sweet curve of her jaw, the worry he saw in her eyes making it difficult to swallow; she cared for him, at least a little. Perhaps that feeling would grow?

"You had incredible presence of mind, Portia. I knew that even in my groggy state."

She squeezed his hand hard enough to hurt. "Please never do that again, Mr. Harrington. Next time I shall be forced to present you with a bill for services."

"I'll keep that in mind." He kissed her hand and they resumed walking. "Tell me, Signora Stefani, what *do* you charge for making a man scream?"

She laughed and the mood lightened for the remainder of their walk.

Chapter Fourteen

THEIR WEDDING DAY dawned sunny, warm, and lovely. It was too bad Portia started the morning by vomiting into her chamber pot. When she'd finished expelling the meager contents of her stomach she pulled the bell; it would be permissible to have breakfast in her room on her wedding day. After she'd ordered a small breakfast and hot bath she climbed back into bed.

By the time her tray arrived she was actually able to eat the contents. In addition to the toast and tea there was an egg, a small piece of ham, and yet more berries.

Daisy grinned at her. "The master had Cook prepare your tray according to his instructions, ma'am."

"He will not be satisfied until I am as plump as a pigeon," Portia grumbled, pushing herself up into a sitting position.

"I've heard men don't mind a curve or two."

"Daisy!" Portia chastised with a teasing laugh.

Her maid might have been all smiles and giggles about some matters, but about her breakfast she was adamant.

"Now, you make sure you eat your breakfast, ma'am, you have a long day ahead of you."

Portia gave the food a sour look. "I suppose those are orders."

"Mr. Harrington only wants what is best for you."

Portia knew that was true and gave in to Daisy's well-meaning hectoring, eating every morsel. As a result, she was feeling well enough that she was ready to leave her warm, comfortable bed.

After her bath she was so relaxed that she allowed Daisy to dry, dress, and primp her like a doll.

Daisy wouldn't allow her to look in the mirror until she'd finished and Portia smiled at her reflection. "You've done a lovely job with your lump of clay."

"You look just like an angel, Signora."

Portia laughed at her maid's wildly inaccurate words. "Come, come Daisy, you'll have me weeping and I'd hate to show up to the altar with a swollen nose and red-rimmed eyes."

When Portia entered the tiny, ancient church a short time later she saw only one person: Stacy. He was so stunning it actually hurt to look at him. He was wearing silk breeches the same ivory as her dress, a wheat-colored coat that hugged his magnificent shoulders, and a waistcoat with tiny embroidered roses that matched those on her gown.

But the most fascinating part of his ensemble were his glasses. Rather than his usual dark blue-black pair, today's spectacles were rose-tinted glass in delicate gold frames. He was breathtaking. As she came closer she saw the glasses were not opaque and she could see his eyes; he'd worn them just for her. He winked at her and she laughed.

The ceremony passed in a blur and it felt like hardly an instant passed before they were leaving the small church to encounter what must surely be every person in the village.

"I daresay the Lawsons are responsible for this," Stacy said as they ran through a shower of flower petals to the waiting carriage. He handed her into the open barouche and took a maroon-velvet bag from a nearby footman, flinging handfuls of coins into the air, distracting the crowd before leaping up beside her.

He offered her the bag and she tossed a glittering clutch of coins into the air as the horses surged forward accompanied by an earsplitting din.

Stacy leaned close, having to shout above the racket. "Jewel,

Hawkins, and Baker were sneaking around like young boys to do this and I didn't have the strength to deny them their entertainment." His warm breath warm tickled her ear and sent a delicious thrill through her body.

He took her hand and raised it to his mouth, his lips hot even through her glove. "Hello, Mrs. Harrington. Did I mention how lovely you look today?"

"Thank you, Mr. Harrington. Is the sun not too bright for those?" She gestured at the rose glasses he still wore, shaded by the brim of his hat.

"I will survive such a brief trip."

Portia suddenly remembered something. "Drat!"

"Did you forget something?"

"I forgot to look at the flowers Frances and Mrs. Lawson spent so much time arranging."

"You only had eyes for me, I take it?" His smile was smug.

"You are as vain as a debutante, Mr. Harrington."

He laughed and the warm, deep sound sent arrows of desire shooting through her body. Was is wrong of her to want to skip the wedding breakfast and go directly to the wedding night?

SOMEHOW THE WEDDING breakfast lasted almost until dinner and by the time their guests departed it was time to eat again. Only Frances joined them for the evening meal and Portia was embarrassed by the obvious haste with which the other woman took her leave after the dessert course.

Stacy grinned across at her. "Do you think my aunt really has crucial matters to discuss with Soames?"

"You shouldn't have teased her, Stacy. The poor woman was redder than a beet."

He stood and came around the table, holding out his hand

and drawing her to her feet, his eyes dark behind the rose-colored glass. "I would much rather be teasing *you*, Mrs. Harrington."

She flushed under his hot gaze and swallowed awkwardly; Portia adored this playful, affectionate side of his personality but was not yet accustomed to it.

"I will join you in your chambers after I finish my port—shall we say an hour." He wore a slight, smug smile; a smile that said it amused him to make her wait.

It should have annoyed her, but it only increased her desire for him. Still, she forced herself to meet his hot stare with a prim, cool gaze. "Perhaps an hour and a quarter."

She gave him a deep curtsey and left to the sound of his laughter.

To her delight there was a bath waiting in her chambers.

"Mr. Harrington ordered it for you ma'am."

Portia smiled. So, he was not tormenting her, after all, but being considerate. How decadent to have not one, but *two*, baths in a single day. He knew she was sore—every muscle in her body seemed to ache these days—and wanted to soothe her pain. The realization left an odd ache in her chest; it had been so long since somebody had taken care of *her*.

Daisy helped Portia change out of her wedding finery and she groaned as she slipped into the steaming tub. She lounged until the water cooled, not washing her hair as she'd done so that morning. Afterward, she put on a nightgown she rarely wore, one made of white lawn and trimmed with cobweb-thin lace.

Daisy brushed Portia's hair until it shone and then set the brush down on her dressing table. "Will there be anything else, Mrs. Harrington?"

Portia smiled at her maid's flaming face. "No, Daisy. That will be all for tonight."

Daisy curtseyed and scuttled from the room.

She was too nervous to get into bed so she inspected her new chambers: the mistress apartment. The rooms were done in soothing shades of green with cream silk wall hangings and emerald velvet drapes. It was twice the size of her original chambers and the bed was an enormous four-poster that made her entire body tingle whenever she looked at it.

The connecting door opened and her husband stood in the doorway, wearing a silk robe the color of his magnificent eyes. He closed the door behind him and Portia stood riveted to the floor, her heart pounding and her breathing shallow as she consumed him. He held a bottle and two glasses in one hand, lifting them wordlessly as he came toward her.

Portia pointed to the half-full glass of milk on the side table and he lifted his brows. "Frances had it sent up. I'm afraid even the thought of wine makes me feel ill."

He set down the glasses and bottle on her dressing table. "I shall remember that. May I?" He gestured toward the glass of milk.

Portia laughed. "Of course."

He took a drink and grimaced. "We shall suffer together."

"You don't care for milk?"

"Not even when I was a boy." He replaced the glass and their eyes locked. He reached out and touched her cheek and she shivered.

"That is a lovely gown," he murmured, running his finger down her jaw and throat and coming to a rest at the top button of the high neck. "But I would like to see your body. All of it."

Her breathing hitched and her fingers were on the buttons before he finished speaking. He rested his hands on her shoulders and watched in silence. Portia thrilled at the flaring of his pupils as she unfastened the tiny buttons. When she reached the last of them he slid his hands beneath her nightgown and pushed it off her shoulders, leaving her naked.

"Good God." His voice was thick and his hands moved to

cover her breasts.

Portia gasped and closed her eyes.

"So beautiful," he murmured, his fingers stroking the hard tips. She felt hot a puff of breath and then the gentle suction of his lips and tongue as he took her nipple into his mouth.

She groaned and leaned into him, taking his head in her hands. "I need you," she whispered, all her plans to let him be the one to initiate their love making flying out the window.

He gave a low, wicked laugh and bit her nipple before sliding an arm beneath her knees and sweeping her into his arms.

"You won't hurry me this time, Mrs. Harrington." His lips curved into a mocking smile. "I plan on taking my time."

"You shouldn't be lifting me, Stacy. You'll tear the stitches."

"Shhhh. Let's make that the last time you mention my stitches, shall we?"

His face was all hard, white planes and she swallowed. "Yes, Stacy."

"Such a good, obedient wife," he praised.

Portia snorted and he grinned.

She moved her hand toward the 'V' of his robe when he laid her on the bed. "Take it off," she said, echoing his words.

He gave the sash a tug and the robe slithered open. Portia stared. He was dusted with hair too pale to hide the quilted musculature of his stomach and chest. Even the two bandages he wore did not distract from his masculine beauty. His erection, she was pleased to see, was as impressive as she recalled and her hand moved toward it.

He caught her wrist, pushing her gently back onto the bed, before shrugging out of his robe, the perfectly defined muscles of his chest and shoulders bunching and flexing.

"Lie back."

She sighed but did as he bade, watching in silence as he spread her legs and knelt between her thighs, looming above her. She was desperate to look at every last part of him.

"You're a god," she said, her voice low and harsh with want.

His jaw tightened and his thick shaft jerked, the slit in the fat, smooth crown leaking freely. Portia smiled at the delicious evidence of his desire; he was so close to spending. It would take only a few touches from her—

"You are a devil."

His words pulled her eyes from his erection. He wrapped one large hand around her throat and held her gently but firmly pinned to the bed. The dominating gesture was unspeakably erotic and she spread wider for him. His violet eyes became twin black pools as he dragged his free hand down her chest, between her breasts, leaving her eager nipples untouched. He had a clear destination and didn't linger until he reached the dark tangle between her legs. He parted her swollen lips and thrust a finger inside. She arched against the sudden invasion, desperate for more.

His expression was a mixture of fierce possession and hunger and he effortlessly held her pinned while he proceeded to pump her, his eyes consuming her as she bucked and thrusted and squirmed.

Portia gave a grunt of frustration as he slowed his stroking and brought her back from the precipice.

"Please, Stacy."

But he maintained his steady, annihilating pace, his smile cruel as he eased a second finger inside her, thrusting harder, deeper. Her climax stole up so quickly it ripped the breath from her chest and she threw back her head, squeezed her eyes shut, and gave herself up to the inevitable.

And then—just as suddenly as he'd started—he stopped.

Portia pushed her hips against his motionless hand. When he didn't move she growled and squeezed her eyes even tighter.

"Open your eyes and watch me, Portia."

She gritted her teeth and forced herself to obey.

"Yes," he murmured, his hand resuming its tantalizing motion. "Watch your husband, darling. Watch as I make you come."

His raw words ignited her and her mind exploded, her body arching so hard she thought her spine would snap in half.

STACY FEASTED ON her pleasure thoroughly, like a glutton sucking the marrow from a bone. When her shuddering diminished to mere twitches he withdrew from her body.

"No, don't leave—" Her hand shot out like a viper and caught his wrist.

"Shhh," he murmured, kissing her clenched fingers. "I'm not leaving."

She released him with a sigh and Stacy slid his hands beneath her bottom, positioned himself at her opening, and thrust hard, filling her as the contractions of her last orgasm tightened around him. Her lush body was flushed and sheened with sweat and he was so hard it was painful. How would he ever make this last when she was so bloody gorgeous? He sank his fingers into her hips and slowly dragged himself out before thrusting back in, his body shaking as he struggled for control.

Slow and deep. Make it last forever.

But his hips ignored him, pounding hard enough to drive her up the bed.

She gave a throaty laugh. "Yes, Stacy." Her sheath tightened and white spangles exploded across his vision. A groan of frustration and desire broke from him and she looked up at him with hooded eyes as her hand slid around the base of his cock, circling him where they were joined, tightening around him while he moved inside her.

He shuddered and pounded into her, his fingers digging cruelly into her flesh. "Are you trying to kill me?"

Her lips curved into a wicked smile and then her beautiful, artistic fingers released him and slid between her legs. She worked herself with a skilled, almost ruthless, efficiency that told him this wasn't the first time she'd done this. The thought of her pleasuring herself in her room down the hall all these weeks sent a punishing bolt of desire from his brain to his groin and any willpower that remained flickered and disappeared like the light from a guttering candle.

He held nothing of himself in reserve, driving as deeply as he could, again and again and again—until his mind went blank and sensation consumed him.

PORTIA WRAPPED HER arms around his heaving body and smiled; this wedding night was as unlike her first one as was possible. Instead of anger and recriminations, she'd been pleasured beyond her wildest expectations. She'd never, in her entire life, been this happy. He was heavy, sweaty, and hot on top of her and she loved it. She licked the salty skin below the bandage on his neck, pleased to see his wound had not bled through with all this activity.

He laughed weakly. "You *are* trying to kill me."

"Perhaps, but you will enjoy it, Mr. Harrington."

He slowly rolled off her, his softening organ sliding out of her body. He lay on his side and pulled her closer, his face inches from hers. They looked into one another's eyes and she became lost in his. They were too perfect, too extraordinary. She could get no sense of *him* by looking at them; it was like gazing into jewels. What was he like behind those magnificent eyes?

He pushed a strand of damp hair behind her ear with one finger. "I've always thought your eyes were black, even though I know that isn't possible. They are velvet brown with a very light gold ring around them. I see also that you have a freckle on the side of your nose. Is it the only one?"

"I have one and a half freckles."

"Do you?" He gave her a skeptical look. "Where is the half?"

"You'll have to find it."

He leaned forward to kiss her freckle and she ran a hand up the side of his body, her fingers digging into the bands of muscle that covered his ribs.

"And you, Mr. Harrington? Do you have any freckles?"

"Not a one."

"But you have other . . . things." Her hand moved back down his side. "Things I don't have."

He lifted one eyebrow and shifted his hips so she could access one of those things. His eyes fluttered shut and he sucked in a breath through his clenched teeth when her hand closed around him.

"Oh, you like that old thing, do you, Mrs. Harrington?" he asked huskily.

"Mmm hmm. This is far better than a freckle, Mr. Harrington."

A blissful smile settled on his lips. "Portia," the word was a sigh. "What did I do to deserve such a perfect wife?"

A chill ran down her spine at his words. She could only hope he would always feel that way.

Chapter Fifteen

PORTIA WOKE TO an empty bed. She sat up and looked at the clock—it was almost ten—and then flopped back on the pillow. She should be up and about as the party would begin at two. It had been Stacy's idea to make the day after their wedding a celebration for his tenants and everyone else who worked on the estate. Portia knew he was making the effort to be more social for her sake, and she was grateful.

"And as long as we're having something of a public day we might as well invite the entire town." *That* suggestion had given her pause. His tenants knew him, but many of the townsfolk rarely saw him unless they had a case before the magistrate.

"Are you quite sure, Stacy?"

He'd given her one of his slight smiles, the one that drove her mad with lust. Well, one of the many that drove her mad. "I want to show off my new wife."

"I'm afraid your new wife has very little experience organizing such things."

"Frances can arrange it."

Portia had tried to help, but the older woman was so efficient that she'd only gotten in her way. So she'd left everything in her hands, but there would be plenty of last-minute things that needed doing today.

She yawned and ran one hand down her pleasantly sore body. In spite of her best intentions she'd been unable to curb her insatiable appetite for him last night. No doubt it was too late to hide her true nature from Stacy. Not that he seemed to mind. In fact, for all that he looked like a man carved from ice, he was just as insatiable.

Thoughts of Ivo came unbidden. He'd believed he was the ultimate lover, just like every other Roman man she'd ever met, but in truth he'd been selfish and quick.

His lack of skill in the bedroom might have been bearable if Portia had not already had Benedict as a lover. The Englishman had taught her women could enjoy bed sport every bit as much as men, and certainly more frequently. He'd shown her how to please herself as well as him. Portia now realized he'd been exceptional for a boy his age.

Not as exceptional as Stacy, but then, her husband was no boy.

Portia wondered how he'd learned his lovemaking skills and her chest tightened with jealousy. It was better for both of them if she did not dwell on such matters. No doubt he'd kept mistresses or had lovers, just like other men of his class. Well, wherever he'd learned his skills he was as generous and considerate in the bedchamber as he was everywhere else.

The door opened and Daisy entered with a breakfast tray. Portia realized she wore only a sheet tangled around her hips and scrambled to cover herself.

Daisy didn't seem to notice. "Good morning, ma'am." She set down the tray and went to fetch Portia's robe, holding it out for her.

"Has everyone else already breakfasted?" Portia asked, tightening the sash about her waist.

"Mr. Harrington insisted you be allowed to sleep and he ordered this breakfast for you."

Portia looked down at the tray, which was laden with more food than she could eat in a month.

"I gather we're anticipating a great many people?" She munched a piece of toast while Daisy laid out her favorite day dress, a gold and yellow gown that had always reminded Portia of a daffodil.

"Oh yes, everyone will come, ma'am. Everyone is mad to see you, Mr. Harrington, and Whitethorn."

"Mr. Harrington has never had a party before?"

"Not as long as I've been here. He hasn't done much socializing since—" Daisy broke off and colored.

"Since what, Daisy?"

"Oh, nothing."

"Come now, you are my source of information in Bude. Since what?" It was shameless to pump one's servant for gossip but Portia could not resist the urge. Besides, who else would tell her anything?

"Well, since he was courting Miss Reynard—she that married Sir Stephen."

Portia suppressed the spurt of jealousy she felt at the thought of Stacy's former fiancée. "They live somewhere between Bude and Stratton, I collect?"

"Yes, ma'am."

"Do you think Lady Watley and Sir Stephen will come?"

"My mum always says Lady Watley is the nosiest woman in all of Cornwall."

Portia laughed at her usually sunny maid's sour look. "Then they'll not be able to resist a visit to Whitethorn."

"No, nor a look at Mr. Harrington's bride. Everyone in the county knows who *you* are."

Portia shivered at that news; she would be glad to leave the famous Stefani name behind her. She'd be even happier if people forgot that Ivo had ever existed.

PORTIA AND STACY were chatting with the Lawsons when a fine carriage rolled down the long drive. "Ah, Sir Stephen and Lady Watley," the vicar said, confirming Portia's suspicions. "We'll move along and let you greet your guests."

Portia watched with interest as her husband greeted the woman he'd once considered marrying. Penelope Watley was everything Portia was not: dainty, blonde, blue-eyed, and beautiful. The green-eyed monster that always lurked close by growled menacingly as Stacy bowed over the other woman's hand. He was as coolly friendly with the pretty blonde and her rather oafish-looking husband as he was with everyone else.

Sir Stephen tore his eyes away from her husband long enough to give Portia a look that made her skin crawl.

"Congratulations, Mrs. Harrington." He leered, eying her from head to toe. "Aren't you looking blooming this morning?"

His wife tittered and Portia just stared. *This* was the man Lady Watley preferred to Stacy?

They chatted for a few stilted moments before another set of guests arrived and the baronet and his wife moved along.

A short time later, when they were alone, Portia looked up at her extraordinarily beautiful husband and smiled. "I understand Lady Watley was once my rival?"

"There is nobody to rival you, Mrs. Harrington." The words were low and intimate but his black lenses glinted and he looked implacable, remote, and cruel; nothing like the hot, tender lover she'd enjoyed several times last night. She realized that side of him—the passionate side—was only for her.

Heat pooled in her stomach and between her thighs and she shook her head, maddened by her desire for him. "It is just as well you are wearing those glasses today, Mr. Harrington."

His lips curved into a slight smile and he was just about to say something when Frances approached. "Will you come and help with the selection of the croquet teams?"

He kissed Portia's cheek. "Duty calls, my dear."

Duty called for Portia, as well, and she greeted at least fifty people over the next half-hour. She was beginning to droop when a small break occurred in the procession of guests, so she slipped around the side of the house, to where tall box hedges offered some privacy from the milling crowds. She'd just slumped onto a stone bench and closed her eyes when voices approached.

"She's not quite what I expected," a female voice said.

A low masculine chuckle answered. "She's certainly nothing to *you*, Penny. And Harrington? My God! The man is a freak of nature. I've seen him before, of course, but never so close up. He looks like a statue come to life."

"Count yourself fortunate his eyes are covered, Stephen."

Portia's blood roared at their words and she stood, preparing to march around the hedge and give them both a nasty set-down. But the next words arrested her.

"I still can't believe you saw him coming out of a brothel only last week," Lady Watley said, her voice oozing with smugness.

Portia's body froze.

"As bold as you please in broad daylight," Sir Stephen confirmed. "Kitty Charring's place over in Plymouth."

"I don't want to know how you learned of such a place, Stephen," his wife chided, her voice growing faint as they moved away.

"Oh, Penny, you don't need to worry about—"

Portia didn't hear the rest of what he said but she'd already heard more than enough. Stacy had visited a bordello in Plymouth? She'd wondered why it took him almost four days to secure a marriage license.

She swallowed hard several times and it felt like crushed glass in her throat.

Yet another man who took lovers—even before they were married? How could this be happening to her all over again? *How*?

PORTIA AVOIDED BEING alone with her husband for the remainder of the afternoon. She didn't want to be near him until she managed, somehow, to get her ferocious temper under control. She hoped she hid her feelings, but later, when they played croquet, she couldn't help the vicious triumph that surged through her when she hit his ball so hard it rolled almost into the woods.

Jeremy Lawson sidled up to her and whispered in her ear. "Marital discord already, my dear Portia?"

Portia had laughed, drawing a puzzled look from her husband before he went to look for his ball.

By the time the last of the guests were persuaded to leave it was past dark and Portia was exhausted. And more furious than ever.

They'd just waved off a final straggler and shut the door when Stacy turned to her. "You must be exhausted, my dear. Why don't you go up to bed and I'll have Cook send up a tray. You really should get some rest tonight." He brushed his lips against her cheek and it was all she could do not to shove him away.

Portia smiled tightly. "Yes, I believe you are right—I *am* tired. Good night, Mr. Harrington." She left him without waiting for a response, storming up the stairs to her chambers and flinging open the door to her room so hard it rattled her teeth and made Daisy jump.

"I will undress myself."

Daisy took one look at Portia's thunderous face and fled.

Portia did not undress. Instead, she commenced to pace her chamber, winding herself up as though she were a watch. By the time she heard the door to Stacy's room close three hours later she was nearly blind with rage. When she could no longer hear movement on the other side of the connecting door she flung it open without bothering to knock.

He was lying in bed, the covers pulled up to his waist, his chest naked, a book in his hands, and clear reading spectacles perched on his perfect nose. He looked from the door, which had bounced off the wall, to Portia.

"You will let me *rest*?" Portia asked in a nasty voice.

His eyebrows shot up and he set aside his book and removed his glasses.

"Good evening, Portia."

"Don't you *dare* 'Portia' me!" Fury roared in her skull like the crashing surf of the ocean, drowning that tiny part of her brain that advised her to get control of her emotions.

"I collect you are angry about something?"

"How bloody perceptive!"

His handsome features turned rigid. "Please don't raise your voice at me."

"Did you go into a brothel in Plymouth when you went to get the marriage license?"

He flinched back, as if she'd struck him. "I beg your pardon?" He spoke slowly and clearly, his words covered in frost.

Portia recklessly ignored both his freezing tone and look. "Perhaps you need me to speak more plainly? When did you last lay with a prostitute?" She enunciated the words in an insulting parody of his.

His eyes narrowed to dangerous red slits. "I would ask you not to use that tone with me, ma'am."

"And I would ask you to answer my question, *sir*."

"I have no intention of doing any such thing."

A vicious wave of anger rolled over her. Portia recognized the feeling although it had been some time since she'd felt it—her last argument with Ivo. Pure fury seized her in its punishing grip; she needed something to throw, break, hurt.

Her eyes flickered over his body and moved to the rest of the room. The chamber was almost completely white: white silk hangings on the walls, a white counterpane, ivory carpets over dark wood floors. The bed was a huge mahogany four-poster that looked as though it had come from some gothic castle. And her husband looked like an angry, haughty god bent on disciplining an unruly human as he lay there with his arms crossed over his chest. Portia's eyes landed on the cabinet beside her, where a wooden statue sat. Her hand moved toward it.

He was out of the bed like a flash of lightning, his hand on her arm as her fingers closed around the wooden projectile.

"No." His voice was ice over iron. "You will not." He squeezed her wrist hard enough that she released the statue. Her right hand moved toward his face, palm open, and again he anticipated her, catching that wrist, as well. He looked down at her with violet eyes blazing, a muscle jumping in his clenched jaw. "What have I done to make you believe I am capable of such behavior? You do me a *grave* injustice."

Portia heard the truth in his words—saw it in his eyes—but jealousy gripped her in its brutal talons and squeezed until all she could think of was him with some phantom woman—two beautiful people writhing in each other's arms. A feral noise tore from her throat and she launched herself at his mouth. He met her with a violence that equaled hers. It wasn't kissing, it certainly wasn't making love. It was battle: it was the unrestrained impulse to dominate, subdue, and consume.

Something inside her began to unravel as he plunged his tongue into her, over and over. Portia couldn't resist him and didn't want to. She released his neck and slid down his body to her knees. He was long, hot, and erect and she took him into her mouth, subjugating him the only way she knew how.

He groaned. "Good God, Portia." His hands came to rest on her head, his fingers threading into her hair.

She closed her eyes and worked him so relentlessly he'd never be able to remember he'd ever had any other woman. She would enslave him the way he'd so effortlessly enslaved her.

Her mind became a blank, empty of anything except the driving need to possess and control him—to make him *hers*.

It could have been a minute or an hour when his body began to shake and shudder. She redoubled her efforts, taking him deep into her throat, driving him over the ledge of self-control.

"Portia," he hissed, trying to pull out of her mouth.

Portia slapped away his hand; she wanted every part of him—she *needed* all of him. When he drove himself deep, she dug her fingers into his hips and pulled him even deeper, until she could take no more. Every muscle in his body went taut and he made a sound of pure animal need, his shaft thickening and jerking as he emptied himself deep inside her.

Portia gloried in her ability to undo him; working him until he had nothing left to give. Only then did she pull back and release him, doubling over and gasping for breath, her lungs on fire. It took several moments before she could look up at him.

He stared down at her with a dazed expression, his lips parted and his chest rising and falling as if he'd been running. He shook his head and then took her arms and lifted her to her feet.

"Portia."

She turned, refusing to look at him.

She hated him.

She loved him.

STACY FELT AS though his head had been emptied of all rational thought as he lifted her to her feet: Holy. Bloody. Hell. She wasn't *on* fire—she *was* fire.

She would not look at him and a hot wave of shame rolled through him. He'd just spent in her mouth, thrusting into her so deeply he'd felt the back of her throat. He squeezed his eyes shut, as if that would somehow erase his savage behavior; once again he'd used her harder than he'd ever used any prostitute.

He had to apologize; he needed to assure her this wouldn't happen again.

He tried to pull back but she clung to him. "I'm sorry, Portia."

She merely clung harder.

"Portia, look at me." He could hear the exhaustion in his voice. It had been a long week.

"No."

He gave a tired chuckle at the petulant sound and took her chin, forcing it up. "I'm sorry—I should have never done—" *Christ, what did one call his behavior of a few moments earlier?*

"I wanted it."

He blinked at the unexpected words and then met her mulish look—a look that dared him to say he'd not enjoyed himself. Well, perhaps he would address the matter of his brutish behavior some other time. He held her gaze. "As much as I enjoyed the second part of this passionate interlude I still don't understand—why are you so angry with me?"

She clenched her jaws tight enough that he could see the sinews and muscles beneath the skin.

Stacy sighed. "I don't know what you heard today but I did not lie with any prostitutes when I went to Plymouth. I have not been with another woman since meeting you. Surely you cannot be angry about what I did before I met you?"

Her black eyebrows shot up in surprise.

"Portia?" he prodded when she didn't say anything, "are you angry about things I did before we met?"

"No." She sounded like she was, anyhow.

Stacy wanted to strangle her. Instead, he took her in his arms and kissed her tangle of wild black hair, inhaling the already familiar scent of her. Lavender on fire. "You are enough woman for me," he murmured and then laughed. "More than enough; I don't want anyone else."

He felt her squirm and released her.

She looked up at him with eyes that were wounded and ashamed. "I'm a jealous woman."

Stacy barely caught his snort of amazement in time.

"I warned you before you married me," she said. "When I think about you with another woman I want to throw something. Or hurt somebody. You, I suppose." She gave him a miserable half-smile and shoved him in the chest with her strong pianist's hands.

"I have no plans to be with any woman other than you. I believe in fidelity. I suppose I should have told you that, but I assumed you knew that." He stared at her, unsure of where this passion came from or what he could say or do to soothe her. "Turn around," he finally said, his fingers going to the torturous row of buttons on her gown. "Why did Daisy not undress you?"

"I was too angry."

"Mmm." He decided to leave the subject alone until he had her naked in bed, where the only thing she could hurl at him was her body.

He released her from her stays and stockings and tucked her beneath the covers before extinguishing the candles and joining her. She snuggled against him, her body deliciously soft and warm.

"Why didn't you want me tonight, Stacy?" she demanded through a yawn.

"I always want you, Portia. In fact, it is rather distracting how often I think of bedding you." *Not to mention embarrassing.* "But you are carrying my child and you looked exhausted. I wanted you, but I was trying to be a considerate husband rather than a rutting beast."

"I want a rutting beast."

"Right now?"

"No. Right now I want to sleep. But I shall want you later. Later tonight," she clarified, her words again distorted by a huge yawn.

He grinned into the darkness. "Very well, I shall be happy to oblige. Just remember it was you who asked for a rutting beast."

"Mm."

Stacy listened to her regular breathing, only able to relax after she'd fallen asleep.

Bloody hell. He'd never met anyone like her. Part of him was thrilled she felt so attached to him and so possessive. But part of him was uneasy. He'd been accustomed to a well-ordered, quiet life. He hadn't even known he had such depths of passion inside him until meeting her. He'd always enjoyed sex, but it had never consumed him. Portia consumed him.

He stroked her hair and stared into the darkness, too exhausted to think and too anxious to sleep. She'd looked almost mad when she'd stormed into the room—as if she'd been bent on murder. He was bloody fortunate she'd aimed her passion toward pleasuring him rather than strangling him.

Stacy laughed weakly as he held her close; God help anyone who *truly* roused her ire.

Chapter Sixteen

THE MORNING AFTER their first marital argument Stacy gave Portia her horse, a dainty black mare she immediately named Dainty.

She threw her arms around him and thanked him. “A black horse, Mr. Harrington?” she teased, covering his face with kisses.

“If you continue in this manner I shall have to take off my glasses and bat my eyelashes and you will never learn to ride.” He kissed the side of her nose where her freckle lay.

“I already know how to ride,” she murmured, reminding him of the second time they’d made love that morning.

His hands tightened. “Mmm, Mrs. Harrington.”

She laughed and shoved him away. “I’d like my lesson first.”

Stacy grunted and adjusted himself.

By the end of the first week she was comfortable enough on horseback to join him on rides and by the end of the second week she was able to gallop, at least for a short distance.

Now, a month later, she was going on her longest ride to date. Stacy was taking her to inspect one of the tenant cottages at the far edge of his property. They had a picnic hamper and Portia’s morning sickness had recently been replaced by a voracious appetite, as if her body was making up for all those weeks of sickness.

Last week they’d finally shared the news about the baby with Frances and Nanny—not that she believed the two women hadn’t already guessed the truth. But if they had, neither woman showed any disapproval.

Portia was relieved at no longer having to hide her condition and today's excursion was a perfect way to celebrate. But by the time they rode up to the Humbolts' cottage, she realized she'd reached the limit of her riding ability. Stacy, of course, noticed her fatigue even before she did.

"I should never have suggested such a long trip."

"I will be fine."

He lifted her off Dainty and she slid down the hard length of his body in a way that made him smile.

"None of that here," he murmured, swatting her on her bottom just as Mr. and Mrs. Humboldt approached.

Stacy greeted the older couple in his quiet, dignified way and smiled down at the plump, slightly flustered woman. "Could I impose on you to take my wife inside and force her to rest, Mrs. Humboldt? She is in a delicate way but will not believe her husband knows anything of such matters."

His words struck exactly the right note and the older woman bristled with pride at his request. Portia glared at Stacy's triumphant smile as she was borne off to have cake and some of Mrs. Humboldt's restorative potion.

She was actually grateful for a rest in the coolness of the cottage as the day had become warm. She spent a little over half an hour with the pleasant woman, who was delighted to expound, in vivid detail, on the gory trials of childbirth, having gone through the process no fewer than nine times. By the time Stacy came to fetch her, Portia was ready to scream.

The two men took a glass of homemade wine while they discussed the matter of roof repair and it was another quarter hour before Stacy stood and begged the Humboldts' leave to get his wife home.

Portia made a frustrated growling noise as they waved to the beaming couple and rode away.

Stacy laughed.

"You are wicked, Mr. Harrington. I spent a good half hour listening to the most blood-curdling stories I've ever had the misfortune to hear."

His smile drained away in an instant. "Childbirth tales? I'm sorry, Portia, I did not think."

"Oh, hush. I am only teasing. I *am* starving again, however. I ate three tea cakes but feel hollow. I shall be the size of a cow soon."

He chuckled. "There is a lovely spot about half an hour ahead if you can wait?"

"Barely." But she was very glad that she did when she saw the tiny glade in the woods Stacy found for them. "Why Mr. Harrington, if I didn't know better I'd think you had ideas in mind."

He lifted her from her horse, kissed her hard on the mouth, and went to untie the hamper. "I have lots of ideas, Mrs. Harrington. But you'd better eat first. What I have in mind will require energy."

Three-quarters of an hour later, as she gasped for breath, Portia realized he hadn't been exaggerating.

"That was divine." She lay on her back and stared up at the cloudless sky as the last tremors of her climax rolled through her. Stacy slowly emerged from beneath her skirt, straightening her clothing as he came up alongside her.

"I believe I've found my new favorite way to stay out of the sun, Mrs. Harrington," he said, collapsing by her side with a happy sigh.

"I'm a wickedly lazy wife, Stacy. I can barely keep my eyes open. How selfish of me." A huge yawn stopped her speech.

"Don't worry, darling. I'll get what I want from you tonight. Take a nap while I pack our belongings."

PORTIA WAS ASLEEP before he'd even finished speaking. Stacy put the remains of their picnic into the basket and went to the edge of the clearing to enjoy one of his cigars, far enough away that the smoke would not disturb her.

He'd just taken the first puffs when he saw George Fant and another man approaching on the road that led toward Bude. He was about to step out from under the trees and greet them when their raised voices drifted toward him. It sounded like the two men were having a disagreement, so he stayed where he was. The road followed the woods where Stacy was standing and soon he could hear them clearly.

"*You* talk to her ladyship. I'm not here to discuss matters with the likes of you," the stranger yelled. His accent was heavy—perhaps French or Spanish—and he was gesticulating in a wild, jerky way that made his mount jumpy.

"You'll bloody well do as I say or you'll get nowt," Fant shouted in his own heavily accented voice.

The other man let out a long string of something that could only have been curse words and Stacy realized he'd heard something very similar from his wife the night he'd been shot; the man was speaking Italian. Or at least he was *cursing* in Italian.

"I want half *now*," he demanded, breathless from his yelling.

"You'll get paid when the woman is gone and not a second before—just as you promised. And if both of you ain't gone by the end of—" the rest of whatever Fant said was cut off when the men disappeared around the bend.

Stacy stared at the empty road, tendrils of unease snaking through his body. *What the bloody hell was that all about?* It hadn't sounded like anything good. He puffed on his cigar and considered the odd scene he'd just witnessed. First thing tomorrow he would go to Nanny's and see if Fant had brought the man back to her cottage. If he had, it would be a perfect time to discharge the pair and move Nanny back to Whitethorn as Portia had suggested.

Portia was still sleeping when he returned to the blanket. Stacy never should have taken her on such a long ride. In fact, he would have to curtail her riding altogether, soon. It was far too dangerous for a woman in her condition. She looked so peaceful he hated to wake her but they needed to leave if they were going to make it back to Whitethorn by dinner.

It took a while for Portia to shake off her grogginess, but he was willing to wait; he didn't want her in the saddle without all her faculties sharp.

As they left the glade Stacy recalled Fant's foreign guest and considered asking if she'd ever met the man at Nanny's. But he shrugged the thought away; after all, Portia would have mentioned a stranger—especially an Italian one.

STACY ESCORTED PORTIA to her room directly after dinner. "You need rest," he said, pulling the bell for Daisy. For once, she didn't argue.

"Come to me tonight, Stacy," she murmured into his chest, her soft, voluptuous body pressed against his.

"You need sleep, darling." He stroked her hair, unable to resist plucking out the pins and releasing the black, glossy coils.

"Mm. Come to me anyhow."

He lightly massaged her temples and she purred, rubbing herself against his quickly stiffening cock in a way designed to destroy his best intentions.

"Very well, I will sleep with you. But don't think for a minute that you will entice me into doing anything else."

"Mmmm."

He turned when the door opened. "Please put her to bed

directly and make sure she drinks a glass of warm milk before going to sleep."

Daisy grinned. "Aye, Mr. Harrington, I'll see to it."

A stack of mail awaited him in the library. He'd been spending so much time with his new bride that his business had gone wanting. Tonight he would work through as much of it as he could while she slept.

He'd gone through a good half of the pile when he came across a letter franked by a very spidery old hand—was that the Earl of Broughton? Stacy's brow wrinkled as he studied the name. Now where had he heard that name before?

The letter was brief and signed by Viscount Pendleton, not an earl. The viscount said he would be in the area on Thursday and asked if he might call on Stacy. The letter had arrived several days ago and tomorrow was Thursday. Perhaps the man would not come since Stacy had not answered? He shrugged. Either way, he had no objections to receiving him, indeed, he was even a little intrigued.

It was almost three by the time he went up to bed. He undressed himself, having sent Powell off earlier. When he went into Portia's room it was to find her reading.

"Stacy." She smiled up at him and set aside her book, tossing back the covers to welcome him. Her open joy at seeing him made his entire body throb. He leaned toward the candle to extinguish it but her voice stopped him.

"No, leave it, please. I want to watch you undress."

He looked down at her eager, waiting face and his breathing became something of an effort. As he slid out of his robe her eyes dropped lower, her lips parted, and he heard the sudden intake of breath that always made him hard—or harder, in this case. He climbed in beside her and her warm arms slid around him.

"I couldn't sleep without you," she murmured into his neck.

"Oh? I make you sleepy, do I?" He cupped her jaw and

brought her closer for a lingering kiss. "Odd how you have the opposite effect on me." Her hand slipped between his legs and he sucked in a breath. "What did I tell you earlier, Mrs. Harrington?" he chided, even as his hips began to move.

"That a slate roof was the most durable kind of roof for this climate?" Her voice was muffled as she ducked beneath the covers.

He laughed and then gasped. "You are very naughty, Mrs. Harrington."

"Yes, I know."

And then she proceeded to show him just how naughty.

THEY'D JUST FINISHED breakfast the following morning and Portia was gathering her things to take the gig into town.

"Please take Daisy with you, my dear," Stacy murmured absently as he looked up from the paper.

She laughed. "I don't need an escort to go to town."

"Yesterday I realized how quickly you become fatigued. I would like you to have somebody with you when you go out, just in case you need help."

"I'm not a piece of glass."

He nodded, amused. "Even so, bring Daisy with you."

Her face settled into mulish lines. "Is that an order, Stacy?"

"Does it need to be, Portia?" He immediately regretted the tinge of annoyance in his voice. But he *was* annoyed, annoyed she couldn't see he was only doing this for her own safety. He suppressed his annoyance and tried again. "It would make me less anxious if you allowed her to accompany you."

Her jaw moved back and forth, as if she was chewing on gristle. She finally nodded. "Very well."

Stacy was more than a little relieved. While he had no wish to argue with her, he would not live under the cat's paw, scared to say anything that might make her angry. "Thank you for understanding, Portia."

She kissed him on the cheek and whispered in his ear, "Thank you for caring so much about my well-being, Mr. Harrington."

Stacy put aside his paper after she left. He would need to work on the way he delivered his requests or they would bicker constantly. She required more careful handling than he'd realized. The thought surprised him; handling? Was that how he dealt with people—by managing them? He shrugged the question away. If he was managing her it was for her own good.

PORTIA AND DAISY returned from town to find a large, elegant traveling coach waiting in the courtyard.

Soames opened the front door before they reached the top of the steps.

"Who does that belong to, Soames?"

"Viscount Pendleton, the Earl of Broughton's heir. The family's name is Harrington, ma'am," he added, obviously pleased about his employer's connection to such an illustrious visitor.

Portia was curious about what a viscount was doing here but she could hardly barge in on the two men without an invitation.

"I'll be up in my chambers if Mr. Harrington wants me."

When they reached her rooms Portia and Daisy spent half an hour looking through her garments, picking out some that Daisy could alter to fit her increasing size.

After they'd finished the men were still closeted in the library, so she decided to walk over to Nanny's and bring her the tatting thread she'd requested. Portia had hoped to walk to the cottage with Stacy but she had no idea when he would be free.

Soames was nowhere to be found, but Daisy knew where she was going so Portia pulled on her gloves, glancing at the darkening sky. She considered waiting to see if the clouds passed but decided she could beat the rain if she hurried.

Portia was hurrying through the thickest part of the woods when the first drops of rain hit her. "Drat!" she muttered. Stacy had shown her the ruins of a very old cottage not far off the trail and she headed for that, lifting her skirts high to scramble over stumps and fallen limbs. It was farther than she remembered and her cloak was wet in spite of the shelter of the tree canopy. For a moment she thought she must have mistaken the spot but then saw a stone wall and a mossy section of roof just beyond several large trees. The rain began to pelt down heavily as she rounded the corner of the building and ducked under the bit of roof.

She stopped short; a fire smoked in a small pit and some bedding and clothing hung over an old table in the opposite corner. Somebody was living here, a man by the look of the clothing.

Portia started to back up and ran into something: something warm, hard, and human.

Chapter Seventeen

STACY GAPED AT the tall blond man seated across from him. "Twin brother?" he repeated for the third time.

Viscount Pendleton nodded for the third time.

Stacy laughed, but not with amusement. "You'll have to excuse me if I sound rather skeptical."

Robert Harrington, Viscount Pendleton, raised a hand. "Please, don't apologize. I did the very same thing when I heard." He ran his hand absently through his thick blond hair. "I'm afraid I rather made a mess of things. Perhaps I should start from the beginning?"

"Perhaps you should. Would you like a drink?"

"God, yes."

After they'd both taken long pulls from their glasses, Robert Harrington began his story.

"Our mother was Victoria Standish, the second wife of the Earl of Broughton—our father. The earl's first wife bore him three daughters and died when the girls were well into their early twenties. The earl remarried exactly a year after his first wife's death. Our mother was younger than the earl's daughters, only seventeen to our father's fifty-three. A year later the two of us arrived. I was born first and seventeen minutes later you came. Our mother died that night." He drained his glass and Stacy refilled it without being asked.

"I'm afraid our father is . . ." He grimaced. "Well, let's just say he is a man of narrow understanding. When he saw your, er, condition, he went to my mother's family and confronted them. Our grandfather, our mother's only surviving parent, confessed he'd known there was a possibility his daughter might bear a child with your, uh, affliction." He took another gulp. "He admitted his infant brother, who'd died before he was a year old, was like you." He frowned and stared at the floor, turning his glass round and round.

Stacy couldn't help wondering why the man was so nervous. Or perhaps it was just his face that made the viscount uncomfortable, as it did so many others?

Pendleton resumed his story. "Our father was livid. He accused our grandfather of sabotaging his lineage, jeopardizing the Harrington bloodline, and all other manner of rubbish." He gave Stacy a pained look. "I learned all this when I confronted our grandfather." He must have seen the surprise on Stacy's face. "Yes, he still lives." He snorted. "He is younger than our father. He's rather a wastrel and he bartered away his daughter to cover gambling debts—and he has accumulated even more in the last thirty odd years." He sighed heavily. "Our father's decision to banish you was appalling and I am aggrieved and angered at having missed the opportunity to know my brother, not to mention the disservice he has done to you. He's old now, nearing ninety. He stands by his decision and insists I would not have been able to marry the daughter of a duke if you were known to exist." His mouth twisted bitterly. "My wife is the daughter of the Duke of Rotherham. My father believes the illustrious connection vindicates his behavior." His bitter tone indicated he felt otherwise.

Stacy stared at the man—his brother—not sure where to begin, or even if he *wanted* to begin. He'd lived thirty-five years without a father; a father who'd rejected him like an ill-bred calf. Why bother with him now? He looked at the stranger across from him and saw real pain in his eyes. Robert Harrington had been hurt by their father's actions, not as badly as Stacy, perhaps, but just as deeply.

"You've not said how you finally learned all this?" Stacy asked.

He hadn't thought it was possible, but Robert looked even more miserable. "My father recently told me when he, uh. . ." he coughed, his face darkening beneath his healthy tan. "It might be easier if you would ring for Frances."

Stacy felt as if he'd been punched in the face. "How the *devil* do you know my aunt?"

Robert Harrington stared fixedly at the floor, as if he'd used up whatever reserves he'd brought with him. "Just summon her."

Stacy ground his teeth but pulled the bell. The men didn't have long to wait before the door opened and Frances entered, as if she'd been waiting.

"Stacy," she hurried toward him and then stopped, her worried eyes flickering to the other occupant in the room. "Have you told him everything, Robert?" She clasped her hands in a vaguely prayerful way as she looked from Pendleton to Stacy.

Stacy gave an ugly bark of laughter. "Just what the hell is going on?"

His aunt, or whoever she was, winced, whether from his tone or his unprecedented swearing, Stacy neither knew nor cared.

"I haven't told him everything, Frances."

Stacy dropped into his chair, not caring that Frances was still standing. "How do you two know each other?" He looked at the woman he had always believed to be his only living relative. "Who the hell are you?"

She rushed toward him and sank down beside his chair. "I'm so very sorry, Stacy, so *very* sorry. I've wanted to tell you for years, but Father forbade it. I never wanted to lie to you." Tears welled and fell and she grabbed his hand.

Stacy shot to his feet and yanked out of her grasp, equal parts confused, angered, and repelled. He gestured to the chair beside the viscount.

"Have a seat." His head was heavy and hot; his thoughts were in a jumble. Who *was* this woman? She'd been the bedrock of his existence all his life and she'd been lying to him for thirty-five years? *Thirty-five years.*

Stacy couldn't bear to look at her and turned back to his brother. "Perhaps you'd be so good as to finish this story, my lord?"

Pendleton glanced at Frances Tate—or whoever she was—and turned back to Stacy. "Frances is the earl's eldest daughter by his first wife. We have two other sisters, Mary and Constance."

Stacy's brain tried to absorb what this man—his brother—was saying. He looked at his . . . *sister* but she was staring at the carpet, tears falling onto her folded hands.

Something else occurred to him. "Wait. How do you know her?" He whirled on his aunt—his sister—before Robert could answer. "You've stayed in contact with them?" His voice vibrated with disbelief and growing anger. Frances covered her face and wept.

"She comes to visit us several times a year—on Father's orders—I'd always believed she lived with a widowed friend in Cornwall."

Stacy's laughed bitterly. "Ah, yes. The widowed friend you go and visit." His head throbbed. She'd lived two separate lives and he'd never known. He was a fool—a pitiful idiot.

Frances reached out, as if to touch him, and waves of rage blurred his sight as he absorbed the depth of her deception—her betrayal.

"I think it would be best if you departed with Lord Pendleton when he leaves."

She stood and took a step toward him. "Stacy, I want to tell you—"

"You've had almost thirty-five bloody years to tell me the truth, Frances." He stared into her familiar—once beloved—blue-gray eyes, more furious and hurt than he could ever recall being in his life. "You may start packing now."

She gave a pitiful cry and stumbled toward the door.

"You're being cruel," the viscount said when the door shut behind her. "She merely did what Father ordered. It was Frances who finally made him tell me the truth about you. She couldn't bear it any longer, now that you are married and to have a child. She was tormented—"

Stacy removed his glasses and looked at his brother. The man stopped talking, his mouth still open. Stacy felt a nasty smile twist his lips. What a powerful effect a simple pair of eyes could have.

"My God," Pendleton breathed.

"Or the devil. Perhaps now you understand why the earl banished me?"

Pendleton flinched as though Stacy had struck him. He shot to his feet, his face a cold, proud mask that looked oddly familiar.

"I knew *nothing* of this. I am just as much a victim as you are. I didn't need to come here today, I wanted to." He shook his head hard, as if to dislodge something. "Like a fool I could hardly wait to meet the brother I never knew I had." He realized he was still clutching his glass and lowered it to the table with a clatter. "If you'd rather I never darken your door again, I will leave."

Stacy saw himself in the other man's face for the first time: haughty, proud, and stiff. Twinges of something arrowed through his body—guilt? Curiosity? Remorse? Pendleton was right: Robert Harrington wasn't the responsible party and Stacy was behaving like a fool.

He dug deep to find the reserve of calm he needed. "I apologize for my ungracious words and behavior." Stacy paused. "Tell me, my lord, what is it you want from me?"

Pendleton frowned uncertainly but resumed his seat. "I don't know. All I know is that when I learned I had a brother I had to meet you. I know your wife is to have a child and I—" he stopped, an agonized spasm distorting his handsome features. "You are my heir; do you understand that? If I have no son—which seems likely as my wife has not been pregnant in eight years of marriage—then *you* will be the next earl."

Stacy gaped. No, he'd *not* realized that.

Indecision and insecurity flitted across his brother's proud features. "All my life I've wished for a brother. I love our sisters but they were so much older than me. When I was young, I used to rattle around Thurlstone Castle and wish I had somebody my own age to play with. Mary and Constance are mad to meet you. This has not been easy on them. None of our sisters have married and likely never will." He laughed but there was no mirth in it. "Our father is a hard man. In some ways you've been lucky to grow up away from him. He crushed the girls and I suppose he did a fair job of crushing me, too." He flushed at his words but did not explain. "I've always admired Frances because I believed she'd somehow gotten away. Now I see he used her even worse than the rest of us. She was twenty-seven when he sent her away with you. Constance told me Frances begged to be the one who raised you." He cut Stacy a hard look, his jaw taut. "You ask what I want? I want to know my brother; I want you to come to Thurlstone. I've already told our father I would ask."

Stacy could only gape; how could he share a father with this stranger—a father who'd banished Stacy at birth? What kind of man did that? The kind of man who would've thrown him over the castle walls still squalling in the Middle Ages. His lips twitched at the melodrama of the notion. Could such a father be worth knowing? He looked at his brother, who was staring at him with open curiosity. Not because of his skin or eyes, but because of *who* he was: his brother—his *twin*—his flesh and blood.

"All *my* life I believed there was only my aunt and myself—a tiny but close family of two. I'm sure you can guess how my appearance has mitigated against too much mixing in society. Indeed, if my wife hadn't come to me it's doubtful I ever would have married." He smiled ruefully. "We've been married a little over a month but already I understand that expanding one's family can be a very comforting thing. I will speak to Mrs. Harrington on the matter and perhaps we will make a visit one day, or perhaps you and your wife will come here. Who knows?" He picked up his spectacles.

"Is Mrs. Harrington at home? I should very much like to offer her my felicitations on both your marriage and upcoming happiness."

Stacy took out his watch. "She should have returned from town by now." He rang the bell and they waited in awkward silence until Soames opened the door.

"Ask Mrs. Harrington to join us."

"She is not in, sir." His eyes drifted to Stacy's distinguished visitor.

"She's not back from Bude? She left hours ago."

"She went out again, sir."

"In this weather?" Stacy glanced out the window he now left uncovered. The sky was an ominous gray and the rain was coming down in buckets.

"Yes, sir, she went out shortly after his lordship arrived."

"I hope Daisy prevailed on her to dress warmly," he said as he stared at the deluge.

"You could ask her, sir. Daisy came downstairs looking for Mrs. Harrington some time ago."

"She did not accompany Mrs. Harrington," Stacy repeated sharply.

"Er, no, sir."

Stacy shook his head. He'd asked her not to go out unattended and already she'd disregarded his request. "That will be all,

Soames."

"Is aught amiss?" Pendleton asked, reminding Stacy he was not alone.

"I daresay I am behaving like an over-protective husband, but I wish she would not wander off without her maid."

Pendleton smiled. "You've only been married a short time. You'll soon learn it's pointless to attempt to direct one's wife. Indeed, more often than not I find that *I'm* the one taking direction." He was smiling, but Stacy thought the other man's voice held an edge. What was his brother's viscountess like?

"How long have you been married?"

"Eight years." He did not sound particularly happy.

There was another scratch on the door and Frances entered. She gave Stacy a slightly defiant look. "I'm only here because I wanted to say goodbye to Portia and Daisy told me she went to Nanny's," she paused, flushing under Stacy's stare. "I think something might be wrong. I came that way myself only an hour ago and I did not see Portia. I should've passed her if she was on the path."

Stacy's anger turned to fear.

"Is it a treacherous path?" Pendleton asked.

Stacy shook his head. "No, but she's been rather short of energy lately. I wonder if she stopped to rest someplace."

"Perhaps she's waiting out the storm?" Pendleton suggested. "I'm sure you're eager to go look for her. I'm not familiar with the area but an extra pair of eyes is never a bad thing."

His mind raced. "Tell Hawkins to saddle Geist and Selene. Lord Pendleton and I will take the road. Tell Baker to walk the trail to Nanny's. Have either Powell or Hawkins search the south end of the forest. She sometimes likes to sit by the stream."

Frances left without a word.

Stacy turned to his brother. "I'm sure it will turn out to be nothing but she tires so easily and—" He sounded like a hysterical fool.

Robert gave him a reassuring smile. "Come, my heavy cloak is in the coach, I'll get my man to fetch it and we can go."

Chapter Eighteen

IT WAS DARK when they finally found her.

She'd burrowed into the hollow of a big tree not far from the road to Bude—nowhere near the trail to Nanny's.

Surprisingly, it was Pendleton who saw her. Their lanterns barely cut the dark, not to mention the torrential rain. The storm broke for half an hour near dusk and then returned with a vengeance. They'd looked for two hours when Pendleton spotted the edge of her cloak, a miracle really, as the garment was rain-darkened and brown. She was unconscious and shivering and Stacy held her in his lap, swaddled in his greatcoat while Pendleton went back to fetch the carriage. He wiped water from her face with his handkerchief. Her lips moved but Stacy couldn't hear what she said. He held her close, keeping her warm with his body and murmuring in her ear.

"Say something if you can hear me, Portia."

She remained silent and he leaned back to look at her face. She was pale and her skin was so cold.

"Ivo, no!" The words were a harsh, weak croak and her eyes flew open.

"Portia, it's Stacy." He pulled her closer.

"Stacy?" Her eyes were wide but unfocused.

Relief screamed through him and he forced himself to loosen his crushing hold. The beads of moisture on her long black lashes glinted like diamonds in the lantern light.

"I was so lost; I couldn't get home. I couldn't see the sky." She shivered violently and her eyes fluttered closed.

"Portia?" He gave her shoulders a light squeeze. Nothing. He lowered his ear to her mouth. She was breathing deeply, as though she'd fallen into an exhausted sleep. If she'd left Whitethorn when Soames believed she had, then she'd been in the rain for hours. Damn stubborn female. This never would have happened if Daisy had been with her—all the locals knew the woods like the backs of their hands. Stacy pulled her to his chest, wrapping his arms around her to keep her warm. She'd bloody well obey him in the future or she wouldn't leave the house.

The minutes crawled past and he kissed the bridge of her proud, Roman nose, her freckle ominously dark against her unnaturally pale skin. He wasn't sure how long he'd been waiting when he heard the wheels of the carriage even over the rain.

"Thank God!" he whispered, closing his eyes and kissing her too-cold mouth.

The rain on his lips tasted of salt.

WHEN THEY REACHED the house his aunt—or sister, he mentally corrected—insisted the first thing they must do was warm her while they waited for the doctor.

"The sooner the better, Stacy."

He ignored her chiding tone, kissed his wife on her pale, clammy brow, and reluctantly left her in the women's hands. By the time Doctor Gates showed up Portia was dry, swathed in a fluffy blanket, and lying in bed drinking from a cup of tea which Frances had to hold for her.

When the doctor finished his examination he turned to Stacy, frowning. "The child is fine, but I would like to cup her."

"No!" Portia sat bolt upright, her hair wild and her dark eyes feverish. "No!"

"Shh, Portia." Frances gently pushed her back against the pillow. "Doctor Gates only wants to do what is best for you and your baby."

Portia paid her no attention, her imploring eyes on Stacy. Stacy went to her and laid a hand on her brow. She was no longer cold, nor was she particularly feverish. Still, if the doctor recommended cupping, that is what he believed was necessary.

He stroked her sweet, rounded jaw. "It will make you feel better, Portia."

She grabbed his wrist, her eyes wide with terror. "No, please, Stacy."

"Hush, darling," he soothed. "You are becoming overwrought. Doctor Gates believes this is for the best, so I really must insist. I will be here with you."

"Please, no!" She sobbed as if her heart were breaking, madly kissing his hand and fingers, begging in a slurred, frightening way.

Stacy glanced up at the doctor. "This is necessary?"

Gates's mouth was compressed in a grim line. "Yes, absolutely. It will help settle her hysteria and—"

"They killed my mother that way." Portia's hands squeezed his forearm hard enough to shift bones. "They bled her until there was nothing left. Please, I beg of you. If you keep him away from me I will do whatever you say. I promise to obey, just don't let him touch me, I'll never argue with you again. I'll obey you." The last words were more of a moan and tears poured from her huge, dark eyes.

Her vehemence was shocking and Stacy realized she'd never spoken of how either of her parents died. But whatever had happened, he could see she had a fear of cupping that verged on phobic. His kissed her brow and held her face close to his.

"Shh, darling, don't make yourself ill. There will be no cupping tonight. But tomorrow, if you're still—"

"I'll be better, I promise. I promise, Stacy."

He stroked her cheek and forced a smile. "I'm going to hold you to this sudden vow of obedience."

Her eyes closed and she sagged against him. "Thank you, Stacy. Thank you. You will not regret it. I'll be good—I *promise.*"

Stacy turned to the doctor. "No bleeding, doctor."

"It is the accepted treatment in such cases, Mr. Harrington."

Stacy knew it was and he hoped to God he was doing the right thing—for Portia *and* their child. "Come again in the morning. If she is not better, we can discuss the matter then."

"This isn't wise," Frances said. "I'm afraid you will regret indulging her. Please—"

Stacy ignored her. "I shall see you in the morning," he said to the doctor.

Gates's expression said he believed Stacy to be another idiotic new husband, but he shrugged and put his implements back in his bag.

"See the doctor out, Frances." Stacy wanted to be alone with his wife. He waited for his sister to move from the bed so he could sit beside Portia. When the door shut he took her hand.

"You've made me a promise and you may start obeying me now," he scolded quietly. "You will rest, do you hear me? You will only leave this bed when I say you may."

She gave him a tremulous smile that squeezed his heart. "I will stay in bed as long as you say. Thank you so much. Thank you, Stacy." Her eyes fluttered closed before she'd even finished speaking.

Stacy waited until she was breathing evenly before releasing her hand and pulling up her blankets. The door open and Daisy entered. "Mr. Soames sent me up to sit with Mrs. Harrington if you want to get ready for dinner."

Stacy blinked: dinner?

The girl gave him a gentle smile. "Viscount Pendleton is still here, Mr. Harrington."

Blast! Stacy had completely forgotten he had a peer of the realm in his house.

He gave an abrupt nod. "If she wakes, send for me."

"Aye, sir."

Stacy opened the connecting door to his room and found Powell waiting with hot water.

He submitted to his valet's ministrations in a trance. And when he was clean, shaved, and dressed he went downstairs to dine with his brother and sister.

PORTIA RAN THROUGH a forest that went on forever. Thorns and limbs tore at her skirt and wicked, grasping branches scratched her face. Everywhere fallen trees, rotting logs, and hidden stumps tried to stop her. She tripped, stumbled, and pitched headlong into a bottomless tangle of brambles. The footsteps behind her got louder and louder and she burrowed into the tearing, gouging thorns to hide. The briars turned into hundreds of hands, pulling and grasping.

Portia! Portia come back, you can't hide from me!

Portia tried to scream but no sound came out. She struggled against the iron grip that held her, kicking and thrashing until she tore free and her eyes flew open. She gasped for breath and her eyes slowly focused.

She wasn't in the woods but back in her very own bed. She felt the bed next to her and found it empty. Where was Stacy? She sat up and squinted through the gloom; he was sitting in the overstuffed chair beside the bed, the dull glow of the fire bathing him with warm, red light. His head rested against the chair back, his eyes were closed, and he was breathing deeply. He was still wearing his evening clothes but had unbuttoned his coat and removed his cravat. His shirt was loose and open, exposing the white, muscular column of his throat; he looked like an angel at rest.

She squinted at her bedside clock; it was three twenty-two in the morning—the witching hour and the loneliest time of the night. Yet she was not alone; he must have fallen asleep watching her. He looked delicious and she wanted him—*needed* his quiet strength and his powerful, sheltering body. She opened her mouth to wake him when it all came crashing down on her.

Ivo. He was back.

Chapter Nineteen

IT HAD BEEN Ivo who'd been camping in the old falling-down cottage. Ivo, who was very much alive. Ivo who had come back for her.

Portia screamed when she saw his face and he'd grabbed her with rough, cold hands, clamping the bent fingers of his damaged hand over her mouth.

"Sh, *mia cara*!" He was not much bigger than Portia, but he was wiry and strong and held her in an unbreakable grasp while uttering a string of placating endearments in Italian—not something he'd done for many years. When he felt the struggle go out of her body he loosened his grip. "I'll remove my hand from your mouth if you will promise not to scream."

Portia nodded and he took away his hand, still keeping an iron grip on her wrist. She stared, shocked by how haggard and gaunt he looked.

"The ship you were on—it went down with you and your w-wife on it—*I read it in the paper*." Portia spoke Italian, the only language adequate to express her anger, loathing, and shock.

His sensual lips twisted in a way that used to make her heart throb faster a long, long time ago. His eyes were the color of brandy, warm and intoxicating. But Portia knew they masked a man who thought of only one thing: Ivo Stefani.

"You look well, Portia. Very well for a grieving widow." Her stomach lurched as his smile twisted into something unpleasant.

"You did not grieve for me, did you? It made you happy that I was not just *pretend* dead, but *real* dead? You simply moved on, eh?" He didn't wait for an answer. "Imagine my surprise when I showed up in London and found my school closed and our house empty."

"*Your* school? The only thing you ever gave to the school was your name—and debt."

Ivo squeezed her wrist until she cried out.

"What a harpy you are, Portia, always on about the same thing." He yanked her close, his eyes dark with fury. "Mrs. Sneed did not turn a hair when I showed up on her doorstep. That is when I knew you never told the newspapermen either the tale of my hero's death in the War or my unfortunate demise at sea. Even when you thought I was dead you didn't mind keeping me alive to use my name and status." He made a clucking sound as he pushed her down onto a pile of mossy stones that must have once been part of the wall. Portia tucked her feet beneath her skirt and buried her hands in her cloak. Ivo sat beside her, his hand like an iron manacle around her wrist.

"It took some work to get your address from Mrs. Sneed without looking like a fool. I told her I was just back from a family emergency and had lost my baggage in a shipping debacle. Ha!" He slapped his thigh, clearly amused by his own cleverness. The suit of clothing he wore had once been one of his better ones. Now the cuffs were ragged and shiny patches showed the coat had been cleaned and pressed to within an inch of its life. His cravat was yellowed and knotted carelessly. And his once beautiful boots—boots he'd commissioned from the great Hoby himself—were a scuffed, battered disaster.

"What happened, Ivo?" Portia prepared herself for the web of lies he would no doubt spin. Ivo could not tell the truth even if it would help his cause. She'd learned long ago, and to her detriment, that he lied for the pure joy of manipulating his listener.

"I might ask you the same thing, *cara.*" He reached out to take her chin and she jerked out of his reach. He laughed. "I hear you are married to a very rich man." His pupils shrank and she noticed the deep grooves beside his mouth and nose. He looked older than he'd done a mere eighteen months ago but he was still a very handsome man. Portia hated him. She wished—God have mercy on her soul—that he really *was* dead at the bottom of the ocean. The only things he'd ever given her were pain, humiliation, and a miscarriage.

"What business is it of yours, Ivo, we were never even married. You are less than nothing to me. Where is your *wife*?" Rage made her body shake. But beneath her rage was fear. Why had he come back?

He laid his right hand over his breast and cast his eyes skyward. "Alas, poor Consuela! She really did perish this time."

Portia gave a rude snort. "I suppose you were the only survivor out of an entire ship?"

Ivo smirked, pleased to illicit emotion from her, no matter what it was. "Not just me, *gattina.* When we saw which way the wind was blowing, pardon my inexcusable pun, another gentleman and I took one of the two lifeboats. My darling Consuela refused to get into such a small craft. I tried coaxing her but she was adamant. She could not swim, you see, and believed that staying on a larger ship that was headed for calamity would somehow save her." He shrugged, demonstrating the same depth of emotion for his wife that he'd felt for Portia.

"We had a few nasty moments, my companion and I, but we were fortunate in that we had ample supplies and encountered propitious currents. We did not have very much remaining to us by the time we made landfall but it was enough that we could bring our few possessions ashore and convince a local fisherman to give us shelter." He stopped and gave her a look of disbelief. "I must tell you, my love, that you and I were fortunate to have left

Rome when we did. The Corsican made a bloody mess of the entire Continent. *Banditti* run rampant and it is worth a man's life to travel anywhere. Unfortunately, it was worth my companion's life. I'm afraid he did not make it to Grenoble—the home of his lovely widow." Ivo's smile made Portia's flesh crawl. When had he become this man? Was it the loss of his hand or had he always been unscrupulous and his beautiful gift had merely masked it?

"I remained with the grateful widow until her officious brother arrived from Paris and made my position untenable. I'd begun to miss you in any case, my pretty Portia." He squeezed her, his hand like a vise. "It breaks my heart to learn you do not feel the same."

Portia didn't bother trying to pull away. That was what he wanted, a struggle. He'd always become violent when thwarted.

"What do you want, Ivo?"

"I want my wife back. But what did I learn? That you were spreading those white thighs for some other man. That you were already carrying some other man's brat, and a freak of a man by all I've heard." He laughed and grabbed her hand before it could make contact with his face. "I'll hit you back, *gattina*, and I'll do it twice as hard."

She wrenched her arm away. "What do you want?"

His features twisted into an expression that was half rage and half something else—jealousy? Portia found that difficult to credit. It was more likely pique that she'd not wasted away after he left her, brokenhearted.

"What would your wealthy freak say if he knew you were already married and that your long-lost husband had returned?" He pushed a finger against her midriff and she flinched back. "And the child in your belly is legally *mine*?"

Fear clamped around her chest until she could barely breathe. She could not show Ivo how terrified she was, it would be the end of her. She pulled from his grasp and sneered at him.

"You forget we were never legally married, Ivo."

"And how will you prove that, my dove? We held ourselves out to the world as blissfully married for almost a decade. It just so happens I have our wedding lines to prove it."

That made her laugh. "Our wedding lines just so happened to survive a shipwreck?"

His smug, ugly smile chilled her. "Oh, darling." He laughed, and it actually sounded genuine. "You don't think I planned to stay away from London *forever*, did you? I only humored Consuela to get her out of England. One way or another, I was coming back so I tucked away money and valuables in my bank in London." He grinned. "Too bad you did not declare me dead, eh? Perhaps then the bank officials would have sought out my unfortunate widow?"

Portia's head throbbed with such rage she could not speak.

"In that bank box I put money, your mother's lovely jewelry, and a few important documents. I'm afraid I had to sell the jewelry, and I've run low on the money, but I still have my documents. So, what will your new husband believe when he sees our marriage lines, eh? I'll bet you were too ashamed to tell him about Consuela, weren't you?" He laughed at whatever he saw on her face. "And now it is too late to disclose the truth without it sounding suspiciously self-serving."

A strange humming noise filled her head. His lips kept moving but Portia could no longer hear his words. She would kill him before she let him claim her child and ruin her life. She would kill him.

He grabbed her shoulders and shook her until her teeth rattled.

"Are you listening to me, you mad bitch? I will not put up with one of your crazy rages, do you hear me?" He slapped her so hard her head snapped back and the metallic tang of blood flooded her mouth. And then he shook her. "I tolerated you for a bloody decade—you will give me recompense, or I will claim what is in your belly for my own."

Her head pounded from the blow, the vicious shaking, and her own rage. They locked eyes, the air around them thick with violence and a fine, cool mist as the rain struck the feeble roof above them with increasing frequency and force.

He squeezed her shoulders until they ached. "Do what I tell you or pay the price."

Portia's stomach churned and her anger slowly drained away until she felt cold and dead inside. "What will it take to make you go away and never, ever come back?"

He grinned and the avarice in his eyes sickened her. "I believe two thousand pounds would set me up quite nicely. Perhaps I will go back home and buy a small villa. Two decades of turmoil has played havoc with the value of land and has created many new opportunities."

"*Two thousand pounds*?" Just saying the amount made her dizzy. "Are you mad, Ivo? Where do you expect me to get that?"

The smile slid from his face. "Use that whore's body, Portia, I'm sure you'll find a way."

The rain pounded overhead and the spray soaked them. Portia didn't know how long they'd sat locked in silent argument when a voice floated toward them from the direction of the path.

"Stefani!"

Ivo leapt to his feet and grabbed her arm, yanking her up. "You must get out of here. I cannot be seen talking to you. Go!" He shoved her so hard she stumbled, landing on her knees beside the broken stone wall.

"What is *wrong* with you?" She shot him a look of pure hatred as she struggled to her feet.

"Go!" he hissed, murder in his eyes.

"With the greatest of pleasure." She began picking her way over a pile of rubble and heading toward the corner of the cottage.

Ivo grabbed her arm and almost yanked it from the socket.

"Not *that* way, *stupida*, you will walk right into him! There is a road in that direction." He gestured vaguely toward the other side of the woods. "You will return to me with the money in a week or—"

"Ten days," she grated out. "I cannot possibly do it in less." It was unlikely she could get so much money even in ten *years*. But she needed as much time to think as she could get.

He let out a string of curse words. "Ten days, no more." He shoved her and she almost fell again.

Portia knew the road in question but had never crossed through the woods to get to it. She glanced back and saw Ivo glaring.

"Go." he mouthed.

Beyond him the underbrush rustled as somebody approached the derelict cottage. Portia was tempted to wait and see who it was just to interfere with whatever Ivo had planned. They stood, eyes locked, and his expression turned from ugly to terrified. What was he afraid of?

Portia decided she did not want to know. She turned and ran.

She staggered blindly through the rain for perhaps a quarter of an hour before she accepted that she was lost. The sky was almost black and it was impossible to tell direction by the position of the sun. For all Portia knew she could have gone in a circle and would soon come back to Ivo and whoever it was he was meeting.

The rain began to fall in solid sheets and thunder sounded somewhere in the distance. She pulled up the collar on her drenched cloak and picked a direction. By the time she found the enormous tree she was stumbling more than walking. It was an ancient monster with a large hollow at its base. The depression was filled with weeds and bracken but it was big enough that she could wedge her body out of the rain. Portia was so tired and wet she no longer cared about rain, insects, Ivo, or anything except closing her eyes. The next time she opened them it had been to find herself cradled in Stacy's arms.

Portia wanted to cry as she looked at her husband asleep in the chair beside her bed. He'd stayed close in case she had need of him. She'd been groggy but she recalled the sick worry she'd heard in his voice as he held her. She'd also heard affection and perhaps even love, or at least the beginnings of that emotion.

Tears were sliding down her cheeks and she was clenching her jaw so tightly her head throbbed. This was a mess, a terrible mess. There was only one way out of it: she would find the money, no matter what she had to do to get it.

FOR A MAN who'd refused to stay in his *own* sickbed after he'd been shot twice Stacy had no sympathy for Portia's desire to get out of bed. He bullied and browbeat her for three full days before he allowed her to leave her bedroom. Not only that, but he refused to make love to her the entire time.

"I will sleep in your bed, Portia, but that is all we will do. The doctor says you are suffering from extreme exhaustion. You've refused his recommended treatment so now you must submit to *mine.*" The stern expression on his face when he issued his orders made her ache for him.

Of course *everything* her husband did made her ache for him.

"Are you listening to me, Portia?" His cool, clipped words interrupted the fantasy that had begun to develop in her mind—yet another fantasy of Stacy without any clothing.

She heaved an exaggerated sigh. "Yes, Stacy. I am listening."

He was wearing his dratted glasses, hiding his thoughts from her along with his beautiful eyes. She was positive he did that to torment her.

His mouth twitched, as though he could read her thoughts. But his humor was short lived. "You will stay in your bed, eat at least three meals per day, and get a full night's sleep for three days. At the end of that time I shall reevaluate your condition and decide accordingly."

He'd said all this while looming over her, arms crossed over his broad, muscular chest, dressed in his riding clothes. Her eyes drifted from his impassive face over his elegant, snug-fitting clawhammer and lingered on the front of his buckskins. They been tanned black, to match his coat, and fit his taut, narrow hips and powerful thighs like a glove. Looking at him made her mouth water.

"Portia?"

"Hmm?" She wrenched her eyes away from his body and looked up.

"What did you promise me?"

She fluttered her lashes and touched a hand to her brow. "I don't remember."

"Do I need to summon Doctor Gates to remind you?"

Portia sat up. "You wouldn't. You promised, Stacy."

He uncrossed his arms and began to turn.

"No, stop. You are a bully," she said when he turned back.

"Yes, but I am *your* bully, thanks to your promise. Now come, it won't be so bad. I will go for a ride while you take your bath. When I return I will entertain you. But first I shall make sure you eat everything on your breakfast tray." He stared down at her, the muffled *tap, tap, tap* of his boot against the thick rug telling her the threat was not an idle one.

And so it went. For three entire days.

It was on the second of those days that Stacy explained his aunt's absence from the house and passed along Viscount Pendleton's startling revelations.

Portia listened to tale with her mouth hanging open. "But this is utterly fantastical, Stacy! What must your father be like to have done such a monstrous thing to his own child?"

"According to Pendleton he is an implacable man who keeps his own counsel. Even now, at almost ninety, he has no regrets."

"So why has he finally told your brother about you now?"

"Robert says he's only thawed because you are with child. The earl didn't want me, but I am my brother's heir if he does not have children. That would make a male child of ours the next in line. Otherwise the title would go to some distant relative. Apparently the earl cannot countenance such a thing." They sat in silence as they considered this new twist for their unborn child's future.

Portia found that she couldn't think about such a possibility right now. "Do you want to accept your brother's invitation to visit?"

"Why should I put myself before such a man?"

"You have a brother and two sisters you've never met. As for your father?" She waved a dismissive hand. "What do you care about a bitter old man? But your brother came to see you the moment he found out the truth. You probably have an entire legion of other relatives. Oh!" she stopped abruptly. "Does this mean you are *Lord Harrington?*"

Stacy laughed. "I do not believe it works that way. Only my brother has a courtesy title, I am still a mere mister."

"Oh." She shrugged. "Well, that is beside the point. The point is you have a *family*, Stacy."

"I already have a family, Portia." The tender expression on his face made her heart swell. It also made her want to weep.

Dear Lord, how could she do anything that might cause her to lose this man?

The answer to that was simple: she couldn't. She realized, with a shiver of apprehension, that she would do whatever it took to keep Ivo away from Stacy, their unborn child, and her marriage.

"Darling? Are you cold?"

Portia looked up and smiled. "All three of your sisters have known about this?"

"It sounds as though they were powerless to say no to the earl. Frances was in her late twenties when she left with me, the other two a few years younger. I know it was too much to expect very young women to defy such a man but I can't help being furious with Frances."

Portia brought his hand to her lips. "You must forgive her, Stacy. She loves you so much and must be in agony that you've banished her."

His face settled into unyielding lines. "The old man sounds like an authoritarian monster, intent on getting his own way no matter who gets hurt in the process." His jaw clenched, making him look a bit authoritarian, himself. "I understand keeping the secret when I was a child but how could Frances continue to do so?"

Portia swallowed. For once she was grateful that she couldn't see his eyes. His face was a cold, hard mask; he had inherited his father's implacability, if nothing else. If he sent Frances away for her deception, what would he do to Portia when he found out?

The answer to that question was terrifyingly clear: he must never find out.

UNDER OTHER CIRCUMSTANCES—THOSE in which Ivo had not risen from the dead and commenced blackmailing her—Portia would have loved the cossetting and extra time with Stacy. But every second of enforced bedrest was agony when she could think of little except Ivo prowling about in the woods, waiting for his money.

Who had been coming to meet Ivo that day? Whoever it was, Ivo had a partner in blackmail—and somebody who frightened him. Judging by his pathetic campsite he could not have much money. What if someone discovered his makeshift quarters and his presence became known before she could get the money?

And that was another crushing worry: the money. Two thousand pounds? Just thinking the number nauseated her. The only money she had was the two hundred pounds Stacy had given her before the wedding. At the time, she'd tried to refuse the money—why would she need so much? Where would she spend it? He'd already paid her mountain of debts, even though it had shamed her to allow him to do so.

Portia bit her lip; how could she ask Stacy for more money? She couldn't ask for two thousand pounds. Her desperate brain moved inexorably to the pearls he'd given her. The thought of selling them made her sick. They had belonged to his mother; how could she even contemplate doing such a thing?

Portia had learned how to pawn her possessions when Ivo was recovering from his accident and she needed money. It was possible to borrow against an item with the intention of retrieving it—although she'd never done so. Perhaps she could take the jewels to a broker who would contrive such an arrangement? But where? How could she do anything with Stacy watching her every move? He would not even let her out of bed, how would she manage to sneak the jewels to a pawnbroker? And where was the nearest one? Stratton? Plymouth?

Thinking about Plymouth made her recall he'd spoken of a bank account and marriage settlement. Where was the account and how much did it hold? And where did a person go to find out such details? Could she ask him without generating suspicion?

Portia groaned and thumped the bed with her fist. Why had she not paid more attention when he'd spoken of those matters before their marriage?

Think, Portia, think!

Stratton or Plymouth?

Stratton was far closer, but also smaller—and she might see someone she knew. It would have to be Plymouth and she would just need to figure out a way to get there.

Portia gave a laugh that contained hysteria rather than humor. How in the world could she go to Plymouth without her husband noticing?

THE OPPORTUNITY CAME far sooner than Portia could have hoped. Two days after Stacy released her from bedrest—a full five days after seeing Ivo—Stacy received an urgent message from his factor in Barnstaple.

Stacy and Portia had been writing letters in the library after breakfast when Soames entered with the note. "The messenger is waiting for your response, sir."

Stacy's frown deepened as he read. He looked up at her. "It seems there is a tempest brewing in Barnstaple. I'm afraid I have to set off as soon as possible." He turned to Soames. "Have Hawkins prepare the coach and tell Powell to pack for three—no four—nights."

"Very good, sir." Soames shut the door behind him.

Stacy turned back to her. "I am sorry, my dear, but Carew wouldn't send for me if it weren't important."

Portia tried not to show her excitement. "Naturally you must go. You needn't worry about me. I shall have my time filled with the nursery." Fixing up the nursery had been Stacy's idea, no doubt something he'd conceived of to keep her occupied while she was under house arrest. "Daisy is already very keen to stitch every part of the room with her own hands."

Stacy nodded absently, his mind on other things. "If you were feeling better I would take you with me, but—" he shrugged the thought aside. "I shan't be longer than a few days. At least I don't think I will." He gave her a rueful smile. "I'm sorry, Portia."

"I will be fine; you must do what you need to do."

"Right now I'm afraid I must finish this letter."

Stacy was packed, changed, and ready to depart in less than two hours.

Portia took his hand before he stepped into his traveling carriage. "I shall miss you, Mr. Harrington." She looked up at two images of herself reflected in his glasses, marveling at the ease with which she could paste such an innocent expression on her face.

He kissed the palm of her hand and the casual, sensual gesture squeezed her heart. "I shall be back before you know it."

Portia watched his carriage roll down the drive, her mind spinning quicker than its wheels.

LEAVING WHITETHORN PROVED much more difficult than she'd anticipated. When Portia made it known that she and Daisy would make an overnight trip to Plymouth she faced opposition in the form of Soames, who balked at having the smaller carriage made ready.

"You were thinking that Bannock would serve as your coachman, ma'am?" His face was impassive but there was a tense awareness in his hazy blue eyes.

"Has Bannock never driven Mr. Harrington's carriage?" Portia asked.

Soames looked pained, as though he suspected her of trying to get him in trouble. "Bannock drove Mr. Harrington when Jewell was ill a few years back," he admitted, every word grudgingly given.

"Then I do not foresee any problem."

Soames's gray brows shot up to his hairline, but his voice remained level. "I'm afraid the master has taken the coach horses, ma'am."

She adopted her loftiest expression, one she'd not needed to use since the night she'd arrived at Whitethorn under a cloud of deception and shame. "Send Bannock to the inn to procure job horses, Soames."

He hesitated a long moment before bowing. "Very good, ma'am."

Daisy proved even more resistant than Soames. "Oh, Mrs. Harrington, wouldn't it be better to wait for the master to come with us?"

"No, it would not. We will be shopping for the nursery. Men do not care for such things. I doubt we will be gone much longer than Mr. Harrington. We shall leave at first light and be back before my husband returns from Barnstaple." Portia very much doubted that would prove to be true and expected to receive a rather severe admonishment when Stacy returned to find her gone. But she had no other choice. "Please see to the packing, Daisy."

Portia almost made it to the door before Daisy's voice stopped her.

"Mr. Harrington told me you should not exert yourself, ma'am."

Portia turned and regarded her servant through slitted eyes. Daisy's pretty face flushed and Portia knew a moment of shame for putting the poor girl into such an uncomfortable position. But what choice did she have?

She adopted the cold and haughty tone Stacy employed to such effect. "I'm grateful for Mr. Harrington's solicitude on the subject of my health. I'm also cognizant of your wish to follow his instructions. I can certainly go without you."

Portia felt like an inhuman monster when the younger woman's thick brown lashes quivered against her creamy cheeks.

"I'll go, ma'am."

"I'll leave you to pack, then." She left the room in a cloud of embarrassment at having become such an ogre. She went directly to the library to fetch the jewels from Stacy's safe, even though she'd spoken to him about her bank account only yesterday.

"I might wish to order some nursery furniture and may need to draw on the account you set up for me. I forget which bank it is."

"The account is in Plymouth, at Nelson's Bank. But that money is for you, Portia, not for household matters. Please send any bills for the nursery or anything else for the house to me." His honest generosity made her feel like a scheming louse, which she was.

She'd not been able to scruple asking him how much money was available, so she'd need to bring the jewelry just in case.

He'd told her the combination to the big wall safe behind his desk when he'd shown her the remainder of his mother's jewelry. If there was not enough money in her account she hoped to raise the remainder by pawning some of the lesser pieces before resorting to the pearls.

There was a roll of bills in the safe but she felt a visceral revulsion at the thought of taking money. She snorted at her asinine scruples; wasn't pawning his mother's possessions worse? Portia bit her lip and pushed the wretched thought aside.

She left the jewelry boxes behind and poured their contents into her needlework bag, the only place Daisy was unlikely to look.

Portia was more than a little surprised the following morning when there was actually a carriage and four waiting. Not only that, but Daisy was packed and ready. Even an hour away from Whitethorn Portia kept expecting Stacy to come thundering up beside the coach and demand she return his mother's jewels.

Daisy looked as nervous as Portia felt and she wondered what Stacy had said to the poor girl. Perhaps she feared for her job? The notion made her feel like a selfish shrew. But she told herself that if she did not get Ivo's money, she wouldn't need the services of a lady's maid. Not that she believed Stacy would throw her out with only the clothing on her back. After all, she was carrying his child. But even if he believed her—in the face of marriage lines he would be powerless to do anything. Under the law, their baby would belong to Ivo. Portia closed her eyes and fought down the wave of sickness that threatened to swamp her. She couldn't think about that or she'd crawl into bed and never leave it.

The carriage was modern and light and they made better time than Portia dared to hope. They changed horses in Launceston and used the new Tavistock Road. The quality of the road easily made up for the frequent stops and they reached Plymouth at just past four.

Portia decided to stay at the Marlborough House, which is where Soames said Stacy always lodged. She was exhausted by travel and worry and ordered a meal to be delivered to her private parlor.

She sent Daisy to ask the innkeeper for directions to the most superior cloth and furniture warehouses in Plymouth, where they would go in the morning. But Portia could hardly ask Daisy to inquire as to the most convenient place to pawn jewels, so she waited until the servants had gone to bed and summoned one of the inn porters, a thin, villainous-looking man with shifty eyes. He gave her directions to a pawn broker—along with an impertinent, knowing leer—in exchange for more money than such information merited.

After he departed Portia collapsed into her bed, too overwrought to sleep. She lay in the dark for hours before drifting into an uneasy sleep filled with dreams in which Ivo chased her through the streets of Plymouth.

PORTIA SPENT AN hour with Daisy at the first cloth warehouse before putting her plan into action. She cupped her forehead and adopted a pained expression.

"It is another of those annoying headaches I've been getting, but we've come too far to quit now. You have the list. Indeed, you know better than I do what we need. I shall go back to the inn while you complete the shopping. Perhaps after I rest for an hour I'll be ready to try again. You keep Baker with you to help with all the parcels."

Daisy's smooth forehead furrowed. "Oh, ma'am, I should go with you. Or at least Baker. I don't need his help. I can return after you—"

"Nonsense, that would be a waste of time." She gave her a reassuring but pained smile. "I know Mr. Harrington wants you to be with me when I'm out and about, but really, I travelled from London to Bude alone. I am perfectly able to take care of myself on a ten-minute journey back to the inn. I shall see you when you've finished." Daisy could not argue when she spoke with such finality.

Baker told the hackney driver to take her to the Marlborough House but once they'd gone half a block Portia rapped on the roof and told him she needed to make a stop at Nelson's Bank first. The bank was in a blocky, gray building not far from the inn. Portia gave the front clerk her name and he whisked her into small but elegant sitting room. She didn't have to wait long until a slim, gray-suited man of indeterminate years bustled into the room.

"What a pleasure to meet you, Mrs. Harrington. I am Reginald Nelson."

It appeared her husband was a significant depositor at their bank and Mr. Nelson was eager to keep his new wife happy. A quarter of an hour elapsed on pleasantries before Portia could work Mr. Nelson around to the point of her visit.

"My husband set up an account for me with your bank."

Mr. Nelson nodded. "Yes, several. One for general use and one that is held in trust."

Portia hadn't known about the trust account. What else had he given her? She wanted to drop her head into her hands and weep with shame but now was not the time.

"I should like to withdraw two thousand pounds."

The banker did not even blink. "Of course, Mrs. Harrington, I will be pleased to arrange matters for you. Are you sure you don't care for tea?" he asked for the fifth time.

"Thank you, but I'm rather pressed for time." Her not so subtle words sent him on his way.

The transaction did not take long but Portia was forced to spend another five minutes reassuring him she would be fine carrying such a large sum and did not need a guard to carry it.

"Very well," he finally agreed. "But I'm afraid I must put my foot down on the issue of a hackney. I've had my carriage brought round for you."

Portia was nearly mad with worry by the time she took leave of the officious little man and settled into his very comfortable carriage. It was an hour and a quarter since she'd left the warehouse. If Daisy and Baker had returned and found her gone it would be more than a little awkward.

She tucked her bulging reticule under her arm as the carriage slowed and the footman opened the door and then handed her out with a flourish.

The first thing Portia saw upon entering the Marlborough House was her husband.

Chapter Twenty

STACY WAS STRUGGLING mightily not to vent his spleen on the innocent innkeeper at his favorite inn. He took a deep breath and tried again.

"I already went to the address your porter gave the hackney driver and the clerk said my wife left for the Marlborough over an hour ago. Her maid confirmed that. Are you *certain* you did not see her return? Perhaps she came back and went out again? Would not your man have—"

"Stacy?"

He spun on his heel and found Portia looking up at him, her big brown eyes worried as they glanced from him to the innkeeper and back. The relief that surged through him at the sound of her voice was instantly replaced by four kinds of anger.

He tamped down his fury with no little effort. "Ah, Mrs. Harrington, there you are." He looked from his anxious wife to the equally anxious innkeeper. "We shall use our private parlor right now, Mr. Withers."

"Very good, sir, your usual rooms are ready for you, Mr. Harrington." The older man glanced nervously from Portia back to Stacy, no doubt fearing a domestic altercation.

"Transfer my wife's possessions to my rooms." He held out his arm. "My dear?" Stacy impressed even himself with his cool, level tone.

When they reached the parlor he removed his driving coat,

hat, and gloves and threw them onto a chair before turning to his silent wife.

She was clutching a large, bulging reticule before her as though it were a shield. When he reached for her cloak she flinched back. He froze, his arm still outstretched. One side of her mouth twitched into an embarrassed smile.

"Why do you flinch from me, Portia?" His tone was harsh and accusatory and he tried to soften it. "Did you think I would strike you?"

"No, of course I didn't think that." She smiled uneasily and pulled at the ribbons on her bonnet. Her hands were shaking.

He saw by her flushed face that he had guessed correctly. "Good God! Did Stefani strike you?"

She yanked at the ribbon, which was already hopelessly knotted. Her fingers pulled so hard her knuckles were white and she dropped her gaze to the floor.

"Portia?" Stacy could barely hear his voice over the claxons screaming in his skull. *Somebody* had hit her. By God he would find whoever it was and thrash them to within an inch of their life, he'd bloody—

Stacy realized his hands were clenching with rage and his heart was thumping like a marching drum. He exhaled slowly.

Once he'd regained control of himself, he removed the mangled ribbon from her unresisting fingers. She watched without speaking as he eased the knot apart, her eyes huge in her pale face. When he'd untied the ribbon, he lifted the hat from her head. Next, he unfastened her cloak. When he went to take her reticule she clutched it to her chest, as if for safety. He let her keep it and led her to a chair.

She stared up at him, her expression oddly blank. "Are you angry I've come shopping?"

Stacy ignored the question and crouched down beside her, his hand on her knee. "Did he hit you?"

She frowned and her face went from afraid to ashamed to angry in the blink of an eye. "What does it matter? You would never hit me. I know that, Stacy."

He wasn't certain if the last part was a statement or a question and the thought left him nauseated. He took her hand in his and held it gently but firmly. "I would never strike a woman, a child, a servant, an animal, or *anyone* who is weaker than me—physically or otherwise."

"I know." She cupped his jaw with her free hand and he leaned into her palm and closed his eyes.

"To answer your question, Portia, yes, I was angry—an anger born of fear. The route you took to Plymouth was the same one I was on when I was shot. You were two women with only two young, inexperienced men to protect you."

Stacy heard her sharp inhalation of breath and opened his eyes. He could see from her stunned expression she'd never considered the possibility of highwaymen. The anger drained from him and left him weak. He released her hand and stood, taking the chair across from her.

"I am so sorry, Stacy, I never thought."

Her expression made him feel even worse. Now she would know the gut-wrenching worry that had eaten at him during that horrible drive from Whitethorn to Plymouth. Stacy removed his glasses and massaged his temples. He had a colossal headache. He'd gone from Barnstaple to Whitethorn at a reckless pace, eager to get home, only to find Portia had left for Plymouth that very morning. It had been too dark to leave again so he'd needed to wait until just before dawn.

He'd come on Geist, hatted, gloved, scarved, and bespectacled until nothing of him was visible. Powell was irritable and tired after the breakneck journey from Barnstaple and hauling him along had been very much like hauling a large sack of stones. Even with his reluctant valet they'd made miraculous time. He'd treated his horse abominably to do it, which had made him even angrier.

The entire time he'd flagellated himself for behaving like a mother hen. And then he'd remember, yet again, that he'd been shot twice on the same bloody road. He felt hands in his hair and opened his eyes.

"I'm sorry." She massaged his temples, unerringly compressing the very spot that was pounding.

He groaned. "Mmmm, that feels good."

"I didn't mean to cause you anxiety. It just seemed like a convenient time to leave as you were away." Her hands moved to where his jaws hinged and he was in too much bliss to speak as she worked his tense muscles all the way down his neck to his shoulders. She kneaded and probed, the pressure of her fingers strong even through the layers of clothing. He was nearly asleep when her fingers stopped. He opened his eyes.

She took his hands and tried to pull him from the chair. "You're too heavy for me to lift."

He gave her a drowsy smile and stood. "Where are you taking me?" he asked even though he knew exactly where she was headed.

She dragged him into the adjacent bedchamber where her bag now sat beside his. She led him to the bed and shoved him hard in the chest. He fell onto the soft bedding and propped himself up on his elbows while she locked both doors and came to stand before him. She gave him a wanton smile and began plucking hairpins from her hair, one black eyebrow arched high.

"You are depraved." He was hard and his breathing had roughened; this woman was his *wife* and he could have her whenever he wanted. The thought made him dizzy with joy.

She pulled the last pin from her hair and shook it loose before leaning over him and unbuttoning his coat and waistcoat, continuing south to his fall and peeling open his buckskins.

He lifted his hips. "I'm filthy, darling."

"I like you filthy." She slid a cool hand around his throbbing cock and stroked him with erotic efficiency. Somewhere in the back of his mind—the very back—he knew he was being manipulated away from their discussion but he didn't care.

Portia stopped as suddenly as she'd started, leaving him hard and wanting. He opened his eyes a crack. She'd hiked her skirt and petticoat and tucked them into the front of her bodice before clambering onto the bed and straddling him. She stared at him as she guided him to her entrance, lowering herself onto him with a violence that robbed his lungs of air. Daylight streamed through the windows and it was brighter than any room they'd ever made love in. Stacy could not keep his eyes from consuming her.

Her lips parted as she rode him. "Tell me what you want, Mr. Harrington." Her head tipped back until he could only see the long white column of her throat. She dropped a hand to where they were joined and circled the base of his shaft with strong, hot fingers while she undulated, taking him deeper with each languorous thrust.

He placed his palms beneath his head and then flexed his aching hips until he was angled for her pleasure, thrusting upward as she came down on him.

She gasped and he thrust again, harder this time.

"I want you to come with me, Portia."

She shuddered at his words and her muscles tightened around him. And then she commenced to ride him harder than he'd ridden Geist.

"DOES YOUR HEAD hurt?" Portia asked.

Stacy rolled onto his side and faced her, wiping his brow with the back of his forearm. "Not anymore. You are a miracle headache cure. But I shan't be bottling and selling you." He lifted the curtain of hair that covered her face and wound it around his fist, holding her head up when she would have lowered her eyes to his chest. "We were having a conversation before you so skillfully distracted me."

She pursed her mouth and rolled onto her back, staring at the ceiling with a petulant expression, as though she were preparing to be catechized on Latin conjugations.

Stacy considered his question and her angry response. Did he really have the right to pry into her last marriage? Would he appreciate similar prying into his past?

You've never told her about Kitty, have you . . . ?

He opened his mouth to tell her it was none of his concern but her voice stopped him.

"He struck me when we argued and he found himself on the losing side, which was frequently, I'm afraid. He pushed me down a short flight of stairs and I had my miscarriage soon afterward." She turned on her side, as if she wanted to see his reaction to her heartbreaking revelation. "Our marriage began badly. I did not come to his bed intact." She ran one finger slowly around his nipple.

Anger, shock, and arousal roiled in his gut and Stacy was more than a little uneasy that she would tell him such dreadful things while stroking him. But he could not find it in himself to stop her. He kept his eyes on her face while her distracting finger danced across his body.

"My first lover is the one who . . ." She stopped and gave him a shy smile. "Well, he taught me about bed sport." She blushed wildly, which made his cock twitch. She glanced down at his half-hard shaft and smiled before continuing her story.

"He was uninhibited and passionate and I thought that is how all men were in bed. On my wedding night I learned differently." She cut him a quick glance. "I was not promiscuous—I loved Benedict, my first lover, but he died and I thought my heart would break. Then I met Ivo. I was swept away by his talent, just like everyone who heard him play. He singled me out among all the girls who were trying to capture his attention. After my father died, I was lonely and Ivo's future was so bright I was blinded by what I thought was love. He showed the same passion for me as he did his playing, at least until he made me his wife. He believed me to be a chaste virgin and did no more than kiss my hand before we wed. When he learned otherwise, on our wedding night, he never forgave me."

A serpent wended its way from his stomach to his chest, tightening around his heart. Stacy fought no small amount of jealousy—for two dead men. The thought of Portia with another man made him want to break something or hurt someone. A reaction that was both foreign and distasteful.

"It was not a happy marriage. Ivo took lovers from the beginning and he made no effort to conceal it. He believed it was his right because I had dishonored and tricked him. There were many fights, a few instances of tempestuous rapprochement, and ever-increasing estrangement." Her hand moved across his chest until she held the side of his waist, her fingers digging into the corded muscles hard enough to hurt. "I've never been this happy before, Stacy. Ever."

Her words sucked the air from his lungs, from the room, even. He stared into her eyes as her hand slipped lower.

"I want to be with you all the time. I want you on top of me, around me, inside me." She rolled onto her back and spread her thighs for him, opening like a butterfly.

Stacy knelt between her open legs and slid into her eager, welcoming body. She was heaven to him and she became more important every day. He thought of his child growing inside her body and plunged into her harder, deeper, faster. She shuddered beneath him again and again and again. And still he rode her, like a man pursued by demons. Like a man who was desperately trying to outrun the nagging fear that nothing this good could ever last.

THE PLYMOUTH TRIP taught Portia two things. First, she was in love with Stacy. Second, she would do *anything* to protect their marriage.

The first realization left her both joyous and terrified. He was the most wonderful thing that had ever happened to her and she refused to lose him. She knew he cared for her and might even come to love her if they had enough time. But that could only happen if Ivo was out of their lives forever.

After the Plymouth trip Stacy was more adamant than ever that Daisy accompany Portia wherever she went. The only time she could get away was at night and there were precious few nights left to get the money to Ivo before he came looking for it.

Two days after they returned from Plymouth she feigned a headache. Portia hated to rouse Stacy's concern but it was the only way she could think of to be alone. She waited until after dinner, when they were both sitting in the library reading.

She put her book down on the table beside her and reached up to massage her temples. "I am developing something of a headache."

He took off his spectacles. "I know a woman who has a cure for that very thing." His suggestive half-smile caused a pulsing between her thighs.

God, how she loved everything about him.

The realization crushed her like a brutal, relentless fist and the pained smile Portia gave him was not contrived. "I'm afraid even that cure won't work tonight. I've had this type of headache in the past. The only relief comes from quiet, darkness, and rest."

His smile disappeared, replaced by concern. "Is there nothing you can take for it?"

"I've never found any draughts helpful and I don't care for laudanum."

He took her hands in his and lifted them to his mouth, his beautiful eyes worried.

"You needn't look so troubled; it is not a serious malady. I shall be right as rain in the morning, I promise."

Yes. Tomorrow everything would be better; it had to be.

SHORTLY AFTER TWO o'clock Portia donned a dark brown gown, heavy cloak, and black gloves before wrapping a dark scarf around her head. She took the pouch of money and jewels from where she'd hidden them inside an old pillowcase and put a candle and flint into the bag. She was tempted to see if Stacy was sleeping but didn't want to risk waking him. The house was as quiet as a tomb when she opened the door to the hall.

First, she would take Ivo his money. If she ran out of time she could always return the jewels to the safe tomorrow night. Portia left the bag of jewelry just inside the sunroom door and took only the money and candleholder with her.

When she could no longer see the house, she lit the candle. It cast abundant light for the path and she could only hope it would be sufficient to find the place where she would need to cut into the woods.

It turned out she needn't have worried. The trail from the path toward the old cottage looked as if a herd of cattle had been trampling it. She cursed Ivo's stupidity under her breath. He might as well have erected a sign with an arrow. People were bound to notice such a well-trod pathway if they hadn't already. Portia picked her way through the woods, resisting the urge to hurry. She could just imagine the fix she'd be in if she twisted her ankle.

She was almost to the cottage when something touched her shoulder. She shrieked, jumped, and flung the candleholder.

"Sh, *cara*, it's only me." A small flare of light illuminated the darkness as he lighted his own candle.

"*Stupido!* Why would you sneak up behind me in such a manner?" Portia dropped to her knees and groped in the weeds for her candle and holder. She found both and stood, stepping back when she realized how close he'd come.

"I knew you would come tonight. I could sense it." His voice was caressing and smug and Portia wanted to slap him.

"I've brought your money."

He crouched to dribble wax on a rotting log and fix the candle stub in it. When he stood, the light was far dimmer but she caught a flash of teeth as he stepped closer. "I've learned a lot about you while I've been living in my little hovel."

Portia refused to think about what he'd learned or who he'd learned it from. "When are you leaving?"

"So hasty!"

Portia dearly wished she had something to hit him with.

He chuckled. "As soon as I receive the money, I will pack my few possessions and be gone."

"You will leave tomorrow?"

There was a pause and then, "I will leave tomorrow."

His finger grazed her cheek and she jumped, swatting at his hand. "Stop it."

Again he laughed.

"I did not come here to play foolish games with you. This is the only money you shall ever get from me—I give you my word on that."

"Calm yourself, *cara.* You can trust me. I will take my money and be gone from your life forever."

"How will you leave the woods without drawing notice? You have no horse." She paused. "How did you get here to begin with?" She raised her hand palm out. "Never mind, I do not wish to know."

He reached for her hand, touching her lightly before she could snatch it away. "Do not vex yourself, my dove. I shall be gone with nobody the wiser." He could not hide the thread of weariness beneath his soothing tone. His life in the woods would not have been pleasant. She took the leather bag from her voluminous cloak pocket and shoved it at him. "It's all there. You must take notes as anything else would have been prohibitively heavy."

"Oh, banknotes shall do very well indeed, *mia bella.*" He paused. "I think—" he stopped and she squinted through the gloom at his face; his full lips were strangely flat.

"You think what, Ivo?" she asked, not bothering to hide her own weariness. Weary of him, weary of this deception, weary of lying to her husband.

He shook his head. "It is nothing, *cara.* I was only going to caution you to take care of yourself. People are not always who you think they are and you've always been far too trusting. Watch out for those who would take advantage of you."

Portia snorted. "People like you?" She turned away before he could answer and pushed a foot ahead of her before fishing around in her cloak pocket for the flint. "I never want to see you again, Ivo," she called over her shoulder.

The only answer was the rustle of trees. Portia sighed and took a moment to light her candle before picking her way through the woods. When she got to the path she ran until she was breathless. She extinguished the flame before she reached the edge of the trees and slowed her pace. Now there was only the jewelry to replace and her nightmare would be over.

STACY REACHED OUT for Portia and found the bed beside him empty. He sighed and turned onto his back, blinking into the darkness. It was difficult to sleep without her. He threw back the blankets, pulled on his robe, and went toward the connecting door to check on her—but not disturb her. He opened the door and squinted into the darkness. The covers had been thrown back and Portia was not in her bed.

Perhaps she had gone to the kitchen for something to eat, not wishing to disturb the servants. She'd barely eaten anything for dinner. He would go find her and they could have a late-night feast—he smiled, his body stirring—and perhaps some dessert after.

He pulled open the drapes, preferring to get dressed by starlight rather than light a candle. He was about to turn away from the window when a flicker of light caught his attention: somebody was coming from the woods. Stacy leaned closer to the glass and squinted; he knew who it was even before he saw her face.

What the devil was she doing? He stared without breathing, as if the sound might frighten her. As she got closer, he saw she was moving at a brisk pace, her head down. She went around the corner of the house and he lost sight of her. She must be heading toward the sunroom, an entrance she favored.

Stacy snatched up his robe, but donned no slippers, moving silently on bare feet. He reached the bottom of the stairs just in time to see her walk past the music room and open the library door, not bothering to close it behind her. He went toward the library, fully intending to let her know he was there without frightening the wits out of her. But when he looked inside, he saw she'd gone directly to the painting that hid the wall safe. He paused and something sour twisted in his stomach as he watched her stealthy movements.

She opened the safe with an ease that told him this wasn't the first time. Next, she removed the marquetry box that held the pearl set, placed it on the desk, and then opened her bag and slid something into the box. She rearranged the contents, closed the box, and replaced it in the safe. She took out the second box, the larger jewel case that held the rest of his mother's jewelry and returned what seemed to be most of the jewels to the box. When she was finished, she shut the safe door and re-hung the painting.

Stacy returned to the foyer and waited at the base of the stairs. He ignored the rabid pounding of his heart. He was sure she had a good reason for what he'd just seen. He was sure of it. She would tell him about it and they would chuckle and spend the night in each other's arms.

Chapter Twenty-One

PORTIA'S PALMS WERE damp and her heart was pounding so loud it deafened her.

You're almost done. The nightmare is almost over, the voice in her head reminded her as she replaced the painting and tucked the pillowcase into the pocket of her cloak.

The worry of the past few weeks suddenly hit her, turning her legs to jelly. She wanted to collapse at Stacy's desk and weep with relief, but she kept moving, closing the library door and heading toward the stairs. Maybe she would surprise Stacy and slip in beside him while he was sleeping. Her lips pulled into a smile as she imagined it.

Portia was so preoccupied with the amorous visions in her head that she collided with the man himself at the bottom of the stairs.

"Stacy! What are you doing?" It was too dark to see his face and only the outline of his body was visible in the gloom.

"I was about to ask you the same thing. Where were you?" He sounded . . . perturbed. What had he seen?

Portia blurted out the first lie that came to mind. "I was hungry. I didn't eat much at dinner."

"You need your cloak for a journey to the kitchen?"

She bit her lip. *Stupid, stupid, stupid.* "I was full after eating so I took a walk. It's lovely out. You enjoy this time of night, do you not?" The only sound in the big foyer was the pounding of her blood in her ears.

He finally spoke. "You are returning to your room?"

"I was hoping to return to *your* room." She let more than a hint of suggestion into her voice. The silence drew out until Portia's face burned. His lack of response was far more insulting than any words could have been. She opened her mouth to ask him if anything was amiss but his voice stopped her.

"I believe you need your rest. We wouldn't want you to suffer a relapse of your dreadful headache." His voice was colder than an arctic wind.

Portia was still trying to think of something to say when she saw a flicker of white moving up the stairs. She ran up after him, fast enough to leave her breathless, reaching the third floor just in time to see a flash of ivory silk and hear the soft but distinctive click of a door.

Her knees buckled and she leaned against the wall.

What had he seen?

THE FIVE DAYS that followed her meeting in the woods were some of the worst in Portia's life. It was even worse than the bad times with Ivo—the times when she could not leave the house without a veil after one of their more violent confrontations. Not that Stacy had laid a hand on her—in any way.

He was pleasant to her in the same way he was pleasant to his servants. He never raised his voice or said anything rude or cutting but his well-modulated kindness was more painful than a whip or fist. He knew she'd lied and he was furious. He'd told her that first day he abhorred lying. And Portia was most certainly a liar.

After a dinner spent discussing pleasantries they retired to the library and he worked on some project while she pretended to read but really watched him. After a few hours he put away his papers, rose from his chair, and bid her a polite good night. When he didn't come to her bed that first night, she checked the connecting door to his room and found it locked. The message was more painful than a slap in the face; she didn't try the door again.

By the fifth day she was nearly ill with despair. She sat in the breakfast room and pushed a piece of toast around her plate. Even their lessons, which they'd both been thrilled to continue after their marriage, passed as bloodless transactions between polite strangers.

Portia had resolved to tell him the truth today; she could not continue to live this way. Besides, she knew in her heart that Ivo would be back. Blackmailers always returned to the source of their money; every fool knew that. She would tell Stacy the truth and *make* him believe her. Eventually he would forgive her for lying and the next time Ivo came they would face him together.

Oh yes, that is exactly what will happen, the dry voice jeered.

Portia shoved away her uneaten food and stood just as the door to the breakfast room opened and Stacy entered. He wore his black glasses and was dressed for riding.

"Ah, you are finished with your breakfast, Portia?"

She lowered herself back into her chair. "I would have another cup of coffee if you would not mind the company." She would tell him after he ate. They would go to the library and she would tell him everything.

"I always enjoy your company, my dear." The words were spoken absently, as if he were commenting on the weather.

Portia turned to the footman. "Would you please bring a fresh pot of coffee?"

Stacy served himself from the sideboard and sat down at the far end of the table.

"I saw you leave on Geist hours ago."

"Yes. I went into Bude, to the Elephant and Castle," he cut a piece of ham and raised it to his mouth. She could not see his eyes but she could *feel* the weight of his stare.

"Did you?" Although he'd begun to go out in public with increasing regularity after their marriage, he still did not go into town very often.

He took a bite of food, chewed, and swallowed, a vision of unruffled poise.

Portia hated his glasses, especially now, when she knew he was using them as a weapon to keep her at a distance.

The footman entered and they both waited while he filled their cups with fresh coffee.

Stacy set down his knife and fork. "I received a message early this morning that a dead body had been found on the beach."

Portia froze, her cup half-way to her mouth. "A dead body?"

"Thank you, Thomas, that will be all for now," Stacy said. When the door closed behind the servant he turned to Portia, "Yes, a body."

"Where?" she asked when it was clear he was not going to volunteer any information.

"It was on the rocks beneath Penhallow's Bluff—what everyone refers to as Lover's Leap. Right below Nanny's."

Portia's hand trembled and coffee spilled over the edge of her cup, missed her saucer, and stained the snowy table linen. She stared at the brown blossom, unable to wrench her eyes away.

"Was it someone crossed in love?" she asked, finally looking up.

He remained motionless for a moment longer and then picked up his fork and knife and resumed eating. "I suppose he might have been someone's lover."

"He?" she repeated. "Was it somebody you knew?"

"It was a foreign gentleman, nobody from around here. He was carrying nothing that gave any clue as to who he was."

Portia frowned. "How do you know he was foreign if he had no identification?"

"His clothing is of fine quality but of foreign make—except for his boots, which bore Hoby's mark. He might be an itinerant actor. Or perhaps a musician." He shrugged. "He is most likely one of the many refugees we've been seeing from the Continent now that the War is over."

Tiny needles of fear began to shoot through her, bouncing and ricocheting and multiplying. "An actor?"

He chewed, swallowed and took another drink of coffee before answering. "Or a musician, although that is not likely as one of his hands had been crushed rather badly at some point."

The conversation was like the bad dreams she'd been having recently, the ones in which she tried to run but got nowhere.

She had to clear her throat several times before she could speak. "When did he die?"

"The doctor believes he must have drifted back to shore after spending several days in the water."

Portia's mind buzzed like a beehive that had been poked with a stick. Several days? What did that mean? Four days? Three days? But Ivo had promised to be gone the next day. Well, that would have been five days. Had he stayed around for another day for some reason? If so, how had he ended up at the bottom of a cliff?

Her frantic mind leapt to the money. Where was the money? Had the person who found him taken it? Had somebody else taken it before he fell to his death? Perhaps he had been robbed? And what about the marriage lines? Had he been foolish enough to have those with him?

She looked from her plate to her husband, who was facing her, as still as a statue.

Portia dropped her gaze. She needed to be alone. Now. She stood and tossed her napkin onto the table.

"I promised Nanny some embroidery silks for the christening bonnet she is making."

Stacy was on his feet in an instant and preceded her to the

door. His hand lowered to the door handle but he did not open it. "Please give Nanny my regards and tell her I shall visit her later today." He stood close enough that Portia could feel the warmth of his body and smell his tantalizing cologne. She swayed toward him, teetering on the brink of flinging herself into his arms and telling him everything.

She opened her mouth and looked up.

He had a polite smile on his face. Polite and cold.

"I will," she said.

She felt his eyes on her back all the way down the hall. When she reached her room, she shut her door and collapsed against it.

Good God. Ivo—dead! What would happen if they found out who he was?

STACY WAITED UNTIL his wife disappeared from view before closing the breakfast room door and resuming his seat. His unfinished breakfast held no appeal and he pushed it away.

He took off his glasses and squeezed the bridge of his nose with his thumb and forefinger until it hurt. He'd cast out his lure about the dead body hoping to be mistaken but Portia's reaction had left him in no doubt: she'd known the man.

What in God's name was she involved in and why wouldn't she tell him? The late-night jaunt and visit to the safe had been one thing; a dead man on his property was something else entirely. What was she so desperate to hide?

As the local magistrate it had been Stacy's duty to examine the body when it was found. The corpse was badly water damaged but he recognized it as the same man who'd been arguing with Fant that day.

He'd stood looking at the body, nauseated, and not just because of the stench. The dead man was an Italian and Stacy's wife was half-Italian. He wanted to believe it was a coincidence, but his wife's reaction this morning proved him wrong.

"Blast and damn," he muttered. Why the bloody hell wouldn't she trust him with whatever was bothering her? Pain and disappointment mingled in his gut and threatened to choke him. He reminded himself that she'd never promised him love or affection and he'd been a fool to expect it. He ground down any regret he felt over the admission and squared his shoulders. He'd go to Nanny's today and see Fant. He might be unable to get the truth from his own wife, but he could bloody well get it from a man in his employ.

THE PEOPLE IN the village spoke of almost nothing but the mysterious body so Portia was able to keep abreast of matters without asking her husband for information.

As nobody came to claim the body, Stacy ordered the man buried in a pauper's grave.

Every day Portia waited for an opportunity to sneak away to Ivo's meager camp site. Every day Daisy stayed so close she might have been stitched to Portia's side. Every day she expected somebody to learn Ivo's identity and come for her.

Even going at night was out of the question. Although Stacy continued to wage his frigid campaign, Portia knew he would be watching for nighttime jaunts.

She also knew she should feel sad about Ivo's death, but she only felt angry that he'd come to such a pitiful end after such a glorious beginning. He'd possessed the kind of talent that occurred only a few times in a generation. Portia mourned the loss of Ivo the musician far more than Ivo the man.

GOING TO CHURCH was one of the few activities Stacy and Portia still engaged in together. They'd stopped their daily rides and no longer spent evenings in companionable silence in the library. Their lessons continued, but only three times a week now, and they'd become polite transactions between strangers.

The Sunday ride back from the church was as uncomfortable and stilted as the ride there had been and Stacy stared out the carriage window rather than at his wife when he said, "Viscountess Pendleton has sent us an invitation to a house party at Thurlstone Castle."

Portia was studying her clasped hands, her profile tense, and did not answer him. What was in her mind at that moment? Would he ever know her any better than this?

"Would you like to go?" he asked when she didn't respond.

She looked up; her face impassive. "Do you care what I like, Stacy?"

There were mauve half-circles beneath her expressive eyes. How long had those been there? Stacy realized he'd not really looked at her since the night he'd caught her sneaking about and lying; it was too painful to look at her without touching her.

But he looked at her now. Was it his behavior that was making her look ill and drawn? Had he done this to her? To the child she was carrying?

Stacy placed his hand over hers, the motion awkward and stiff. "I do care what you like." He'd meant to be kind but his voice came out even colder than usual. He sighed as he looked at her distant profile. There was a part of him—the part accustomed to being obeyed—that wanted to demand she tell him the truth. Just who the devil had that man been and what the hell happened in the woods that night?

But there was another part of him, a part that became more pronounced every day, and it had only one question: did he really want to hear what she said?

The truth was Stacy was afraid of whatever she was hiding.

What would he do if she'd done something terrible? Had she known the man? Had he been some lover from her past? Had he been Ivo Stefani—her husband? The crushed hand certainly suggested that was a possibility. Whoever he was, why had he come here? Had he been blackmailing her? Had she brought the jewels to silence him and then shoved him off the cliff instead? Perhaps the man had struck her and she fought back? Perhaps somebody pushed him off the cliff before she met him?

Stacy ground his teeth as the questions whirled. He'd gone to shake some answers out of Fant but Mrs. Fant said her husband was visiting family in Yorkshire. The dour woman claimed to know nothing of the man Stacy described. Had Fant and the stranger merely travelled together for a time, as people frequently did to minimize danger? Stacy wanted to believe that, but it didn't sit right. The two men had been arguing in a way that seemed far too personal for mere traveling companions.

He knew he should just ask Portia and clear up the matter, but he couldn't. When he'd asked her to marry him, he'd believed he was merely obsessed with her body, her talent, and the child she carried. Now that he'd lost her companionship—her friendship—the truth was unavoidable: He loved her and was afraid to learn what had really happened that night.

Stacy snorted; he loved her but he did not trust or believe her. What kind of man did that make him?

"Do you want to accept your brother's invitation?" Her voice jerked him from his self-loathing.

Did he want to get to know his family or did he just want to get his wife away from whatever might have happened that night at Lover's Leap? Robert's face flickered through his mind. "I would like to meet my sisters and spend time with my brother."

"What of Frances? Will you forgive her?" The words were soft but accusatory.

"I don't know." It was the truth. Stacy was still too furious to think clearly about her betrayal. Besides, he was far more concerned about Portia and whatever it was *she'd* done. Good God. What if she'd killed that man? Did he love her enough to forgive and forget the crime of murder? He didn't want to know the answer to that.

"It would be nice to get away for a while." The words were so quiet Stacy almost missed them. He studied her unreadable profile. *Could* he get away, especially when the source of the trouble would be right there beside him? He removed his hand from her arm and turned back toward the window.

"Very well," he said. "We shall go to Thurlstone Castle."

Chapter Twenty-Two

IT WAS LESS than seventy miles to Thurlstone but Stacy decided they would break the journey in Plymouth.

"You will need your rest," he told Portia in his cool, implacable way. She was tempted to argue—just because—but he spoke the truth: she did tire easily lately.

He rode alongside the carriage with his valet, hatted and gloved and scarved, leaving Portia and Daisy to entertain each other inside the traveling coach. When they reached Marlborough House, they found it crowded with revelers who'd come to watch a mill that was to take place that night.

"We just have the one room, Mr. Harrington. If you'd like, I could move one or two of the gentlemen who—"

"That won't be necessary," Stacy assured the haggard innkeeper. "We'll take the room you have."

Stacy sent the servants to a nearby inn, clearly preferring to wait on himself rather than have Powell and Daisy view their frigid interactions in such an intimate space. Not that either servant could have failed to notice their master and mistress no longer visited each other's beds.

Portia lay down on the bed they would share for the first time in weeks and rested while Stacy arranged their meal. Would he go to the brothel tonight—where he'd claimed to have done nothing more than visited a friend? Jealousy burned hot in her belly at the thought.

She heard a sound and opened her eyes.

Stacy stood in the open doorway. "I'm sorry—I didn't realize you were sleeping." He turned on his heel to go.

She scrambled up onto her elbows. "I was only resting. I daresay you wish for a bath after a day on horseback."

He gave her a faint smile and Portia saw new lines of strain around his mouth. As usual he wore glasses; she'd not seen his eyes in weeks. The realization brought an odd, painful lump to her throat. He'd found the perfect way to punish her: depriving her of every last form of contact, even looking into his eyes. Did he know ignoring her was the best punishment he could conceive? She doubted it. Her nature was so different from his. She needed contact, interaction—even if it was only conflict. He seemed to need nothing; nothing from her, in any case.

He rang for a bath and busied himself in the small dressing room adjacent to the bedroom. She listened to the normal sounds of domesticity and pondered her life. How much longer would this continue? Each day that passed made telling him one notch more difficult. He was an impenetrable wall of ice: hard and cold and unyielding. Not for a second had he melted toward her or given any sign that he missed their nights of passion or their days of friendship.

It is your *fault you are estranged,* the prim schoolmistress in her head scolded.

Shut up.

Tell him the truth.

Portia groaned and sat up; trying to rest was pointless.

A parade of servants passed through the room to fill the large bath and she busied herself with the contents of her valise until the last servant deposited his steaming bucket and departed. She flopped onto the bed with a book and then noticed the door to the dressing room was open a sliver, just enough that she could see Stacy as he disrobed.

She lowered the book and stared, silently willing him not to notice the door. By the time he bent to remove his buckskins and drawers she had difficulty breathing normally. He stepped out of the clothes, leaving them strewn on the floor while he leaned back and stretched. He extended his muscular arms over his head, cords and sinews rippling like steel beneath white silk as he worked the soreness out of his body. When he finished stretching, he absently scratched one perfect buttock and then lifted a foot to test the water. He jerked his foot back before lowering it again and slowly easing into the tub.

It took him a full minute before he submerged himself. It was the best minute of the past month and Portia wished it would go on forever. But all too soon the only things she could see were his shoulders and head.

She was shaking when she stood, the place between her thighs every bit as wet as his body. She unfastened her carriage gown as though she were in a daze, never taking her eyes from the narrow slit between the door and frame. He was splashing about while he soaped his body, and by the time she removed her chemise and stockings he'd submerged his head. She paused to watch as he emerged, the water flowing off snow-white hair and beading on flawless skin.

He turned when she pushed open the door and his translucent violet gaze swept her naked body and kindled. They took one another's measure, probing without touching, looking for secrets, lies, the truth, anything other than the terrifying detachment that had settled between them. His eyes left a scorched trail in their wake until every inch of her body was on fire.

"Come here." The words were quiet and controlled, just like his face—just like everything except his eyes. His eyes told the truth about what he was feeling, his pupils huge and black and bottomless. She closed the distance between them.

"Straddle the tub." His words were clipped and his lids lowered as he reclined against the high, slanted backrest.

She raised one leg over the side and his eyes dropped to the curls between her thighs. His lips tightened and his chest expanded as he inhaled. She lowered both thighs until they rested on warm metal, holding herself upright by gripping the metal rim behind her, leaning back slightly to do so.

"Come closer."

She pushed herself closer, the motions awkward, like a crab forced to walk forward.

"Closer." The single guttural word made her shudder and Portia scooted until she was close enough to feel the heat of his uneven breathing on the sensitive skin of her thighs. He lifted wet hands and parted her lips, his touch warm and feather-light. When he looked up the violet was no more than a ring around swollen black pupils. He slid low in the water before leaning into her, his eyes holding hers while the very tip of his tongue found her peak.

She gasped and gritted her teeth to keep from giving orders; or worse, begging.

Again he flicked her, the same light, taunting touch tormenting her while he gently but inexorably pushed her legs wider, until her hip sockets pulsed with an exquisite pain.

"Please, Stacy."

He stopped teasing and began to stroke her in earnest. Unspeakable pleasure flooded her body and reduced every thought to one: want. He sucked her swollen bud into the soft heat of his mouth and slid a finger inside her. She tightened around him while he found the spot that seemed to be his very own discovery. While he worked her from within, his clever lips and tongue teased out her first climax.

Indecent sounds and words burst from her and her hands gripped the tub until they were numb and still he didn't stop. A second wave of pleasure obliterated the small piece of her mind that remained and left her gasping for breath. Her head fell back and she lowered her shaking arms until her elbows rested on the rim of the tub, her body spread wantonly before him.

She was on a blissful cloud when he pushed to his feet, his abrupt motion sending waves over the high copper sides and water fanning out over the wooden floor.

In a few brusque motions he lifted her, set her on her feet, and bent her over the tub, shoving her knees wide before stroking her hot cleft with his equally hot shaft. And then he thrust into her so hard she had to brace her hands to keep from falling over the rim and into the water.

He pulled all the way out and teased her entrance with his swollen head as he wound her hair around his hand, the motion arching her back and back and back until she felt her spine might snap. He held her body taut and immobile while he breached her only with the fat crown.

The demonstration of raw power made her tighten around him and he gasped, slamming deeply into her, holding her arched, stretched, and filled.

"Have you missed this?" he hissed, his chest slick and hard against her back, his breath hot against her ear. "Have you missed my cock inside your body? My fingers? My tongue?" he taunted before pounding her with a series of savage thrusts that left her dizzy. He stopped again, buried to the hilt, his shaft so hard she could feel him pulsing inside her.

"Did you pleasure yourself, Portia?" His voice throbbed with a tangle of desire, anger, and hurt. "I did. I stroked myself raw thinking about you." He pulled out with agonizing slowness and then impaled her with a brutal thrust.

Portia almost climaxed from his words alone.

"Did you slide your fingers inside your body and imagine they were mine? Can you make yourself wet the way I do?" He didn't wait for an answer but rode her with a violent intensity that obliterated her wits.

She knew, for the first time in all their lovemaking, he was not considering her needs, but using her for his own pleasure.

That unexpected streak of selfish cruelty only made her want him more.

He gave a last flurry of brutal, sharp thrusts, and then hilted himself, his fingers digging into her hips, his shaft thickening and jerking as he pumped his release deep inside her body.

For one blinding moment she was complete—at one with him—but his tremors hadn't even receded before he stepped back and left her empty.

Portia's arms were shaky as she pushed up from the hard rim of the tub, echoes of her climax still rippling through her body. She watched through a pleasure-drenched haze as he picked up one of the towels, cleaned his still tumescent organ, and tossed the linen to the floor without looking at her.

And then he strode from the room and shut the door behind him with a decisive click.

PORTIA HADN'T GIVEN much thought to what Thurlstone Castle would look like but she'd assumed the country seat of an earl—and a castle, at that—would be impressive. Nothing prepared her for what greeted them when their carriage crested the rise. The house was an endless succession of structures that sprawled in all directions, more impressive for its sheer size than its elegant architecture. Indeed, it looked wholly English and nothing like the castles of Europe. The central portion—a crenelated tower that lent the edifice its name—must have served a defensive purpose in the distant past. But the once-majestic tower was now ringed by buildings and additions and resembled a squat debutante in a dress that bore too many furbelows and flounces.

The land that surrounded it, by contrast, was as meticulously and mathematically laid out as an ancient Roman military encampment. An immense formal garden extended to the south and west and a thin ribbon of blue led to a placid pond surrounded by carefully orchestrated clusters of trees.

It was closer to the sea than Whitethorn and one could hear the sound of breakers and smell the tang of salty air. As they descended the hill the ancient trees that lined the drive obstructed most of their view. The only thing visible inside the tunnel of autumn foliage was the entrance to Thurlstone some distance ahead. The entire estate was impressive, but Portia could not help thinking the less structured wilderness that held sway around Whitethorn was more to her taste.

Not that she would have cared if the place had been a hovel. After their torrid encounter at the inn and Stacy's frigid indifference, she'd hardly been able to keep from running back to Whitethorn on foot.

When she'd finally emerged from the dressing room last night, he'd behaved toward her with the same icy courtesy he'd employed for over a month. If she'd had any feelings of remorse about lying to him before, she had an entirely different set of feelings toward him now. If a battle of wills was what he wanted, that was exactly what she would give him. Last night was the last time she would show her desire for him. Ever.

"Oh look, ma'am," Daisy interrupted Portia's venomous musings to point out a distant sliver of blue between two massive tree trunks. Portia ignored the sight and looked instead at her husband, who rode on that side of the carriage. He chose that moment to look at the window, as if sensing somebody watching him. Portia gave him a blinding smile and was childishly pleased when his lips parted in surprise. She turned to see Daisy watching them, a disapproving wrinkle between her eyes. Portia ignored her and stared out the opposite window.

The carriage rolled to a stop in front of two lines of people that stretched from the huge, metal-studded castle doors to the middle of the drive. It looked as if her new sister and brother-in-law had assembled every servant on the property to greet them.

Viscount Pendleton himself lowered the carriage steps and opened the door.

"Mrs. Harrington," the viscount exclaimed, his handsome face wearing a genuine smile. "Welcome to Thurlstone."

Prinny himself could not have received a warmer welcome.

Lord Pendleton's wife waited for them at the top of the shallow, worn steps, her exquisite pale green gown making Portia feel travel-stained and frumpy.

"It's a pleasure to meet you," the viscountess and duke's daughter murmured, her lips flexing into a slight smile. Her cool manner matched her icy blonde exterior. She was not as thrilled by their visit—or at least not as demonstrative—as her exuberant spouse. She was to be addressed as Lady Rowena, rather than Lady Pendleton. It appeared she preferred to use her courtesy title as a duke's daughter.

The next half hour passed in a blur of introductions and greetings. By the time it was over the only person they hadn't met was the earl. Portia glanced at her husband but he was as impassive as ever.

Stacy gave Frances a brief nod but Portia embraced the tall, bone-thin woman and whispered in her ear, "I've missed you, and so does he, even if he is too proud to show it. We will have you back at Whitethorn before you know it."

Frances gave her a tremulous smile and quick squeeze before releasing her.

Stacy's other sisters were considerably shorter than Frances but all four siblings shared the same sandy blond hair and blue-gray eyes. Although they must have heard about Stacy over the years, neither sister could take their eyes from him. Portia couldn't blame them. She saw him every day and still found it difficult to look at anything or anyone else when he was in the vicinity; even when she wanted to club him over the head with a brick.

By the time they'd been escorted to their chambers, which were twice the size of those at Whitethorn, Portia was exhausted. But there would be no rest. They'd agreed to freshen up and meet in the Red Drawing Room for tea.

Portia was sitting in front of her dressing table trying to keep from falling asleep while Daisy fixed her hair when Stacy came through the connecting door. They met each other's eyes in the mirror. Well, at least she thought they did, he was wearing his impenetrable glasses. She smiled bitterly. She should probably be grateful he hadn't stopped to put them on before their torrid encounter at the inn last night. She glanced at her reflection and was proud to see no sign of either her anger or amorous thoughts showed on her face.

"If you wish, I will tell them you mean to rest before dinner, Portia." The offer was considerate, even if his delivery was aloof.

"I am quite refreshed," she lied. "Should we ring for a servant or do you recall the way?"

Daisy stepped back and Portia stood and took her husband's arm. Even that slight contact caused intense churning in her stomach.

"I believe I can get us to our destination without precipitating the need for a search party," he said, causing Daisy to giggle.

Portia ignored him.

The house was just as rambling on the inside as it appeared from the outside. The original portion had been built in the Plantagenet period and had sprouted a new wing with each succeeding monarch. It felt like it took an hour to reach the appointed room, but that might have been the uncomfortable silence.

Portia wondered how a person decided which of the dozens of rooms and salons to use each day. If she and Stacy lived in this house they would never need to see one another again. She turned slightly to look at her husband's handsome, sharp-edged profile and then wished she had not. It was tragic that he was so attractive.

Stacy's sisters and brother were already in the room when they arrived. The earl was not in attendance. Did the man really exist?

The five siblings tried to bridge the yawning gap between them with conversation about the unseasonably cold weather, the exceptionally poor harvest, and the state of the roads. While the three sisters resembled one another quite closely, Stacy and Robert Harrington were only alike in that they were both tall, well-built, and handsome. The one characteristic all five seemed to share was a certain reserve. Yet as reserved as they were, Portia could see they wished to know each other.

Lady Rowena, however, appeared to have no interest in anyone other than Portia. The woman's pale green eyes bore all the warmth of a snake's and her piercing gaze slithered over Portia's face and person in a way that left her feeling . . . invaded.

"I understand congratulations are in order," the viscountess said, breaking into something Mary was saying to Stacy about the nearby Bishop Caverns. "When is your confinement?"

"March."

The Harrington sisters greeted this information with nods and soft murmurs. The men drank their tea and the sound of cups clinking against saucers filled the silence. Portia almost laughed; this was agonizing. Was the entire two-week period going to be like this?

"I understand your last husband was the pianist Ivo Stefani."

Stacy stepped in before she could answer. "Portia is also a remarkable musician in her own right."

Portia slid him an astonished look while trying to appear modest at his display of husbandly pride.

"Perhaps you will play for us?" Robert Harrington asked,

giving her a warm, charming smile.

Portia instinctively liked Lord Pendleton. His enthusiasm about Stacy was unfeigned and he appeared thrilled to have discovered his brother.

His wife, however, was a duke's daughter first, an earl's daughter-in-law second, a viscount's wife third, and a human being last. The woman had a ridiculous sense of self-consequence. Her clothing was more formal and grander than what her three sisters-in-law were wearing and it was evident she spent a good deal of time and money on her appearance.

Portia smiled at her brother-in-law. "I would be delighted to play for you. Does anyone else play?"

"Father insisted we all have lessons but I'm afraid only Mary was worth our poor instructor's patience." Frances's eyes flickered to Stacy, as though she thought he might chastise her for having the audacity to speak in his presence.

"Do you still play?" Portia asked Mary.

Her blushing sister-in-law gave a breathy laugh that was more suited to a girl of eight-and-ten than a woman who must surely be over fifty. "I shan't be playing in front of *you,* Mrs. Harrington, nor . . . er, Eustace." She looked from Frances to Stacy, uncertain what to call her brother.

Again, Portia filled the embarrassed silence. "Stacy is quite accomplished. Perhaps he can be persuaded to play, as well."

"My wife has to say that. She is, after all, my teacher."

The siblings laughed and Stacy looked at Portia and smiled. How oddly competent he was at behaving as though they were a loving, happy couple. Portia wanted to throw her teacup at his head.

"Indeed. Stacy is my most promising student." She smirked to demonstrate that she, too, could behave with amused sophistication.

"You still teach music?" The viscountess could not have

sounded more surprised if Portia had confessed to running naked through the streets of Mayfair.

"My wife is jesting. I am her only pupil and a very demanding one." Stacy gave Portia the first genuine smile she'd seen in a month while his sisters and brother laughed with more enthusiasm than the comment merited. Still, it served to lighten the atmosphere and the seven of them broke into smaller, more conversable groups. Portia found herself with the four women while Stacy and his brother spoke quietly together.

"How are the plans for the nursery progressing?" Frances asked, the yearning in her voice making Portia even angrier at Stacy for banishing the woman from Whitethorn.

"Very well. Nanny helped me pick out the colors for the new drapes and wall hangings and Daisy has been stitching her fingers to nubbins."

"How are Mr. and Mrs. Lawson? Has Jeremy's new assistant arrived?"

"They are well and Jeremy is pleased with the young man who has joined his practice."

Rowena must have decided the conversation had gone on long enough without the mistress of the house contributing.

"Is this a physician you are speaking of?" Something in the way the viscountess said 'physician' made Portia's hackles rise.

"He is also a friend"

"Yes, he is," Frances agreed. "He's the vicar's son."

The viscountess looked amused. "Ah. The vicar's son." She took control of the conversation after that and it revolved around the entertainments she'd planned for their two-week visit. The first week was for family but more guests would arrive the following week. There were to be alfresco parties, dinners with local luminaries added to the pool of guests, shooting for the men, a riding party to the Bishop Caverns, and other activities usual at country house parties.

"His lordship has not been well so we've not had such an entertainment at Thurlstone Castle in years—not since before my arrival," the viscountess told her, an odd gleam in her eyes.

Portia could only assume Stacy's return was the reason for the sudden change and wondered if that irritated the woman.

"A grand ball will take place next week, after the guests have arrived."

As she listened to her sisters-in-law discuss the ball, she realized she did not have a suitable garment.

Frances leaned toward her. "Did you bring a ball gown?"

"I have never owned one. Is there a *modiste* nearby?" The area on the way to the castle had looked as remote as that around Whitethorn.

"We'll take a trip into Plymouth. My sisters and I go to a woman who does lovely work." She shot a glance at the others to ensure they were not listening and then asked, "How is he?"

They both looked at the man in question, who was engaged in a conversation with his brother. A stranger might overlook the subtle signs of tension, but Portia knew him well enough to see the tightness around his mouth and the stiffness in his shoulders. He was far from relaxed.

"He is hurt, but I know he misses you. It will take time." Her words were inadequate but there was not much more she could offer given her own position. "This visit is a very good sign, in my opinion."

"And you? Are you still ill in the mornings?"

"I am no longer sick, but now I eat everything in sight and tire very easily."

"This is your first child, Mrs. Harrington?" The viscountess's voice startled her and Portia looked up to find her rather avid green eyes boring down into her. Why did Portia feel like Lady Rowena was trying to make some obscure point with everything she said?

She decided to see what effect raw honesty would have on the noblewoman's supercilious demeanor. "I've had a disappointment in the past."

Mary and Constance murmured soft platitudes but the viscountess merely raised her pale eyebrows. "I feel certain you will be successful this time. After all, life in the country must be so much healthier than the hectic life you led with your first husband."

What kind of musician did she think Ivo had been—a strolling minstrel?

Portia held the woman's cold green stare. "Yes, life at Whitethorn is quite lovely and relaxing. Are you from this part of England, my lady?"

"My father has a hunting cottage between Thurlstone and Plymouth. It is where I first met Lord Pendleton."

"I wouldn't call it a cottage," Robert said as both he and Stacy came to join the conversation. He smiled at Portia and sat beside her. "The duke's hunting lodge is quite commodious."

The viscountess gave her husband the same coldly amused look she seemed to bestow on everyone. "Pendleton stays with my brothers and father every year for a few weeks, hunting and also spending some time in Plymouth. You rather enjoy Plymouth, don't you, my lord?"

The question was for her husband but her eyes were on Stacy.

Stacy's eyes were . . .well, Portia could not see what he was looking at.

Pendleton gave his wife a formal smile that did not reach his eyes. "I've had some of the best times of my life there."

An awkward silence filled the room while the two spouses held each other's gaze.

Just what is going on?

Robert turned to Portia and broke the spell. "I'm going to steal your husband for a few moments, if you do not mind?"

Portia looked from his smiling face to Stacy's unreadable one.

"As long as you bring him back, my lord."

Harrington chuckled and even Stacy's mouth twitched.

"There is some resemblance between them, is there not?" The viscountess asked as they watched the men depart.

"That is to be expected. They are brothers, after all," Frances said sharply, indicating what Portia had already guessed: that there was no love lost between the two women. Frances turned to Portia with a look that seemed all the more affectionate in contrast. "You must be exhausted, Portia. Would like to rest before dinner?"

"That would be wonderful."

"Come, my dear, let's get you to your chambers." Frances took her arm. "You will soon find your way," she promised as she led her up a particularly grand staircase Portia had no recollection of using before. "I daresay it is you who persuaded Stacy to come."

"No, he was eager to meet his family and I believe he feels your absence keenly." Portia squeezed Frances's hand. "Everyone misses you. I'm afraid managing a household is not one of my skills. I dearly miss you in that regard as well as others."

Frances flushed at the compliment and then stopped in front of a door Portia didn't recognize. "Well, here you are, my dear. Get some rest and I shall see you at dinner."

Daisy was busy in the large dressing room when Portia entered.

"Where have they put you?"

"I couldn't say, ma'am. I doubt I'll ever find my room again. Powell brought me here. Without him I would have wandered for days."

Portia collapsed on the bed without even removing her slippers.

"I'm so tired I'm afraid I might sleep through dinner."

Daisy removed her shoes, lifted her legs onto the bed and pulled a blanket up over her. "Don't you worry, ma'am. I'll wake you in time."

Portia closed her eyes and within seconds the dream started.

It began the same way it always did. She was on the cliff in front of Nanny Kemble's cottage, running and getting nowhere. The sky was dark with rain and her gown was soaked and whipped by the wind. She was looking west and there was Ivo, silhouetted against the sea. She tried to run toward him but her body refused to move. He was standing too close to the edge and she tried to warn him but the wind tore away her words.

Ivo stared at something over her shoulder and shook his head. His large brown eyes were sad and held compassion, a look she'd not seen in them since her father died.

Portia remembered Ivo was already dead and she could not save him. But he had to leave; he had to go back where he belonged. She tried to scream when he took a step into thin air and disappeared over the edge. Only when he was gone could she make a sound.

"*No!*" Her eyes flew open and she lurched upright. She blinked rapidly, her vision blurry; she wasn't on a cliff watching Ivo die, she was in her bed, in Thurlstone Castle.

And she was alone.

Chapter Twenty-Three

BY HIS THIRD day at Thurlstone Stacy realized he genuinely liked his brother. Indeed, it would have been difficult not to. Robert did everything in his power to make their visit enjoyable and comfortable. When Stacy contrasted his brother's behavior with his father's, Robert's kindness was even more noticeable.

Stacy hadn't been expecting much from the man who had banished him at birth and that turned out to be a very good thing. The Earl of Broughton was an old man but the years had done nothing to soften him. At first Stacy thought his father's conspicuous absence was because the old man was ashamed of his behavior; it had taken only a few minutes in the earl's presence to dismiss that thought.

He doubted the earl even knew the meaning of the word shame. Or love. Or kindness. He treated Stacy with the same contempt he displayed toward all his children. Even Robert, his heir, appeared not to merit any interest or kindness. If anything, the earl seemed to like Robert's cold wife best. That didn't surprise him—father-and daughter-in-law were stamped from the same mold: aristocrats more concerned with position than anything else.

Like his sons, the Earl of Broughton was tall and broad-shouldered, or at least he had been. His big frame had been ravaged by time and he was now confined to a wheeled chair. Not even the chair and his bone-thin body could diminish his presence, however. He resembled an ancient falcon that had been hooded but was still dangerous if one came within range of its razor-sharp beak and talons.

His gray eyes were the only part of him that looked alive and they burned with fierce loathing whenever they rested on Stacy. The Earl of Broughton hated him; the realization did not sadden him, but it did confuse him. Why had he disclosed Stacy's existence if he despised him so much? Stacy pondered that question far more than he wished. He knew his father was a twisted, bitter, hateful old man who deserved nothing from him. Yet he was fascinated by him all the same.

The earl might ignore his children, but he was not immune to Portia—at least not to her music.

The second night of their visit Portia played the Beethoven sonata Stacy loved. By the time she was finished there wasn't a dry eye in the room and that included the harsh gray eyes of his parent.

"I say!" Robert exclaimed, clapping his hands hard enough to leave bruises. "You are absolutely brilliant, the best I've ever heard."

Portia accepted his brother's words—the praise of a person who knew next to nothing about music—with a tolerant smile.

Not only had she played magnificently but she looked good enough to eat. She had on the red gown that enflamed him every time she wore it. The red made her hair and eyes look even darker and her skin was the ivory velvet of a magnolia blossom. Around her elegant throat were his mother's pearls. Stacy saw his father's raptor-like eyes rest on the jewels and wondered if he was recalling his long-dead wife.

He'd seen the portrait of his mother—a full-length painting by no less than Gainsborough—his first day at Thurlstone. The portrait had been done only a few months after her marriage to the earl. She hung in the gallery, depicted in life-sized brilliance beside a portrait of the earl. Even at half a century Broughton had been a powerful, formidable man, his lips twisted into a cruel, confident smile, his cold gray eyes scorning the viewer.

The second Countess of Broughton had been fair and fragile with startling blue eyes—heartbreakingly lovely. Stacy was stunned by how extremely young she'd been: only seventeen.

And she'd married the monster who hung beside her, borne him two sons, and then died.

Stacy wondered if she ever knew she'd given birth to twin sons. He hoped for her sake that his demon eyes had not been the last thing she'd seen before dying.

He shook away the disturbing, pointless thought and looked over at his older brother, who rode beside him on an elegant bay hack. They were accompanying the ladies on a shopping trip to Plymouth. The women rode inside the Broughton coach, which rumbled along beside them.

"Let us go with them, Stacy," Robert had said last night when the plan came up at dinner. "I know of a pub in Plymouth where they have remarkable homebrew. I will stand you a pint while I thrash you at darts."

Stacy smiled now as he remembered his brother's boastful threat. Darts were something he'd always enjoyed and played often with Hawkins and the grooms. They kept a board in the barn and had a game or two most weeks. Stacy rarely beat Hawkins, but then his stable master was a pub champion in their part of Cornwall and he'd taught Stacy well.

Pendleton was in for a surprise.

"You've got a mare in foal by your Geist?" Robert asked him, eyeing the big stallion enviously. Robert's mount was a fine piece of horseflesh but could not compare to Geist.

"Yes, it will be her first." Thinking of Snezana always made Stacy recall that night in the stables. He grimaced. The last thing he needed right now was to think of Portia and what had transpired between them that night—or any other time they'd made love. He wasn't sure how much longer he could take the distance between them. Portia seemed to become more remote and resolute by the hour. He'd hoped she would have sought rapprochement by now, but he was beginning to believe it would have to be him—especially after the way he'd behaved in Plymouth. She'd been stubborn before, but his appalling behavior that night had served to make her doubly so.

Stacy knew he should not admire her ability to be more stubborn than he could be, but he did.

"Will you come to town for the Season?" Robert asked, interrupting Stacy's unproductive musings.

"I've never gone in the past."

"Then it is time you *do* come. Surely your wife would like to experience a London Season?"

Stacy had no idea what Portia wanted. Well, other than to make him suffer and eventually come begging.

"Portia enjoys the country."

"But she's lived most of her life in cities. She told me she's been to fourteen European capitals."

Stacy felt a stab of jealousy that she'd never shared that fact with him. He glanced through the carriage window and saw her laughing about something. The sight made his temples ache. What the devil were they doing? They'd already wasted an entire month of their lives engaging in a pointless argument.

"I believe she has things to hold her at Whitethorn," Stacy said. "She has made friends in the area and is also very close with my old nurse. I doubt Portia would want to leave her life in Bude."

"Your nurse lives with you?"

"In a cottage on my land. She came from around here, I believe. I don't know her maiden name but she married a man named Kemble." Thinking about Nanny made him recall how she'd cried with joy when he told her he knew the truth behind his birth. It seemed to have knocked ten years off the old woman's age. She'd never wanted the deception but as an employee had had no choice but to lie. Not like Frances. Stacy's jaw tightened at the thought of his duplicitous sister.

"Hm, Kemble? No, I've not heard that name." Robert sounded uninterested in the provenance of Stacy's nurse and the conversation moved to the topic of Plymouth, each of them apologizing in advance for annihilating the other at darts.

A FEW DAYS after their arrival in Plymouth—where Portia found a particularly lovely mauve silk for her first ball gown—she finally gave in to one of Lady Rowena's many offers to go riding. At first, Portia had begged off going with Rowena, an excellent horsewoman, but she couldn't continue to do so after the viscountess caught her talking about going riding with Frances.

She took a last look in her mirror as Daisy placed the high-crowned riding hat on her head. Her habit, if not her riding skills, was flawless. Stacy had presented her with three outfits when he'd given her Dainty.

The stark black was only relieved by a burgundy cravat that matched the feather in her hat. Portia believed she looked better in her riding habit than any other clothing but that might be because Stacy had selected it for her. It aroused her to think of him taking the time and effort to choose things that would touch her body, even if *he* no longer wanted to do so.

She'd just shut the door to her chambers when she encountered the man who was never far from her thoughts. He must have just returned from his own ride. When he saw her, he stopped in front of his door and looked her up and down, tapping his crop absently against his boot as he did so. Something about his cool inspection set her back up.

"You are going riding?" he asked, his eyebrows arched.

"As you see."

"With whom?"

She resented his tone but refused to let him see her irritation. "Lady Rowena." She turned to go but his voice stopped her.

"The viscountess is a bruising rider, Portia. Make sure you don't let her lead you in above your head."

She swung around. "I appreciate your concern for my welfare, *Stacy*, not to mention your confidence in my riding skill and overall intelligence."

His mouth tightened and the crop stilled. "Must I remind you that it is not only *your* welfare I am concerned with?"

"I believe you just *did*," she snapped, furious at his impassivity, his superior attitude, and the nearly overwhelming desire she felt for him no matter how much she hated him.

He closed the gap between them with two long strides, until their bodies were mere inches apart. She swallowed and took a deep breath, refusing to step back or look away. He smelled of horse, sweat, and leather and it brought to mind vivid memories of their first coupling.

"I should hate to have to restrict your riding privileges, my dear." The words were softly spoken but she heard the threat beneath them. She felt something on her leg and looked down. He was lightly tapping his crop against her thigh. The message was clear: it was he who had the whip hand and she would do well to remember it. Her breath caught at the blatantly dominating gesture and she looked up into his unsmiling face, her eyes reflected back at her.

Her heart was pounding, doing its best to betray the desire she felt for him.

"I should hate to make you issue a restriction I'd be forced to ignore," she said just as softly and then spun on her heel, forcing herself to walk at a leisurely pace when all she wanted to do was run from his brooding stare.

When she reached the stables, it was to find Rowena already mounted on a gray stallion who matched Geist for size, magnificence, and enthusiasm. The woman sat her horse as if she'd sprung fully formed from the saddle.

"Heavens," Portia murmured as the big gray pawed the ground. "Please tell me you've got something a bit less . . . volatile for me?"

The viscountess laughed, the first time Portia had heard her do so. The sound was light and musical but held no warmth or mirth.

"No, I believe Frost would be a bit much for you. I've had Watts saddle Honey. You'll like her; we give her to visiting children. Please excuse me for a moment." She turned away and trotted over to one of the grooms before Portia could reply. That was just as well. What could she say about her ladyship's cutting words when they were true? No doubt all the children who came to Thurlstone already rode far better than she ever would.

The groom led a placid-looking honey-colored horse up to her.

"This is Honey, ma'am. She's a good girl, eh?" This last part he addressed to the horse, who gave Portia a sly look as if to say, *Maybe I am, or maybe I'm not.*

He helped Portia into the saddle and handed up her whip.

Lady Rowena called over her shoulder, "I thought I would take you through our small wood."

They'd hardly left the stables behind when Honey decided to test Portia's mettle, ambling off the trail and grabbing a mouthful of what was probably one of the earl's prize topiaries.

Portia hauled on the reins, but Honey continued chewing her treat. "You *villain,*" she hissed.

Her sister-in-law half-turned, an amused look on her face. "Honey," she said, not even raising her voice. The blasted creature released the shrub and hurried forward.

"Hateful, odious beast," Portia muttered beneath her voice as the horse trotted up beside the other woman's massive horse.

The viscountess glanced down at her. "Don't worry, the ride we'll take today is quite gentle." Her thin lips twisted while her pale eyes glinted. Could that be humor?

Rowena's gray habit was exquisite, just as all her clothes were. Portia wouldn't be surprised to learn she had a habit to match each horse. With her pale skin and light blond hair she looked and rode like a Valkyrie. Portia tried not to hate her but the woman did not make that an easy proposition.

"You did not grow up around horses, Mrs. Harrington?"

"I grew up in Rome. Horses were neither feasible nor necessary." Portia wasn't entirely able to keep the sharpness from her voice. "You, I see, are an expert. You said your father keeps a hunting box; do you hunt?"

"Yes, I quite enjoy hunting."

Portia wasn't surprised to hear it. "Do you go often to your father's property?"

"A few times a year."

"It is close to here?"

"It is almost directly inland from here—in the hunting country, north of Modbury." The viscountess turned away, clearly not interested in making conversation.

Portia couldn't help wondering why the woman had been so insistent on dragging her out riding if she didn't wish to speak to her. No doubt she'd just wanted to humiliate her on horseback. They took a narrow path that led toward the nearby woods. The trees swallowed them up and the castle disappeared from view. The air was humid and heavy and sound was muffled by the lush canopy of greenery. Portia quickly realized the small forest was more extensive than it appeared. Most of it was below the level of the park and sloped toward the stream.

"Do you feel it?" Lady Pendleton asked her.

"Feel it?" Portia repeated.

"This wood is ancient—some of these trees are hundreds and hundreds of years old. Many were here long before the Harringtons and they'll be here after we're gone." Portia could not see her face but her voice throbbed with hushed reverence.

Interesting. Here, it seemed, was something the disdainful daughter of a duke appreciated: land, the badge of the English aristocracy. Before Portia could pursue the topic the viscountess spoke.

"How are you enjoying your visit to Thurlstone so far?"

"Very much, thank you. Your hospitality means a great deal to both my husband and me."

"You must forgive the earl if he seems rather rigid in his behavior. I'm afraid he is not a demonstrative man."

Portia was tempted to point out he was very demonstrative when it came to exhibiting his disdain, but held her tongue. She could well believe this cold woman thought such haughty behavior admirable. Indeed, she was rather *undemonstrative* herself, except when it came to demonstrating scorn.

The path narrowed and the viscountess slowed. "You go ahead of me, Mrs. Harrington. This is wide enough only for one. It is also somewhat steep, but only for a short while."

The branches of the surrounding trees almost touched them and the path sloped sharply. They rode in silence for a few minutes as the trail cut back and forth, zigzagging down the steep hill. The trail had just begun to straighten when the sound of hooves came from behind them.

Portia tensed, hoping the rider would see them before they ended up on top of them. She risked a quick glance behind her even though she was terrified of the steep, narrow path ahead.

"Do you hear—"

"Hallo! Hallo, Portia!" a voice called.

Portia sighed with relief: it was Frances, and the hooves thundered to a halt.

"Frances, what are you doing here?" Rowena asked, sounding irritated.

"I ran into Stacy and he said you were going for a ride with Portia. I thought I'd join you as I missed my usual ride this morning."

Portia couldn't help smiling. So, she'd actually exchanged words with Stacy? Good for Frances! She was about to tell Frances she was glad she'd joined them when she heard a loud *crack* and her hat was torn from her head. Honey reared and made a noise that sounded very much like a baby screaming.

And then she bolted.

Chapter Twenty-Four

PORTIA'S SCREAMS JOINED Honey's as the reins flew from her hands and the horse surged forward. Voices rang out behind her as she fumbled for a handful of Honey's mane. She grabbed for the reins and almost flew over Honey's head. By some miracle she managed to snag one of the reins. She pulled back with all her might but the horse had the bit and no amount of yanking would stop her.

The forest flickered past in a green-brown blur and a low-hanging branch ripped painfully at her hair. She hunkered low just in time to feel Honey gather her strength, bunch her hind legs, and sail over something that lay across the path.

Portia screamed as they flew. She wanted to squeeze her eyes shut but suppressed the foolish urge and stared with wide, tearing eyes as they burst from the woods and entered a gently sloping vale. Emboldened by the lack of obstacles, Honey doubled her speed.

Something wet hit Portia in the face, blotting the vision in one eye and she gripped Honey's mane in one hand and the solitary rein in the other, blinking rapidly to clear her vision.

A dark shape thundered into her peripheral vision and a hand shot out and grabbed Honey's bridle, pulling the horse to a stop so abruptly Portia had to hug the horse's neck to keep from flying over her head.

Portia buried her face in Honey's hot, damp mane until a

strong hand grabbed her shoulder and pulled her upright. She brushed at her eye and saw blood on the York tan glove.

"Are you all right?" Frances's face was white except for two slashes of color over her high cheekbones.

"Blood." Portia held up her hand as if Frances might not believe her without proof.

"It is Honey's, she's been shot. The bullet clipped your hat and hit her ear. That is what set her off."

"Shot?" Portia repeated, her voice sounding oddly sleepy.

Rowena came cantering up on her other side. "Are you hurt, Mrs. Harrington? My heart was in my mouth when I saw you bolt."

Fury distorted Frances's normally impassive features as she whirled on the viscountess. "Somebody shot at her, Rowena."

Rowena flushed at the accusation in the other woman's tone. "It must have been somebody shooting hares or wood pigeons, a poacher. I daresay they never even realized we were there or that anyone had been hit. It looks as though Honey has lost the tip of her ear." Her pale eyes moved from the horse to Portia. "You are extremely fortunate, Mrs. Harrington, the bullet passed less than an inch from your head."

Portia's mouth fell open. Why, in the name of all that was holy, would the woman feel the need to reiterate such a horrible thing?

Frances must have wondered the same thing and made an irritated noise and pushed her horse closer. "I will take you back, Portia. You must be scared witless and poor Honey will need her ear seen to." She turned her back on Rowena and leaned over to grab Honey's reins.

The return trip took forever and the entire way through the woods Portia's scalp itched, as if waiting for another bullet. She was shaking so badly by the time they reached the house the groom had to lift her off the horse.

"Carry her up to the house," Frances ordered.

Portia rebelled at the thought of being carried anywhere. "Oh, no, please, Frances. I am perfectly able to walk. I am just a little shaky but will be fine in a moment." Portia turned to the strapping groom who'd already bent down as if to scoop her up. "I shall be fine, really." She was ashamed by the wobbly sound of her voice.

"I will go and arrange that a bath and tea be sent up immediately," the viscountess said.

Frances watched her depart with a hard look before taking Portia's hand. "Come, Portia, you will feel far better once you are in a nice hot bath."

PORTIA WAS LYING in the bath and wondering if she would ever stop shaking when the door flew open so hard it bounced off the wall.

Stacy crossed the floor in a few long strides, dropped down beside the enormous tub and took her wet soapy hand in his. "Good God! I just heard. Are you all right?"

She thrilled at his worried expression and the unrestrained anxiety in his voice.

"I am unharmed, it is the poor horse who lost a piece of her ear."

Stacy exhaled noisily, as though he'd been holding his breath. He lowered his head and reached up to take off his glasses with a shaking hand. When he looked up, she could see the terror in his arresting eyes. He squeezed her hand so hard it hurt.

"Robert thinks it was a poacher they've been having trouble with lately. He has men combing the woods." He shook his head, his lips thin. "I should never have allowed Lady Rowena to choose your horse. She has no idea of your skill level." He frowned. "But I cannot stay. I should go and help them search. I just wanted to make sure you were unharmed first."

Now that the immediacy of the moment had passed, he looked awkward.

"The child . . ?"

"I do not feel anything amiss, either with the child or myself." She gave him a teasing look, hoping to lighten the mood. "Does this mean I'm forbidden to ride from now on?"

His expression became even haughtier. "It means I'm not going to let you out of my bloody sight."

Portia's mouth fell open. Was he blaming *her* because some idiot poacher shot her horse?

She glared up at him. "That won't be an easy task—not with the connecting door locked and you on the other side of it." Portia wished she could bite off her tongue. The last thing in the world she wanted him to think was that she missed him in her bed, even if it was true. *Especially* because it was true.

He slid his glasses over his eyes. "If you lock the door you'd better expect it to be broken down," he promised, striding from the room.

Portia threw her wash cloth at him but it missed him by several feet and smacked wetly against the wall. "It wasn't me who locked it in the first place!" she yelled, not caring who heard.

His answer was to slam the door.

IN SPITE OF everyone's urging, Portia went down to dinner that night. What was the point of lying around in her room when she was not injured? Besides, she did not feel like being alone. She hated to admit it, but she was horribly shaken by the episode.

Stacy came to her room just as Daisy was leaving. Neither of them spoke and the walk to the dining room seemed to take two hours. It was Stacy who finally broke the silence. "You look beautiful tonight, Portia." He issued the compliment with an aloofness which annoyed her.

"Life-threatening situations must flatter me."

She felt him turn to look at her but she refused to look up at twin reflections of her own face.

"Please tell me you will not make a habit of such situations."

Portia stopped, yanked her hand from his arm, and spun to face him. "I am to tell you that I will not make a habit of being shot at?" She gave him no time to answer the question. "Hmm," she said, taking her chin between thumb and forefinger, as if giving the matter serious consideration. "No," she said. "No, I'm afraid I do not feel comfortable promising that." She turned on her heel and strode down the hall.

"Portia."

She refused to stop.

"Portia, you are going back the way we just came." Even from twenty feet away she could hear the amusement in his voice. She wanted to scream and was sorely tempted to just keep walking. She *would* have kept going but she knew she'd never find her room. She stopped, too furious to turn. Instead, she closed her eyes and counted to ten. A light, warm, touch settled on her arm.

"Come, let us go to dinner before they send out men with dogs and torches. You must know I am not angry with you, Portia. I was merely very frightened." Portia felt herself weakening toward him and took a breath to say something rude. But when she opened her mouth nothing came out.

"Yes?" His voice was close to her ear, his breath warm and ticklish.

She placed her hand on his arm and they resumed their trek. "Did they find anything in the woods?"

"Nothing. No doubt the poacher heard the commotion and hastened to get as far away from the scene as possible."

That was what Portia had expected. It was probably some farmer with a failed crop trying to feed his starving children.

When they reached the drawing room, they found the entire family awaiting the arrival of the other dinner guests and Portia suddenly recalled this was the first dinner they would have with outsiders. She grimaced. Perhaps she *should* have stayed in her room.

Robert approached her without outstretched hands, his forehead furrowed with concern. "I am so sorry this happened to you, Portia, of all people."

Portia laughed. "Well, I suppose there isn't anyone here who *would* have enjoyed it, my lord."

"You're determined to be a good sport about it. That is what your husband said you would do."

Portia shot a startled look at Stacy. The annoying man remained his usual impassive self.

"How is Honey faring? She is the true victim."

"She will be fine, although minus the tip of her ear. No doubt it will lend her a certain gravitas among her fellows. Her bravery will be spoken of in the equine world for decades to come."

Portia bit back a smile. "Perhaps she should append something to her name that proclaims her battle worthiness?"

Robert laughed. "Yes, did not the Vikings distinguish themselves in such a manner?"

"Perhaps something like Honey Cleft-Ear would be suitable," Stacy suggested with a straight face.

The men laughed and Portia shook her finger in admonishment, hardly able to suppress her own laughter. "You are terrible to make fun of my valiant mount."

They were making up additional, equally ludicrous, Viking names when Constance approached them. All Stacy's sisters were shy but Constance was the most retiring.

"Father wonders if you would join him, Mrs. Harrington."

She gave Stacy a fearful look as she delivered her message, as if she were worried that he might insist on joining his wife.

"Will you excuse me?" Portia murmured to Robert and Stacy.

The earl sat in state beside the massive fireplace, his back to his family. He looked up when Portia approached and gestured to the chair a footman had just placed across from him. She sat, able to see not only the earl but the rest of the family behind him. She looked at the old man and they locked eyes. His were a very different color from his son's but they were shapely and long, set deep beneath well-marked brows. There was not even a particle of softness in those eyes. They raked, weighed, and assessed her as efficiently as a piece of meat at the butchers. His mouth curled into a contemptuous smile, as if he'd found something to entertain him.

"I heard your husband play once." His voice was deep and hollow, the clipped consonants elegant.

Portia smiled slightly but did not respond. She loathed what he'd done to his family and the way he was behaving toward Stacy.

He watched her face like a raptor sizing up a potential kill and one corner of his thin mouth twitched. "You are recovered from today's mishap in the west wood." It was not a question.

"I was not hit. The bullet clipped the ear of one of your horses. I daresay she will not forget the incident any time soon."

That drew a sharp bark of laughter. "Horses are stupid creatures, much like most people. They forget what they choose. You are new to riding, Frances tells me. Grew up in Rome, did you?" Something about that seemed to amuse him.

"Yes. My father was Italian but my mother was English. They met while my father was teaching music here in England."

His smile became more derisive. "Married one of his students, eh?"

"Yes. He married the Earl of Marldon's daughter." Portia hated herself for dropping the name of her illustrious relative and trying to impress the supercilious man. Her disclosure made the earl laugh again, but this time it was a bellow that turned into a choking fit.

Constance appeared in an instant, her mouth puckered as though someone had pulled it with a drawstring.

"Father?"

He flapped his hand over his shoulder, not bothering to turn. "Get away! Quit fussing." The words came between gasps. He turned back to Portia, his breathing labored and his expression twice as venomous.

"Marldon had nothing but *females* and hardly two pence to split between 'em." He gloated at the thought of the other peer's surfeit of daughters and impoverished state. "He's dead now. I hear the new earl is not half the idiot the old one was." He saw her face and his expression grew avid. "Did you visit the new earl when you returned to England and impress him with your famous husband?" The notion seemed to tickle him.

"I am not acquainted with the new earl."

He laughed outright this time. "So the new sprig would have nothing to do with you, eh?"

Portia refused to either confirm or deny his accurate reading of the situation but it seemed he didn't need her to carry on a conversation.

"Well, you've done well enough for yourself even without their help, eh? Your new husband has accumulated quite the fortune for himself." Portia heard aristocratic disgust, but it was tempered with pride. Portia's lip curled; as if *he'd* had any hand in Stacy's success.

Again, he seemed to read her as easily as a ledger.

"I don't claim any credit for his situation—nor would I want to. Well, only for the part of me he was lucky enough to inherit, that is." He gave another of his raucous coughing laughs. This time his daughter was wise enough to keep her distance. When he'd ceased hacking, he pinioned Portia with his pitiless gaze. "You will play after dinner for my guests." It was not a request. He chewed the inside of his mouth, the action an unprecedented show of emotion, although Portia knew not which one. He glared at her like a magistrate judging a felon. "It is my opinion your playing puts Stefani's to shame." The words were grudging and he looked pained to have uttered them.

Portia felt one of her eyebrows arch in response to his unwillingly bestowed accolade.

He saw the expression and snorted.

"Why, thank you, my lord." Portia didn't bother keeping the ironic amusement from her tone.

Just then the first visitors were announced and the Earl of Broughton turned his chair away from her.

The interview was over.

STACY COULD NOT take his gaze from his wife's usually expressive face as she spoke with his father. But, for once, he could read nothing. He guessed this was what she looked like when she spoke to a stranger—a stranger she did not much care for.

He also realized she'd never turned such an expression on him. When she spoke to Stacy, she showed what she was feeling: anger, fury, passion, lust, affection, concern, pain. Her openness was—he now understood—a gift she gave to him. It was also a gift he was singularly ill-equipped to handle. He'd never been the recipient of any great passion before, nor had he felt any. Until now.

"Don't worry, Stacy, your wife will be able to manage him," Robert said in a low voice. Neither of them could take their eyes from the unprecedented sight of their father having a *tête-à-tête* with anyone. Stacy looked at his brother and saw a wrinkle between his friendly blue-gray eyes, as if he didn't quite believe his own words.

"I have every confidence in her," Stacy said. And he did. He'd never lacked for admiration or respect when it came to Portia. He just wished he trusted her.

PORTIA WAS SEATED between a local squire and a rather handsome widowed baron. Conversation with both men was lively and, after her uncomfortable grilling by the earl, pleasant.

Stacy sat at the far end of the long table between two blushing young women. Over the course of the meal Portia watched them go from terrified awe of the pale god between them to competing for his attention and rare smiles. Her husband looked magnificent. He wore a waistcoat she'd never seen before, ivory silk embroidered with pale violet roses, the same shade as his eyes. He wore his dark spectacles, which seemed to be causing an almost paralyzing giddiness among the women. Portia looked at his elegant, chiseled profile as he bent his head to listen to one of them and realized her jaw was clenched. She lowered her eyes and swept the table beneath her lashes. The only person looking at her was her father-in-law, who was watching her with gleeful amusement.

Portia scowled at the extremely unpleasant old man and turned her attention to her food.

Once the last course had been removed, the women left the men to their port and retired to the big drawing room that connected to the music room.

The viscountess hovered beside her before she could sit. "I trust you are recovered enough to play for our guests tonight, Mrs. Harrington?"

Portia had asked the woman to call her by her first name at least a half-dozen times. "Of course, my lady, have you anything particular in mind?"

"I'm sure your taste is far superior to mine in such matters." The viscountess's eyes flickered over her dark blue gown as if to say Portia's taste needed to be superior in *some* way. Portia almost applauded her performance. She really was a virtuosa when it came to casting aspersions with a smile on her face.

"Most of the house guests begin to arrive tomorrow?" Portia asked, hoping the harmless question might cause the woman to sheath her ever-ready claws.

"Yes. We shall have a full house over the next few days." She gave a laugh that contained no humor. "Well, not entirely full. Thurlstone contains many rooms which are, I'm afraid, no longer habitable."

The admission surprised her. Not only did the castle look well-maintained, but the haughty duke's daughter did not seem like the kind of woman who would admit to either a lack of perfection or the money to achieve that state.

"I would love to see the house."

Her sister-in-law's thin lips twitched into an indulgent smile. "Perhaps I could give you a tour tomorrow?"

First the horse ride and now this? Maybe the woman really *was* trying to be friendly but didn't know how.

"That would be lovely, if you are not too busy preparing for your guests."

"I have servants to see to all that, Mrs. Harrington." The words were spoken gently but the meaning was clear: If you were not such plebian speck you would know that.

Portia almost laughed at the stunning set-down.

Frances approached with the two young women who'd been flirting with Stacy at dinner.

"Portia, I'd like to introduce Lady Elizabeth, the Duke of Beaconridge's daughter and Miss Jennings, Sir Jerome Staunton's daughter. Lady Elizabeth is visiting Miss Jennings."

Curtseys were exchanged all around.

"We are *very* excited to hear you are going to play for us tonight, Mrs. Harrington," Lady Elizabeth gushed, her soft brown eyes glowing with admiration. Well, here was *one* duke's daughter who did not radiate contempt for lesser beings.

"Do you play, Lady Elizabeth?" Portia asked the obligatory question, resigning herself to spending the next ten minutes engaged in a conversation that moved as torpidly as a carp.

"I adore the piano! My piano instructor says I am the most promising of his pupils."

Portia could imagine. She'd frequently told the same lie, particularly after Ivo left and her pool of pupils began to shrink. It was Portia's experience that a student's skill was usually inversely proportional to their wealth.

"Perhaps you will play for us tonight?" Portia asked, aware she'd said the correct words when Lady Elizabeth smiled enchantingly.

Portia could not recall how it felt to blush in such innocuous circumstances. Once you'd begged a man to fuck you, most other situations seemed tame by comparison. Her lips twitched at the thought.

"Oh, I couldn't," Lady Elizabeth demurred, looking at the viscountess expectantly.

"You absolutely must, my dear. You can play something before Mrs. Harrington entertains us." The not very subtle point of her suggestion being it would be a disaster to go *after* Portia. Lady Elizabeth's thoughtful frown made her look like rather like a kitten that had just been kicked.

Rowena turned to Miss Jennings. "And you, Miss Jennings?"

Miss Jennings, unlike her friend, was no fool. "I hurt my wrist riding the other day."

"Oh? Was that the day I saw you riding Thunder?"

Miss Jennings blushed. "Yes, I knew I shouldn't have, but

Jonathan dared me."

Rowena laughed and it almost sounded genuine. "You should never let a brother lead you into imprudence, my dear."

Miss Jenkins's rather plain features twisted with mortification. "I know, but he is so dreadfully teasing." She stopped, her expression becoming more serious. "I say, just after we saw you, we ran across a rather frightening man in the woods. Did you see him, too?"

"Frightening?"

"Yes, a stout, lurching sort of man. He was headed in your direction."

"No doubt it was just another trespasser who'd gotten lost in the woods looking for the path to the old flint mine."

"Oh yes, we are always discovering them crawling about our land. Father believes the old mines should not be mentioned in guidebooks. He says it attracts the wrong sort."

Portia found it difficult to keep from laughing at the notion that guidebook-toting tourists were "the wrong sort."

The men entered the drawing room and Lady Elizabeth as well as two other females were prevailed upon to play. Stacy, naturally, declined to play when his sister-in-law approached him. Portia knew it was not worry that his father would sneer that stopped him, but that her husband played only for those he liked.

The footmen opened the doors to the music room and the guests arranged themselves on the various settees and chairs. Portia found herself seated beside her brother-in-law on the small sofa she'd chosen at the back of the room. Stacy was seated between Miss Jennings and a woman who could only be her mother. Both women wore nervous, pleased grins, their bums barely resting on the settee, as if they were too excited to sit. Stacy turned in her direction but his expression didn't alter. Even so, Portia could practically hear his thoughts.

"Stacy looks resigned," Lord Pendleton said.

"You have learned to read him quickly, my lord. Most people have difficulty seeing past his façade."

"Yes, he does look rather like a marble statue, doesn't he?"

Portia was tempted to tell him that he sometimes behaved like one.

Instead she said, "It is deceptive, my lord. He has an exceptionally warm and generous heart, although, like most men, he would shudder to hear himself described thus."

The viscount laughed. "You have us poor males properly sorted, I see."

Portia did not answer as the playing had begun. They listened in silence for a few moments before Pendleton leaned toward her and whispered. "Is this painful for you, Mrs. Harrington?"

It was, but Portia was not rude enough to say so. "Are you worried I might rush across the room and smack her knuckles with a ruler, my lord?"

He snickered. "I was more concerned you might suffer some sort of aural hemorrhage."

"You are very cruel, my lord. Besides, my eardrums are as hardened as a rake's conscience."

His body shook with suppressed laughter and it was a few moments before he spoke. "Won't you please call me Robert? I feel like I know you after listening to Stacy talk of you."

Portia's eyes moved to her husband. Although she could not see them, she felt his eyes on her.

"I would be honored, Robert. You must call me Portia."

"Your name suits you down to the ground, Portia."

Portia again wondered why a man as pleasant and affectionate as Robert had sought the hand of such a frosty woman. And then she dismissed the foolish thought. Naturally he'd married at his father's direction. It was clear the earl thought Rowena the perfect broodmare, although one could not help wondering what he felt about his son's childless state. Was that because they could not stand to bed one another? Portia could not recall a single instance when she'd seen the two speaking to each other. It did not look like a happy marriage but, then again, neither was hers just now.

They listened to the remainder of Lady Elizabeth's competent but uninspired performance in respectful silence. The two women who followed her were much the same. Neither would lead an audience to tears—either from joy or agony.

Rowena stood up. "We will have a brief intermission before Mrs. Harrington entertains us."

"What will you play, Portia?" Robert asked, leaning close to her on the small settee.

"What would you like me to play, Robert?" She echoed his teasing, flirtatious tone.

"What do you have music for? Will that not decide the matter?"

His naïveté charmed her. Portia could play for twelve hours without opening her eyes. So could any musician worth their salt. "I've committed a few things to memory. What do you like?"

"Bach?" he said with a hopeful smile.

"I believe I can accommodate your request."

Stacy approached and held a glass toward her. "I thought you might enjoy something to sustain you."

Portia took the glass of lemonade. "Thank you."

He turned to his brother. "Sorry old man, I should have brought you a brandy."

Robert grinned. "I want nothing that will dull my senses. I wish to be astoundingly alert when Portia plays. She has allowed me to choose the music."

Stacy's brows rose at his brother's use of her Christian name.

Portia sensed an odd tension between the two men, as though they'd gone a lifetime without brotherly competition and were now taking up their roles with a vengeance. She'd heard them taunting one another about the dart games they'd played in some

Plymouth pub. They had been playful but there was rivalry beneath the laughter.

A footman rolled her father-in-law's chair to a halt not far from them and Portia realized he'd not been in the room for the earlier playing. The man really was objectionable and took no pains to hide it. He glanced over at her and gave her a sneering smile, as if he'd heard her thoughts.

Portia ignored him and turned to the other guests, all of whom were taking their seats and looking expectant. She handed Stacy her glass and stood. She never felt nervous performing, whereas Ivo became so sick before some of his performances it had been unclear whether he'd be able to go on. Of course he'd played before monarchs all over Europe, not in family drawing rooms.

Portia surveyed her small audience. "I've had a request for Bach."

She sat at the piano, stretched her hands, closed her eyes, and played.

STACY COULD HARDLY tear his eyes away from his wife long enough to look at the faces in the room. His brother was thoroughly captivated and Stacy could not blame the man, especially given the iceberg he'd married.

The desiccated old man in the wheeled chair sat with his eyes closed, a beatific expression on his gaunt, age-ravaged face. The quote *"music hath charms to soothe a savage breast,"* came to mind. Not that the old bastard deserved soothing of any kind: physical, spiritual, or emotional. A twinge of shame shot through him at the uncharitable thought and Stacy ruthlessly suppressed it. The Earl of Broughton deserved no pity and surely did not want any.

He turned away from the bitter old man and back to the piano, the usual chaos of emotions assaulting him as he studied his wife: admiration, pride, frustration, possession, lust, desire, regret, and on and on.

Portia looked magnificent. She wore dark blue tonight and the color created yet another version of her. Red turned her into human fire but this dark shade of blue made her precision and grace personified. Her arms were delicate yet strong, drawing notes of surpassing beauty from the instrument before her. He drank in her gently sloping shoulders, her elegant throat, and her distinctive, kissable nose. Stacy's body heated and his vision blurred; as usual, he became hard just looking at her.

He would end the foolishness between them tonight. The door between their rooms would not remain locked any longer. He felt eyes on him and turned. His father was staring at him. It was perhaps the first time he'd looked the man square in the face. The amount of malice he saw took his breath away. This man—his father—*hated* him.

For the first time Stacy truly understood: there would be no tender father-son reconciliation; there would be no apology forthcoming for his banishment; there would only be unrelenting loathing. This was a man who'd discarded his own child the way other people discarded rubbish. How could Stacy ever expect anything other than contempt from such a person? He smiled at the foolish thought and saw his father recoil, as if he'd not imagined such a freak was capable of humor.

When Portia's final notes settled over the room the applause was deafening for such a modestly sized audience. Even the earl raised his hands for a few seconds.

"She is *magnificent*!" Robert sprang to his feet, his eyes blazing with admiration.

Stacy smiled up at his older brother, yet another man who'd fallen under Portia's spell. Well, he thought, rising to his feet beside him, who could blame the man for showing excellent taste?

Chapter Twenty-Five

PORTIA HAD JUST given her earrings to Daisy to put away when the connecting door to Stacy's room opened and her husband entered. He'd not yet undressed as they'd just come from the drawing room minutes before.

"Would you please excuse us, Daisy?"

Daisy dropped a hurried curtsey before leaving.

Stacy gestured to the door through which he had come. "Will you join me in the sitting room, Portia?"

The elegant sitting room attached to his suite had a fire burning and Portia took the chair that was closest; she was always cold.

Stacy went to pour a drink. "Do you care for any brandy? Or should I ring for something else—milk?"

"Not tonight."

He took the seat across from her and stretched out his long legs. Her eyes were drawn to the flexing muscles beneath the snug-fitting pantaloons, her hands itching to touch him.

He took a sip and then set down his glass. "I would like to put an end to the strain between us, Portia. I know you were acquainted with the Italian man who died in Bude. Who was he to you?"

HER LIPS PARTED and Stacy realized he'd surprised her. Indeed, he'd surprised himself with his directness. Her skin flushed a shade of red that shrieked of guilt.

"It was Ivo."

He snorted and momentarily closed his eyes before facing her. "Why did you not tell me this before?" All the fury and fear he'd held in check for weeks broke free.

Rather than look contrite Portia's eye's blazed at him. "Because I was ashamed, Stacy, that is why."

"Ashamed your husband was alive?" Ashamed was not the word he would have chosen. Appalled or stunned he could have understood—even overjoyed, although he wouldn't have liked it—but ashamed?

"Ashamed he *wasn't* my husband!"

Stacy realized his mouth was open and shut it.

"I can see what you are thinking," she accused.

"What a wonderful skill you possess, Portia. But have you ever thought you might sometimes *misread* my mind?" Stacy had no interest in her answer. "Would you please do me the honor of explaining what happened before condemning me?" He was one step away from escorting her back to her room and locking the damn door.

For a moment he thought she might do the same thing—after hurling something at his headfirst—but she sighed.

"The explanation is simple, if sordid. Ivo was married before we met. I did not know this until his first wife—his legal wife—came to England to find him. Ivo claimed he'd believed her dead or he never would have married me." She snorted. "It made no difference to me what he knew or when he knew it. The only thing that mattered was that it would destroy me if it were made public. So, I gave him the tiny bit of money I'd saved and he promised to change his name and leave quietly and never, ever come back to England.

"We agreed I'd wait a few months and then claim he'd died

during the War. I knew how the news of his death would damage the school so I was in no hurry. And then, a few weeks after he departed, I read about the shipwreck. The paper listed the names of those who'd died and Ivo's assumed name was among them. Part of me could not believe it, but there it was, in print."

She smoothed her skirt over her lap, the motion abrupt. "I didn't bother to spread the story—the newspapermen would have seized on it like ducks on breadcrumbs and the school, already in trouble, would have collapsed. Oh, I know I should have told the truth when I closed the school but it was hardly a priority." She pulled her eyes away from the past and looked at him, her creamy cheeks tinting. "I never told you this, but I had less than two pounds when I showed up at Whitethorn. I was truly desperate."

Her full lips compressed into a grim line but she continued. "Ivo turned up at Whitethorn not long after we married. He claimed his wife died in the shipwreck." Portia shrugged. "Maybe she did, maybe she didn't. Who knows? He said he would tell you we were still married and that you would never believe me because he had our marriage lines." Her eyes flickered around the room as if she sought the words. "Even without such damning proof I doubted you would believe me. After all, you and I were just beginning to know each other." She exhaled and tipped her head back, staring at the ceiling.

Stacy studied the column of her throat and his heart ached for her. It was everything he could do not to take her in his arms. But he wanted to hear the rest of her story—no matter how much he dreaded it.

"I could not take the risk you might believe him, so I paid him the money and he promised to leave. I knew he would probably come back but I thought the next time he came our marriage would be . . . stronger.

"I took the jewels to Plymouth in case I did not have enough money in the account you created for me." She gave him a wry smile. "I'm afraid I did not listen when we discussed the settlement you generously bestowed on me." Her smile disappeared. "I returned the jewels to the safe that night after paying Ivo the two thousand pounds."

Stacy sucked in a breath at the sum and held it for a long moment before letting it out slowly.

Portia continued. "Whoever found Ivo's body must have taken the money. Or perhaps he showed it to someone and that was why he was killed. I don't know. Two thousand pounds would be enough to tempt anyone."

"Is that . . . all?"

Her eyes came back into focus and she arched her shapely brows. "Are you asking if there are there *more* non-husbands I haven't told you about? Or are you asking if I am the one who shoved him off the cliff?" She stood and closed the distance between them before sinking gracefully to her knees beside his chair. "I should not jest; the subject is not funny. I am *so* sorry I did not tell you. I was scared at first and stupidly lied to you. And then I became hurt and furious at you for treating me so coldly and my temper seized control." She took his hand. "I calmed down and was about to confess everything and then Ivo's body was discovered. Given what you saw that night, I was even more terrified of what you might think." She squeezed his hand. "I should have confessed everything even though I was ashamed. But my temper—" she shrugged, her expression one of resignation.

Stacy looked down at her glossy dark hair, warm brown eyes, and lush pink mouth and became as aroused as he always did whenever she was near.

"I'm sorry about deceiving you, but Ivo was such an accomplished liar, I just thought—" she bit her plump lip. "I swear I won't keep anything from you again." She slid one hand from his knee up his thigh, her eyes holding his, one eyebrow arched, as though daring him to stop her. "Do you forgive me?"

"Of course I forgive you—I only wish you'd trusted me. I also owe you an apology for my stubborn, childish behavior, and also for how I acted at the inn. Do you forgive me?"

She chuckled. "I forgive you for part of it."

Stacy knew this discussion was far from over, but he was a besotted fool and powerless to stop her wicked, questing hand as she reached for him.

STACY COLLAPSED BESIDE her after a particularly impressive display of sexual prowess, his hair damp and curly around his face, his chest slick with sweat.

"What do you think of my brother and his wife?" he asked, his chest heaving.

Portia eyed his nipples; something about their diminutive size was irresistible. She lowered her mouth and suckled one for a moment while his body stiffened and she considered his question.

Stacy groaned. "I'm an old man, darling. I need some time."

She reluctantly released the hard pebble and rested her chin on his chest. "Your brother is lovely. Warm, handsome, amusing, intelligent—"

"Thank you, that is quite enough," he interrupted, punctuating his point with a sharp spank on her bare bottom.

"You didn't let me finish, my jealous husband." She wiggled her bottom against the hand now resting there. "I was about to say that, despite all that, he could not hold a candle to my own Harrington male."

"That's better," he grumbled.

"You are happy we came?"

"Yes, I am happy. I am enjoying getting to know Robert and my sisters—although that is not easy given their reserved natures."

Portia smiled at that, thinking of her husband's reserved nature. "And Frances? Have you forgiven her?" She felt him stiffen at the question, and not in a good way.

"I'm trying, Portia."

She let the subject be.

He tilted his chin down until their eyes met. "And you? Are you glad you came?"

"I am. I like your brother and sisters, very much. Although your father . . ." she stopped.

"Yes, let us agree to avoid speaking of my father."

Portia knew it was cowardly, but she was grateful to leave the subject of the earl untouched—for now.

"And Lady Pendleton?" Stacy asked.

"Ah, the viscountess . . . I believe she is trying to be accommodating and welcoming but I think the experience is novel. I can only suppose her life as the daughter of a duke lacked any training in the area of pleasing mere commoners."

"I think you've accurately summed up our proud sister-in-law. I don't think Robert and his wife like each other, sometimes it feels as if it might even go beyond dislike."

Portia thought they hated each other but kept that thought to herself. "I believe that is common among the aristocracy. If you'd been raised within your father's grasp then you, too, would most likely be wedded to the appropriate article." She ran a single finger from his nipple to the tantalizing line of white hair that ran over the taut muscles of his abdomen toward his slumbering organ. She lightly dragged a finger over the astonishingly soft skin on the crown and he leapt against her hand and she laughed.

He plunged a hand into her hair, wrapping a length of it around his fist and forcing her to meet his eyes. "And what type of article are *you*, Mrs. Harrington? I'll bet you were the kind of little girl who enjoyed teasing all the boys. Did you? Did you eat sweets in front of them without sharing? Promise them kisses and then run away? Yes, I would wager that you reveled in such diabolical and wholly female behavior."

She gave him an innocent, wide-eyed stare. "I was the ideal child. Perfect in every way."

"Just as you are the perfect wife?" He laughed and she nipped his chin.

And then she lowered her mouth over his swiftly hardening shaft and showed him—yet again—just how ideal and perfect she was.

WHEN PORTIA WOKE the following morning, she was alone in bed. She was also sore in places she'd never realized could be sore. They'd been like a pair of starving castaways who'd stumbled upon a banquet, pulling every last ounce of pleasure from each other's bodies and then returning for second and third helpings. In between bouts both savage and tender they'd talked as they'd never done before, neither of them sleeping much in their eagerness to make up for lost time.

Portia was smirking to herself and reliving the evening when Daisy entered. The state of her bedroom spoke louder than words and Daisy gave her a huge smile; well, at least the servants were happy again.

"Mr. Harrington said I should let you sleep, ma'am. Would you like breakfast in your room?"

Portia glanced at the bedside clock and saw it was almost eleven. She was to meet Rowena for a tour of the castle at one.

"I'd better be up and about. Do you know where Mr. Harrington went?" She stepped into the robe her maid held out for her and went to sit at her dressing table so Daisy could untangle her hair before she bathed.

"Powell said the master left earlier with his lordship." Daisy began the long, painful process of brushing out the knots. Her hair was quite coarse and Portia had hated it until lately, when Stacy couldn't seem to resist playing with it and wrapping strands of it around parts of his body.

"I think I'll wear the new burgundy dress, Daisy. Have you heard anything about who will be arriving today?" Portia had spent enough time hovering between the servants' hall and the upper levels of various houses to realize servants always knew the comings and goings better than the master or mistress of the house.

Daisy took the hair pins she'd held clamped between her teeth and laid them on the dresser's glossy surface.

"I believe there will be nine couples and four singles." Her voice dropped to a whisper. "There is quite a bit of worry about Lady and Lord Kenwich. They had a mad row the last time they visited and threw the entire contents of a tea tray at one another."

Portia laughed. "Goodness. A passionate pair, are they?"

"Aye, but not about one another." Daisy's eyebrows were near her hairline.

It was a little after twelve by the time Daisy had her dressed and ready for the world. Portia arrived in the breakfast room and found only Rowena eating.

"Good morning, my lady." Portia smiled at her sister-in-law and then turned to one of the numerous footmen. "Could I have a glass of milk, please?"

"Milk?" Rowena repeated once the footman had gone, her expression scandalized, as though Portia had ordered a floating island and a magnum of champagne. Predictably, the viscountess was sipping black tea and eating dry toast, which no doubt was how she maintained her trim figure. "I don't believe I have ever seen an adult drink milk."

"My husband is a bit of a tyrant and says the proper diet for a woman in my condition includes milk. Lots of milk."

The viscountess frowned at that information, and then chose

to ignore it. "Are you ready to see Thurlstone today?"

"I am looking forward to it. Frances tells me you are quite the expert on the castle. Did you grow up in a house like this?"

"There is no other house like Thurlstone." Her voice held an odd, almost fierce, intensity. "My father's seat is Bent Park, not far from Chelmsford. It is a Tudor structure." She set down her empty cup and motioned for a footman to remove it before she stood. "I'm afraid I must leave you now. Shall we meet in the long gallery at one?"

Portia watched her stiff figure disappear, grateful the woman was gone. No matter what subject she raised with the viscountess it always felt awkward and hostile. She felt genuine sympathy for her brother-in-law—not to mention the three sisters who would need to live on her bounty when Lady Pendleton eventually became mistress of Thurlstone.

Portia dawdled over her breakfast and read the paper. When she finished eating it was time to make her way to the long gallery, where she perused portraits of long-dead Harringtons while she waited. The room had been designed to awe visitors and descendants alike. Sun filtered through the stained glass of massive mullioned windows, which allowed in light to illuminate the room but not enough to damage the precious paintings that covered every square inch of the wood-paneled walls. Portia had grown up in Rome, where buildings far grander than this had been common when the Harringtons' ancestors had still been painting themselves blue and fighting with sticks. Even so, it was one thing to view such opulence in a public setting but quite another to realize you'd married into it.

Portia was examining a pair of young girls dressed in the fashion of the early seventeenth century when she heard footsteps behind her.

She turned to find Frances and gave her sister-in-law a genuine smile. "What a pleasant surprise." Portia gestured to the identical girls. "Do you know who these young ladies are?"

"Those were the twin sisters of Charles Harrington, the fifth earl. I believe their names were Constance and Faith, two family names. They never married," she added. "I will find you a book my great uncle James Harrington wrote on the history of the family." She smiled fondly. "He was still alive and living here when I was a young girl. He never married and spent his entire life in the east wing. After he died, we found hundreds of bundles of foolscap, all the books he'd worked on during his lifetime but never showed to anyone. I had his book about the family portraits bound." Her pale cheeks stained, as if she was embarrassed by her enthusiasm on the subject. "I came to see if you wished to go to the summer pergola. This is not the best year for it, but there will be some beautiful foliage."

"Could we could go a little later? I'm meeting Lady Rowena in a few minutes for a tour of the castle."

Frances's mouth tightened at the sound of her sister-in-law's name. "I daresay you've only seen the wing in which you are staying and this addition?"

"When was this added?" Portia gazed up at the soaring ceiling and ornate crossbeams.

"This is late gothic, I believe 1537. The oldest part of the building dates to the eleventh century, and then there are ruins that run down to the cliff closest to the sea. That collection of tumbled down masonry is what is left of the Saxon stronghold."

The sound of clapping made Portia jump.

"Brava, Frances." Rowena's voice came from the far end of the hall. "You really *are* an expert on this house and everything Harrington. I do believe you must know all the family secrets." Rowena's smile was mocking as she turned to Portia. "Are you ready for your tour, Mrs. Harrington?" The viscountess's hard green eyes made Portia regret promising to spend more time than necessary in her presence.

She glanced at Frances; her face looked as though it were carved from stone. "Shall we meet after my tour, Frances?"

"I believe I shall tag along," Frances spoke to Portia but her eyes were on Rowena. "It has been a long time since I've looked at the old north wing. Perhaps Rowena will be able to teach *me* something about the castle as she's been working toward its restoration."

Rowena inclined her head. "As you wish."

An hour into Rowena's tour Portia was grateful to have eaten such a large breakfast. The rambling house was comprised of endless warrens and dark hallways, many of which smelled of damp and decay.

"I've lost track of the rooms," she said as they looked at a third set of state apartments. This one occupied by Queen Elizabeth for two weeks in 1559, with her alleged lover, Robert Dudley, staying only two doors away.

"We are some thirty rooms shy of being a 'calendar house,'" Frances said, frowning while examining the corner of a rotting tapestry that hung behind the bed where Elizabeth had slept.

"Calendar house?"

"Yes, like Knole House, in Kent, or the Duke of Plimpton's family seat, Whitcomb House—a house that has a room for every day of the year."

"I feel like I've been through at least that many," Portia murmured. She wished they would leave the state apartments, which were decayed and depressing and made one think of better days.

"We can finish the tour in the minstrel's gallery. From there it is convenient to go back to the main house through the east wing," Rowena said over her shoulder as she led them down a particularly dank hallway which opened into a spectacular rotunda the size of a large ballroom.

"How lovely," Portia breathed. The spherical room had a dizzyingly intricate black-and-white floor and an ornate balcony that wrapped around the walls about three-quarters of the way up to the ceiling. An enormous rose window illuminated the room like a blazing chandelier. She could imagine the scene: the minstrels arrayed in a semicircle on the balcony and playing for their wealthy, powerful patrons below. The guests would dance roundels and voltas while the musicians observed their peccadillos and machinations from afar.

"Oh no, look at this, Frances." Emotion pulsed in the viscountess's voice as she examined one of the casement windows that looked out over the knot garden. Portia could see several panes of glass were broken. While the two women examined the windows Portia went up to look at the minstrel's gallery. As she climbed the narrow rickety stairs, she realized it would be a miserable trek for those carrying heavy instruments. When she reached the balcony, she saw remnants of once spectacular tapestries hanging from the walls, concealing storage nooks cut into the stone wall. There had been no pianos in those days, but perhaps there might still be a harpsichord or virginal. She'd only walked five or six steps when a blood-curdling scream stopped her in her tracks.

Chapter Twenty-Six

"PORTIA *STOP*! THAT section of the balcony is extremely unstable."

Portia froze, her heart in her throat.

Frances wheeled on Rowena. "What happened to the barricade I had Thompson put up last year?" She didn't wait for Rowena's answer before striding toward the stairs. "Just stay right there and don't move. That newel post near you is rotted, so don't touch it. Now, if you look down you'll see there are some broken slats beneath your feet."

Portia looked down and then wished she hadn't. It wasn't far to the ground, but she became dizzy looking at the open air beneath her feet. How had she missed it? There were dozens of gaps, some as large as an inch, places where the decorative parquet had splintered and fallen away, exposing either the blackened beams below or open air.

"Can you reach that section near the wall?" Frances pointed to the spot she meant; she'd come up the stairs, stopping a few steps shy of the balcony.

The floor right in front of Portia looked the worst, but just beyond that it appeared solid, so she nodded. "I can reach it if I take a very large stride."

Frances raised a staying hand. "No, don't do that." She looked down at Rowena. "Get Thompson and tell him to bring the tallest ladder, a good length of rope, and two footmen—the biggest.

Hurry, Rowena!" She turned back to Portia. "Stay as still as you can, she'll be back soon and we'll take you down by ladder."

They listened to Rowena's footsteps recede until there was nothing.

Portia couldn't have moved if she'd wanted to; her body was rigid with fear. She might come away from the fall with nothing more than broken bones but it could kill her baby. She swallowed and exhaled slowly.

"Tell me something to take my mind off this, Frances. Tell me what it was like growing up here."

"Our mother was wonderful. She was mad for horses and had us all in the saddle almost before we could walk. It was how my mother had been raised and she argued with our father about letting us roam the property without a groom." Frances smiled. "She was the only person who ever argued with him."

Even in the grip of fear, Portia ached at how haggard Frances looked.

"I never had a Season." She gave a short, unhappy bark of laughter. "Who would look twice at a woman my size other than to stare? So when the opportunity came to take Stacy I seized my chance to raise a child. It was not easy at times, and it made my heart bleed to watch other children shun or taunt him. He was always strong and cheerful, but I knew he suffered. I worried that a part of him died when he overheard that dreadful Penelope call him a freak while gossiping with her friends."

Something odd flickered across her face. "What my father did was wrong—beyond wrong, criminal—but I want you to understand that none of us had a choice. Constance and Mary should have had their chances to find husbands but they were needed here to raise Robert." She lifted her shoulders, shrugging beneath ancient, heavy burdens. "I will never forgive my father for rejecting his own son but I can't regret my life with Stacy. He is my brother, but I love him like my own child."

Portia understood something about the love Frances was feeling now that she was standing fifteen feet above a marble floor, her mind fixed on only one thing: saving the life inside her.

"He loves you too, Frances. I know he will—"

A low, ominous groaning sound vibrated through the rotted boards beneath her and she screamed, reaching out for the balustrade by reflex.

"*Portia! No—*

The structure beneath her shivered almost lazily and the staccato snapping of wood cracking filled the air. The heel of her right foot tilted back and Portia staggered, the railing breaking like a dry twig as the parquet beneath one foot disappeared.

Later, when she would try to recall what happened, Portia couldn't remember Frances grabbing her arm. The older woman must have moved like lightning to get up the crumbling stairs as the balcony disintegrated beneath Portia's feet.

Frances held her in arms like iron bands and the two of them slipped and fell through crumbling steps before coming to an abrupt halt on a third step. The stop was bone-jarring and Portia bit her tongue, her mouth flooding with blood.

Above them, the balcony screamed like a wayward child and then pulled away from the wall with the ponderous slowness of a giant.

Portia pressed her body against the wall but skidded down another couple steps as the stairs pulled away from the wall. Frances tried to keep her upright, but they both slipped and staggered drunkenly as step after step collapsed beneath them.

Portia's feet struck marble with another bone-jarring *thump* and Frances fell backward, pulling Portia down on top of her.

The deafening shriek of twisting wood that filled the room was followed by a moment of ominous silence as the balcony teetered almost gracefully.

And then four hundred years of wood, stone, and metal

crashed against unforgiving marble. Plaster, dust, and pulverized wood rose from the floor like a filthy snowstorm. A resilient newel post hit the ground, bounced high into the air, and struck the wall less than a foot from her head, sending chips of plaster flying. Portia and Frances screamed and wrapped their arms around their heads as debris ricocheted around them like artillery.

The room became silent almost as suddenly as it had exploded and Portia forced her eyes open; a thick cloud of fine powder obscured the room, clinging to her eyelashes and plugging her nostrils. She clamped a hand over her mouth and fanned her face with the other, as if that might dissipate the haze.

"Portia? Frances?"

It was Stacy's voice, or at least Portia thought it was. Her head was ringing so loudly it was a miracle she could hear anything.

"We're over here," Frances called in a raw voice.

"Stay where you are. I'll come to you."

It seemed like a year but was probably closer to a minute before the dust in front of her shifted to reveal a pale and beloved face.

He dropped down beside her and Portia broke, sobbing out his name. "Stacy!"

His arms went around her so tightly he squeezed a squeak out of her. They were still holding each other when the men Rowena went to fetch arrived and began opening doors and windows to clear out the choking dust.

Other than some bruises and shaking so badly she could barely stand, Portia appeared unharmed.

Stacy molded her trembling body to his and stroked her hair. "Shhh, sweetheart, everything will be all right. I've got you."

"Frances," Portia began, desperate to tell her husband how his sister had saved their child's life.

"I'm here, Portia."

Portia broke away from Stacy just enough to grab Frances's

shoulder and pull her toward her brother. And then the three of them collapsed into a shaking huddle while she sobbed, this time with relief.

THAT NIGHT PORTIA decided to eat dinner in her bedroom, not that Stacy would have allowed anything else. And Robert, who was almost as bad as his brother, insisted on calling the local doctor to check on Portia.

"You are doing remarkably well, Mrs. Harrington, as is your baby. But rest can never hurt, especially for a woman in your condition."

"How long should she stay in bed?" Stacy's arms were crossed over his chest.

The doctor looked from Stacy to Portia and frowned, uncertain which of them to please.

"She is physically unharmed and very healthy. So, unless she shows any sign of shock, I think she will be fine after a good night's sleep."

Portia could see her husband did not care for that advice. "I still want you to call again tomorrow."

"But Stacy—" She couldn't see his eyes, but his jaw tightened and his expression was pitiless. Portia closed her mouth with a snap.

"I think that is an excellent idea," the doctor agreed nervously.

"Thank you, Doctor." Stacy escorted him to the door and shut it behind him. When he turned, he shook his head.

"Bloody hell, Portia."

Portia raised her eyebrows at his language, which was usually gentlemanly and proper—unless they were in bed. Stacy raked his hands through his disheveled hair, the motion dislodging a cloud of dust. He pulled off his dirty spectacles and tossed them onto her nightstand before grasping her shoulders, looming over her, his expression wild. "Are you trying to put me in the madhouse?"

Portia gaped in amazement. "Surely you don't think I destroyed your family's minstrel's gallery on purpose?"

He laughed weakly. "No, but I'm beginning to believe you are cursed, Mrs. Harrington."

"You aren't the only one," she retorted, and then looked into his agonized eyes and relented. She raised his hand to her lips and kissed his dusty palm before placing it against her cheek and leaning into his warm strength. She closed her eyes and luxuriated in his touch. "Maybe I should stay in bed until the baby is born. You could stay with me and make certain I avoided dangerous situations."

"But then you would be in danger of physical exhaustion." He leaned down to kiss her soundly. "One of us should make an appearance at dinner and I suppose it shall have to be me. I'd better go and begin the bathing process. I daresay it will take half a dozen tubs before I'm clean." He slapped his buckskins and made a gray cloud. "Daisy is seeing to your dinner and will sit with you; try not to do anything dangerous."

"Ha!" Portia threw a pillow at him as he walked toward the connecting doors. After he'd gone she sighed sleepily. She doubted she'd stay awake until her dinner tray arrived.

ASTONISHINGLY, PORTIA SLEPT all the way through to the following morning, waking only moments before Stacy came to tell her he was going for an early ride with Robert.

"I think I liked it far better when you slept until ten o'clock every day and went out at midnight," she grumbled.

"Mmmm." He kissed her cheek and reached under the covers, stroking the first thing he found, which just happened to be one of her breasts. His hand felt divine and she was suddenly wide awake. She arched toward him.

He laughed. "You need your rest and I need a good, hard ride after yesterday—on Geist," he qualified when he saw her eager expression.

Portia opened her mouth to argue but a yawn came out.

He raised his eyebrows. "You see?" He pinched her nipple and was gone.

The next time Portia woke it was to find a cup of hot chocolate beside her bed and Daisy supervising the filling of her bath. She took a drink of chocolate and wandered into the lovely marble bathing chamber.

"You read my mind, Daisy."

"No, ma'am, it was Mr. Harrington who sent the bath—and the chocolate. He said I was to have you in the breakfast room by noon." She gave Portia a little smirk, as though she found a husband ordering his wife around charming. So did Portia in this instance. She'd been afraid he would try to make her remain in bed for the remainder of their visit.

When she arrived in the breakfast room there were at least a dozen people, Stacy among them. He rose and led her to a vacant seat while Lord Pendleton performed introductions to all of the people who'd arrived the day before while Portia was lying in her bedchamber.

She said the appropriate words, smiled, and assured everyone she was fine. She would have preferred to answer all the questions and meet all the guests *after* she'd had coffee but that was not to be. One thing about the group of people surprised her greatly: none of them appeared to find it odd that a full-grown son and his wife had magically appeared at Thurlstone. If they did think it was strange, they were too polite to mention it or stare.

She'd just acquired her first cup and taken a long, steadying draught when Rowena entered the room, her eyes sweeping the table before settling on Portia. Portia groaned inwardly; what now?

"How are you this morning, Mrs. Harrington?" Her disconcerting eyes crinkled in solicitude, but the expression in them was as hard as the agates they so resembled.

"I am well, my lady." She changed the subject. "Lord Pendleton was just about to share the plans you've made for our entertainment." Portia turned back to Robert.

"We have an alfresco lunch prepared for our trip to the Temple of Music on our neighbor's estate, Hillcombe Park."

"Oh Lord Pendleton, how wicked," a woman named Miss Creasy teased. She was one of the new arrivals, a pretty girl with honey-colored hair who was making her interest in Robert quite evident.

But Robert merely smiled coolly and turned to Portia "Miss Creasy is referring to the history of Hillcombe Park, of course. One of the prior masters of Hillcombe was very good friends with the infamous Sir Francis Dashwood, the founder of the Hellfire Club. Lord Bishop built a tribute to Dashwood on his property."

The conversation grew noisy after that, as everyone vied to share their knowledge on the taboo subjects of orgies and satanic rituals. A plate of ham and eggs mysteriously appeared before her and she looked up to find her husband's eyebrows raised in challenge.

"Thank you, Stacy."

He gave her the slight, sensual smile that drove her mad—and also made her achingly grateful they'd bridged their differences. Never again, she promised herself. Never again would she let her dreadful temper come between them.

Stacy leaned closer as she lifted a forkful of food. "Perhaps this is one appetite of yours I can actually satiate."

Portia almost choked and had to take a sip of coffee. She looked up to see Robert watching their intimate interplay with an expression of envy and yearning. Portia darted a glance at Rowena;

the cool blonde was watching her husband with an amused, mocking smile.

Portia felt like an actor in a French farce.

The young man on Portia's other side asked her a question and she turned away from her disturbing in-laws.

THE GROUP WHO assembled for the picnic was noisy, gay, and far larger than Portia expected. Many of the houseguests had breakfasted in their rooms and were only now trickling down to the portico, where carriages waited for those who didn't wish to walk to the picnic area.

Stacy and Portia were engaged in a heated discussion about her presence in one of the carriages when he stopped in mid-sentence and stared at something over her shoulder, his jaw dropping. "Kitty?" His voice was high-pitched and unnatural.

Portia turned and encountered one of the most beautiful women she'd ever seen.

"Stacy?"

They stood enrapt, as if only the two of them existed. Stacy emerged from his shock first, turning to Portia as if he'd only now remembered her presence. His pale cheeks flushed a dull, angry red. "Portia . . ." he began, laughed weakly, and then turned back to the other woman. "Portia, this is Mrs. Katherine Charring. Kitty, this is my wife, Mrs. Harrington."

The woman pulled her gaze from Stacy with obvious effort and gave Portia a nervous smile. "It is a pleasure to meet you."

"Likewise," was all she could force out between stiff lips. But she might as well not have spoken as the beautiful woman and her husband only saw each other. The woman looked at Stacy with open affection, as if he were her savior. And Stacy? Well, he was looking at the lovely stranger as if he could not get enough.

The familiar jealous, jangling sensation began to make her head hot and she knew she had to get away, now. She needed privacy to calm herself.

So she pasted a smile on her face. "If you'll excuse me, I believe I will go and see if there is space in one of the carriages."

Her words jarred Stacy into action. "Wait, Portia—"

Robert came around the corner of the house, barely stopping in time to avoid a collision. He grinned at Portia and steadied her with his hands on her shoulders. "Ah, the woman I was seeking. Your carriage awaits, madam." He looked over to where Stacy stood with his beautiful, mysterious friend, and then every drop of color drained from his face and he staggered back, his hand scrabbling blindly for the wall. For a moment, Portia thought he might actually faint.

Mrs. Charring clutched at Stacy, who slid an arm around her slim body with an easy familiarity that set Portia's hackles up. "Are you all right, Kitty?"

Kitty. Yes, the woman did have a long, kittenish upper lip—although it was compressed in shock just now. It was clear to Portia that Kitty was *not* all right. But she seemed to recall herself and blinked rapidly while stepping away from Stacy.

"Yes, yes of course, I'm fine." She looked up at Stacy. Something—Portia didn't know what—passed between the two before Stacy turned to his brother.

"This is Katherine Charring, Robert. She is from Plymouth. Kitty, this is my brother, Viscount Pendleton."

Mrs. Charring's perfect, coral-pink lips hung open but no sound came from between them. Once again, she swayed alarmingly. Once again, Stacy's arm went around her, but this time it stayed.

Robert strode forward, his face its usual mask of polite charm. "Mrs. Charring, what a pleasure to meet you."

"Lord Pendleton," she murmured.

Portia could not look away from the trio, who'd all forgotten her existence they were so transfixed on each other.

Just what the devil was going on?

Chapter Twenty-Seven

PORTIA CUT A glance at her brother-in-law's taut profile. "Thank you for driving me yourself, I'm sorry you'll miss what must be a lovely walk."

He made a soft *clucking* sound and the lively bays leapt forward. "I've taken the walk hundreds of time but I've never had a drive with my charming sister-in-law."

"What a honey-tongued devil you are, my lord."

"You must call me Robert, otherwise I cannot call you Portia," he reminded her. "And I do love the sound of your name on my honeyed tongue." He flashed her one of his charming smiles, his mask firmly in place.

"Have we far to go?" Portia asked. Maybe if she talked, she wouldn't have to think about the bizarre scene she'd left behind her. The last she'd seen of Stacy he'd been walking some distance behind the others, his head bent close to the gorgeous Katherine Charring.

"It is not far at all on foot, but we will take a slightly longer route, which is prettier than the more direct road."

Portia tried to think of something to say—some pleasantry—but found nothing. Instead, she watched him handle the reins, his hands competent and elegant in their tan gloves.

"What do you think of Thurlstone so far, Portia?"

"It is fascinating and overwhelming." And so were the people who occupied it—not to mention some of the guests.

"I am terribly sorry you've had such brushes with danger on your brief trip. I hope it will not keep you from visiting again?"

She knew Robert meant the stray bullet and collapsing balcony, but the only danger she could think of right now had red hair and green eyes. She tried to swallow the raw jealousy that threatened to choke her.

"Portia?"

Robert was looking down at her, his brow furrowed. "Do you not feel well?"

Hysterical laughter joined raging jealousy and it took every bit of self-control she had not to unravel. Instead, she smiled. "I am just a little tired." Portia was still scrambling for something to say when Robert spoke.

"Have you known Mrs. Charring long?"

"I met her a few moments before you did."

His hands tightened on the reins. "Ah, I see. I thought Stacy seemed to know her."

"Yes, he does."

A muscle in his jaw twitched. "Do you know how they met?"

"No, I don't. But surely Lady Pendleton must have invited her, so she must know her?"

His lips twisted into a smile that sent a chill through her. "Oh yes, my wife certainly knows her."

Portia waited for more, but he remained frustratingly silent and she changed the uncomfortable subject. "Will it be difficult to find the craftsmen to repair the minstrel's gallery?" she asked, keeping the conversation for the remainder of the ride centered on the safe subject of maintaining an ancient building.

When they reached the drive to Hillcombe Park they saw several other carriages already parked on the verge. Robert turned the horses over to a groom and lifted Portia down.

"I'm afraid it's all by foot from here. Do you feel up to the task?"

"I'm ready for a walk. I am also, I'm disgusted to confess, quite hungry again."

"Well, it is your lucky day as a feast awaits." He led her toward a narrow, stepped path. "The lake is in the shape of a swan, yet another homage to West Wycombe Park in Buckinghamshire," he said.

"The owners do not mind us trespassing?'

"We've always been amiable neighbors, although relations have been scant these past years as the family is rarely here. The new Lord Bishop is around my age and we were slightly acquainted at Eton. My father was a contemporary of his grandfather and the two locked horns on more than one occasion. Even so, we've always availed ourselves of each other's properties."

The park was nothing short of spectacular, even if it was rather neglected. They followed the trail in companionable silence, passing a small reflecting pond, complete with stone benches, enormous goldfish, and an ancient-looking grotto.

When Portia commented on the structure Robert chuckled. "It's probably not much older than I am, but the last Lord Bishop was an expert at reproducing antiquity."

The path meandered through a small glade and on the other side were the shores of the picturesque lake. Guests strolled near a generously sized pavilion set with comfortable-looking chairs, colorful awnings, and food enough to feed ten times the crowd. Portia could not see her husband. Or Katherine Charring. Misery and fury surged inside her but she forced them down.

You promised to think before you became overly emotional, her inner, hectoring voice reminded her.

I did promise him that, but he's not making the promise easy to keep.

Remember the last time you made a fool of yourself—mere weeks ago.

Portia gritted her teeth. *I'm trying.* And she was; she couldn't recall trying to restrain her temper quite this much. Ever. But he deserved the benefit of the doubt.

"Let's get you something to eat before you expire from hunger," Robert teased, breaking into her annoying thoughts.

"Are you rested, Mrs. Harrington, or has my husband been exerting you?"

Portia turned to find Rowena had come up behind them, her smile sly. "I am quite rested, thank you. What a lovely display." Not that Portia could take any enjoyment from it.

"You really must try the liver mousse and our very own ham, sliced tissue thin. It is far superior to what is offered at Vauxhall Gardens."

A young couple approached. "Where should we set up the croquet, my lady?"

"I'll leave you in my husband's care." Rowena gave Portia a lingering look before turning to the young man.

Portia heaved a sigh of relief; she was not in a mood to deal with Rowena's cutting, oblique comments just now.

Robert cast a cool, speculative glance at his wife's retreating back before turning to Portia and smiling. "Why don't you have a seat while I wait on you?"

Portia did not demur and he left her in a chair beneath one of the striped awnings, her mind racing until he returned a short time later with a heaping plate.

Portia laughed. "You plan to share this with me, I hope?"

"Save some for me—I'll be back in a moment. I'm going to find Stacy and tell him you've arrived." He left without waiting for a response.

That was just as well as Portia didn't want to think about her husband and what he was doing, or with whom he was doing it. Instead, she demolished her heaping plate and watched Rowena order the young guests about as though she were a field marshal with poorly trained troops. She ate her way through the mountain of food and was just finishing a piece of creamy gold cheese when Rowena returned.

"Did you enjoy the ham?"

"I enjoyed it too much." She gestured at her empty plate.

Rowena looked around. "Where did Robert disappear to?"

"He went to find Stacy."

"Ah. He should have asked me. I saw your husband go in the direction of the gothic chapel with Mrs. Charring, they appear to be great friends."

Portia burned to ask the viscountess who the beautiful Katherine Charring was and why Rowena had invited her, but for some odd reason she sensed the woman would enjoy that. So instead she turned away from her sister-in-law's probing eyes, toward the croquet players, and felt, rather than saw, Rowena drift away.

Her eyelids became heavy and she soon succumbed to her body's demand for rest and closed her eyes. The voices became a hum and she drifted into the type of dreamless slumber she'd not experienced since she was a child. Her limbs were immobile and leaden but her mind was strangely light and floated just above her body. She was beginning to sink deeper into sleep when a high-pitched female squeal jarred her awake.

Her sluggish brain took a moment to sort reality from dream. Clouds were covering the sun and Portia could not have said how long she slept. It couldn't have been too long, as the croquet players had not yet finished their game. She rose from the comfort of her chaise and went to the buffet, where a footman stood ready to serve.

"Do you know what time it is?"

"It is two-thirty, ma'am."

So, she'd slept no more than thirty minutes. She searched the groups milling about, unable to find Robert, Rowena, Stacy, or Mrs. Charring.

"Have you seen Lord Pendleton?" she asked the footman.

"I believe he went toward the chapel."

Where Stacy and Kitty had gone, according Rowena. "How far is that?"

"Perhaps a quarter of an hour walk."

"I'm going to walk to the chapel, if anyone should ask for me."

"Of course, Mrs. Harrington."

As Portia made her way toward the cluster of trees she couldn't help wondering why she was going after Stacy and the beautiful redhead. She knew what Rowena had been trying to insinuate with her sly smile and she couldn't help wondering why Stacy had not simply told her how he'd met Mrs. Charring.

You've just promised him you would not jump to conclusions, her rational side accused yet again.

I'm not *jumping to conclusions—I hardly even need to take a* step *toward them—they are coming toward me. Besides, I have not lost my temper.*

Her mental bickering continued as Portia entered the trees. She followed the path for perhaps five or ten minutes before coming to a large clearing. At the opposite end was a tiny, ornate gothic church that seemed to have grown right out of the hill behind it. The air was heavy and motionless and debris cluttered the courtyard in front of the chapel. Weeds had been busy buckling and pulling apart every joint, split, and crack between the cobbles.

There must have been double doors on the chapel at one point but both were gone and someone had even torn the hinges out of the stone wall. The jagged opening resembled a mouth with sharp, broken teeth and beyond the bricks was an inky black maw.

Nothing in the world would have lured Portia into the liquid blackness.

Nothing, that is, except the sound of her husband's voice.

"Shhh, darling, don't cry." Stacy must have been some distance inside the old chapel as he was barely audible.

Portia opened her mouth to call out and then froze when a voice answered, "I'm so sorry, Stacy. It's just too—too *dreadful.*"

"Things are never as bad as they seem, my dearest Kitty." His voice was tender and the endearment was like acid on Portia's heart. She knew she should run in the opposite direction as fast as her legs would carry her. Instead, she took another step into the darkness.

"What am I going to do?" Katherine Charring's voice throbbed with pain.

"We'll think of something."

Portia's foot came down on a piece of broken stone and she stumbled, flailing in the darkness. She grazed her knuckles on the rough wall but stopped herself from falling.

"What was that?" Mrs. Charring's voice was suddenly very loud.

"Probably just some vermin," Stacy assured her.

If only you knew.

Portia remained where she was, unwilling to risk either discovery or injury by going any farther. Besides, she could hear more than enough from her current position.

A delicate sniff floated through the darkness. "I thought I'd squashed my love and come to terms with my life but now I see I was just lying to myself."

"You poor darling. Come here." It was the same comforting voice he often used on Portia and the long pause could only mean they were embracing. And maybe kissing.

She swallowed so hard she was amazed they couldn't hear it.

They're distracted; the only thing they are hearing is each other.

Portia closed her eyes, as if that would somehow stop the voice in her head.

"There's nothing that can be done now, I'm afraid. You must know a divorce is out of the question?"

Divorce? He wanted a divorce? Portia could barely hear the soft sound of crying above the roaring in her ears.

"Oh, Stacy, I thought I'd gotten beyond it all, but coming here has made my heart break all over again—" the sound of soft sobbing filled the air and it was a long moment before the woman could gain control of herself and continue. "I know I told you I was no longer in love, but I was lying, Stacy."

"Shh, sweetheart. God, how I wish you'd told me all this a long time ago. If you want to leave today I will take you back to Plymouth. But I want to tell Portia the truth before I go and—"

"No! Please don't, Stacy, I should hate for her to know everything. It's not as though we could ever do anything about it. I don't want anyone to know about this."

Portia tasted the salt of her own tears and roughly scrubbed at her eyes with the back of her hand. She stumbled backward, blinded by pain as she listened to her husband comfort a woman who'd obviously decided too late that she loved him.

As she ran from the clearing she wondered if a person could actually hear the sound of their heart breaking.

PORTIA DID NOT stop running until she was out of the trees. She slumped breathlessly against a boulder beside the path and squeezed her pounding temples, as if she could squeeze out the horrible thoughts.

Stacy had only married her because she was with child and now this woman—a woman he clearly cared a great deal for—had decided she wanted him. Portia winced at the memory of the anguish in his voice as he'd soothed his lover's pain.

Agony, fear, and jealousy twisted inside her and her gorge rose. She covered her mouth—she could not be sick now; it would only draw unwanted attention. She dug her fingernails into the palms of her hands until the pain distracted her. When she unclenched her hands there were bloody half-moons. She was still staring at her palms when she heard her name and looked up.

Robert was coming toward her from the direction of the trysting couple. Good God! Had he—

"You went for a stroll, Portia?" His gaze flickered toward the direction she'd just come from and Portia knew, in that instant, that he'd heard the lovers. The smile he gave her was taut and fixed, and lines of strain bracketed his eyes. The expression in them was one of pity.

"Yes, just a short one," Portia said, struggling against a powerful urge to run and run and run. "The viscountess was looking for you," she said absently.

"Yes, she found me." He glanced over her shoulder and his face tightened. "Ah, here are Stacy and Mrs. Charring." The false jollity in his voice was worse than a knife in her chest.

Portia dug deeply for the strength to face him. She told herself this was not the worst she'd endured. If she could survive the miscarriage Ivo had caused with his fists, she could survive this, and so would her baby.

Stacy smiled, looking almost as if he was glad to see her.

Mrs. Charring looked from Portia to Robert, her beautiful face showing no sign she'd been crying a short time ago.

"Did you find the chapel?" Robert asked.

"Yes, we did. It's quite a fascinating little structure."

Nobody seemed to have anything to say, and an uncomfortable silence settled over them.

"Shall we return to the pavilion?" Robert finally asked.

They were able to walk four abreast as they were out of the trees.

Stacy put his hand on Portia's arm and she looked up at him. "How are you feeling, my dear?" His face was tender as he reached out to tuck a stray strand of hair behind her ear. It was all Portia could do not to flinch away. She darted a look at Mrs. Charring. What must she be thinking of her lover's behavior?

But the other woman was staring into the distance, her face expressionless.

Portia took a step back and broke contact with his hand. "I've already eaten, napped, and even taken a walk."

"Is that all? No game of croquet?" Stacy asked playfully. "Were you just waiting for the right partner?"

Portia was sickened by the ease with which he played his part; who knew he had such duplicity in him? "I shall have to pass on the croquet today."

He was immediately solicitous. "Are you tired? Would you like to go back to Thurlstone? You have a long evening ahead of you." He looked at his brother. "I'm sure Robert wouldn't mind if I used his curricle to take you back."

Robert, who'd been staring at Kitty Charring, tore his eyes away from the beautiful woman with obvious effort. "Absolutely, Bains can have the team hitched in a trice."

The last thing Portia wanted was to ride back to the castle alone with Stacy. That would be a disaster; she needed time to get control of her temper. "There is no need to rush off before you've had a chance to eat. And you should join the next game as they are desperate for fresh blood. I'll relax under the awning and watch for a while." Portia moved away quickly, heading for the same chair she'd used before, this time angling it away from the buffet table. She didn't want to look at either food or her husband. But Stacy followed her and dragged a chair up beside her. He was lowering himself into it when Lady Elizabeth and two other women approached.

"Will you be playing, Mrs. Harrington?"

Portia forced yet another smile. "I'm afraid I don't have the energy for it today."

Lady Elizabeth fought unsuccessfully to hide her pleasure.

"Then may we steal your husband?" The younger woman's body swayed toward Stacy's in a way that made Portia want to rip off her head and smack *it* with a mallet.

Stacy looked from the flirtatious girl to Portia. "I think perhaps—"

"I'm going to rest. There is no reason you cannot play."

He paused and smiled at Lady Elizabeth. "Very well. But you must allow me to eat first."

It was agreed he would have a quarter of an hour before they would collect him. When they left Stacy sat beside her.

"Is aught amiss, Portia?"

Portia looked at her husband, a man she'd come to love with every fiber of her being. He'd done the proper thing when he found out she was pregnant, even though he was in love with another. It was beyond unfortunate that Mrs. Charring had only realized her true feelings for him when it was too late. Portia knew she shouldn't hate him for who he loved; a person did not get to choose—she knew that better than most. He did not love her, but he'd been kind to her. Clearly he was determined to be a good husband and father even though his heart belonged to another. Portia just wanted to be alone and weep.

Instead she smiled. "I'm fine, but *you* will be in trouble if you are not ready to play when your admirers return."

Stacy leaned toward her. "You know very well there is only one admirer I want, Portia. Are you sure you don't wish to go back?" His voice was low and intimate and it made Portia's heart ache.

How could he mouth such words when less than an hour ago he'd been holding his weeping lover? She wanted to tell him to quit acting. She wanted to run away and hide where nobody would find her. But she could do neither—at least not until after they left Thurlstone. She'd wait to tell him she wanted a separation until they'd returned home. Surely he would not wish for a divorce until after the child was born?

Portia smiled at him, her cheeks aching. "I'm certain—now go eat; I wish to close my eyes for a while."

He looked like he wanted to argue, but he stood and left her alone. She stole a look from beneath her lashes a few minutes later and saw that Rowena had descended on Stacy and dragged him to join another group.

She waited until the game was well underway before going to find Robert. He was watching three other men compete for Kitty Charring's attention; the woman was some sort of siren.

"I hate to interrupt, Robert, but would it be possible to have one of the grooms take me back to Thurlstone?" The inevitable clucking and fussing transpired before Portia could convince everyone concerned that she refused to tear any of the revelers away from the fun.

"You cannot leave your guests, Robert. Please tell Stacy where I've gone. I hate to disturb him as he seems dangerously close to winning."

Portia didn't fully relax until the carriage started down the lane. And then it took all her strength not to weep.

BY THE TIME Stacy learned Portia was gone it was too late to catch up with her.

"I'm sorry, old man," Robert said. "She didn't want to make a fuss. She said she was going to have a rest before dinner and the ball."

Stacy gestured toward the twittering collection of females. "They want another game. Will you step in for me?"

Robert gave his shoulder a reassuring squeeze. "Of course. If you take the same shortcut you took to get here, you'll most likely get there just about the same time she does."

Stacy was taking his leave of the players when Kitty approached. "Is everything all right, Stacy?"

"I want to check on Portia. She hasn't been feeling up to snuff, even though she does a good job of hiding it."

"I'll come with you, if you don't mind." She looked significantly at Robert's back and Stacy understood. They spoke very little on their way to Thurlstone. Stacy was worried about Portia and he knew Kitty had concerns of her own.

He encountered Daisy leaving Portia's chambers. "Is she in?"

"She just dropped off to sleep, sir. She was exhausted."

Stacy nodded, torn between the desire to go to her and relief he would be spared from having to divulge this mess with Kitty for a little bit longer. He *knew* she would've noticed his awkward behavior and cursed himself for not pulling her aside earlier. But Kitty had been a wreck, so he'd gone off with her.

Once back in his room Stacy poured himself a hefty brandy and dropped into the nearest chair with a groan. What a bloody, unbelievable, coincidental disaster.

Chapter Twenty-Eight

SLEEP WAS IMPOSSIBLE. Instead, Portia lay in the dark, her mind churning. If only she could leave—run away. But there was this wretched ball to be endured and two more days after that. She refused to give Rowena the satisfaction she so clearly desired. It was obvious the woman had invited Katherine Charring for her own twisted amusement, although how she'd known about Stacy and the woman was a mystery. Or perhaps it was mere coincidence and she was imagining things? Could she really be so paranoid?

She knew her dislike of Rowena was petty, but at least it gave her something to think about other than the agonizing knowledge that her husband was in love with another woman.

Portia bit her lip to keep from sobbing like a child. Instead, she tossed and turned, her mind an endless blur of questions with no palatable answers. Did she stay with him, knowing she was a duty to him? Knowing she would be a burden for him to bear if he wanted to know his child? Or did she leave, taking the child with her? Because she could never leave her child, she knew that.

Where would she go? Back to London? Portia knew her friends would take her in, but what would happen to their reputations—their lives—to have a divorced woman with a child living with them?

She couldn't stay, and she couldn't go.

By the time Daisy came to dress her for the evening she was far more exhausted than she'd been hours earlier. She took strength in the knowledge that she only needed to maintain a convincing façade for another few days.

Daisy chatted happily as she dressed Portia's hair, thrilled beyond anything to be preparing her mistress for a ball in a castle with actual peers. Portia closed her eyes and let the sound of her maid's excited voice wash over her. A knock on the door a few moments later made Portia's entire body stiffen. *Please don't let it be Stacy.*

"Good evening, my dear."

She opened her eyes. Stacy looked even more godlike than usual. He wore a black coat and pantaloons and his waistcoat was ivory silk embroidered with mauve birds that matched Portia's gown perfectly.

He smiled. "Do you like it? It is Daisy's doing."

Portia's eyes became unaccountably hot and she was afraid she would begin weeping.

She swallowed convulsively. "Daisy, you truly are a wizard."

"'Twas nothing, ma'am," she murmured, her face red as she rummaged through the jewel box looking for the earrings Portia would wear.

Stacy came to stand behind Portia, facing her reflection. Of course she couldn't see his eyes. He held a black velvet box toward her.

"What is it?" Her voice was sharper than she'd intended.

The corners of his mouth turned down. "You sound so . . . *fierce.* Am I not allowed to give my wife a gift?"

Portia couldn't look at him, she was afraid she would collapse into a puddle of tears. *Why was he doing this to her?*

"You shouldn't have." Her voice broke on the last word but at least she wasn't crying.

Stacy's hand settled on her shoulder, his brow furrowing with concern. "Will you excuse us, Daisy?"

Portia watched her servant leave the room as though she was

bidding farewell to her last great hope. The door closed and she turned back to the mirror.

"Are you sure everything is all right, Portia?"

"I'm sorry I was sharp. I'm afraid I have been experiencing the most exhausting swings in mood." That was true enough, at least.

"Are you sure you want to go downstairs?"

Anything was better than sitting alone in this room. She smiled. "I'm looking forward to it," she lied.

He nodded, and then turned to the box in his hand. "I commissioned this for you when I was in Barnstaple. It took the man longer than he expected. When I learned of this ball I sent him a message requesting that he make haste to finish it."

Portia took the box as though it were a live snake, her hands trembling. She lifted the lid and gasped. It was more pearls, but unlike any she'd ever seen. She glanced from the beautiful necklace to her husband's reflection. "Why, they're almost . . . black."

He smiled at her amazement and reached into the box. "Yes. Black pearls, uncommon, precious, and beautiful. Just like you, Portia." He draped the double strand around her neck and clasped it. It fit snugly. "This is called a collar." His elegant white fingers stroked the pearls, the contrast between black and white arresting. "Now you wear my collar, Portia." He bent low and nuzzled the side of her neck, his mouth hot against her skin. "You belong to me."

Portia felt as though he'd reached into her chest and crushed her heart. How could he be so cruel? Just what game was he playing?

He saw her stricken expression in the glass and frowned. "What is it, why—"

A knock on the door interrupted whatever he was going to say.

"Come in!" Portia called, beyond grateful for whomever was on the other side of the door. Frances stood in the doorway, her eyes flickering nervously from Stacy to Portia before settling on the necklace and widening.

"My goodness," she breathed.

Stacy took a step back and clasped his hands behind his back. "Good evening, Frances. You look lovely."

Portia was momentarily distracted from her misery by Stacy's kind words. But he was right, Frances did look striking in a gown of verdigris silk, an unusual shade which brought out the gold in her hair and made her blue eyes look almost turquoise. Her high cheekbones tinted at his words and she came forward, one of her hands outstretched.

"This is for you, Portia. It belonged to my mother and I would like you to have it."

Portia glanced from the small velvet covered box to Frances and could no longer hold back the tears.

"Here! What is this?" Stacy was beside her in an instant.

Portia shook her head, capable only of making gulping sounds like some sort of fish.

Frances placed the box on her dresser and held out a handkerchief before taking Portia's free hand. "It is normal for a woman in your condition to be emotional—especially with this most recent shock."

Portia gave the other woman a startled look. Did she know about Kitty Charring?

"You might not have taken physical harm from the incident with the balcony," Frances continued, stroking her hand, "but it would have been a terrible stress on you."

Portia didn't know whether to be happy or miserable that the other woman didn't know the worst of it. Oh, how she wished she had somebody to confide in. Instead, she dabbed her eyes and nodded. "Thank you, Frances. You are correct, it has been a strain."

"You don't need to do this tonight, darling. Everyone will

understand if you decide to rest," Stacy said.

Especially Rowena.

Portia shook her head. She'd endured years of misery at Ivo's hands; surely she could endure a few hours of this wretched evening. She turned to Frances and smiled. "I would love to see what is in the box."

THE HUGE DRAWING room was filled with beautifully dressed, coiffured, and bejeweled house guests when they entered a short time later. While Stacy wished Portia had taken his suggestion and stayed in bed, he could not deny he was pleased to have her beside him.

"Will you both excuse me?" Frances asked. "I promised Rowena I would speak with the new pastry chef. He is a bit . . . temperamental."

Stacy nodded and then said, "The ring was a lovely gesture, Frances."

Portia held up her right hand and the diamond ring sparkled. She smiled at his sister. "Yes, thank you. It is beautiful."

Stacy watched his sister walk away and slid his hand down Portia's back until it rested at the base of her spine. Her sharp intake of breath sent blood rushing to his groin. The mauve silk was thin and he could not resist sliding his hand lower, until it rested on the generous swell of her bottom. Her cheekbones stained a delicate rose and a flare of possessive heat churned in his gut at the way her body responded to his touch. He should have said to hell with this bloody ball and taken her to his bed. They could have made love and he could have left Kitty, Robert, and Robert's scheming wife to sort out their own problems.

But instead he'd behaved like a responsible adult and now it would be hours and hours before he could hold her, soothe her . . .

be inside her delicious body. He needed to stop thinking about it before he embarrassed them both in public.

Of course he'd have to tell her about Kitty first—an unpleasant conversation—not about her connection to Robert, but certainly about their friendship. Now that he knew Portia better, he could not relish introducing her to a former lover.

Thoughts of that discussion were enough to stop the pleasurable sensation in his groin.

"Would you like something to drink, Portia?"

"Perhaps a glass of lemonade."

"I will return before you know it." He headed for the drinks table and poured a lemonade for Portia and small glass of wine for himself. He surveyed the room for Robert, whom he'd hoped to pull aside for a few moments before they all sat down to dinner. Even if they only—

"Good evening, Mr. Harrington," the viscountess's purr came from his other side and he turned. Stacy had to admit his brother's wife was a beautiful woman. Even so, he could not understand how Robert had been persuaded to marry her. She was cold, untouchable, and more than a little devious. And he was going to get to the bottom of her invitation to Kitty before this bloody visit was over.

Stacy took her proffered hand and bowed over it. "Good evening, my lady, you look lovely. Something to drink?" Her smile was odd—almost flirtatious—as though he'd just asked to put his hand up her skirt.

"Nothing for me, thank you." She turned from the table and swept the room as she fingered the hideous diamond choker around her neck. Her décolletage was so low he thought he could see the top of her areolae.

"That is an impressive necklace."

Her throaty chuckle held no warmth. "It belonged to the earl's first wife, a woman endowed with more money than breeding, I'm afraid."

Stacy frowned at the distasteful comment.

She smiled, as if he'd spoken out loud. "One could not say the same about *your* mother, of course."

"I know very little about my mother." He did not care to discuss his family, or anything else, with such a venomous person.

"You look very like her, more so than Pendleton. Your mother was a beautiful woman."

Stacy's eyebrows rose. Was she *flirting* with him?

Robert entered the ballroom just then, spotted Stacy, and headed in his direction. Whatever his sister-in-law was up to, Stacy could only hope Robert's arrival would put a stop to it.

"Good evening Stacy, Rowena." The look he gave his wife was markedly colder than the one he bestowed on Stacy. He poured himself a hefty brandy and pointedly ignored his wife.

Stacy glanced across to where Portia stood, wishing he were beside her right now. She was talking to a young couple who'd gone to the picnic today. The door behind Portia opened and Kitty entered. It wasn't his imagination that the conversation in the room briefly stuttered. Robert stopped in the process of drinking; the rim of the glass resting against his lower lip, as if he'd lost the strength to tip the liquid into his mouth.

Stacy couldn't help being amused by how Kitty drew every eye in the room, her beauty was like a flame. She might appear magnificent in her emerald gown—which looked as if it had been stitched to her body—but he could see she was nervous. Stacy knew she'd likely donned her garment like battle armor. The question was, just who would she have to do battle with?

Kitty glanced around the room before going to stand beside Portia, who—after a brief look of surprise—smiled and introduced her to the others beside her. Stacy was proud of his wife for the kindness she was showing Kitty. Most of the other female guests were glaring at the beautiful woman as if she were a serpent that had slithered through a crack in the door.

He shot a look at Robert. His brother had finally completed the action of drinking. In fact, his glass was empty. The viscountess was also looking at Kitty and when her eyes swiveled from the other woman to her husband Stacy inhaled sharply at the raw hatred he saw. His brother did not notice. In fact, Robert looked as though he'd forgotten everyone's existence but one. He set the glass blindly on the table and started toward Kitty like a sleepwalker.

Lady Pendleton's eyes sank into her husband's back like pale, lethal blades.

"If you'll excuse me, my lady." Stacy took long strides to reach Portia and Kitty before Robert could do anything foolish—like try to take Kitty into dinner. The gorgeous redhead might look strong, but Stacy knew she was hanging on to her sanity by a thread.

"Here you are, darling." Stacy pushed the glass into Portia's hand and turned to Kitty. "Kitty, you look smashing. Will you allow me to accompany you into dinner?"

He turned to give Portia a reassuring smile, but her face had hardened into the polite mask he recognized too well.

Blast and damn! She couldn't be jealous, could she—not after their conversation less than twenty-four hours ago? He reached for her elbow and leaned toward her but she turned away to answer the young man on her other side, pulling her arm from his grasp.

Yes, she is angry. Stacy wanted to go after her but Robert had come around Stacy and stopped in front of Kitty, looking like a man who'd been struck between the eyes with a mallet.

"Kitty." The single word was ragged, as though it had been dragged over rocks before escaping his mouth. "I need—"

"She's already agreed to go to dinner with me, old man." Stacy cut Robert a look that should have brought him to his senses. Really, was his brother an idiot? Did he not see how his wife was watching? Did he not notice how Kitty was as fragile as glass? Stacy added in an undervoice, "You can talk to Mrs. Charring *later,* Robert."

Stacy turned to talk to Portia, but she was walking away on the arm of a young man.

The dinner gong rang and Stacy gritted his teeth to keep from howling. Instead, he smiled down at Kitty and guided her toward the dining room.

"Thank you, Stacy." Kitty's voice was almost inaudible, but Stacy could feel the tremors shaking her delicate body.

"Don't let her see your suffering."

They both knew who he meant, and Kitty stiffened. "No, you're right."

He placed his hand over hers and smiled at another couple who approached the door. "I cannot imagine you will be seated near him at dinner," he murmured, not really sure of any such thing. Who knew what his sister-in-law was up to? And Stacy was positive it must have been Rowena who'd invited Kitty here, luring her with promises of information about her child. And if she'd invited Robert's old lover why would she draw the line at seating them together? He could only hope her respect for precedence superseded her desire for making mischief. He twisted around to look for Portia. She was taking her seat and smiling up at the young man beside her, laughing at something he said. She looked happy and seemed to be enjoying herself.

Stacy heaved a sigh of relief; he must have been wrong about her reaction to Kitty.

IT WAS THE longest meal of Portia's life. Stacy sat directly across from her and she was forced to watch as he charmed his two dinner partners in between darting glances at Mrs. Charring, who was seated almost all the way at the other end, not far from Robert.

It was all Portia could do to make basic responses to the two men beside her as she doggedly ate her way through three courses, planning her escape.

As soon as dinner finished, she stood with unseemly haste, grateful for the brief escape from Stacy the thirty minutes of port and cigars would afford her. In the drawing room she planted herself between two matrons who were discussing their servant problems. Half an hour later the women had moved on to the subject of the best London warehouses to find draperies when Katherine Charring stopped in front of Portia, her smile uncertain.

Portia wanted to scream. Why in God's name did the woman insist on attaching herself to Portia like a limpet? She resisted the urge to claw out her gorgeous green eyes and gestured to a vacant chair, her smile as brittle as glass.

"Please, join us." What else could she say? "We are thrashing out the important topic of new draperies."

Portia was still wondering how to escape ten minutes later when two footmen opened the enormous double doors that led to the grand ballroom and a hush fell over the group.

"My goodness," one of the other women whispered.

Hundreds of candles burned in giant chandeliers—the light reflecting off the gilt ceiling and bathing the dark wood walls in a warm glow. The floor was breathtaking, an ornate design that looked almost Moorish and radiated out from a massive medallion in the center. An elevated pavilion off to one side held a full orchestra.

Katherine Charring shot to her feet, her eyes on something on the far side of the room. "Will you excuse me?" she asked, not waiting for a response before she fled. Thank God.

A few moments later the two matrons stood. "Shall we move closer?"

Portia followed them until she saw Stacy's distinctive white head in front of them, and then she turned right, which conveniently led to the long bank of tables along the far side of the room that had been set up with refreshments. She looked at the heaping platters of food and her stomach rumbled. She had to laugh; dinner had ended less than three-quarters of an hour ago and her body was hungry, even though the mere thought of more food made her ill.

She looked out over the crowd and quickly located her husband. Right beside him was a distinctive redhead. She turned her back to the room, took a plate and filled it with cakes, no longer caring if she ended up weighing twenty stone.

Portia had just declined her second invitation to dance and was systematically consuming the contents of the buffet when a footman wheeled the earl toward her. Hysterical laughter bubbled up in her throat; this was *exactly* what she needed to make the evening completely miserable.

She resisted the urge to scream and run. Instead she swallowed her mouthful of cream cake and prayed he would bypass her and go somewhere else, perhaps America. But the poisonous old bastard rolled toward her as inexorably as bad weather. Portia was in no mood to tolerate his snide comments tonight. He'd better mind his nasty mouth or he might find himself the recipient of some of his own medicine.

"Good evening, Mrs. Harrington." He smiled; the expression as festive as a funeral procession.

He was up to something.

She gave him a mockery of a curtsey. "My lord."

Her terse greeting amused rather than insulted him and he chuckled. Portia stared at the dance floor, hoping he would go away if she ignored him. Unfortunately, the first thing she saw was Stacy leading Kitty out for the next set.

"That redheaded chit is causing quite a bit of heartburn tonight, eh?" He laughed and Portia turned to glare down at him. He gave her an ingratiating smile, as if they were partners in an amusing caper. Portia entertained herself with a vision of pushing his chair down the stairs with him in it and was able to smile back.

"I see your husband managed to get her for a waltz. Perhaps he has more of me in him than I gave him credit for." His unpleasant cackling drew curious looks from several people standing nearby.

"My husband and Mrs. Charring have a prior acquaintance. They are friends," she said in the most repressive tone she could muster.

"Is that what you call it in Italian? *Friends*?" He guffawed. "I believe Robert might be her *friend*, too. I believe she is the sort of woman who has lots of *friends*."

Portia's gaze flickered across the faces of the observers until she found Robert. He did look rather . . . intent. Just what was going on?

"He's an idiot," the earl said, slicing through her thoughts with his harsh indictment. His tone was no longer amused and he wasn't staring at his son, but at the viscountess, who was chatting with a handsome older man, the same cool, supercilious smile on her face. "His wife is the perfect woman. The very pinnacle of breeding—everything our class has striven to produce."

"You sound as though you're describing a horse, my lord."

The footman who'd been stationed behind him snorted, and then coughed to cover it.

The old man twisted in his chair. "You may go," he snapped.

The unfortunate footman fled the ballroom as if the hangman of death was on his heels and the earl shot Portia a poisonous look. "You can be the one to push me about now, missy."

"Ah, but you might not like where I push you, my lord."

He laughed, his hawkish eyes narrow and hard. "Oh you've got fire, I'll give you that. No doubt a gift from your mongrel father."

Portia refused to take the bait and shrugged. "A fair trade for the musical ability I inherited."

His skull-like face shifted into something that might have been a genuine smile. The expression was awkward, as though he hadn't used it in at least fifty years. "You are correct in that; I wish you were playing tonight instead of this claptrap. My head is pounding already."

"I did not see you in the receiving line, my lord."

He gave another of his barking laughs. "I'm master here, not court jester."

One of the houseguests, Baron Langston, strolled over to engage Broughton in conversation—or at least tried to. Portia listened with one ear, watching the dancers as she tried to think of a way to leave the ball without drawing attention. Stacy led Lady Elizabeth into the next set. He saw her watching and flashed her a quick smile. Portia returned his smile before she recalled he was in love with another woman, and then wrenched her eyes away only to encounter her father-in-law's sharp stare. He was ignoring Langston, who was droning on about a hunter that was short in the back or some such drivel.

The earl's smile was distilled spite; the man saw too much.

One of the young men who'd sat beside her at dinner came to request her hand for the next set but Portia declined. "I'm afraid I lack the energy this evening. But I do thank you for your kind offer." Portia wasn't lying; she was exhausted. She wasn't even sure she could walk all the way back to her room—if she could find it.

Langston asked her a few unanswerable questions about horses and hunting and then began to pontificate on both topics and required no responses from either Portia or the earl. She looked over the couples on the dance floor but could not see Stacy. The group of men who'd been standing with him had dispersed and now three older ladies occupied the spot. Portia wondered if he'd gone to the room Rowena had set up for those who preferred cards to dancing. Without thinking she scanned the room for a distinctive redhead. But Katherine Charring was nowhere to be seen. Portia swallowed and kept her eyes on the dance floor, unwilling to let her father-in-law see her pain.

Two more sets passed and Portia declined yet another offer to dance. Stacy and Mrs. Charring had not returned and Langston, amazingly, was still talking about hunters and withers.

The Earl of Broughton yanked on her hand. "I've had quite enough of this foolishness." He made no effort to keep his voice down and glared at the rotund peer beside him, whose plump, pleasant face was gaping down at him in shock.

"Take me out to the hall and send somebody to fetch my man," Broughton said, using the same tone he would on the lowest scullery maid. Portia stared at him, considering her choice of responses. She finally decided she would carry him to his chambers *herself* if it meant being shed of his company.

"Excuse me, my lord," Portia said to the stunned Langston. She pushed the earl through the clusters of people forming up for the next set.

"Goddamned windbag," Broughton muttered loud enough that several people cast startled looks in their direction.

"At least he has good manners."

"Ha! Manners, hey miss? What would the likes of *you* know about manners?"

"I know I have enough of them not to launch you and this chair off the balcony into the rose garden, my lord."

Her threat tickled him so much she thought he might choke to death. Unfortunately, he recovered by the time they reached the grand staircase. While he caught his breath, Portia locked the brake on his chair and sent one of the footmen to fetch the earl's valet.

"I've laughed more in your company than I have in years."

The old man wheezed, looking at her as though she should be proud of such a miraculous feat.

"I haven't."

He went into another fit of laughter mixed with coughing. Portia was staring at the handsome marble floor and listening to the last of the earl's paroxysm when an enormous man hastened toward them.

"It's about damn time," the earl snarled. "What the devil have you been doing up there? Drinking my port, I'll wager." He gave his servant the same evil stare he bestowed on every living thing.

"Good night, my lord." *And good riddance!* Portia turned to go but he reached out and caught her hand with one skeletal claw and yanked her back toward his chair. He was surprisingly strong for such a frail-looking old man.

She sighed and raised her eyebrows, not bothering to hide her irritation. "What?"

He squeezed her hand so hard it hurt. "You keep that son of mine in hand, do you hear?"

Portia pursed her lips in irritation, not sure what he meant or what she was supposed to say.

He saw her perplexed look and laughed. "Don't you fret about whores, missy, he's a man, goddammit. Men have needs." He let out another bark of humorless laughter and his eyes dropped to her slightly protruding midriff. "You just hold his interest enough to make sure he mounts you regularly—not like my *heir.*" He spat the word; his grip unbreakable. "Just concentrate on giving me a few grandsons and you'll be amply rewarded." He released her hand and turned to his waiting servant. "What the *devil* are you gawking at, you fool? Get me to my room. I've had my fill of foppery."

The muscular servant lifted the fragile old man from the chair and began the long journey to the earl's chambers. A footman followed, carrying the wheeled chair. Portia watched them until they disappeared up the stairs.

She looked through the doors into the ballroom and saw the floor was full of dancers. Nobody was paying her any mind and now was a perfect time to escape to her room. Unfortunately, she needed to find the necessary and use it first.

The retiring room was overflowing with women repairing loose curls, torn hems, and a variety of other sartorial disasters. There was a wait, but Portia did not think she would make it all the way back to her room—if she could actually find it. It took far longer than she hoped—not to complete her business, but to get away from at least two dozen nosey women, all of whom wanted to have a chat with her—before she could escape.

Her chambers lay in the west wing, which could only be reached by going to the great hall and taking a smaller set of stairs. Her feet were heavy and it was an effort to walk.

And five minutes later she realized she was lost.

Portia stood in the middle of the dimly lighted hallway and considered curling up in the nearest corner and going to sleep.

"Mrs. Harrington?"

She screamed and whirled around.

"I'm so sorry to have startled you," the viscountess said.

Portia gaped at her sister-in-law, her hands fisted at her sides. "What are you doing?" she demanded, even though she knew it was beyond rude to interrogate the woman in her own house.

Rowena's smile was not her usual supercilious sneer. "I was looking for you, actually." She bit her lower lip in an uncharacteristic display of agitation.

"What is it?"

Rowena looked away. "I daresay you will not thank me for this. . . but—" She grimaced and her face twisted in misery, almost as if she were fighting tears. "I overheard your husband and Mrs. Charring—they have arranged a . . .a meeting of sorts for tonight."

Portia could only stare; of all the people to know about the relationship between Stacy and Kitty, why did this woman have to be the one?

She crossed her arms. "I already know about them, my lady. What do you want me to do about it?"

Rowena opened her mouth, paused, and then took Portia's arm. "Come with me." She led Portia back up the stairs, turning right instead of left at the top. She stopped in front of massive double doors Portia knew led to an enormous library at least five times the size of the one at Whitethorn.

Portia pulled her arm from the other woman's grasp. "They're in *there*?"

"No, but I know where they are going."

"Isn't this what you wanted? Isn't this why you invited Katherine Charring to this party?" Portia demanded.

Rowena's eyes widened. "But I didn't—I never met her before today."

Portia stared. "If you didn't, who did?"

The viscountess opened her mouth, and then closed it.

"Who?"

"I'm afraid it was the earl."

"The *earl*? Why would he do such a thing?" *Especially after telling me I'd better keep breeding,* she thought, but did not say.

Rowena took a deep breath, released it, and then took another, as if she needed to fortify herself. "This is exactly the kind of thing he enjoys, watching people tear each other apart."

Portia recalled the earl's gleeful venom in the ballroom. "Who does such things?"

"The kind of man who throws out his own son."

Portia stared at the other woman, whose expression, for once, was one of compassion. Rowena laid a hand on her arm. "I know how you are feeling—Robert has paraded his mistresses in front of me for years. I suppose that makes me sympathetic to you. I want to help you—not just because you may be carrying the heir, but—" she chewed her lip, her pale cheeks reddening. "I've grown to like you."

Portia gawked at her in disbelief; would the surprises never end? She shook her head and pulled away from the woman; she needed to sit. She opened the library door and went inside, slumping into a chair and dropping her head in her hands. Rowena moved away, but Portia could hear sounds coming from the far side of the vast room.

"Come and help me," she called to Portia.

Portia groaned and sat up. She just wanted to go to bed—forever. But she forced herself to her feet and went to join the viscountess, who'd begun pulling books off the shelf and piling them on the floor.

Portia stared; the woman had run *mad.* "What on earth are you—?"

A low grinding sound filled the room as the entire bookshelf—a good ten feet high—slowly swung inward. Her mouth fell open.

Rowena took a candle from the candelabrum and turned to her. "This passage will get us to the chapel much faster than following them above ground."

"The chapel? But what—"

The viscountess disappeared into the darkness and Portia's feet followed before her brain could stop them. Rowena was standing just inside the entrance and feeling for something in the panel beside the moving section of wall. Portia glanced around, her eyes adjusting to the gloom. At the end of the short hall was a set of stairs.

"Where do those lead? To the chapel?" When Rowena didn't answer, Portia turned around, just in time to hear the scraping noise and watch the bookshelf door swing shut.

"Why did you shut it?" Her voice was shrill.

Rowena's pale eyes glinted in the candlelight. "Don't worry, the mechanism to open it is here." She gestured toward a large wooden lever sticking out of the panel. "Come, follow me." Rowena squeezed around Portia and headed toward the stairs.

"Follow you where? And why did you shut it?" Portia demanded as she hurried after Rowena, who was now the only source of light.

"I doubt you want an audience for this meeting."

Portia didn't want Rowena, either. "I didn't say I *wanted* to go, did I?"

The other woman stopped so abruptly that Portia ran into her. "Are you saying you wish to go back? Will you give up what is yours so easily?"

"And have you confronted all your *husband's* mistresses?" Portia shot back.

"No, I have not—but then I am not carrying Robert's child. I heard them speaking, Mrs. Harrington, That *woman* will have him if you do not fight for him. You might be carrying the *heir.*"

Ahh, now Portia understood—it always came back to status and blood lines and the future of the bloody earldom with this woman.

She opened her mouth to demand Rowena take her back, but the scorn in the other woman's eyes was too much to bear. Portia threw up her hands. "Fine, lead on."

Rowena turned without a word.

Portia had to trot to keep up with her and she stubbed the toe of her thin satin slipper against something hard. "Will you please slow down," she called out as the light disappeared around a corner. She rested one hand against the wall and massaged her aching toe until Rowena came back.

The viscountess reached up to a wall sconce and Portia saw there were others evenly spaced down the narrow hall. She plucked out the candle and lit it. When it flared to life it bathed the space between them with twice as much light.

She came back to Portia, her pale face eerie. "Here." She handed her the candle and resumed her journey.

Portia scrambled after her down the hall but paused when they reached a second, longer, set of stairs.

"Hold carefully to the railing and watch your step," Rowena called over her shoulder.

"I thought you said they were going to the chapel?" Portia asked Rowena's retreating back. "This feels like we're headed down the side of the cliff."

"The tunnels run to Thurlstone and beyond. We must go down and then come up again in another section. They are very old—far older than the chapel itself, which is not even a hundred years old."

Portia's stomach was in knots; did she really want to find them? "Perhaps—"

"Perhaps what?" Rowena asked without pausing.

Portia stared at the other woman's back. What should she tell her? She didn't know what to think, herself.

You need to see them, don't you, Portia? You need to rub salt in the wound.

She grimaced; is that why she was following? To torment herself? Or maybe. . .

Maybe what?

Maybe Rowena is right—maybe I should fight for him.

But what of your pride, Portia?

The thought surprised her so much she stumbled, glad to be holding the railing. Was pride really the only thing standing in her way? No, surely that couldn't be true. Could it?

They reached the bottom of the stairs and continued down a narrow, windy corridor with a wood-plank door at the far end.

Rowena opened the door and paused. "Perhaps, what, Mrs. Harrington?" She gestured for Portia to take the lead.

Portia preceded her. "Perhaps we should not be doing this," she said lamely, not wishing to put her thoughts into words. "I would rather talk to my husband alone—later." That much was true, at least.

Rowena laughed, her pupils tiny black dots in the candlelight.

"This is no laughing matter to me." Portia's voice shook with suppressed anger, not all of it for the woman across from her.

Rowena laughed even harder, shaking her head as she struggled to catch her breath.

"What is wrong with you? Why would laugh at such a thing?"

"I'm laughing because it is not *your* husband she wants, *Portia*, it is *mine*." She snorted at Portia's shocked face and then roughly shoved past her.

Portia hurried to catch up, a tiny spark of hope burning in her chest. "What?"

"Yes, it is Robert. He and the whore had a child together years ago, you see. The two met in Plymouth while he was staying in my father's house, if you can believe it. She was a governess somewhere—I don't recall now. But I *do* recall Robert met her *after* we were betrothed. Even before we married he was whoring." She laughed and the sound sent an uncomfortable tingling sensation down Portia's spine. Something was very wrong.

Portia stopped, and then began to back up.

Rowena spun around. The hand that wasn't holding the candle held a pistol, which she was pointing at Portia.

"Stop where you are, Mrs. Harrington."

Portia froze and the other woman advanced on her, the gun pointed at her midriff.

"You are not going back, Mrs. Harrington. Ever." Her smile was terrifying, but not as terrifying as the look in her eyes. For the first time since Portia had met the woman her face wore a genuine expression: madness.

She reached out and tapped Portia's stomach with the barrel

of the gun. "You will walk or I will shoot you right now."

Portia's brain spun like a toothless gear, unable to find purchase.

Rowena gestured to the corridor ahead. "*Now.* Start walking."

Portia looked from the gun to the other woman's face; hatred blazed in her pale green eyes and she prodded Portia's stomach hard enough to hurt. "This is the last time I will say it. Walk."

Portia turned and took several hasty steps while holding the candle high and squinting into the darkness. She could see nothing ahead of her other than the narrow, dark tunnel.

Rowena poked her shoulder with the gun. "Faster."

Portia walked faster. "Why?" she finally asked.

Her question elicited another frightening laugh.

"Why must you die? Why must your child die? And, most importantly, why must your husband die? Because I married the wrong brother, you idiot. Because our interfering, controlling, monster of a father-in-law threatened to expose everything unless I produced an heir. Did you not hear what he said to you tonight? *You* are his new broodmare."

Portia stumbled over an uneven spot in the floor and came to a fork in the tunnel.

"To the right," Rowena barked. "Our wretched father-in-law has threatened to tell everything if I do not let his disgusting son touch me. He gave me a year, and it is almost over. He will tell the truth and I will live out the rest of my life as nothing more than the wife of a cheating, worthless second son."

Rowena's words rang in Portia's ears and her head spun. "Good God!" she said, her voice a wheeze. "Stacy is the elder."

"Ah, congratulations, my dear Mrs. Harrington, indeed he is. I suppose I should call you Lady Pendleton?"

Portia had no response for that.

"For thirty-five years the secret held." Portia felt the pistol jab her in the back. "It most likely would have continued to hold but for *you.* It is *your* fault, *my lady*. But for *you* the earl would have had no weapon to use against me. But for you the freak would never have found a woman to marry him and would have continued going to whores. Without *you* the freak would have gone to his grave without ever siring offspring."

Her brutal words and horrible insults made Portia stiffen—but with rage rather than fear. She squared her shoulders and stopped.

Rowena pressed the gun against the back of her skull before she could turn. "Don't get any foolish notions. I can shoot you in the back as easily as in the front."

"Why should I do what you say if you are just going to shoot me? Why should I make it any easier for you?"

"Because I can let you die slowly while I shoot you through the leg, the other leg, the arm, and so on. Or I can offer you something that will give you a painless release." She spoke with a quiet, menacing certitude that turned Portia's anger to terror. "Now walk."

Portia walked.

"Trust me, dear sister, this is not my choice. I tried to do things the easy way. Both you and your husband must have been born under fortunate stars. First he escaped those inept highwaymen I hired. And then, just when I thought I might actually have to shoot you myself, your dearly departed came back to life."

Portia gasped. "You know about Ivo?"

She gave a bark of laughter. "Know about him? Good Lord! I paid the man to take you away. But what does he do? He decides to make a little *more* money and blackmail you."

"So you killed him?"

"Don't be stupid. Fant killed him."

"Fant?"

"Yes, the Fants have worked for my family for generations. They are very loyal—and I pay them well, of course. Unfortunately, even money can buy only so much. Fant became frightened that he would hang after killing Stefani so he came running to *me* to help him out of his fix. He is far more willing to do my bidding now, not that he is any more effective—as he demonstrated by shooting off your horse's ear instead of your head."

Portia was too astonished to speak.

"Imagine my irritation when you not only managed to dodge the bullet but stay in the saddle of a half-mad horse." Her bitter laughter made Portia's scalp tingle. "I suppose I will have to accept the blame for the minstrel's gallery myself. Not one of my most inspired ideas but it would have worked if not for Frances." She paused. "And so, my dear sister-in-law, I came to the conclusion that I would have to take care of matters myself. If you behave, it will be painless. I've got something that will make you drift off to sleep. After you are gone I'll let the truth about your husband's relationship with the whore be known and there won't be any doubt in people's minds why you took your life.

"Then I shall take care of your husband at my leisure. Who knows, maybe he will be so devastated by your death he will do away with himself? I've seen the way he looks at you—everyone has. Except you, it seems." Her voice brimmed with malicious amusement. "You must be an idiot to believe he was planning to run off with the whore. What did you hear in the chapel, I wonder?" She didn't wait for an answer. "As annoying as all this has been it has given me a good deal of pleasure to watch my own dear husband stew in his miserable juices. If I'd known how enjoyable it would be to watch him suffer and pant I would have thrown the two of them together years ago, instead of working so hard at keeping them apart."

A small, iron-strapped door appeared ahead in the gloom.

Rowena thrust a large key over Portia's shoulder. "Open it."

Portia fumbled with the lock before it made a dull *click*.

Rowena reached around her and opened the door. "So, here we are dear sister-in-law." And then she knocked the candle out of Portia's hand and shoved her into darkness.

Chapter Twenty-Nine

"I'M SO SORRY to pull you away from your family's ball, Stacy," Kitty said yet again as they ascended the stairs to the third story. "I feel like such a fool, but I just could not bear another moment. Robert wouldn't—"

Stacy patted her hand. "He's not thinking clearly. I believe he and his wife have been playing these nasty games for years. You are well away from it while I get to the bottom of everything. Jewell will take you to Plymouth and then return for us." She began to protest and he cut her off. "No, that is what will happen. This situation is intolerable. I don't know what that woman is about, but I plan to find out."

He took her through a large set of double doors that separated the main wing from one of the older sections. He looked around the dark hallway and frowned. The smell of damp and mildew was stifling.

"Good Lord, who put you all the way over here? This is dreadful—the viscountess should be flogged," he muttered. She stopped walking and he turned. "What is it, Kitty?"

Her eyes brimmed with tears. "I'm so ashamed at having brought all this on you."

Stacy took both of her shoulders and gently shook her. "Stop it right now, Kitty. You are not to blame for any of this. It's obvious the viscountess is playing some sort of game with Robert."

Her beautiful face twisted into an expression of misery. "I

wouldn't have come but when the letter mentioned the baby—"

"Kitty," he said sternly, "I'll find out everything I can—including the truth about your child. Do you understand me? The woman is poison and has driven my brother half mad—you must leave. All you need to worry about is—"

"Stacy!"

Frances was running toward them, clutching her ball gown in her fists. "It's Portia," she gasped in between breaths. "You must come with me now!"

PORTIA FELL INTO the darkened room and bumped into something hard.

"Stay put," Rowena snapped, entering the room and shedding light in the darkness, slamming the door behind them.

The room was perhaps three times as wide as the tunnel they'd just left behind and there was a second door across from the one they'd just come through. The only furniture was a spindly side table against one wall and a large, rough-hewn table in the center of the room, which is what she'd hit.

Wide leather straps were attached to the top, middle, and bottom of the bigger table and Portia could barely pull her eyes away. When she looked up, she wished she hadn't. The walls had dozens of carved niches and each one held a hideous mask. It felt as though dozens of hate-filled eyes were watching.

Rowena dribbled a daub of wax on the side table and stuck her candle in it. The determined grimace on her face was far more frightening than any of the masks on the wall.

"Get on the table." She pushed the pistol into Portia's side to encourage obedience. Her eyes slewed toward the second door and her mouth tightened with irritation as it slowly creaked open. Mr. Fant stood in the narrow doorway, his eyes wide.

"Close the door, you idiot," Rowena snapped. "What took you so long?"

The dour-faced man flushed. "I got lost, my lady. There's miles of tunnels down here." He carried a big wooden tool box in one hand and a shielded lantern in the other.

A look of intense annoyance spasmed across Rowena's face and for a moment the hand holding the pistol wavered, as if she were considering shooting her accomplice.

"Do you have it?" she asked through clenched jaws.

Fant's eyes flickered from his mistress to Portia and moved quickly to the wooden box. He set it on the floor beside the lamp and dug into its depths, extracting a large piece of folded canvas and a small round clay jar. "The woman said it only took a mouthful."

"Put that out," she gestured to the lamp in his hand and held out her pistol. "Take this." She waited impatiently as he complied. "Can you keep this trained on her without shooting either yourself or me?"

Fant's lips tightened at her belittling tone but he took the gun without comment, aiming it at Portia, his expression even grimmer than usual.

Rowena pulled the bung out of the earthenware jar and thrust it Portia. "You're going to take at least two mouthfuls and then lie back on the table. It will happen fast and there will be very little pain. Do you understand? I'll strap you down if you—"

The heavy plank door behind her flew open and slammed into her shoulder. She cried out and staggered sideways, knocking into the table where she'd set the candle. Her hand scrabbled for purchase and she knocked the candle to the floor, plunging the room into darkness.

"Put down your weapon Fant, I know you have a pistol," a calm, familiar voice demanded. "There are five men with me and more approaching from the other direction. You are trapped. Do as I tell you, and you might live."

Portia jumped off the table and took a step. And then an arm snaked around her neck.

"Stacy!" Her scream came out a choked gurgle as she struggled against Rowena's surprisingly strong hold, clutching her stomach protectively. Rowena's arm tightened around her throat and Portia gagged.

"Fant, hand me the gun," Rowena demanded.

"Do not give her the pistol, Mr. Fant." Stacy's voice was almost bored. "My pistol is aimed at your heart. You know very well that I can see better in the dark than a cat. I can see you right now, in fact, backing toward the other door. You've got a lamp in your hand."

"*Give me the gun*!" Rowena screamed, shoving something against Portia's lips.

Portia realized it was the flask of poison and clamped her jaws shut tighter than a vise. A mindless fury swept through her trembling body and she drove her elbow back with all the force she could muster. Rowena grunted and staggered back, her arm loosening. Portia dropped to her hands and knees and crawled between the legs of the big table, curling her body into a tight ball.

"Fant!" Rowena screamed.

Portia heard the sound of scuffling feet and a muffled curse as somebody struck the tool box and sent the contents clanging and banging across the flagstone. The deafening crack of a pistol filled the room and what sounded to be at least a dozen male voices shouted just before a second gun went off, followed by a sickening grunt and the unmistakable *thud* of a body hitting the floor.

"Fant is down, Lady Rowena. It is over." Stacy's voice came from someplace close by and Portia had to bite her tongue to keep from calling out.

The sound of pottery shattering on the flagstone was followed by a watery, choked laugh. A light flared and Portia looked up to see Stacy holding a candle away from his face and staring at something on the other side of the small room.

"My God. What did you do?" His voice was thick with dread.

"You didn't think I was going to let you lock me up, did you?" Rowena's gurgling laughter turned into an animal scream of pure pain. Her pale green eyes bulged with the torment she'd promised Portia she would not feel and she slid down the wall until she sat slumped on the floor.

The door Fant had come through exploded and Robert stood panting in the doorway, his lantern illuminating the carnage, a giant man beside him holding an ax.

He saw Fant's body first. "The devil!" he hissed.

"Ah, my darling husband has arrived."

Robert turned at the sound of his wife's voice.

"Rowena! What have you done?" He closed the short distance in one long stride and dropped down beside her. Blood oozed from her mouth and she coughed and spat blood at his feet.

"You poor fool," she rasped. "I did all this for you. And it was all for—"

Portia closed her eyes at the sickening sounds and felt a light touch on her shoulder and looked up to find Stacy's beautiful eyes only inches away. He took her hand and lifted her to her feet. "Are you hurt, darling?"

She launched herself at him. "I am so sorry, Stacy."

"Sorry for what, sweetheart?"

Portia further embarrassed herself by dissolving into tears, the love in his voice making her feel like the world's greatest fool. She squeezed him until she hurt.

He stroked her hair. "Don't cry, Portia, you're safe now."

"I never cry." She sobbed into his neckcloth.

"I know you don't, love," he agreed, his laughter a low rumble in his chest. "But I think you may have earned this one. In fact, do you mind if I join you?"

She laughed but it turned into wracking sobs, her body shaking so hard she could barely stand.

"Are you going to faint, Portia?" He pressed his lips against her head over and over.

"I never faint."

And then everything went black.

THE FIRST THING Portia saw when she woke after the nightmare in the tunnels was her husband, reading a book in a wingback chair close to her bed. A slow smile spread across his face when he saw she was awake. He took off his reading glasses and put down his book.

"I thought you would sleep today away," he murmured, coming to sit on the bed.

Portia took his hand and looked up into his beautiful eyes, "I am so sorry, Stacy," she said, the enormity of her idiocy the first thing to enter her mind.

"You kept saying that all the way back to the house last night, even after you fainted. You'd wake from time to time and mutter how sorry you were. Would you mind telling me exactly what you are sorry for?" He reached out and pushed a strand of hair behind her ear. "Or do I want to know?"

Her face became hot and she kissed his palm before holding his hand against her face. "I heard you and Mrs. Charring in the chapel yesterday."

He looked blank. "So?"

"I believe I didn't listen quite closely enough to what you were saying. I'm afraid I thought something quite different." His brow wrinkled and she groaned. "I thought you were the one she loved and you regretted marrying me. I am an idiot." Tears built behind her eyes and that made her even angrier. When had she turned into such a watering pot? She closed her eyes and hot lines made their way down her cheeks.

He took both her hands in his. "Look at me." She heard the sternness in his voice and her stomach clenched painfully. "Portia, open your eyes and look at me."

She opened her eyes; he looked angry. "I love you."

She blinked. "What did you say?"

He gave her a look of helpless amusement. "I love you. I'd hoped you might understand how I felt based on my behavior. I see now that I could not have been more wrong. I love you, Portia. Can you get that idea into your beautiful head?"

Portia did not trust herself to speak so she nodded.

"Good. I will tell you again in five minutes. Just to make certain you heard me."

"And . . . Kitty?" Portia seemed to have lost her ability to concoct complete sentences.

"I was Kitty's lover years ago—almost a decade ago. We've been nothing but friends for a very long time. I know I should have told you as soon as she arrived but she had a dreadful shock when she saw Robert and she needed help." He grimaced. "I suppose I should have guessed you would draw the worst possible conclusion from the way Kitty and I were behaving. I love Kitty as a friend and would do anything for her, but that is all."

Jealousy flared at the thought of him with another woman but this time the emotion flickered and then died; he loved her.

"Please, tell me what happened."

"Are you sure? It is not a pretty story—nor is it short."

"I'm sure."

"On the face of things, this whole mess appears to be a coincidence of almost mythic proportions. However, most of it happened by design—Rowena's design. Robert met Kitty years ago—before he married Rowena." He stopped. "But I'm getting ahead of myself. Kitty grew up in a vicarage, the youngest of two daughters. She was eighteen when her father died and she needed to find work. She took a governess position just outside Plymouth. Her young charge had an elder brother who came down from Oxford with friends from time-to-time. One of them was Robert. It doesn't take much imagination to guess what happened, next. They fell in love. Unfortunately, Robert was already engaged."

"That's what Rowena told me," Portia said.

"Well, Robert knew Rowena was not in love with him and he felt certain he could convince her to release him. He told Kitty what he was going to do and promised to return as soon as he'd spoken to Rowena, the duke, and his father.

"Robert told Rowena the truth and she agreed that she didn't want to marry a man in love with another woman. Rowena said she would go to her father and claim that she'd changed her mind. She didn't seem upset, and she even invited him to stay the night and dine with her and her brothers.

"The next morning, on his way to Thurlstone Castle, Robert's horse was shot from under him while he was crossing a bridge." He gave her a grim look. "Based on Rowena's recent behavior, Robert and I have assumed it was no accident. A local squire found his body beside the river, not far from his dead horse. He had a broken leg and was badly concussed; there was nothing that identified him. It was weeks before he returned to Plymouth and by then Kitty was gone."

"This is like a novel from the Minerva Press," Portia said.

Stacy nodded and continued. "The family Kitty was working for found out that she was with child. It's not wild conjecture to think Rowena was behind that, as well. They discharged Kitty without references."

Portia could hardly imagine the young girl's terror. At least when Ivo had abandoned her, she'd had her friends to turn to.

"She waited for him until she ran out of money, and then she sold the only thing she had left."

"Dear God," Portia said. "And Robert?"

"Her former employer told him Kitty had gone to an aunt up north but they didn't have the woman's direction. Robert went to her father's old vicarage, but the new vicar knew nothing about Kitty's family and nobody in the village had ever heard of an aunt. He had nowhere else to look."

"What a horrible story."

"There is more. Rowena knew exactly where Kitty ended up because she made sure the Fants were there to offer her a place to stay."

"The Fants!"

"They've worked at the duke's Yorkshire property for generations. So when the time came for Kitty to give birth to Robert's baby, Rowena paid the midwife who attended the birth to claim the baby died." He gave Portia a chilling look. "The reason Kitty came to Thurlstone was because she received a letter telling her the child was still alive. The letter said that if she wanted her child she would come to the house party."

Portia shook her head. "But *why?* Why would Rowena do such a thing?"

Stacy shrugged. "Revenge? Anger? We'll never know, now."

"How did you learn about the child?"

"Fant told us."

"But I thought he was shot?"

"His wound was mortal but he lingered for several hours and was conscious. He told us the truth in exchange for letting his wife go free. He claimed she knew nothing about any of it."

Portia pictured the shrewish woman and her small, mean eyes. "I don't believe that."

"Neither do I, but it was the only way to get the rest of the story." He continued. "Several years ago Rowena became curious about Frances and didn't believe the story about her living with a school friend, so she had her followed."

"Why?" Portia asked.

"Frances thinks Rowena might have heard something from Nanny's elder sister—a woman named Elsa who was the midwife who delivered us. Elsa lived in a cottage on the estate and Rowena, doing her duty as the future mistress of Thurlstone, met the woman while delivering calf's foot jelly or whatever it is that angels of mercy think the poor, old, and infirm need. Elsa would have known the truth, and perhaps she decided to share it. Or maybe, like Nanny, her mind simply wandered and the story came out. In any case, it is telling that Elsa died not long afterward."

Portia shivered. "More like an angel of death. How did the Fants begin working for Nanny?"

"Fant said Rowena told them about the position when Frances advertised for it. Fant said part of his duties were to keep an eye on me and he was the one who found out I knew Kitty and reported that odd coincidence to his employer. Rowena had no use for that information until recently, when she decided Kitty would be the perfect weapon to punish both me and Robert."

He stopped, a muscle in his jaw flexing. "Did Rowena tell you about the earl?"

"What about him?"

"She must have smothered him in his bed just before she came after you."

"Oh God!" Portia covered her mouth with both hands.

"She thought it would stop the secret from going any further, but the murder of my father would have been her undoing. You see, he left sealed letters explaining the truth for both Robert and me in the event of his death." Stacy's lips curled with disgust. "I'm never happy when anyone dies, but my father truly deserved what he got."

"Do you think he knew Rowena was behind all those accidents?"

"I don't want to know, and I'm glad the truth died with him."

Portia remembered something else from the night before. "She paid Ivo to come to Cornwall, but I don't understand how she even knew about him."

"She never met him, but she sent Fant to check up on you when she began to worry you and I might be getting fond of each other. She sent him to London to your old house."

Portia grimaced. "Mrs. Sneed was our landlady. She is a dreadful woman; I daresay she was thrilled to bits to sell any information she had. So, Fant killed Ivo?"

"With his dying breath Fant claimed Ivo's death was an accident. He also said he knew nothing about the money Ivo blackmailed from you."

"Do you believe him?"

"No, I think his wife has the money, but she will have hidden it well." He shrugged. "I didn't trust the woman and before we came to Thurlstone I had Hawkins's oldest daughter move into Nanny's cottage to keep her safe."

Portia blinked. "What made you do that?"

"I saw Fant talking to Ivo."

"What?" Portia sat up straighter.

"Yes, the day we went to look at the Humboldts' roof. The same day we had a picnic in the woods."

Portia remembered the day very well. From the look on his face, so did Stacy. He smiled and ran a hand over her stomach, the gesture both tender and possessive.

"Why didn't you tell me?"

"What was there to say? I suspected there was something odd about Fant but I had no proof. When I went to ask him about Ivo's death later, his wife said he'd gone up north for a visit." The candles illuminated his sculpted features and stunning eyes. "You're staring, Lady Broughton."

Portia gasped. "How is Robert taking all of this—he must be devastated?"

"He's like a man in a dream. He hasn't said much about his marriage to Rowena but I gather the two of them made each other fairly miserable."

Portia thought about the woman who'd tried to kill her at least three times and shivered. "She was ready to murder all of us for a ridiculous title."

Stacy squeezed her hand. "I know, darling."

"What about Kitty and Robert—was it true about their child?"

"Fant said his brother raised the child. Robert has already told me he will be leaving in the morning to fetch their daughter."

"What do you think Robert and Kitty will do?"

"I don't know. But whatever happens he told me he would no longer live here."

She frowned. "Are *we* moving here?"

"No. At least not until after the baby is born. Robert has agreed to stay until then."

"Thank God. I want our child to be born at Whitethorn."

"As do I, my love." He pulled her into his arms, holding her so tight she couldn't breathe. "I love you, darling. Do you think we could have a week without you forgetting that?"

She laughed. "I promise. Maybe even two weeks."

Epilogue

Several Months Later
Whitethorn

STACY HEARD A tentative scratch on the library door and leapt to his feet.

"Come," he called, his voice rough from disuse.

It was Soames. "The countess is asking for you, my lord." His lips twitched and Stacy could see he was struggling to contain a smile.

He stared at his generally somber butler and opened his mouth. And then closed it. And then opened it again. "Thank you, Soames, I shall be up directly." He remained standing and staring at the door even after it had closed. He'd wanted to be upstairs with her for hours and now, quite suddenly, he was . . . nervous.

Robert lowered the paper he'd been reading and regarded him with an amused, tolerant smirk. "Well, are you ready, old man?"

Stacy looked at his brother—his younger brother—his mind a whirl. Poor Robert had not had an easy time these past months. He'd stayed to manage their father's holdings, but Kitty had wanted nothing to do with him. Fortunately, he'd seen their daughter, April, quite often, even bringing her to Thurlestone to meet their aunts. Stacy and Portia had met the girl, as well, but Kitty never brought up the subject of his brother, and Stacy did not feel right about prying. Who knew what would happen between those two after such a tortured past?

"Are you just going to stand there all day, Stacy?"

He shook himself, and took a deep breath, Robert's laughter following him from the room.

Stacy was only vaguely aware of the faces of most of his servants as he made his way toward the master suite. It felt as though the distance between the library and their bedchambers had tripled at some point during the last twenty-two hours. He took the steps two at a time and almost collided with his sister Mary at the top of the stairs.

She beamed and seized his hand. "Come, they are waiting."

They? Oh, yes, it wasn't just Portia he was going to see.

There seemed to be a hundred people in Portia's bedchamber: her friends from the academy—all but Miles and Honoria—had made the long journey and had been here almost a week. Stacy had met all of the former teachers during a visit to London last Christmas, and he liked all of them—even the far-too-handsome Miles. He was glad her friends had been here for her, but right now he only had eyes for his wife. Portia was propped up on a mound of cushions, her wild black hair loose about her shoulders, her beautiful face exhausted but glowing with pride.

She held out her hands. "Oh, Stacy!"

He kissed her brow and squeezed her hands so hard she winced. "How do you feel, darling? You look beautiful. They would not let me in. Frances and Serena stopped me at the door and would not let me pass."

She laughed and glanced over his shoulder and he turned.

Frances held a child in her arms.

And so did Serena, Portia's closest friend, a fiery young widow much like his own wife, and a woman he was coming to like very much.

Stacy's jaw hit the floor. "Two?"

"Our son and daughter, Stacy." Portia's voice was soft and full of wonder.

"Twins?" he asked stupidly. A chill expanded in his chest; were they like him?

He got to his feet slowly and approached the bundle Frances held. He looked down on a pink face with a scant fluff of black hair and smiled.

"This is your daughter, your first-born," Frances said. "She is twelve minutes older than your son."

Stacy touched her tiny pink cheek with one finger and she squirmed but continued sleeping.

He turned to Serena. The usually gregarious Frenchwoman was even more disheveled than usual, her long, wild hair sticking out in all directions. She met Stacy's eye with an uncharacteristically solemn look. "This is your son, my lord."

Stacy pulled back the blanket. His son was not sleeping. He was pale with no hint of color except for his eyes; eyes that were a pale, pale blue. Stacy stared into those eyes for a long moment, his emotions a confusing welter of love, joy, fear, and a little sadness at what his son would have to face. He swallowed hard at the thought of the boy's future. He would endure the same stares and cruelty as Stacy had and his life would never be easy. But then, whose life was? And at least he wouldn't have to face it alone.

His son gurgled and his hand shot out and grabbed Stacy's finger, his grip fierce for such a tiny thing.

Stacy laughed and looked toward the bed, meeting Portia's worried gaze. "He's got your hands. Our children are beautiful, my love. Both of them."

Relief flooded her face and Stacy frowned. Had she been worried he would not love his own child?

Had *he* been worried about the same thing?

He turned to Frances and Serena, who were both grinning broadly, and held out his arms.

"Both of them?" Serena asked, hesitating.

"I'd better become accustomed to it."

They felt so light in his arms; they weighed nothing but had already changed everything.

He sat on the bed with a baby carefully balanced in the crook of each arm and looked at his wife.

"You were wise to stop with two, Portia, I do not have another arm to spare."

She gave a tired chuckle and looked from their daughter, to their son, and then at him, her dark eyes glowing with love. "They are perfect, Stacy."

Stacy looked at the woman who'd brought so much light and joy into his colorless life and nodded.

"Yes, my dear, they are perfect. And they will grow up together and know the love of their parents, family, and each other."

Thanks so much for reading THE MUSIC OF LOVE!

If you enjoyed reading about Stacy and Portia's world you can meet more of their friends in THE ACADEMY OF LOVE series, which features seven out-of-work Regency schoolteachers who are about to get some serious lessons in love!

Here's an exclusive excerpt from

A FIGURE OF LOVE

BOOK 2 in

THE ACADEMY OF LOVE SERIES....

Chapter One

Kent

1817

GARETH LOCKHEART LOOKED down at the snuffling brown and white balls of fur in some perplexity. "Do I really need so many?" he asked the Honorable Sandford Featherstone.

The puppies stirred and whimpered at the sound of his voice and the mother dog—or bitch, Gareth supposed she was called—gave him a look of reproach for waking her sleeping brood. Or flock. Or whatever one called a herd of puppies; puppies with a finer pedigree than Gareth Lockheart could claim.

Featherstone's head bobbed up and down with an enthusiasm Gareth found exhausting. "Oh yes, this many and more if you are to hunt."

Ah, hunting. He'd forgotten all about the supposed need for hunting. Gareth frowned at the prospect but didn't bother arguing with the fussy, fine-boned aristocrat. After all, this was exactly the type of information he was paying Featherstone for: how to behave like a nob; how to build and furnish a house that looked as if toffs had been living in it for centuries.

Gareth had to pause for a moment in order to remind himself *why* he was doing this.

Ah yes, he recalled now: He was enduring all this upheaval and irritating discussion and excessive expenditure because his business partner—Declan McElroy—claimed they needed to present a civilized front if they were ever to gain credibility with the aristocracy and Gareth was more likely to be successful in such a venture. Gareth supposed the man had a point, although why he should trust Declan's judgement on anything English was beyond him. After all, Declan despised the English and took great joy in acting *more* Irish *than* Irish, even though he'd never stepped foot on the Emerald Isle.

"And about those hunters, Mr. Lockheart."

Gareth looked up from the sleeping puppies at the sound of Featherstone's voice; a grating voice with its clipped consonants and condescending cadence. The smaller man was watching him closely; his expression one of concern mingled with . . . *something.*

While Gareth might not be good at reading people he knew what aristocrats saw when they looked at him: an upstart cit with more money and influence than such a mongrel deserved. He found such an attitude neither offensive nor amusing; just irrelevant.

The truth was that the thick walls of the aristocracy had been breached by wealthy merchant princes like Gareth; the power of the peerage was leaking through that breach like water draining from a ship's scuppers.

But the change was happening slowly and England's ancient, landed families still wielded influence in government that was disproportionate to their numbers or wealth.

The resulting equation was simple: aristocrats needed men like Gareth as much as he needed them.

Featherstone shifted from foot to foot under Gareth's silent regard. "My cousin has a very well-respected stud farm in Yorkshire and—" words poured out of his mouth and filled the close air of the stables like a cloud of gnats. Words, words, and more words.

Gareth began to get the flying-apart feeling that invaded him whenever he was too long in Featherstone's company—or in the company of anyone who wasted his time with trivial matters that had already been discussed.

Controlling the unpleasant sensation required mental gymnastics and a great deal of effort on his part.

First, Gareth directed his attention away from his current situation. Next, he focused on the Goldbach Conjecture, an open mathematical problem dating from 1742, as yet unsolved. Pondering such a conundrum never failed to calm him.

Every even integer greater than two is the sum of two primes—

"Mr. Lockheart?"

Gareth forced his eyes to refocus on Featherstone's narrow, anxious face and recall what he'd been babbling about. Horses. He'd been talking about horses.

Gareth frowned. "I've already told you to purchase whatever stock you think fitting, Featherstone. I have entrusted you with such decisions so that *I* will not be taxed by them." *And yet you are taxing me with them,* he wanted to add, but didn't.

Instead, he pivoted on the heel of his boot and strode toward the exit. He'd hoped the other man might stay behind, but he could hear his footsteps struggling to keep up.

"But Mr. Lockheart, you don't even want to talk about your own hunters—"

"No." The sound of their footfalls echoed through the vast and, as yet, unoccupied stables like the sharp reports of a pistol. Gareth deliberately changed the subject. "When does Hiram Beech arrive?"

"Mr. Beech will be here late in the afternoon."

Gareth bit back the irritation he felt whenever he thought of Beech. He'd wanted Amon Henry Wilds to design Rushton Park but the famous architect refused to take a commission so far from his beloved Brighton. Gareth had not been able to lure him away even by offering triple his usual fee. A man without a price was singular in Gareth's experience and he discovered he did not like it.

Instead of Wilds he'd chosen Beech, who was highly recommended as an architect known to favor the Indo-Saracenic style; a style which Gareth had been told was all the rage. He could not care less what style the country house was built in—he only wanted it to be built by the best. Otherwise, what was the point of all this?

To be honest, Garth had lost interest in the sprawling pile of bricks after the construction phase ended. He had no aptitude for design, décor, or furnishings and had only enjoyed the engineering aspects of the project.

Oh, he was pleased enough with the house, he supposed. Not that he spent much time in it. He'd hoped all the fuss and mess would be over last spring, when the structure had been completed. But now he'd been told he needed some sort of pleasure garden or ancient ruin or other such nonsense. It seemed Beech was the man to arrange the design and building of such things as he already knew the property, and to Gareth, employing him sounded like the least painful and time-consuming option.

They reached the steps to the front entrance—twenty of them, made of the finest breccia marble quarried and transported from the Continent, now that the War was over—and Gareth stopped and turned to Featherstone, eager to be shed of him.

"I have a great deal of work to do and will be in the library, I trust you will handle whatever arrangements need to be made for Beech." Even to Gareth's untutored ears his words sounded abrupt and uncivil. "I will leave you to your business," he added to soften the rude directive.

Featherstone nodded, his hands moving in the compulsive washing gesture Gareth found distasteful and annoying. The man was an unpleasant combination of condescending and unctuous, but Beech had recommended him. "Mr. Beech will be bringing—"

Gareth held up a hand. "Yes, you've already said. He will be bringing a stone-worker or sculptor or gardener or what-have-you. I will speak with both or all of them before we dine this evening." Gareth tossed the words over his shoulder, impatient to get back to work.

He strode through the great hall and then turned right to pass through the portrait-less portrait gallery on his way to the residential wing of the house. He spent most of his time at Rushton Park in the library, which was composed of three massive rooms linked together. The size seemed excessive to Gareth but the design apparently aped an ancient library from some place Gareth had never heard of. All he'd requested of Beech was that it be well-lighted and commodious enough to contain a desk, his journal collection, and a comfortable chair. And all Gareth had required of Featherstone when the man began stuffing the house with furniture and other frippery was that the library remain free of distracting clutter.

Two footmen stood at attention outside the double doors, waiting for nothing other than his arrival. Gareth ignored the unease he felt at such excess; after all, this was what he'd wanted, a country home that was as gratuitously sized and overstaffed as one of the royal dukes' residences. Actually, Gareth had more servants *and* a larger house.

Since coming down from London two days ago he'd had his correspondence delivered twice daily by couriers. The pile of letters was easily three inches tall. There would be reports from all his businesses, but most of the stack would be about the new pottery he was building in London, his most ambitious project thus far.

Gareth was only half-way through the pile when the sound of somebody clearing their throat made him look up. His butler, Jessup, stood in the doorway.

"I asked not to be disturbed."

The towering, bone-thin man gave a slight nod, but his expression remained as fixed as a totemic carving. He was, Gareth knew, utterly unflappable. Gareth had poached him from the Duke of Remington's household, where Jessup's family had been employed as butlers for two hundred years. Remington could not compete with the pay Gareth offered.

"You have a visitor, Mr. Lockheart, Mrs. Serena Lombard."

Gareth shook his head. "I am not acquainted with, nor am I expecting any such person."

"She is here at the behest of Mr. Beech, sir, about the gardens."

"Ah, I see." Although he did not. He cleared his throat. "You say Beech has engaged a woman gardener?"

"Yes, sir. Mrs. Lombard is a woman. And a gardener," Jessup agreed.

Sometimes—just occasionally—Gareth wondered if his butler made mock of him. He shrugged the thought away. What did he know of gardeners? For all he knew, they might all be females. Well, whoever she was and whatever she did, Gareth would find out at the appropriate time. He cut Jessup an impatient look. "Have Featherstone see to her, Jessup."

"Mr. Featherstone has gone to the village, sir."

Gareth stared at the man.

Jessup nodded, just as if he'd spoken. "I shall put her in the sitting room and offer her tea."

"Yes, very good. Put her in a room with tea." Lord knew there were enough rooms in the house—seventy-three—certainly one of them would be appropriate for accommodating unexpected female visitors.

Gareth's eyes and attention drifted back to the neat column of figures in front of him.

"Very good, sir."

He barely heard the butler, his mind already back on his numbers, the woman forgotten.

Serena eyed the generously loaded tea tray with approval and helped herself to three different types of biscuits and the loveliest fairy cake she'd ever seen. Such delicacies were rare these days. Even when she paid a visit to the home of her dead husband's parents, the Duke and Duchess of Remington, the offerings were rather thin; the powerful duke had suffered since the War ended, forced to retrench at his six houses.

Serena examined the huge sitting room—the gaudiest specimen she'd ever sat in—and enjoyed her delicacies. The butler returned after she'd been alone for about a quarter of an hour.

"Do you have everything you need, Mrs. Lombard?" The hesitation before her name was almost imperceptible, but she noticed it all the same.

Serena cocked her head and smiled up at him. "What? Are we no longer friends, Jessup? How are you? I have not been to Keeting yet this year, but I was there at Christmas. His Grace speaks fondly of you, you know." Keeting Hall was the country seat of the Duke of Remington.

The slightest dusting of color appeared on the butler's high, sharp cheekbones. "And I often think of His and Her Graces as well as the rest of the family." He looked as if he wished to say something else, but hesitated.

"His Grace does not blame you for leaving, Jessup," she said.

Well, that was a bit of a fib. Her in-laws *had* been devastated by their family retainer's desertion. But Mr. Lockheart—a man reputed to be among the ten richest in Britain—had offered a wage too high for Robert Jessup to resist.

Jessup's lips flexed in what passed for a smile. "You are very kind, madam."

"So, how do you find it here?" Serena glanced around the cavernous room, which evoked a seraglio with its bold fuchsia, gold, and green color scheme, opulent silk and velvet window coverings, and Egyptian-style furniture.

"I find my position suits me admirably, Mrs. Lombard."

Again she heard the hesitation before her name. She knew that Jessup, like her dead husband's family, were unhappy that she refused to use her honorific. Serena allowed them all to believe her resistance to aristocratic titles was because of her French Republican upbringing, rather than the truth; a truth they could never know.

She realized the butler was waiting for her answer. "I'm pleased to hear you are happy here, Jessup." And she was. It was too bad he'd needed to leave his home of many years, but—as she knew all too well—everyone deserved a chance at a better life.

Serena returned her cup and saucer to the massive tea tray. "Mr. Beech has asked me to work with him on the new gardens for Rushton Park." Jessup knew what Serena did for a living. He'd worked for the Lombard family when she had first arrived in England almost ten years ago. He'd been there when Serena—after living her first year under the care of the duke and duchess, who were very kind to their youngest son's foreign widow—had scandalized her new relations by moving to London to take up a position teaching art and sculpture at a girls' school.

Once again, her husband's family blamed her mad French blood—but, thankfully, hadn't tried to stop her—for taking her infant son from the comfort of Keeting Hall and moving them both to a town house with two other women teachers. It had been a difficult decision, but she did not regret it.

"If you will permit me to say so, madam, I have seen your work, and it is quite lovely."

The Jessup of old would never have offered an unsolicited opinion. Perhaps working in a Whig household had given him a more egalitarian outlook.

"Thank you, Jessup." She stood and smoothed down the skirt

of her dark green traveling costume. "I'm refreshed and eager to see Rushton Park. Would it be possible to take a stroll around the grounds?"

"Of course, madam."

Serena opened the flap of the large leather satchel she was rarely without and took out her sketchpad.

She smiled up at him. "I'm ready."

As he moved to open the door for her, Serena studied his familiar narrow form and black-clad shoulders and decided she was more pleased than she would have expected to find an old family ally and retainer. Of course she'd known Jessup worked for the reclusive Gareth Lockheart, but the man kept houses in London, Edinburgh, and Bristol. If she'd given the matter more than a passing thought, she would have assumed Lockheart kept the unparalleled butler in his London house, where it was rumored he spent most of his time.

Jessup escorted her down a staircase wide enough to accommodate seven soldiers marching abreast and paused on the ground floor.

"Shall I take you out through the orangery, madam?"

"Yes, please. I didn't see it from the drive, but I've seen it on Beech's drawings."

The house resembled an Elizabethan "E" but with many modifications—some rather. . . unconventional.

"How long have you been here, Jessup?"

"I came down with Mr. Lockheart two days ago, madam. I have been at his London house but accompanied him here to see to some unfinished household matters."

Serena had never seen a house quite like it. It was a *corps de logis,* comprised of a central block with two wings that were three stories and curved to form a three-sided courtyard—or *cour d'honneur*—on each side of the central block.

Either Lockheart or Beech must have been very fond of onion

domes, as there were no fewer than five of them. The blinding white façade was festooned with multitudinous cusped arches, minaret-shaped finials, and vacant plinths waiting for statuary. The mishmash of Orientalism and Indo-Saracenic styles was so like the Royal Pavilion that she kept thinking she must have taken a wrong turn and ended up in Brighton.

The interior lacked the chinoiserie so far as she had seen. Indeed, the décor was far less definite than the exterior and felt like the rather halfhearted result of a committee.

The hall flooded with light and ahead was a wall of leaded glass.

"My, how lovely," Serena said as Jessup opened one of the massive double doors to the empty conservatory, which was without even a stick, plant, leaf, or crumb of dirt. "When was this finished?" She turned in a circle, gazing overhead at the spectacular glass walls and canopy.

"Last spring, ma'am."

Serena couldn't help thinking of the orangery at Keeting Hall, which was perhaps a quarter of this size and so choked with plants it had felt like a jungle. It might be old and crowded, its glass hazed and cracked, but it was alive. Which was more than she could say for this empty glass box. Beech had not mentioned the orangery, but Serena couldn't help feeling a frisson of excitement as she imagined filling such a beautiful space with living things.

Jessup opened one of the French doors and they stepped out into the cool spring sunshine. She turned to him. "I will walk the immediate area until Mr. Beech arrives."

The butler's eyebrows arched.

"What is it, Jessup?"

"Mr. Beech is not expected until late afternoon, ma'am."

Serena frowned. "He told me it was to be a midday meeting. I have engaged the post chaise to return for me at four."

"Mr. Beech is to arrive at five o'clock and will stay the night."

Serena wanted to howl with frustration but it was hardly Jessup's fault. "I'm afraid Mr. Beech neglected to inform me of either the correct time or duration of our meeting." She sighed and glanced around her without seeing anything, her mind churning. The expensive journey out and back had been paid for by Mr. Lockheart, of course, so she was not concerned about that. But she had brought no change of clothing or any other items for an overnight stay. She also had not told Lady Winifred, her friend and housemate, that she would be gone overnight. And of course Oliver would be expecting to see her tomorrow morning.

She looked up half a foot to meet Jessup's impassive eyes and shrugged. "Well, Jessup, this is a bit of a muddle. I did not come prepared for an overnight stay, nor did I tell anyone I would be away that long." She caught her lower lip between her teeth and worried it. "You know the way of things here, what do you advise?"

His expression didn't change, but his dark brown eyes glinted with approval at her calm reaction.

"Mr. Lockheart is a gentleman who does not stay long in one place, ma'am. It is his plan to leave Rushton Park tomorrow. He will return to London for a few days but then I believe he is headed to the North. It may be some time before he returns to Rushton Park for another meeting."

That was his way of saying she should stay. "I see."

Jessup's mouth opened a crack, but then he closed it.

"What is it you are thinking? Don't be shy."

"Do you need to be back in London tonight?"

"No, but my son and the woman we live with will worry if I'm not back by this evening."

"If I could make arrangements to provide you with the items necessary for an overnight stay and send a message to reassure your friend and Master Oliver, would you have any objections to staying?"

It was not ideal, but she knew this commission would be worth a great deal of money.

"Thank you, Jessup, that would serve admirably."

"If you will excuse me, I will see to it. I will leave you to enjoy your walk and return for you in half an hour."

GARETH HAD THE big rolls of plans for the new pottery spread out on the vast trestle table he'd had made for this exact purpose. He was examining it with a magnifying glass, studying the details for the massive kilns.

He was so enrapt he nearly jumped out of his skin when a throat cleared behind him. He ignored his rapidly beating heart and sighed. "Yes, Jessup, what is it now?"

"I am terribly sorry to disturb you, sir, but there appears to have been something of a misunderstanding."

Chapter Two

SERENA STARED AT the immense book-lined room. Three rooms linked together, actually. A library unlike anything she'd ever seen. Of course the entire property was singular, from the lush countryside that surrounded the gargantuan house, to the vast suite of rooms she'd been given for her brief stay. Rooms that were twice as large as any she could recall at Keeting Hall.

Jessup had taken care of her as if she were a queen, sending one messenger speeding off to London and another all the way to Ayelford—the nearest town with a dress shop—to purchase a nightgown and dressing robe. These, as well as a selection of toiletries, combs, and brushes—all new—awaited her in her sumptuous chambers. Serena would have to wear her clothing to dinner and again tomorrow when she left, but Jessup told her Mr. Lockheart had been apprised of the matter and tonight's dinner would be informal.

All in all, she could not be unhappy to be staying an evening in such a house. The library alone was worth the inconvenience. Bookshelves began only a few inches off the floor and did not stop until the ceiling, which she believed to be at least fifteen feet high. The book ladder was precariously tall, and she could imagine herself scaling it and risking life and limb for the sake of a book.

She was examining a rather exquisite set of six volumes of illuminated French poetry when the door opened behind her. She turned to find Sandy Featherstone, her deceased husband's cousin, twice removed.

"Hallo, Serena, Beech told me you'd agreed to come." He came toward her with his arms outstretched and Serena submitted with resignation to his embrace. He was a sticky-handed man whom she had only ever tolerated because of his connection to the family.

Serena stepped away when it became apparent he was not going to voluntarily release her. He eyed her in a way that made her jaw tighten, his small-fingered hands moving in their habitual hand-washing motions.

"Hallo, Sandy." Serena forced a smile. "So, it appears I have you to thank for this." She made a gesture which encompassed everything around them.

He grinned, the sight somewhat alarming as he seemed to have twice the normal complement of teeth. "It was nothing, my dear—merely family looking after family. Besides, I told Beech we had better snap you up before your fees became exorbitant." He chortled, clearly tickled at the thought of such a thing happening.

Serena's smile became even stiffer. "Well, whatever the reason, I do appreciate it. I've just finished a series of small commissions and was at loose ends."

"What are cousins for, my dear?" He gestured toward a cluster of decanters sitting on a granite slab supported by massive gold lion's feet. "Would you like a drink before dinner, Serena?" His hand trembled slightly, making it clear *he* would like a drink.

"A glass of sherry, if you have it."

"Mr. Lockheart has everything." He smirked and then turned to fix their drinks. "Oh, and I'm afraid I've got some rather disappointing news," Sandy said over the sound of glass clinking against glass. "It seems Beech was delayed in London."

Serena closed the volume she'd taken down and replaced it on the shelf. Of course he was. It had been exactly that kind of day.

Sandy came toward her with their drinks. "Not to worry,

though. He sent his plans down and we can study them after dinner."

Serena perked up. That was actually better than having Beech here as she'd noticed the successful architect had a tendency to talk over-much about himself and his achievements. The two times she had met with him it had taken him more than a half hour before he could come to the point.

Serena sat on a gilt settee that had been upholstered in a rather shocking chartreuse while Sandy took the chair closest to her, a gothic thing with dragons for armrests.

"So, what have you been up to since we last saw one another—Lord!" He examined the ornately coffered ceiling, as if it might contain the information he sought. "Was that five years ago?"

"Has it been that long?" But she knew it had. Sandy had done something to displease the duke and had not received an invitation to the famous house party the duke and duchess had every year around Christmas. She took a sip of excellent sherry and set down her glass on a side table that appeared to be a Sphinx.

"Yes, Oliver was towing around that wooden horse, if I recall correctly. You were on holiday from the school." He wore a sly smile, clearly amused by her method of supporting herself.

Serena was surprised he remembered her son's name. "The Stefani Academy closed last year."

"I'd heard that." His pointy nose quivered, putting her in mind of a rat. "I'd also heard the woman who owned it was rather dodgy and hared off abruptly—almost as if there was something scandalous she wished to leave behind?"

Serena felt a surge of distaste for both him and his characterization of her friend Portia Stefani. The school in question had been an oasis of friendship and security, and she sorely missed it. She changed the topic before she said something to Sandy she would regret.

"I have had a series of commissions since then. Most notably a project for the Mannerings.

"I heard about that, too—some rather ostentatious work on an undercroft in their private church."

It always amazed her how Sandy seemed to know everything that went on in *ton* circles, even though he was perpetually on the fringes of it.

"And you, Sandy, how have you been occupying yourself?" Besides drinking and gambling, she could have added.

"As you see." He waved a hand in the air, his other hand holding the glass which already held just half of what it had only a moment earlier. Sandy had always had too much of a taste for spirits.

"What exactly do you do for Mr. Lockheart?"

"This and that. In truth, I am no more than a well-paid secretary, although he does not use me for his matters of business." He smirked. "You might say I act as his wife, until he can buy one."

"Oh? Is he in that market?"

He gave her a smile that made her feel dirty. "You sound interested, Cuz."

"I am quite happy as I am, Sandy."

His raised brows told her what he thought of that claim. "I selected many of his servants, furnished all his houses except the London townhouse, and advise him in his acquisition of art. Right now I am busy with his stables, which he wants to have ready for use by the fall."

Serena suddenly understood the hideous furnishings. "Mr. Lockheart hunts?" She could not recall hearing much about the man, other than he was rich and rather odd.

"No."

The door opened before Sandy could explain, and their host entered the room. Serena was surprised—he was not only younger than she had expected, he was also elegantly dressed and strikingly handsome. Serena realized she'd given in to preconceived notions and had expected a brawny merchant or flashy cit.

He crossed the long expanse of carpet and Sandy leapt to his feet to make introductions.

"Mr. Lockheart, may I present Mrs. Lombard."

The tall, well-proportioned Adonis took her hand and made a perfunctory bow over it.

"I am pleased to make your acquaintance, madam." His eyes were slate gray and the most opaque Serena had ever seen, observing her without a hint of interest or any other emotion. His lips, sinfully lush and shapely, bore no trace of a smile.

He was perhaps a head taller than she, his dark blond hair on the longish side. Like Sandy, he was dressed informally to accommodate her lack of evening dress, in a bottle-green coat, rich brown waistcoat, and buff pantaloons tucked into coffee-colored Hessians polished to a blinding shine. His snowy white neck cloth was tied with simple elegance; he wore a plain gold watch with no fobs at his waist. His clothing had been made by a master and tailored to fit his form as snuggly as a well-made glove.

"Thank you for inviting me to Rushton Park, Mr. Lockheart."

He nodded abruptly and glanced at his watch, his sensuous mouth turning down slightly at the corners. "There are still seventeen minutes until dinner." He looked up, his gaze flickering over Serena's untouched sherry to Sandy's empty glass. "What are you having, Featherstone, I will refill it."

"Ah, thank you, sir. Brandy."

He took the glass without speaking and went to the sideboard.

Sandy smiled at her and gave a slight shrug. So, her prospective employer was a gloriously handsome man who was also brusque and without social graces. Well, she had heard he was different.

"I daresay Jessup has informed you Mr. Beech will not be here for dinner," Sandy said, his flickering eyes proclaiming his discomfort with silence.

"I received his plans by courier. We will proceed without him," Lockheart said. "After dinner we will examine what he has drawn up." His voice was as devoid of expression as his face. No irritation, regret, or anger at Beech's absence. He returned to where they were seated and took a chair across from Serena after giving Sandy his drink. A double, if Serena was not mistaken.

He fixed Serena with his rather unnerving cool gray stare and took a sip from his glass. His hands, like his person, were slim, elegant, and devoid of jewelry. Serena had expected the stereotype merchant, a beefy, bluff man in his later years. But Lockheart not only resembled a gentleman, he spoke like one, too. While his accent was not exactly aristocratic, it was refined and precise, definitely not that of a man said to have come from the stews of London. There was more here than met the eye.

"I understand you inspected the property this afternoon, Mrs. Lombard."

"Nothing so thorough as an inspection, but I did wander as far as the stream and then along the small wood."

"And did you have any ideas?"

Serena chuckled. "I always have ideas." She smiled at him, but he only blinked calmly back at her. So, he was lacking in humor. She tried again. "My understanding was Mr. Beech would submit a general design and I would see to the details and statuary."

"It is true I have engaged Mr. Beech to create a plan. Have you designed and laid out gardens yourself?"

"Yes," she admitted, surprised by the question. "But never anything as large as this."

"What would you do if it were yours?"

Now *that* was an interesting question, and one she had never been asked by any other client, most of whom had had their own ideas, many of them quite bad.

"I would lay out a parterre directly off the orangery. Beyond it, I would leave things as they are. I believe the terrain on the south side, with its gentle slope, is similar to Badminton and would be perfect for a Brown-like lake, which could be achieved by some clever damming of your stream. Right now there is an old wooden footbridge over the stream. I would replace that with something more interesting." She smiled. "Naturally I would recommend something in stone. If you wish for a folly there is a nice rise on the far side, and once you've created a lake it would be a lovely situation with the addition of a few trees. A rose garden, with a walk to the woods on the east side. You have the two *cour d'honneur* that face the drive and they could be given greenery, a fountain, more roses, intimate seating areas. Of course I did not inspect anything beyond the immediate area and could see more of the estate, more quickly, if I had a horse." She paused. "But those are my first impressions and what I would consider if it were mine." Serena took a sip of claret and never took her eyes from her host, whose expression had not flickered while she spoke. He was not an easy person to talk to; he gave no facial or physical cues to put the speaker at ease. He sat silently for a long, uncomfortable moment, as if considering her words, and then nodded.

"It sounds perfect." He turned to Sandy, who again had his glass raised to his lips. "Will you recall everything Mrs. Lombard said, Mr. Featherstone?"

Sandy gulped down a mouthful of brandy, coughed, and set down his glass. His eyes slid in Serena's direction and then snapped back to his employer. "If I do not, I'm sure Mrs. Lombard will be able to tell me in greater detail."

Mr. Lockheart turned back to her. "You have several ideas I approve of, ma'am. Would you be able to implement such plans without further consultation with Mr. Beech?"

Serena's eyebrows shot up. "Are you asking *me* to design your gardens and park, Mr. Lockheart?"

"Yes."

"But haven't you an agreement with Mr. Beech?" Serena would hate to gain a reputation for poaching commissions.

He continued to regard her with his flat, disorienting gaze. "I have not engaged Mr. Beech, but asked for his bid. He would not go uncompensated for the work he has done. Is Mr. Beech your only objection to accepting such work?"

"I have no experience with anything this large."

Still he did not speak.

And I'm a woman, or don't you care? Or haven't you noticed. Good Lord! Design an entire estate's grounds? Why, that would be—

"Do you think you could accomplish what you described, ma'am?"

She felt a flutter of anticipation at the thought of being paid to experiment with such interesting concepts at someone else's expense. It would be a creative endeavour that would be beyond her dreams—and also one that would be a glorious fit with her talents. She could design a garden to showcase her work, rather than the other way around.

Serena looked up at his impassive face, met his cool gaze, and said, "Yes, Mr. Lockheart, I believe I could."

I hope you'll grab a copy!

So who IS Minerva Spencer?

Minerva has been a criminal prosecutor, college history teacher, B&B operator, dock worker, ice cream manufacturer, reader for the blind, motel maid, and bounty hunter.

Okay, so the part about being a bounty hunter is a lie.

Minerva does, however, know how to hypnotize a Dungeness crab, sew her own Regency Era clothing, knit a frog hat, juggle, rebuild a 1959 American Rambler, and gain control of Asia (and hold on to it) in the game of RISK.

Read more about Minerva at:
www.MinervaSpencer.com

Follow Minerva
On BookBub
On Goodreads

Minerva's OUTCASTS SERIES
DANGEROUS
BARBAROUS
SCANDALOUS

ANTHOLOGIES:
BACHELORS OF BOND STREET
THE ARRANGEMENT

Made in the USA
Monee, IL
05 February 2021